THE MAN WHO WOULD BE KING

Krispos rose when the service was finished and turned to Tanilis. "Thanks again for making room," he told her.

"The privilege was mine, eminent sir," Tanilis said.

"Why do you keep calling me that?" he snapped, irritation getting the better of his manners. "I'm just a groom, and glad to be one—otherwise I expect I'd be starving somewhere. Come to think of it, I've done that, too, once or twice. It doesn't make you eminent, believe me."

Tanilis raised her head to look at him again. He started to stutter out an apology for his outburst—then, looking into her face, he stopped. The last time he had seen that almost blind stare of perfect concentration was on the face of a healer-priest in trance. He watched her eyes go huge and black, saw her expression turn fixed. Her lips parted. Ice ran through him as he heard the word she whispered.

"Majesty."

She slumped forward in a faint.

By Harry Turtledove
Published by Ballantine Books:

*Forthcoming

KRISPOS RISING

Book One of
The Tale of Krispos

Harry Turtledove

A Del Rey Book
BALLANTINE BOOKS • NEW YORK

A Del Rey Book
Published by Ballantine Books
Copyright © 1991 by Harry Turtledove

Library of Congress Catalog Card Number: 90-93460

ISBN 0-345-36118-0

Manufactured in the United States of America

First Edition: February 1991

Cover Art by Romas

This one is for Rebecca
(who arrived during Chapter V)
and for her grandmothers,
Gertrude and Nancy.

AUTHOR'S NOTE

Krispos Rising and the second book in *The Tale of Krispos, Krispos of Videssos*, are set in the same universe as the four books of *The Videssos Cycle: The Misplaced Legion, An Emperor for the Legion, The Legion of Videssos,* and *Swords of the Legion.* The events described in *The Tale of Krispos* take place about five hundred years before those chronicled in *The Videssos Cycle.* Thus the map that precedes the text is different from the one in front of the books of *The Videssos Cycle.* So, too, are some of the customs that appear here: nations, even imaginary ones, do not stand still over five hundred years.

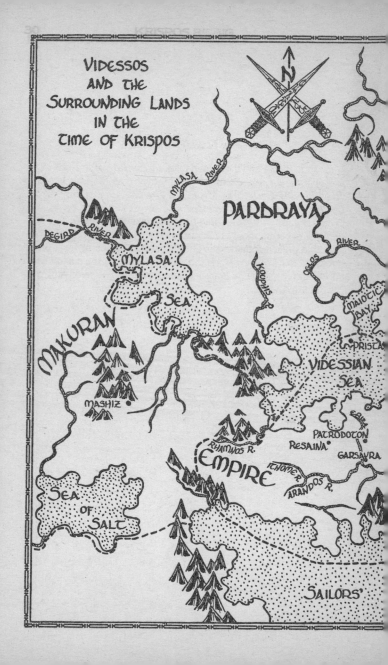

I

THE THUNDER OF HOOFBEATS. SHOUTS IN A HARSH TONGUE.

Krispos opened one eye. It was still dark. It felt like the middle of the night. He shook his head. He did not like noise that woke him up when he should have been asleep. He closed the eye and snuggled down between his mother and father on the straw paillasse he and they and his little sister used for a bed.

His parents woke, too, just when he was trying to go back to sleep. Krispos felt their bodies stiffen on either side of him. His sister Evdokia slept on. *Some people have all the luck*, he thought, though he'd never thought of Evdokia as particularly lucky before. Not only was she three—half his age—she was a *girl*.

The shouts turned to screams. One of the screams had words: "The Kubratoi! The Kubratoi are in the village!"

His mother gasped. "Phos save us!" she said, her voice almost as shrill as the cries of terror in the darkness outside.

"The good god saves through what people do," his father said. The farmer sprang to his feet. That woke Evdokia, where nothing else had. She started to cry. "Keep her quiet, Tatze!" Krispos' father growled. His mother cuddled Evdokia, softly crooned to her.

Krispos wondered whether he'd get cuddled if he started crying. He thought he'd be more likely to get his father's hand on his backside or across his face. Like every farm boy from anywhere near the town of Imbros, he knew who the Kubratoi were: wild men from north of the mountains. "Will we fight them,

1

Father?'' he asked. Just the other day, with a stick for a sword, he'd slain a dozen make-believe robbers.

But his father shook his head. "Real fighting is for soldiers. The Kubratoi, curse 'em, are soldiers. We aren't. They'd kill us, and we couldn't do much in the way of fighting back. This isn't play, boy.''

"What *will* we do, Phostis?'' his mother asked above Evdokia's sniffles. She sounded almost ready to cry herself. That frightened Krispos more than all the racket outside. What could be worse than something bad enough to frighten his mother?

The answer came in a moment: something bad enough to frighten his father. "We run,'' Phostis said grimly, "unless you'd sooner be dragged north by the two-legged wolves out there. That's why I built close to the forest; that's why I built the door facing away from most of the houses: to give us a chance to run, if the Kubratoi ever came down again.''

His mother bent, rose again. "I have the baby.''

In her arms, Evdokia said indignantly, "Not a baby!'' Then she started to cry again.

No one paid any attention to her. Krispos' father took him by the shoulder, so hard that his flimsy nightshirt might as well not have stood between man's flesh and boy's. "Can you run to the trees, son, fast as you can, and hide yourself till the bad men go away?''

"Yes, Father.'' Put that way, it sounded like a game. Krispos had played more games in the forest than he could count.

"Then run!'' His father threw open the door. Out he darted. His mother followed, still holding Evdokia. Last came his father. Krispos knew his father could run faster than he could, but his father didn't try, not tonight. He stayed between his family and the village.

Bare feet skimming across the ground, Krispos looked back over his shoulder. He'd never seen so many horses or so many torches in his life before. All the horses had strangers on them—the fearsome Kubratoi, he supposed. He could see a lot of villagers, too. The horsemen rounded up more of them every second.

"Don't look, boy! Run!'' his father said. Krispos ran. The blessed trees drew nearer and nearer. But a new shout was up, too, and horses drummed their way. The sound of pursuit grew with horrid quickness. Breath sobbing in his throat, Krispos thought how unfair it was that horses could run so fast.

"You stop, or we shoot you!" a voice called from behind. Krispos could hardly understand it; he had never heard Videssian spoken with any accent but the country twang of his own village.

"Keep running!" his father said. But riders flashed by Krispos on either side, so close he could feel the wind from their horses, so close he could smell the beasts. They wheeled, blocking him and his family from the safety of the woods.

Still with the feeling it was all a game, Krispos wheeled to dash off in some new direction. Then he saw the other horsemen, the pair who had gone after his father. One carried a torch, to give them both light to see by. It also let Krispos clearly see them, see their fur caps, the matted beards that seemed to complement those caps, their boiled-leather armor, the curved swords on their hips, the way they sat their mounts as if part of them. Frozen in time, the moment stayed with Krispos as long as he lived.

The second rider, the one without a torch, held a bow. It had an arrow in it, an arrow drawn and pointed at Krispos' father. That was when it stopped being play for the boy. He knew about bows, and how people were supposed to be careful with them. If these wild men didn't know that, time someone taught them.

He marched straight up to the Kubratoi. "You turn the aim of that arrow aside this instant," he told them. "You might hurt someone with it."

Both Kubratoi stared at him. The one with the bow threw back his head and howled laughter. The wild man *did* sound like a wolf, Krispos thought, shivering. He wished his voice had been big and deep like his father's, not a boy's squeak. The rider wouldn't have laughed then.

The rider probably would have shot him, but he did not think of that until years later. As it was, the Kubrati, still laughing, set down his bow, made an extravagant salute from the saddle. "Anything you say, little khagan, anything you say." He chuckled, wiping his face with the back of his hand. Then he raised his eyes to meet those of Krispos' father, who had hurried up to do what he could for the boy. "Not need to shoot now, eh, farmer-man?"

"No," Krispos' father agreed bitterly. "You've caught us, all right."

Along with his parents and Evdokia, Krispos walked slowly back to the village. A couple of horsemen stayed with them; the other two rode ahead so they could get back to doing whatever Kubratoi did. That, Krispos already suspected, was nothing good.

He remembered the strange word the rider with the bow had used. "Father, what does 'khagan' mean?"

"It's what the Kubratoi call their chieftain. If he'd been a Videssian, he would have called you 'Avtokrator' instead."

"Emperor? That's silly." Even with his world coming apart, Krispos found he could still laugh.

"So it is, boy," his father said grimly. He paused, then went on in a different tone, as if beginning to enjoy the joke himself: "Although there's said to be Vaspurakaner blood on my side of the family, and the Vaspurs all style themselves 'prince.' Bet you didn't know your father was a prince, eh, son?"

"Stop it, Phostis!" Krispos' mother said. "The priest says that nonsense about princes is heresy and nothing else but. Don't pass it on to the boy."

"Heresy is what the priest is supposed to know about," his father agreed, "but I won't argue about the nonsense part. Who ever heard of a prince going hungry?"

His mother sniffed, but made no further answer. They were inside the village by then, back where other people could hear them—not good, not if they wanted to talk of heresy. "What will they do with us?" was a safer question to ask, though not one, necessarily, with a surer answer. The villagers stood around under the bows of the Kubratoi, waiting.

Then more riders came up, these leading not people but the village's herds and flocks. "Are the animals coming with us, Father?" Krispos asked. He had not expected the Kubratoi to be so considerate.

"With us, aye, but not for us," was all his father said.

The Kubratoi started shouting, both those who spoke Videssian and those who did not. The villagers looked at one another, trying to figure out what the wild men meant. Then they saw the direction in which the cattle and sheep were going. They followed the beasts northward.

For Krispos, the trek to Kubrat was the best adventure he'd ever had. Tramping along all day was no harder than the chores he would have been doing had the raiders not descended on his village, and he always had something new to see. He'd never imagined, before, how big the world was.

That the march was forced hardly entered his mind. He ate better on it than he had at home; the Kubrati he'd defied that first night decided to make a pet of him and brought him chunks of roast lamb and beef. Soon other riders took up the game, so the "little khagan" sometimes found himself with more than he could eat.

At his father's urging, he never let on. Whenever the Kubratoi did not insist on having him eat in front of them, he passed their tidbits on to the rest of the family. The way he made the food disappear earned him a reputation as a bottomless pit, which only brought more his way.

By the end of the third day on the road north, the raiders who had descended on his village met with other bands bringing captives and booty back to Kubrat. That took Krispos by surprise. He had never given any thought to the world beyond the fields he knew. Now he saw he and his family were caught up in something larger than a local upheaval.

"Where are those people from, Father?" he asked as yet another group of bewildered, bedraggled peasants came stumbling into the larger stream.

His father shrugged, which made Evdokia giggle—she was riding on his shoulders. "Who can say?" Phostis answered. "Just another village of farmers that happened to be unlucky like ours."

"Unlucky." Krispos tasted the word, found it odd. He was enjoying himself. Sleeping under the stars was no great handicap, not to a six-year-old in summer. But his father, he could tell, did not like the Kubratoi and would have hit back at them if he could. That made Krispos ask another question, one he had not thought of till now. "Why are they taking farmers back to Kubrat?"

"Here comes one." His father waited till the wild man rode by, then pointed at his back. "Tell me what you see."

"A man on a horse with a big bushy beard."

"Horses don't have beards," Evdokia said. "That's dumb, Krispos."

"Hush," their father told her. "That's right, son—a man on a horse. Kubratoi hardly ever come down from their horses. They travel on them, go to war on them, and follow their flocks on them, too. But you can't be a farmer if you stay on your horse all the time."

"They don't want to be farmers, though," Krispos said.

"No, they don't," his father agreed. "But they need farmers, whether they want to farm themselves or not. Everybody needs farmers. Flocks can't give you all the food you need and flocks won't feed your horses at all. So they come down into Videssos and steal folk like—well, folk like us."

"Maybe it won't be so bad, Phostis," Krispos' mother said. "They can't take more from us than the imperial tax collectors do."

"Who says they can't?" his father answered. "Phos the lord of the great and good mind knows I have no love for the tax collectors, but year in, year out they leave us enough to get by on. They shear us—they don't flay us. If the Kubratoi were so fine as all that, Tatze, they wouldn't need to raid every few years to get more peasants. They'd be able to keep the ones they had."

There was a commotion among the captives that night. Evidently a good many of them agreed with Krispos' father and tried to escape from the Kubratoi. The screams were far worse than the ones in the village the night the wild men came.

"Fools," Phostis said. "Now they'll come down harder on all of us."

He was right. The men from the north started traveling before dawn and did not stop to feed the peasants till well after noon. They pushed the pace after the meager meal, too, halting only when it got too dark for them to see where they were going. By then, the Paristrian Mountains loomed tall against the northern skyline.

A small stream ran through the campsite the Kubratoi had picked. "Shuck out of your shirt and wash yourself," Krispos' mother told him.

He took off his shirt—the only one he had—but did not get into the water. It looked chilly. "Why don't you take a bath, too, Mama?" he said. "You're dirtier than I am." Under the dirt, he knew, she was one of the best-looking ladies in his village.

His mother's eyes flicked to the Kubratoi. "I'm all right the way I am, for now." She ran a grimy hand across her grimy face.

"But—"

The swat of his father's hand on his bare behind sent him skittering into the stream. It was as cold as it looked, but his bottom still felt aflame when he came out. His father nodded to him in a strange new way, almost as if they were both grown men. "Are you going to argue with your mother the next time she tells you to do something?" he asked.

"No, Father," Krispos said.

His father laughed. "Not until your backside cools off, anyway. Well, good enough. Here's your shirt." He got out of his own and walked down to the stream, to come back a few minutes later wet and dripping and running his hands through his hair.

Krispos watched him dress, then said carefully, "Father, is it arguing if I ask why you and I should take baths, but Mama shouldn't?"

For a bad moment he thought it was, and braced himself for another smack. But then his father said, "Hmm—maybe it isn't. Put it like this—no matter how clean we are, no Kubrati will find you or me pretty. You follow that?"

"Yes," Krispos said, although he thought his father—with his wide shoulders, neat black beard, and dark eyes set so deep beneath shaggy brows that sometimes the laughter lurking there was almost hidden—a fine and splendid man. But, he had to admit, that wasn't the same as pretty.

"All right, then. Now you've already seen how the Kubratoi are thieves. Phos, boy, they've stolen all of us, and our animals, too. And if one of them saw your mother looking especially pretty, the way she can—" Listening, she smiled at Krispos' father, but did not speak. "—he might want to take her away for his very own. We don't want that to happen, do we?"

"No!" Krispos' eyes got wide as he saw how clever his mother and father were. "I see! I understand! It's a trick, like when the wizard made Gemistos' hair turn green at the show he gave."

"A little like that, anyhow," his father agreed. "But that was real magic. Gemistos' hair really *was* green, till the wizard changed it back to brown again. This is more a game, like when men and women switch clothes sometimes on the Midwinter's Day festival. Do I turn into your mama because I'm wearing a dress?"

"Of course not!" Krispos giggled. But that wasn't supposed to fool anyone; as his father said, it was only a game. Here, now, his mother's prettiness remained, though she was trying to hide it so no one noticed. And if hiding something in plain sight wasn't magic, Krispos didn't know what was.

He had that thought again the next day, when the wild men took their captives into Kubrat. A couple of passes opened invitingly, but the Kubratoi headed for neither of them. Instead, they led the Videssian farmers down a forest track that seemed destined only to run straight into the side of the mountains.

But it did not run into the mountains—rather, into a narrow defile the trees and a last spur of hill screened from view. Though the sky stayed blue overhead, everything in the gorge was lost in shadow, as if it were twilight. Somewhere a nightjar hooted, thinking its time had come.

Strung out along the bottom of that steep, twisting gorge, people and animals could move but slowly. True evening came when they were only part of the way through the mountains.

"It's a good trick," Krispos' father said grudgingly as they settled down to camp. "Even if imperial soldiers do come after us, a handful of men could hold them out of this pass forever."

"Soldiers?" Krispos said, amazed. That Videssian troopers might be riding after the Kubratoi had never crossed his mind. "You mean the Empire cares enough about us to fight to get us back?"

His father's chuckle had little real amusement in it. "I know the only time you ever saw soldiers was that time a couple of years ago, when the harvest was so bad they didn't trust us to sit still for the tax collector unless he had archers at his back. But aye, they might fight to get us back. Videssos needs farmers on the ground as much as Kubrat does. Everybody needs farmers, boy; it'd be a hungry world without 'em."

Most of that went over Krispos' head. "Soldiers," he said again, softly. So he—for that was how he thought of it—was so important the Avtokrator would send soldiers to return him to his proper place! Then it was as if—well, almost as if—he had caused those soldiers to be sent. And surely that was as if—well, perhaps as if—he were Avtokrator himself. It was a good enough dream to fall asleep on, anyhow.

When he woke up the next morning, he was certain something was wrong. He kept peering around, trying to figure out what it was. At last his eyes went up to the strip of rock far overhead that the rising sun was painting with light. "That's the wrong direction!" he blurted. "Look! The sun's coming up in the west!"

"Phos have mercy, I think the lad's right!" Tzykalas the cobbler said close by. He drew a circle on his breast, itself the sign of the good god's sun. Other people started babbling; Krispos heard the fear in their voices.

Then his father yelled "Stop it!" so loudly that they actually did. Into that sudden silence, Phostis went on, "What's more likely, that the world has turned upside down or that this canyon's wound around so we couldn't guess east from west?"

Krispos felt foolish. From the expressions on the folk nearby, so did they. In a surly voice, Tzykalas said, "Your boy was the one who started us hopping, Phostis."

"Well, so he was. What about it? Who's the bigger fool, a silly boy or the grown man who takes him seriously?"

Someone laughed at that. Tzykalas flushed. His hands curled into fists. Krispos' father stood still and quiet, waiting. Shaking his head and muttering to himself, Tzykalas turned away. Two or three more people laughed then.

Krispos' father took no notice of them. Quietly he said, "The next time things aren't the way you expect, son, think before you talk, eh?"

Krispos nodded. He felt foolish now himself. One more thing to remember, he thought. The bigger he got, the more such things he found. He wondered how grown people managed to keep everything straight.

Late that afternoon, the canyon opened up. Green land lay ahead, land not much different from the fields and forests around Krispos' home village. "Is that Kubrat?" he asked, pointing.

One of the wild men overheard him. "Is Kubrat. Is good to be back. Is home," he said in halting Videssian.

Till then, Krispos hadn't thought about the raiders having homes—to him, they had seemed a phenomenon of nature, like a blizzard or a flood. Now, though, a happy smile was on the Kubrati's face. He looked like a man heading home after some hard work. Maybe he had little boys at that home, or little girls. Krispos hadn't thought about the raiders having children, either.

He hadn't thought about a lot of things, he realized. When he said that out loud, his father laughed. "That's because you're still a child. As you grow, you'll work through the ones that matter to you."

"But I want to be able to know about all those things now," Krispos said. "It isn't fair."

"Maybe not." No longer laughing, his father put a hand on his shoulder. "But I'll tell you this—a chicken comes out of its egg knowing everything it needs to know to be a chicken. There's more to being a man; it takes a while to learn. So which would you rather be, son, a chicken or a man?"

Krispos folded his hands into his armpits and flapped imaginary wings. He let out a couple of loud clucks, then squealed when his father tickled his ribs.

The next morning, Krispos saw in the distance several—well, what were they? Neither tents nor houses, but something in between. They had wheels and looked as if animals could pull them. His father did not know what to call them, either.

"May I ask one of the Kubratoi?" Krispos said.

His mother started to shake her head, but his father said, "Let him, Tatze. We may as well get used to them, and they've liked the boy ever since he stood up to them that first night."

So he asked one of the wild men trotting by on his pony. The Kubrati stared at him and started to laugh. "So the little khagan does not know of yurts, eh? Those are yurts you see, the perfect homes for following the flocks."

"Will you put us in yurts, too?" Krispos liked the idea of being able to live now one place, now another.

But the horseman shook his head. "You are farmer folk, good only for raising plants. And as plants are rooted to the ground, your houses will be rooted, too." He spat to show his contempt for people who had to stay in one spot, then touched the heels of his boots to his horse's flanks and rode off.

Krispos looked after him, a little hurt. "I'll travel, too, one day," he said loudly. The Kubrati paid no attention to him. He sighed and went back to his parents. "I *will* travel!" he told his father. "I will."

"You'll travel in a few minutes," his father answered. "They're getting ready to move us along again."

"That's not what I meant," Krispos said. "I meant travel when *I* want to, and go where *I* want to."

"Maybe you will, son." His father sighed, rose, and stretched. "But not today."

Just as captives from many Videssian villages had joined together to make one large band on the way to Kubrat, so now they were taken away from the main group—five, ten, twenty families at a time, to go off to the lands they would work for their new masters.

Most of the people the Kubratoi told to go off with the group that included Krispos' father were from his village, but some were not, and some of the villagers had to go someplace else. When they protested being broken up, the wild men ignored their pleas. "Not as if you were a clan the gods formed," a raider said, the same scorn in his voice that Krispos had heard from the Kubrati who explained what yurts were. And, like that rider, he rode away without listening to any reply.

"What does he mean, gods?" Krispos asked. "Isn't there just Phos? And Skotos," he added after a moment, naming the good god's wicked foe in a smaller voice.

"The Kubratoi don't know of Phos," his father told him. "They worship demons and spirits and who knows what. After they die, they'll spend forever in Skotos' ice for their wickedness, too."

"I hope there are priests here," Tatze said nervously.

"We'll get along, whether or not," Phostis said. "We know what the good is, and we'll follow it." Krispos nodded. That made sense to him. He always tried to be good—unless being bad looked like a lot more fun. He hoped Phos would forgive him. His father usually did, and in his mind the good god was a larger version of his father, one who watched the whole world instead of just a farm.

Later that day, one of the Kubratoi pointed ahead and said, "There your new village."

"It's big!" Krispos said. "Look at all the houses!"

His father had a better idea of what to look for. "Aye, lots of houses. Where are the people, though? Hardly any in the fields, hardly any in the village." He sighed. "I expect the reason I don't see 'em is that they're not there to see."

As the party of Kubratoi and captives drew near, a few men and women did emerge from their thatch-roofed cottages to stare at the newcomers. Krispos had never had much. These thin, poorly clad wretches, though, showed him other folk could have even less.

The wild men waved the village's new inhabitants forward to meet the old. Then they wheeled their horses and rode away . . . rode, Krispos supposed, back to their yurts.

As he came into the village, he saw that many of the houses stood empty; some were only half thatched, others had rafters falling down, still others had chunks of clay gone from the wall to reveal the woven branches within.

His father sighed again. "I suppose I should be glad we'll have roofs over our heads." He turned to the families uprooted from Videssos. "We might as well pick out the places we'll want to live in. Me, I have my eye on that house right there."

He pointed to an abandoned dwelling as dilapidated as any of the others, set near the edge of the village.

As he and Tatze, followed by Krispos and Evdokia, headed toward the home they had chosen, one of the men who belonged to this village came up to confront him. "Who do you think you are, to take a house without so much as a by-your-leave?" the fellow asked. Even to a farm boy like Krispos, his accent sounded rustic.

"My name's Phostis," Krispos' father said. "Who are you to tell me I can't, when this place is falling to pieces around you?"

The other newcomers added their voices to his. The man looked from them to his own followers, who were fewer and less sure of themselves. He lost his bluster as a punctured bladder loses air. "I'm Roukhas," he said. "Headman here, at least until all you folk came."

"We don't want what's yours, Roukhas," Krispos' father assured him. He smiled a sour smile. "Truth is, I'd be just as glad never to have met you, because that'd mean I was still back in Videssos." Even Roukhas nodded at that, managing a wry chuckle. Phostis went on, "We're here, though, and I don't see much point in having to build from scratch when there're all these places ready to hand."

"Aye, well, put that way, I suppose you have a point." Roukhas stepped backward and waved Phostis toward the house he had chosen.

As if his concession were some sort of signal, the rest of the longtime inhabitants of the village hurried up to mingle with the new arrivals. Indeed, they fell on them like long-lost cousins— as, Krispos thought, a little surprised at himself, they were.

"They didn't even know what the Avtokrator's name was," Krispos' mother marveled as the family settled down to sleep on the ground inside their new house.

"Aye, well, they need to worry about the khagan more," his father answered. Phostis yawned an enormous yawn. "A lot of 'em, too, were born right here, not back home. I shouldn't be surprised if they didn't even remember there *was* an Avtokrator."

"But still," Krispos' mother said, "they talked with us as we would with someone from the capital, from Videssos the city— someone besides the tax man, I mean. And we're from the back of beyond."

"No, Tatze, we just got there," his father answered. "If you doubt it, wait till you see how busy we're going to be." He yawned again. "Tomorrow."

Life on a farm is never easy. Over the next weeks and months, Krispos found out just how hard it could be. If he was not gathering straw for his father to bind into yealms and put up on the roof to repair the thatch, then he was fetching clay from the streambank to mix with roots and more straw and goat hair and dung to make daub to patch the walls.

Making and slapping on the daub was at least fun. He had the chance to get filthy while doing just what his parents told him. He carried more clay for his mother to shape into a baking oven. Like the one back at his old village, it looked like a beehive.

He spent a lot of time with his mother and little sister, working in the vegetable plots close by the houses. Except for the few still kept up by the handful of people here before the newcomers arrived, those had been allowed to run down. He and Evdokia weeded until their hands blistered, then kept right on. They plucked bugs and snails from the beans and cabbages, the onions and vetch, the beets and turnips. Krispos yelled and screamed and jumped up and down to scare away marauding crows and sparrows and starlings. That was fun, too.

He also kept the village chickens and ducks away from the vegetables. Soon his father got a couple of laying hens by doing some timber cutting for one of the established villagers. Krispos took care of them, too, and spread their manure over the vegetables.

He did more scarecrow duty out in the fields of wheat and oats and barley, along with the rest of the children. With more new arrivals than boys and girls born in the village, that time in the fields was also a time of testing, to see who was strong and who was clever. Krispos held his own and then some; even boys who had two more summers than he did soon learned to give him a wide berth.

He managed to find time for mischief. Roukhas never figured out who put the rotten egg under the straw, right where he liked to lay his head. The farmer and his family did sleep outdoors for the next two days, until their house aired out enough to be livable again. And Evdokia ran calling for her mother one day when she came back from washing herself in the stream and found her clothes moving by themselves.

Unlike Roukhas, Tatze had no trouble deducing how the toad had got into Evdokia's shift. Krispos slept on his stomach that night.

Helping one of the slower newcomers get his roof into shape for the approaching fall rains earned Krispos' father a piglet—and Krispos the job of looking after it. "It's a sow, too," his father said with some satisfaction. "Next year we'll breed it and have plenty of pigs of our own." Krispos looked forward to pork stew and ham and bacon—but not to more pig-tending.

Sheep the village also had, a small flock owned in common, more for wool than for meat. With so many people arriving with only the clothes on their backs, the sheep were sheared a second time that year, and the lambs, too. Krispos' mother spent a while each evening spinning thread and she began to teach Evdokia the art. She set up a loom between two forked posts outside the house, so she could turn the spun yarn into cloth.

There were no cattle. The Kubratoi kept them all. Cattle, in Kubrat, were wealth, almost like gold. A pair of donkeys plowed for the villagers instead of oxen.

Krispos' father fretted over that, saying, "Oxen have horns to attach the yoke to, but with donkeys you have to fasten it round their necks, so they choke if they pull hard against it." But Roukhas showed him the special donkey-collars they had, modeled after the ones the Kubratoi used for the horses that pulled their yurts. He came away from the demonstration impressed. "Who would have thought the barbarians could come up with something so useful?"

What they had not come up with was any way to make grapes grow north of the mountains. Everyone ate apples and pears, instead, and drank beer. The newcomers never stopped grumbling about that, though some of the beer had honey added to it so it was almost as sweet as wine.

Not having grapes made life different in small ways as well as large. One day Krispos' father brought home a couple of rabbits he had killed in the field. His mother chopped the meat fine, spiced it with garlic—and then stopped short. "How can I stuff it into grape leaves if there aren't any grape leaves?" She sounded more upset at not being able to cook what she wanted than she had over being uprooted and forced to trek to Kubrat; it made the uprooting hit home.

Phostis patted her on the shoulder, turned to his son. "Run

over to Roukhas' house and find out what Ivera uses in place of grape leaves. Quick, now!''

Krispos soon came scampering back. "Cabbage," he announced importantly.

"It won't be the same," his mother said. It wasn't, but Krispos thought it was good.

Harvest came sooner than it would have in the warmer south. The grown men cut first the barley, then the oats and wheat, going through the fields with sickles. Krispos and the rest of the children followed to pick up the grains that fell to the ground. Most went into the sacks they carried; a few they ate. And after the grain was gathered, the men went through the fields again, cutting down the golden straw and tying it into sheaves. Then the children, two to a sheaf, dragged it back to the village. Finally, the men and women hauled buckets of dung from the middens to manure the ground for the next planting.

Once the grain was harvested, it was time to pick the beans and to chop down the plants so they could be fed to the pigs. And then, with the grain and beans in deep storage pits—except for some of the barley, which was set aside for brewing—the whole village seemed to take a deep breath.

"I was worried, when we came here, whether we'd be able to grow enough to get all of us through the winter," Krispos' father said one evening, taking a long pull on a mug of beer. "Now, though, Phos the lord of the great and good mind be praised, I think we have enough and to spare."

His mother said, "Don't speak too soon."

"Come on, Tatze, what could go wrong?" his father answered, smiling. "It's in the ground and safe."

Two days later, the Kubratoi came. They came in greater numbers and with more weapons than they'd had escorting the new villagers away from the mass of Videssian captives. At their shouted orders, the villagers opened one storage pit in three and loaded the precious grain onto packhorses the wild men had brought with them. When they were done, the Kubratoi trotted off to plunder the next village.

Krispos' father stood a long time, staring down into the empty yard-deep holes in the sandy soil back of the village. Finally, with great deliberation, he spat into one of them. "Locusts," he said bitterly. "They ate us out just like locusts. We would have had plenty, but we'll all be hungry before spring comes."

"We ought to fight them next time, Phostis," said one of the younger men who had come from the same village as Krispos and his family. "Make them pay for what they steal."

But Krispos' father sadly shook his head. "I wish we could, Stankos, when I see what they've done to us. They'd massacre us, though, I fear. They're soldiers, and it's the nature of soldiers to take. Farmers endure."

Roukhas was still Phostis' rival for influence in the village, but now he agreed with him. "Four or five years ago the village of Gomatou, over a couple of days west of here, tried rising up against the Kubratoi," he said.

"Well? What happened to it?" Stankos asked.

"It's not there any more," Roukhas said bleakly. "We watched the smoke go up into the sky."

No one spoke of rebellion again. To Krispos, charging out against the Kubratoi with sword and lance and bow and driving them all back north over the Astris River to the plains from which they'd come would have been the most glorious thing in the world. It was one of his playmates' favorite games. In truth, though, the wild men were the ones with the arms and armor and horses and, more important still, both the skill and will to use them.

Farmers endure, Krispos thought. He didn't like just enduring. He wondered if that meant he shouldn't be a farmer. What else could he be, though? He had no idea.

The village got through the winter, which was fiercer than any Krispos remembered. Even the feast and celebrations of Midwinter's Day, the day when the sun finally turned north in the sky, had to be forgotten because of the blizzard raging outside.

Krispos grew to hate being cooped up and idle in the house for weeks on end. South of the mountains, even midwinter gave days when he could go out to play in the snow. Those were few and far between here. Even a freezing trip out to empty the chamber pot on the dung heap or help his father haul back firewood made him glad to return to the warm—if stuffy and smoky—air inside.

Spring came at last and brought with it mud almost as oppressive as the snow had been. Plowing, harrowing, sowing, and weeding followed, plunging Krispos back into the endless round of farm work and making him long for the lazy days of winter once more. That fall, the Kubratoi came to take their unfair share of the harvest once more.

The year after that, they came a couple of other times, riding through the fields and trampling down long swathes of growing grain. As they rode, they whooped and yelled and grinned at the helpless farmers whose labor they were wrecking.

"Drunk, the lot of 'em," Krispos' father said the night after it happened the first time, his mouth tight with disgust. "Pity they didn't fall off their horses and break their fool necks—that'd send 'em down to Skotos where they belong."

"Better to thank Phos that they didn't come into the village and hurt people instead of plants," Krispos' mother said. Phostis only scowled and shook his head.

Listening, Krispos found himself agreeing with his father. What the Kubratoi had done was wrong, and they'd done it on purpose. If he deliberately did something wrong, he got walloped for it. The villagers were not strong enough to wallop the Kubratoi, so let them spend eternity with the dark god and see how they liked that.

When fall came, of course, the Kubratoi took as much grain as they had before. If, thanks to them, less was left for the village, that was the village's hard luck.

The wild men played those same games the next year. That year, too, a woman who had gone down to the stream to bathe never came back. When the villagers went looking for her, they found hoofprints from several horses in the clay by the streambank.

Krispos' father held his mother very close when the news swept through the village. "*Now* I will thank Phos, Tatze," he said. "It could have been you."

One dawn late in the third spring after Krispos came to Kubrat, barking dogs woke the villagers even before they would have risen on their own. Rubbing their eyes, they stumbled from their houses to find themselves staring at a couple of dozen armed and mounted Kubratoi. The riders carried torches. They scowled down from horseback at the confused and frightened farmers.

Krispos' hair tried to rise at the back of his neck. He hadn't thought, lately, about the night the Kubratoi had kidnapped him and everyone else in his village. Now the memories—and the terror—of that night flooded back. But where else could the wild men take them from here? Why would they want to?

One of the riders drew his sword. The villagers drew back a pace. Someone moaned. But the Kubrati did not attack with the curved blade. He pointed instead, westward. "You come with us," he said in gutturally accented Videssian. "Now."

Krispos' father asked the questions the boy was thinking: "Where? Why?"

"Where I say, man bound to the earth. Because I say." This time the horseman's gesture with the sword was threatening.

At nine, Krispos knew more of the world and its harsh ways than he had at six. Still, he did not hesitate. He sprang toward the Kubrati. His father grabbed at him to haul him back, too late. "You leave him alone!" Krispos shouted up at the rider.

The man snarled at him, teeth gleaming white in the torchlight's flicker. The sword swung up. Krispos' mother screamed. Then the wild man hesitated. He thrust his torch down almost into Krispos' face. Suddenly, astonishingly, the snarl became a grin. The Kubrati said something in his own language. His comrades exclaimed, then roared laughter.

He dropped back into Videssian. "Ha, little khagan, you forget me? Good thing I remember you, or you die this morning. You defy me once before, in Videssos. How does farmer boy come to have man's—Kubrati man's—spirit in him?"

Krispos hadn't recognized the rider who'd captured him and his family. If the man recognized him, though, he would turn it to his advantage. "Why are you here? What do you want with us now?"

"To take you away." The scowl came back to the Kubrati's face. "Videssos has paid ransom for you. We have to let you go." He sounded anything but delighted at the prospect.

"Ransom?" The word spread through the villagers, at first slowly and in hushed, disbelieving tones, then louder and louder till they all shouted it, nearly delirious with joy. "Ransom!"

They danced round the Kubratoi, past hatred and fear dissolved in the powerful water of freedom. It was, Krispos thought, like a Midwinter's Day celebration somehow magically dropped into springtime. Soon riders and villagers were hoisting wooden mugs of beer together. Barrel after barrel was broken open. Little would be left for later, but what did that matter? They would not be here later. A new cry took the place of "Ransom!"

"We're going home!"

Evdokia was puzzled. "What does everyone mean, Krispos, we're going home? Isn't this home?"

"No, silly, the place Mother and Father talk about all the time is our real home."

"Oh." His sister barely remembered Videssos. "How is it different?"

"It's . . ." Krispos wasn't too clear on that himself, not after almost three years. "It's better," he finished at last. That seemed to satisfy her. He wondered if it was true. His own memories of life south of the mountains had grown hazy.

The Kubratoi seemed in as big a hurry to get rid of their Videssian captives as they had been to get them into Kubrat in the first place. Evdokia had trouble keeping up; sometimes Krispos' father had to carry her for a stretch, even if it shamed her. Krispos made the three days of hard marching on his own, but they left his feet blistered and him sleeping like a dead man each night.

At last the villagers and hundreds more like them reached a broad, shallow valley. With an eye rapidly growing wiser to the ways of farming, Krispos saw that it was better land than what his village tilled. He also saw several large and splendid yurts and, in the distance, the flocks by which the Kubratoi lived. That explained why the valley was not farmed.

The wild men herded the Videssians into pens much like those in which the peasants kept goats. They posted guards around them so no one would even think of clambering over the branches and sneaking off. Fear began to replace the farmer's jubilation. "Are we truly to be ransomed," someone shouted, "or sold like so many beasts?"

"You keep still! Big ceremony coming tomorrow," yelled a Kubrati who spoke Videssian. He climbed up onto the fencing of the pen and pointed. "See over there. There tents of Videssos' men, and Empire's banner, too. No tricks now."

Krispos looked in the direction the man's arm had given. He was too short to see out of the pen. "Pick me up, Father!"

His father did, then, with a grunt of effort, set the boy on his shoulders. Krispos saw the tops of several square tents not far from the yurts he'd noticed before. Sure enough, a sky-blue flag with a gold sunburst on it snapped in front of one of them. "*Is* that Videssos' banner?" he asked. Try as he would, he could not recall it.

"Aye, it's ours," his father said. "The tax collector always used to show it when he came. I'm gladder to see it now than I was then, I'll tell you that." He put Krispos down.

"Let me see! My turn! Let me see!" Evdokia squealed. Phostis sighed, then smiled. He picked up his daughter.

* * *

The next morning, the peasants got far better fare than they'd had on the trek to the valley: roasted mutton and beef, with plenty of the flat wheatcakes the Kubratoi baked in place of leavened bread. Krispos ate till his belly felt like bursting from joy and he washed down the meat with a long swig from a leather bucket of mare's milk.

"I wonder what the ceremony the wild man talked about will be like," his mother said.

"I wish we could see more of it," his father added. "Weren't for us, after all, it wouldn't be happening. Not right to leave us penned up while it's going on."

A little later, the Kubratoi let the farmers out of the pens. "This way! This way!" the nomads who spoke Videssian shouted, urging the crowd along toward the yurts and tents.

Krispos spotted the wild men he had yelled at on the day he was captured and on the day he started back to freedom. The Kubrati was peering into the mass of peasants as they walked by him. His eye caught Krispos'. He grinned. "Ho, little kha-gan, I look for you. You come with me—you part of ceremony."

"What, me? Why?" As he spoke, though, Krispos cut across the flow of people toward the Kubrati.

The now-dismounted rider took him by the shoulder, as his father did sometimes. "Khagan Omurtag, he want some Vides-sian to talk to envoy from Empire, stand for all you people in magic, while envoy paying gold to get you back. I tell him about you, how bold you are. He say all right."

"Oh. Oh, my!" Excitement ousted fear. Khagan Omurtag, in Krispos' imagination, was nine feet high, with teeth like a wolf's. And an envoy from the Avtokrator should be even more magnificent—tall, handsome, heroic, clad in gilded chain mail, and carrying an enormous sword. . . .

Reality was less dramatic, as reality has a way of being. The Kubratoi had built a little platform of hides stretched across timbers. None of the four men who stood on it was nine feet tall, none wore gilded chain mail. Then the wild man lifted Krispos, and he was on the platform, too.

"Pretty boy," murmured a short, sour-faced man in a robe of green silk shot through with silver threads. He turned to the Kubrati standing across from him. "All right, Omurtag, he's here. Get on with your miserable heathen rite, if you think you must."

Krispos waited for the sky to fall. No matter that the khagan of Kubrat was neither especially tall nor especially lupine—was, in fact, quite an ordinary-looking Kubrati save that his furs were of marten and sable, not fox and rabbit. He was the khagan. Talking that way to him had to cost a man his head.

But Omurtag only threw back his head and laughed. "Sweet as always, Iakovitzes," he said. His Videssian was as smooth and polished as the envoy's, and a good deal more so than Krispos'. "The magic seals the bargain, as well you know."

"Phos watches over all bargains from above the sun." Iakovitzes nodded to the man in a blue robe behind him. Dim memories stirred in Krispos. He'd seen such men with shaved heads before, though not in Kubrat; the fellow was a priest.

"So you say," Omurtag answered. "My *enaree* here knows the spirits of ground and wind. They are closer than any lofty god above the sun, and I trust them further."

The *enaree* was the first grown man Krispos had ever seen who cut off his beard. It made him look like an enormous little boy—till one looked into his eyes. They saw farther than boys' . . . farther than men's had any business seeing, too, Krispos thought nervously.

The khagan turned to him. "Come here, lad."

For a split second, Krispos hung back. Then he thought that he had been chosen for his boldness. He straightened his back, put his chin up, and walked over to Omurtag. The tight-stretched hides vibrated under his feet, as if they were an enormous drumhead.

"We have your people," Omurtag intoned, taking hold of Krispos' arm with his left hand. His grip was firm and hard. His right hand plucked a dagger from his belt, set it at the boy's throat. Krispos stood very still. The khagan went on, "They are ours, to do with as we will."

"The Empire has gold and will pay for their safe return." Iakovitzes sounded, of all things, bored. Krispos was suddenly sure he'd performed this ceremony many times before.

"Let us see that gold," the khagan said. His voice was still formal, but anything but bored. He stared avidly at the pouch Iakovitzes withdrew from within a fold of his robe.

The Videssian envoy drew out a single bright coin, gave it to Omurtag. "Let this goldpiece stand for all, as the boy does," Iakovitzes said.

Omurtag passed the coin to the *enaree*. He muttered over it;

the hand that was not holding it moved in tiny passes. Krispos saw the Videssian priest scowl, but the man held his peace. The *enaree* spoke in the Kubrati tongue. "He declares it is good gold," Omurtag said to Iakovitzes.

"Of course it's good gold," Iakovitzes snapped, breaking the ritual. "The Empire hasn't coined anything else for hundreds of years. Should we start now, it would be for something more important than ransoming ragged peasants."

The khagan laughed out loud. "I think your tongue was stung by a wasp one day, Iakovitzes," he said, then returned to the pattern of the ceremony. "He declares it is good gold. Thus the people are yours." He gently pushed Krispos toward Iakovitzes.

The envoy's touch was warm, alive. He moved his hand on Krispos' back in a way that was strange and familiar at the same time. "Hello, pretty boy," Iakovitzes murmured. Krispos recognized the tone and realized why the caress had that familiarity to it: his father and mother acted like this with each other when they felt like making love.

Having lived all his life in a one-room house with his parents, having slept in the same bed with them, he knew what sex was about. That variations could exist, variations that might include him and Iakovitzes, had not occurred to him before, though. Now that it did, he found he did not much care for it. He moved half a step away from the Avtokrator's envoy.

Iakovitzes jerked back his hand as if surprised to discover what it had been up to. Glancing at him, Krispos doubted he was. His face was a mask that must have taken years to perfect. Seeing Krispos' eye upon him, he gave a tiny shrug. *If you don't want it, too bad for you,* he seemed to say.

Aloud, the words he spoke were quite different. "It is accomplished," he said loudly. Then he turned to the crowd of peasants gathered in front of the platform. "People of Videssos, you are redeemed!" he cried. "The Phos-guarded Avtokrator Rhaptes redeems you from your long and horrid captivity in this dark and barbarous land, from your toil under the degrading domination of brutal and terrible masters. Masters? No, rather let me call them robbers, for they robbed you of the liberty rightfully yours . . ."

The speech went on for some time. Krispos was at first impressed and then overwhelmed with the buckets of big words Iakovitzes poured over the heads of the farmers. *Over our heads is right,* the boy thought. He was missing one word in three, and doubted anyone else in the crowd was doing much better.

He yawned. Seeing that, Omurtag grinned and winked. Iakovitzes, caught up now in the full flow of his rhetoric, never noticed.

The khagan waggled a finger. Krispos walked back over to him. Again Iakovitzes paid no attention, though Krispos felt the eyes of both priest and *enaree* upon him.

"Here, lad," Omurtag said—softly, so as not to disrupt Iakovitzes' speech. "You take this, as a reminder of the day." He handed Krispos the goldpiece Iakovitzes had given him to symbolize the Videssians' ransoming.

Behind Iakovitzes, the blue-robed priest of Phos jerked violently, as if a bee had stung him. He made the circular sun-sign over the left side of his breast. And Omurtag's own *enaree* grabbed the khagan and whispered harshly and urgently into his ear.

Omurtag shoved the seer aside, so hard that the *enaree* almost tumbled off the edge of the platform. The khagan snarled something at him in the Kubrati tongue, then returned to Videssian to tell Krispos, "The fool says that, since this coin was used in our ceremony here, with it I have given you the Videssian people. Whatever will you do with them, little farmer boy?"

He laughed uproariously at his own wit, loud enough to make Iakovitzes pause and glare at him before resuming his harangue. Krispos laughed, too. Past tunic and sandals—and now this coin—had never owned anything. And the idea of having a whole people was absurd, anyhow.

"Go on back to your mother and father," Omurtag said when he had control of himself again. Krispos hopped down from the platform. He kept tight hold of the goldpiece Omurtag had given him.

"The sooner we're out of Kubrat and the faster we're back in civilization, the better," Iakovitzes declared to whoever would listen. He pressed the pace back to Videssos harder than the Kubratoi had when they were taking the peasants away.

The redeemed Videssians did not leave by the same winding, narrow pass through which they had entered Kubrat. They used a wider, easier route some miles farther west. An old graveled highway ran down it, one that became broad and well maintained on the Videssian side of the mountains.

"You'd think the Kubrati road used to be part of this one here," Krispos remarked.

Neither of his parents answered. They were too worn with walking and with keeping Evdokia on her feet to have energy left over for speculation.

But the priest who had gone to Kubrat with Iakovitzes heard. His name, Krispos had learned, was Pyrrhos. Ever since Omurtag gave the boy that goldpiece, Pyrrhos had been around a good deal, as if keeping an eye on him. Now, from muleback, the priest said, "You speak the truth, lad. Once the road was one, for once the land was one. Once the whole world, near enough, was one."

Krispos frowned. "One world? Well, of course it is, sir priest. What else could it be?" Trudging along beside him, Phostis smiled; in that moment, son sounded very much like father.

"One world ruled by Videssos, I mean," Pyrrhos said. "But then, three hundred years ago, on account of the sins of the Videssian people, Phos suffered the wild Khamorth tribes to roll off the Pardrayan plain and rape away the great tracts of land that are now the khaganates of Thatagush, Khatrish—and Kubrat. Those lands remain rightfully ours. One day, when Phos the lord of the great and good mind judges us worthy, we shall reclaim them." He sketched the sun-symbol over his heart.

Krispos walked a while in silence, thinking about what the priest had said. Three hundred years meant nothing to him; Pyrrhos might as well have said *a long time ago* or even *once upon a time*. But sin, now—that was interesting. "What sort of sins?" the boy asked.

Pyrrhos' long, narrow face grew even longer and narrower as his thin-lipped mouth pursed in disapproval. "The same sins Skotos—" He spat in the roadway to show his hatred of the dark god. "—always sets forth as snares for mankind: the sin of division, from which sprang civil war; the sin of arrogance, which led the fools of that time to scorn the barbarians till too late; the sin of luxury, which made them cling to the great riches they had and not exert themselves to preserve those riches for future generations."

At that, Krispos' father lifted his head. "Reckon the sin of luxury's one we don't have to worry about here," he said, "seeing as I don't think there's above three people in this whole crowd with a second shirt to call their own."

"You are better for it!" the priest exclaimed. "Yet the sin of

luxury lives on; doubt it not. In Videssos the city, scores of
nobles have robes for each day of the year, sir, yet bend all their
energy not to helping their neighbors who have less but rather
only to acquiring more, more, and ever more. Their robes will
not warm them against the chill of Skotos' ice.''

His sermon did not have the effect he'd hoped. ''A robe for
each day of the year,'' Krispos' father said in wonder. Scowling
angrily, Pyrrhos rode off. Phostis turned to Krispos. ''How'd
you like to have that many robes, son?''

''That sounds like too many to me,'' Krispos said. ''But I
would like a second shirt.''

''So would I, boy,'' his father said, laughing. ''So would I.''

A day or so later, a company of Videssian troopers joined the
returning peasants. Their chain-mail shirts jingled as they came
up, an accompaniment to the heavy drumroll of their horses'
hooves. Iakovitzes handed their leader a scroll. The captain read
it, glanced at the farmers, and nodded. He gave Iakovitzes a
formal salute, with clenched right fist over his heart.

Iakovitzes returned the salute, then rode south at a trot so fast
it was almost a gallop. Pyrrhos left the peasants at the same
time, but Iakovitzes' horse quickly outdistanced his mule. ''My
lord, be so good as to wait for your servant,'' Pyrrhos called
after him.

Iakovitzes was so far ahead by then that Krispos, who was
near the front of the band of peasants, could barely hear his
reply: ''If you think I'll crawl to the city at the pace of a shambling mule, priest, you can bloody well think again!'' The noble
soon disappeared round a bend in the road. More sedately, Pyrrhos followed.

Later that day, a dirt track from the east ran into the highway.
The Videssian captain halted the farmers while he checked the
scroll Iakovitzes had given him. ''Fifteen here,'' he told his
soldiers. They counted off the fifteen men they saw, and in a
moment fifteen families, escorted by three or four horsemen,
headed down that track. The rest started south again.

Another stop came before long. This time, twenty families
were detached from the main group. ''They're treating us just
like the Kubratoi did,'' Krispos' mother said in some dismay.

''Did you expect we'd get to go back to our old village,
Tatze?'' his father said. She nodded. ''I didn't,'' he told her.
''We've been gone a good while now. Someone else will be

working our fields; I suppose we'll go to fill some holes that've opened up since."

So it proved. The next morning, Phostis was one of a group of thirty peasant men told off by the Videssian soldiers. Along with the others and their kinsfolk, he, Tatze, Krispos, and Evdokia left the main road for a winding path that led west.

They reached their new village late that afternoon. At the sight of it, even Phostis' resignation wore thin. He glared up at one of the troopers who had come with the farmers. "The Kubratoi gave us more to work with than this," he said bitterly. Krispos watched his father's shoulders slump. Having to start over from nothing twice in three years could make any man lose heart.

But the Videssian soldier said, "Take another look at the fellows waiting there for you, farmer. Might be you'll change your mind."

Phostis looked. So did Krispos. All he'd noticed before was that there weren't very many men in the village. He remembered arriving at the one in Kubrat. His father was right: more people had been waiting there than here. And he saw no one out in the fields. So what good could this handful of men be?

Something about the way they stood as they waited for the newcomers to reach them made Krispos scratch his head. It was different from the way the villagers in Kubrat had stood, but he could not put his finger on how.

His father could. "I don't believe those are farmers at all," he said slowly.

"Right the first time." The trooper grinned at him. "They're pensioned-off veterans. The Avtokrator, Phos bless him, has established five or six like them in every village we're resettling with you people."

"But what good will they be to us, save maybe as strong backs?" Phostis said. "If they're not farmers, we'll have to show them how to do everything."

"Maybe you will, at first," the soldier said, "but you won't have to show 'em the same thing twice very often, I'll warrant. And could be they'll have a thing or two to teach you folk, as well."

Krispos' father snorted. "What could they teach us?"

He'd meant that for a scornful rhetorical question, but the horseman answered it. "Bow and sword, spear and shield, maybe even a bit of horsework. The next time the Kubratoi come to haul you people away, could be you'll give 'em a bit of a surprise. Tell me now, wouldn't you like that?''

Before his father could answer, Krispos threw back his head and howled like a wolf. Phostis started to laugh, then stopped abruptly. His hands curled into fists, and he bayed, too, a deep, solid underpinning to his son's high yips.

More and more farmers began to howl, and finally even some of the soldiers. They entered the new village like a pack at full cry. *If the Kubratoi could only hear us*, Krispos thought proudly, *they'd never dare come south of the mountains again.*

He was, after all, still a boy.

II

For some years, the Kubratoi did not raid into Videssos. Sometimes, in absent moments, Krispos wondered if Phos had heard his thought and struck fear into the wild men's hearts. Once, when he was about twelve, he said as much to one of the retired veterans, a tough graybeard called Varades.

Varades laughed till tears came. "Ah, lad, I wish it were that easy. I'd sooner spend my time thinking bad thoughts at my foes than fighting, any day. But more likely, I reckon, is that old Omurtag still hasn't gone through all the gold Rhaptes sent him to buy you back. When he does—"

"When he does, we'll drive the Kubratoi away!" Krispos made cut-and-thrust motions with the wooden sword he was holding. Grown men, these days, practiced with real weapons; the veterans had been issued enough for everyone. A spear and a hunting bow hung on the wall of Krispos' house.

"Maybe," Varades said. "Just maybe, if it's a small band bent on robbery instead of a full-sized invasion. The Kubratoi know how to fight; not much else, maybe, but that for certain. You farmers won't ever be anything but amateur soldiers, so I wouldn't even try taking 'em on without a good advantage in numbers."

"What then?" Krispos said. "If there's too many, do we let them herd us off to Kubrat again?"

"Better that than getting killed to no purpose and having them herd off your mother and sisters even so."

Krispos' second sister, Kosta, had just turned two. He thought of her being forced to trek north, and of his mother trying to care for her and Evdokia both. After a moment, he thought of his mother trying to do all that while mourning his father and him. He did not like any of those thoughts.

"Maybe the Kubratoi just won't come," he said at last.

Varades laughed again, as boisterously as before. "Oh, aye, and maybe one of the village jackasses'd win all the hippodrome races down in Videssos the city. But you'd better not count on it." He grew serious. "I don't want you to mistake my meaning, boy. Sooner or later, they'll come. The whoresons always do."

By the time Krispos was fourteen, he was close to being as tall as his father. The down on his face began to turn dark; his voice cracked and broke, generally at moments when he least wanted it to.

He was already doing a man's work in the fields. Now, though, Varades and the other veterans let him start using real arms. The wire-wound hilt of a steel sword felt nothing like the wooden toy he'd swung before. With it in his hand, he felt like a soldier— more, like a hero.

He felt like a hero, that is, until Idalkos—the veteran who had given him the blade—proceeded to disarm him half a dozen times in the next ten minutes. The last time, instead of letting him pick up the sword and go on with the lesson, Idalkos chased him halfway across the village. "You'd better run!" he roared, pounding after Krispos. "If I catch you, I'll carve hams off you." Only one thing saved Krispos from being even more humiliated than he was: the veteran had terrorized a good many people the same way—some of them Phostis' age.

Finally, puffing, Idalkos stopped. "Here, come back, Krispos," he called. "You've had your first lesson now, which is that it's not as easy as it looks."

"It sure isn't," Krispos said. As he walked slowly back toward Idalkos, he heard someone giggle. His head whipped around. There in her doorway stood Zoranne the daughter of Tzykalas the cobbler, a pretty girl about Krispos' age. His ears felt on fire. If she'd watched his whole ignominious flight—

"Pay the chit no mind," Idalkos said, as if reading his thoughts. "You did what you had to do: I had a sword and you didn't. But suppose you didn't have room to run. Suppose you were in the middle of a whole knot of men when you lost your blade. What would you do then?"

Die, Krispos thought. He wished he could die, so he wouldn't have to remember Zoranne's giggle. But that wasn't the answer Idalkos was looking for. "Wrestle, I suppose," he said after a moment.

"Would you?" Krispos put down the sword. He set himself, leaning forward slightly from the waist, feet wide apart. "Here, I'm an old man. See if you can throw me."

Krispos sprang at him. He'd always done well in the scuffles among boys. He was bigger and stronger than the ones his own age, and quicker, too. If he could pay back Idalkos for some of his embarrassment—

The next thing he knew, his face was in the dirt, the veteran riding his back. He heard Zoranne laugh again and had to fight back tears of fury. "You fight dirty," he snarled.

"You bet I do," Idalkos said cheerfully. "Want to learn how? Maybe you'll toss me right through a dung heap one fine day, impress your girl there."

"She's not my girl," Krispos said as the veteran let him up. Still, the picture was attractive—and so was the idea of throwing Idalkos through a dung heap. "All right, show me what you did."

"A hand on the arm, a push on the back, and then you twist— so—and take the fellow you're fighting down over your leg. Here, I'll run you through it slow, a couple of times."

"I see," Krispos said after a while. By then they were both filthy, from spilling each other in the dirt. "Now how do I block it when someone tries to do it to me?"

Idalkos' scar-seamed face lit up. "You know, lad, I've taught my little trick to half a dozen men here, maybe more. You're the first one with the wit to ask that question. What you do is this. . . ."

That was the start of it. For the rest of that summer and into fall, until it got too cold to spend much time outside, Krispos learned wrestling from Idalkos in every spare moment he had. Those moments were never enough to suit him, not squeezed as they were into the work of the harvest, care for the village's livestock, and occasional work with weapons other than Krispos' increasingly well-honed body.

"Thing is, you're pretty good, and you'll get better," Idalkos said one chilly day in early autumn. He flexed his wrist, winced, flexed it again. "No, that's not broken after all. But I won't be sorry when the snow comes, no indeed I won't—give me a chance to stay indoors and heal up till spring."

All the veterans talked like that, and all of them were in better shape than any farmer their age—or ten years younger, too. Just when someone started to believe them, they'd do something like what Idalkos had done the first time they wrestled.

So Krispos only snorted. "I suppose that means you'll be too battered to come out with the rest of us on Midwinter's Day," he said, voice full of syrupy regret.

"Think you're smart, don't you?" Idalkos made as if to grab Krispos. He sprang back—one of the things he'd learned was to take nothing for granted. The veteran went on, "The first year I don't celebrate Midwinter's Day, sonny, you go out to my grave and make the sun-sign over it, 'cause that's where I'll be."

Snow started falling six weeks before Midwinter's Day, the day of the winter solstice. Most of the veterans had served in the far west against Makuran. They complained about what a hard winter it was going to be. No one who had spent time in Kubrat paid any attention to them. The farmers went about their business, mending fences, repairing plows and other tools, doing woodwork . . . and getting ready for the chief festival of their year.

Midwinter's Day dawned freezing but clear. Low in the south, the sun hurried across the sky. The villagers' prayers went with it, to keep Skotos from snatching it out of the heavens altogether and plunging the world into eternal darkness.

As if to add to the light, bonfires burned in the village square. Krispos ran at one, his hide boots kicking up snow. He leaped over the blaze. "Burn, ill-luck!" he shouted when he was right above it. A moment later, more snow flew as he thudded down.

Evdokia came right behind him. Her wish against bad luck came out more as a scream—this was the first year she was big enough to leap fires. Krispos steadied her when she landed clumsily. She grinned up at him. Her cheeks glowed with cold and excitement.

"Who's that?" she said, peering back through the shimmering air above the flames to see who came next. "Oh, it's Zoranne. Come on, let's get out of her way."

Pushed by his sister, Krispos walked away from the fire. His eyes were not the only ones in the village that followed Zoranne as she flew through the air over it. She landed almost as heavily as Evdokia had. If Evdokia hadn't made him move, he thought, he could have been the one to help Zoranne back up.

"Younger sisters really are a nuisance," he declared loftily.

Evdokia showed him he was right: she scooped up a handful of snow and pressed it against the side of his neck, then ran away while he was still writhing. Bellowing mingled outrage and laughter, he chased her, pausing a couple of times to make a snowball and fling it at her.

One snowball missed Evdokia but caught Varades in the shoulder. "So you want to play that way, do you?" the veteran roared. He threw one back at Krispos. Krispos ducked. The snowball hit someone behind him. Soon everyone was throwing them—at friends, foes, and whoever happened to be in the wrong place at the right time. People's hats and sheepskin coats were so splashed with white that the village began to look as if it had been taken over by snowmen.

Out came several men, Phostis among them, wearing dresses they must have borrowed from a couple of the biggest, heaviest women in the village. They put on a wicked burlesque of what they imagined their wives and daughters did while they were out working in the fields. It consisted of gossiping, pointing fingers while they gossiped, eating, and drinking wine, lots of wine. Krispos' father did a fine turn as a tipsy lady who was talking so furiously she never noticed falling off her stool but lay on the ground, still chattering away.

The male spectators chortled. The women pelted the actors with more snowballs. Krispos ducked back into his house for a cup of wine for himself. He wished it was hot, but no one wanted to stay indoors and tend a pot of mulled wine, not today.

The sun set as he came back to the square. The village's women and girls were having their revenge. Dressed in men's short tunics and doing their best not to shiver, several of them pretended to be hunters bragging about the immense size of their kill—till one of them, fastidiously holding it by the tail, displayed a mouse.

This time, the watching women cheered and most of the men jeered and threw snow. Krispos did neither. One of the female "hunters" was Zoranne. The tunic she wore came down only to mid-thigh; her nipples, stiff from the cold, pressed against its thin fabric. As he looked and looked, he felt a heat grow in him that had nothing to do with the wine he'd drunk.

At last the women skipped away, to thunderous applause. More skits came in quick succession, these mocking the foibles of particular villagers: Tzykalas' efforts to grow hair on his bald head—in the skit, he raised a fine crop of hay—Varades' habit of breaking wind, and more.

Then Krispos watched in dismay as a couple of farmers, plainly intended to be Idalkos and him, practiced wrestling. The embrace in which they ended was more obscene than athletic. The villagers whooped and cheered them on.

Krispos stamped away, head down. He was at an age where he could laugh at others, but could not bear to have them laugh at him. All he wanted to do was get away from the hateful noise.

Because he was not watching where he was going, he almost ran into someone coming back toward the center of the village. "Sorry," he muttered and kept walking.

"What's wrong, Krispos?" He looked up, startled. It was Zoranne's voice. She'd changed back into her own long skirt and a coat, and looked a good deal warmer for it. "What's wrong?" she said again.

"Those stupid jokers back there, that's what," he burst out, "making as if when Idalkos and I wrestle, we don't just wrestle." Half his rage evaporated as soon as he said out loud what was bothering him. He began to feel foolish instead.

Zoranne did not help by starting to laugh. "It's Midwinter's Day, Krispos," she said. "It's all in fun." He knew that, which only made matters worse. She went on, "Anything can happen on Midwinter's Day, and no one will pay any mind to it the day after. Am I right?"

"I suppose so." He sounded surly, even to himself.

"Besides," she said, "it's not as if what they made out was true, is it?"

"Of course not," he said, so indignantly that his changing voice left the last word a high-pitched squeak. As if from nowhere, the memory of Iakovitzes' hand on his back stirred in his mind. Maybe that was part of why the skit had got under his skin so.

She did not seem to notice. "Well, then," she said.

Back by the bonfires, most of the villagers erupted in laughter at some new skit. Krispos realized how quiet it was out here near the edge of the village, how alone he and Zoranne were. The memory of how she'd looked capering in that brief tunic rose again. Without his conscious mind willing it, he took a step toward her.

At the same moment, she was taking a step toward him. They

almost bumped into each other. She laughed again. "Anything can happen on Midwinter's Day," she said softly.

When Krispos fled that embarrassing skit, he hadn't worried about picking a direction. Perhaps not surprisingly, he'd ended up not far from his own house; as usual, his father had preferred one on the outskirts of the village. Suddenly that seemed like a blessing from Phos. Krispos gathered his courage, reached out, and took Zoranne's arm. She pressed herself to his side.

His heart hammering, he led her to his doorway. They went inside together. He quickly shut the door behind them to keep the heat from the firepit in the middle of the floor from getting out.

"We'd better hurry," he said anxiously.

Just then, more laughter came from the center of the village. Zoranne smiled. "We have some time, I think." She shrugged off her coat, got out of her skirt. Krispos tried to undress and watch her at the same time, and almost fell over. Finally, after what seemed much too long, they sank to the straw bedding.

Krispos soon learned what everyone must: that knowing how man and woman join is not enough to keep that first joining from being one surprise after another. Nothing he thought he knew made him ready for the taste of Zoranne's soft skin against his lips; the feel of her breast in his hand; the way the whole world seemed to disappear but for her body and his.

As it does, it returned all too quickly. "You're squashing me," Zoranne said. Brisk and practical, she sat up and picked bits of straw from her hair, then from his.

Given a little more time and a little less nervousness, he might have enjoyed that. As it was, her touch made him spring up and scramble into his clothes. She dressed, too—not with that frantic haste, but not taking her time, either.

Something else he did not know was whether he'd pleased her, or even how to find out. "Will we . . . ?" he began. The rest of the question seemed stuck in his mouth.

Zoranne did not help much. "I don't know. Will we?"

"I hope so," Krispos blurted.

"Men always hope so—that's what women always say, anyhow." She unbent a bit then. "Well, maybe we will—but not now. Now we ought to get back to where everyone else is."

He opened the door. The freezing air outside hit him like a blow. Zoranne said, "We should go back separately. The grandmothers have enough to gossip about already."

"Oh." Krispos had wanted to shout it from the housetops. If Zoranne didn't . . . "All right." He could not keep the disappointment out of his voice, though.

"Come on," she said impatiently. "I told you this wouldn't be the last time." As a matter of fact, she hadn't quite said that before. Thus encouraged, Krispos willingly shut the door again and watched Zoranne slip off into the night.

She kept her word, if not as often as Krispos would have liked. Every taste he had of her, every time the two of them managed not to be busy and to be able to find privacy, only made him want her more. Not knowing a better name, he thought of that as love.

Then, for a while, his own afternoons were occupied: Varades taught him and a couple of younger boys their letters. He learned them without too much trouble; being able to read and write his own name was almost as exciting, in its own way, as sporting with Zoranne.

He would have liked it even more had the village had anything much to read. "Why did you show us our letters if we can't use them?" he complained to Varades.

"To give myself something to do, as much as any other reason," the veteran answered frankly. He thought for a moment. "Tell you what. We might beg a copy of Phos' scripture the next time a blue-robe comes around. I'll go through it with you, best I can."

When Varades asked him, a couple of weeks later, the priest nodded. "I'll have one copied out for you straightaway," he promised. Krispos, who was standing behind Varades, felt like cheering until the man went on, "You understand, it will take a few months. The monasteries' scriptoria are always behind, I'm sorry to say."

"Months!" Krispos said in dismay. He was sure he would forget everything before the book arrived.

But he did not. His father made him scratch letters in the dirt every day. "High time we had somebody in the family who can read," Phostis said. "You'll be able to keep the tax man from cheating us any worse than tax men always do."

Krispos got another chance to use his skill that spring, before either the scripture or the tax collector arrived. Zoranne's father Tzykalas had spent the winter months making half a dozen pairs of fancy boots. When the roads dried out enough to be passable, he took them to Imbros to sell. He came back with several goldpieces—and portentous news.

"The old Avtokrator, Phos guard his soul, has died," he declared to the men he met in the village square.

Everyone made the sun-sign. The passing of an Emperor was never to be taken lightly. Phostis put into words what they were all thinking: "His son's but a boy, not so?"

Tzykalas nodded. "Aye, about the age of Krispos here, I'd say, judging by his coin." The cobbler dug it out of his pouch to show the other villagers the new portrait. "His name is—"

"Let me read it!" Krispos exclaimed. "Please!" He held out his hand for the goldpiece. Reluctantly Tzykalas passed it to him. It was only a little wider than his thumbnail. All he could make out from the image was that the new Avtokrator was, as Tzykalas had said, too young to have a beard. He put the coin close to his face so he could make out the tiny letters of its inscription. "His name is Anthimos."

"So it is," Tzykalas said grumpily. He snatched the goldpiece out of Kripsos' hand. Too late, it occurred to the youth that he had just stolen a big part of Tzykalas' news. *Too bad*, he thought. No matter how he felt about Zoranne, he'd never been fond of her father. That was one reason he hadn't proposed to her: the idea of having the cobbler as a father-in-law was anything but appealing.

What he wanted to do was go home and dig up the goldpiece he'd got from Omurtag so he could read it. He'd buried it beside the house for luck when his family came to this new village, and they'd never been desperate enough to make him dig it up and spend it. But no, he decided, not now; if he did leave, Tzykalas would only think him ruder yet.

"A boy for Avtokrator?" someone said. "That won't be good—who'll keep the plow's furrow straight till he learns how to guide it?"

"That I can tell you," Tzykalas said, sounding important again. "The talk in Imbros is that Rhaptes' brother Petronas will be regent for his nephew until Anthimos comes of age."

"Petronas, eh? Things won't be too bad, then." Drawn by the sight of several men standing around talking, Varades had come up in time to hear Tzykalas' last bit of news. The veteran went on, "I fought under him against Makuran. He's an able soldier, and no one's fool, either."

"What if he seizes the throne for himself, then?" Krispos' father said.

"What if he does, Phostis?" Varades said. "Why would it matter to the likes of us, one way or the other?"

Krispos' father thought about it for a moment. He spread his hands. "There you have me, Varades. Why indeed?"

Zoranne stood in the doorway of Tzykalas' house. She shook her head. "No."

"Why not?" Surprised and irritated, Krispos waved his hand to show how empty the village was. "Everyone's in the farther fields for the rest of the day, and probably tomorrow, too. Even your father's gone off to buy some new awls, you said. We've never had a better chance."

"No," she repeated.

"But why not?" He put a hand on her arm.

She didn't pull away, not physically, but she might as well have. He let his hand fall. "I just don't want to," she said.

"Why?" he persisted.

"Do you really want to know?" She waited till she saw him nod. "All right, I'll tell you why. Yphantes asked me to marry him the other day, and I told him yes."

The last time Krispos had felt so stunned and breathless was when Idalkos kicked him in the pit of the stomach one day while they were wrestling. He'd never paid any particular attention to Yphantes before. Along with everyone else in the village, he'd been sad when the man's wife died in childbirth a couple of years before, but . . . "He's old," Krispos blurted.

"He's years away from thirty," Zoranne said, "and he's already well set up. If I had to wait for you, I'd be past twenty myself by the time you were even close to where Yphantes is now, and that's too long a time."

"But—but then you, but then you and he—" Krispos found he could not make his mouth work the way it was supposed to.

Zoranne understood anyway. "What if we were?" she said defiantly. "You never gave me any promise, Krispos, or asked for one from me."

"I never thought I needed to," he mumbled.

"Too bad for you, then. No woman wants to be taken for granted. Maybe you'll remember that next time with someone else, and end up happier for it." Her face softened. "Krispos, we'll probably live here together in this village the rest of our lives. No point in us hating each other, is there? Please?''

For want of anything better to say, he said, ''All right.'' Then he turned and quickly walked away. If he had any tears, Zoranne was not going to see them. He owned too much pride for that.

That evening he was so quiet that his sister teased him about it, and then he was quiet through the teasing, too. ''Are you feeling well, Krispos?'' Evdokia asked, real worry in her voice; when she could not get a rise out of him, something had to be wrong.

''I'm all right,'' he said. ''I just want you to leave me alone, that's all.''

''I know what it is,'' she said suddenly. ''It's something to do with Zoranne, isn't it?''

He very carefully put down the bowl of barley and turnip soup from which he had been eating; had he not been so deliberately careful with his hands, he might have thrown it at her. He got up and stamped out of the house, off into the woods.

He took longer than he should have to realize that sitting by himself among the trees wasn't accomplishing anything, but after a while he did figure it out. It was quite dark when he finally came home. Then he almost turned around and went back; his father was waiting for him, a few steps outside the door.

He kept on. He would have to deal with his father sooner or later; better sooner, he thought. ''I'm sorry,'' he said.

His father nodded, the motion barely visible in the gloom. ''You should be.'' Phostis hesitated a moment before he said, ''Evdokia was right, I gather—you've had some trouble with your girl?''

''She's not my girl,'' Krispos said sullenly. ''She's going to marry Yphantes.''

''Good,'' his father said. ''I hoped she would. I told Yphantes as much, earlier this year. In the long run, it'll save you trouble, son, believe me.''

''When you what?'' Krispos stared at him, appalled. That moment of shock also let him notice something he'd missed before: both his father and his sister knew about Zoranne. ''How did you find out about us? We were so careful—''

''Maybe you think so,'' Phostis said, ''but I'd bet the only person in the village who doesn't know is Tzykalas, and he would if he weren't a fool who'd sooner talk than see. I'd be just as well pleased not to have a marriage connection with him, I can tell you.''

Krispos had been angry at his father often enough. Till now, he'd never imagined wanting to hate him. In a voice like ice, he asked, ''Is that why you egged Yphantes on?''

''That's part of the reason, aye,'' Phostis answered calmly. Before Krispos' rage could overflow, he went on, ''But it's not the biggest part. Yphantes needs to marry. He needs a wife to help him now and he needs to get an heir to carry on. And Zoranne needs to marry; at fourteen, a girl's a woman, near enough. But you, son, you don't need to marry. At fourteen, a man's still a boy.''

''I'm not a boy,'' Krispos snarled.

''No? Does a man pitch a tantrum when he's teased? You were acting the way Kosta does when I tell her I won't carry her piggyback any more. Am I wrong or am I right? Think before you answer me.''

That last sentence kept Krispos from blowing up in fury. He *did* think; in cold—or at least cooler—blood, what he'd done seemed foolish. ''Right, I suppose, Father, but—''

''But me no buts. Finding a girl who'll say yes to you is wonderful; Phos knows I don't deny it. Why, I remember—'' His father stopped, laughed a small, self-conscious laugh. ''But never mind me. Just because she says yes doesn't mean you want to live with her the rest of your life. That should take more looking than just one girl, don't you think?''

Krispos remembered his own misgivings about Tzykalas the day before. Without much wanting to, he found himself nodding. ''I guess so.''

''Good.'' His father put a hand on his shoulder, the way he'd been doing since Krispos was a little boy. ''What you have to remember is, bad as you feel today, today's not forever. Things'll feel better inside you after a while. You just have to learn the patience to wait till they do.''

Krispos thought about that. It made sense. Even so, though . . . ''It sounds like something that's easier to tell someone else than to do,'' he said.

''Doesn't it just?'' Phostis laughed that small laugh again. ''And don't I know it?''

Greatly daring, Krispos asked, ''Father, what was she like?''

''She?''

"The one you talked about—sort of talked about—a few minutes ago."

"Oh." Phostis walked farther away from the house. He glanced back toward it before going on more quietly, "Her name was Sabellia. Your mother knows of her. Truly, I don't think Tatze'd mind my speaking about her, save only that no woman ever really takes kindly to her man going on about times before he was with her. Can't say I blame her; I'm as glad she doesn't chatter on about her old flames, too. But Sabellia? Well, I must have been right around your age when I met her . . ."

Krispos rubbed his chin. Whiskers rasped under his fingers, not the fuzz he'd had since his voice started changing but the beginnings of a real man's crop. *About time,* he thought. A couple of fifteen-year-olds grew beards as good as his, though he'd had two more summers in which to raise his.

He rubbed again. A beard, even a thin one, was a useful thing to be thoughtful with. Last time out in the woods, somewhere not far from here, he'd spotted an elm branch that had exactly the right curve for a plow handle. He would have paid more attention to it had he not been with a girl.

That oak looked familiar, or so he thought till he got close to it. He walked on. He didn't remember the hazel tree beyond the oak. Sighing, he kept walking. By now he was sure he had come too far, but he didn't want to go back, either. It would have been too much like an admission of failure.

Faint in the distance, he heard noise ahead. He frowned. Few villagers came this far east of home. He'd brought Likinia out here precisely because he had felt sure they'd get to be alone. He supposed men from the next village over could be doing some lumbering, but they'd have to drag the wood a long way back if they were.

The noise didn't sound like lumbering, anyhow. He heard no axes, no sounds of falling branches or toppling trees. As he moved closer, a horse neighed softly. That confused him worse than ever. A horse would have been handy for hauling timber, but there was no timber.

What did that leave? His frown deepened—the most obvious answer was bandits. He hadn't thought the nearby road had enough traffic to support a robber band, but he could have been wrong. He kept moving toward the noise, but now with all the caution he could muster. He just wanted to see if these really were bandits and then, if they were, to get back to the village and bring as many armed men here as he could.

He was flat on his belly by the time he wriggled up to the last brush that screened him from the noise-makers, whoever they were. Slowly, slowly, he raised his head until he could peer between two leafy branches whose shadows helped hide his face.

"Phos!" His lips shaped the word, but no sound came from between them. The men relaxing by the side of the road were not bandits. They were Kubratoi.

His lips moved silently again—twelve, thirteen, fourteen Kubratoi. The village had not had any word of invasion, but that meant nothing. The first word of trouble they'd had when he was a boy was the wild men howling out of darkness. He shivered; suddenly, reliving the terror of that night, he felt like a boy again.

The remembered fear also told him what he had wondered before—why the Kubratoi were sitting around taking their ease instead of storming straight for the village. They would hit at night, just as that other band had. With the advantage of surprise, with darkness making them seem three times as many as they really were, they would be irresistible.

Krispos gauged the shadows around him as he slithered backward even more carefully than he had approached. The sun was not far past noon. He could deal with the Kubratoi as he'd intended to treat the bandits. The villagers had learned weapons from the veterans settled with them to be ready for just this sort of moment.

Soon Krispos was far enough away from the wild men to get back to his feet. Fast and quiet as he could, he headed toward the village. He thought about cutting back to the road and running down it. That would be quickest—if the Kubratoi didn't have a sentry posted somewhere along there to make sure no one gave the alarm. He decided he could not take the chance. Through the woods it would have to be.

He burst out of the forest an hour and a half later, his tunic torn, his arms and face scratched. His first try at a cry of alarm yielded only a rusty croak. He rushed over to the well, drew up the bucket, and drank deep. "The Kubratoi!" he shouted, loud as he could.

The men and women who heard him spun and stared. One of them was Idalkos. "How many, boy?" he barked. "Where?"

"I saw fourteen," Krispos told him. "Down at the edge of the road . . ." He gasped out the story.

"Only fourteen, you say?" A fierce light kindled in Idalkos' eyes. "If that's all there really are, we can take 'em."

"I thought so, too," Krispos said. "You get the people here armed. I'll go out to the fields and bring in the rest of the men."

"Right you are." Idalkos had been an underofficer for many years; when he heard orders that made sense, he started carrying them out without worrying about where they came from. Krispos never noticed he'd given an order. He was already running toward the largest group of men that he saw, shouting as he ran.

"The Kubratoi!" someone said fearfully. "How can we fight the Kubratoi?"

"How can we not?" Krispos shot back. "Do you want to go back to the other side of the mountains again? There's only a dozen or so of them, and they won't be expecting us to hit first. With three times as many men as they have, how can we lose? Idalkos thinks we can win, too."

That brought around some of the farmers who stood there indecisively. Soon they all went pounding back toward the village. Idalkos and a couple of other men were already passing out weapons when they got there. Krispos found himself clutching a shield and a stout spear.

"We go through the woods?"

Idalkos made it sound like a question, but Krispos did not think he was really asking. "Aye," he said. "If they have someone watching the road, he could ride back and warn the rest."

"Right you are," Idalkos said again. He went on, "And speaking of warning—Stankos, you saddle up one of those mules and ride for Imbros, fast as you can, cross-country. If you see the whole landscape crawling with Kubratoi, come back. I'm not sending you out to get yourself killed. But if you think you can make it through, well, I wouldn't mind seeing a few garrison soldiers up this way. How about the rest of you, lads?"

Nods and nervous grins showed him his guess was good. The villagers had nerved themselves to fight, but they were not eager.

Or most of them, the older, more settled farmers, were not. They kept looking back at the fields; their homes; their wives and daughters, who crowded round the knot of would-be warriors, some just standing silently, others wringing their hands and trying not to weep.

Krispos, though, was almost wild with excitement. "Come on!" he shouted.

Some of the other young men also raised a cry. They pelted after Krispos into the woods. The rest of the villagers followed more slowly. "Come on, come on, if we all fight we can do it," Idalkos said. He and Varades and the rest of the veterans kept their amateur companions moving.

Before long, Idalkos had pushed his way up beside Krispos. "You're going to have to lead us, at least till we get to the buggers," he said. "You're the one who knows where they are. It'd be good if we tried to get as quiet as we could *before* we're close enough that they're likely to hear us."

"That makes sense," Krispos said, wondering why he hadn't thought of it himself. "I'll remember."

"Good." Idalkos grinned at him. "Glad you're not too proud to use a notion just on account of somebody else thought of it."

"Of course not," Krispos said, surprised. "That would be stupid."

"So it would, but you'd be amazed how many captains are idiots."

"Well, but then I'm no cap—" Krispos paused. He seemed to be leading the villagers, if anyone was. He shrugged. It was only because he'd been the one to find the Kubratoi, he thought.

He was still a mile away from the wild men when he walked past the elm with the curving branch he'd been looking for. He tried to note just where the tree was. Next time, he told himself, he'd find it on the first try.

A few minutes later, he stopped and waited for everyone to catch up. Only then did he think to wonder if there would be a next time after the fight ahead. He sternly suppressed that thought. Turning to the farmers, he said, "It isn't far. From here on out, pretend you're hunting deer—quiet as you go."

"Not deer," Varades said. "Wolves. The Kubratoi have teeth. And when we hit 'em, we all yell 'Phos!' That way nobody has any doubts about who's who. Nothing to make you want to piss your breeches faster'n almost getting killed by your own side."

The villagers stole forward. Soon Krispos heard men chattering, heard a horse snort. His comrades heard, too, and looked at one another. The Kubratoi were making no secret of where they were. "Quiet as we can now," Krispos whispered. "Pass it along." The whisper traveled through the group.

Try as they would, the farmers could not keep their presence secret as long as they wanted. They were still more than a hundred yards from the Kubratoi when the buzz of talk from the wild men suddenly changed. Idalkos bared his teeth, as if he were a fox realizing a rabbit had taken its scent. "Come on, lads," he said. "They know we're here. Phos!" The last word was a bellowed war cry.

"Phos!" The villagers shouted, too. They crashed through the brush toward the Kubratoi. "Phos!" Krispos yelled as loud as anyone. The idea of rushing into battle was enormously exciting. Soon, he thought, he would be a hero.

Then the brush was gone. Before Krispos could do more than catch sight of the Kubratoi, an arrow hissed past his face and another grazed his arm. He heard a meaty *thunk* as a shaft pierced a man beside him. The farmer fell, shrieking and writhing and clawing at it. Fear and pain suddenly seemed realer than glory.

Whether for glory or not, the fight was still before him. Peering over the top of his shield, he rushed at the nearest wild man. The Kubrati snatched for an arrow. Perhaps realizing he could not shoot before Krispos was upon him, he threw down the arrow and grabbed his sword.

Krispos thrust with his spear. He missed. The Kubrati closed with him. As much by luck as by skill, he turned the fellow's first slash with his shield. The Kubrati cut at him again. He backpedaled, trying to get room to use the spearhead against the wild man. The Kubrati pursued. Feinting with the sword, he stuck out a foot and tripped Krispos.

He managed to keep his shield above him as he went down. Two villagers drove the wild man away before he could finish Krispos. Krispos scrambled to his feet. A couple of Kubratoi were down for good, and two or three villagers. He saw a man from north of the mountains trading sword strokes with Varades. Fighting a veteran, the wild man was fully occupied. He never noticed Krispos until the youth's spear tore into his side.

The wild man grunted, then stared in absurd surprise at the red-dripping spearpoint that burst out through his belly. Then Varades' sword bit his neck. More blood sprayed; some splashed Krispos in the face. The Kubrati folded in on himself and fell.

"Pull your spear out, boy!" Varades yelled in Krispos' ear. "You think they're going to wait for you?" Gulping, Krispos set a foot on the wild man's hip and yanked the spear free. The soft resistance the Kubrati's flesh gave reminded him of nothing so much as butchering time. *No, no glory here,* he thought again.

All across the small field, the villagers were swarming over the Kubratoi, two against one here, three against one there. Individually, each Kubrati was a better warrior than his foes. The wild men seldom got the chance to prove it. Soon only four or five of them were left on their feet. Krispos saw one look around, heard him yell something to his comrades.

Though he'd never learned the Kubrati tongue, he was sure he knew what the wild man had said. He shouted, "Don't let them make it back to their horses! They still might get away."

As he spoke, the Kubratoi broke off combat and ran toward the tethered animals. Along with the rest of the villagers, Krispos dashed after them. He wondered why they hadn't mounted and fled when they first heard the villagers coming; probably, he supposed, because they'd imagined farmers would be easy meat. That had been true a decade ago. It wasn't true any more.

Krispos speared one of the Kubratoi in the back. The man flung his arms wide. Three villagers piled onto him. His scream cut off. In a moment, the rest of the Kubratoi were dragged down and slain. A couple of villagers took cuts in the last frantic seconds of the fight, but none seemed serious.

Krispos could hardly believe the little battle had ended so abruptly. He stared this way and that for more wild men to kill. All he saw was farmers doing the same thing. "We won!" he said. Then he started to laugh, surprised at how surprised he sounded.

"We won!" "By Phos, we won!" "We beat 'em!" The villagers took up the cry. They embraced, slapped one another on the back, showed off cuts and bruises. Krispos found himself clasping hands with Yphantes. The older farmer wore an enormous grin. "I saw you get two of the bastards, Krispos," he said. "By the good god, you made me jealous. I think I wounded one, but I'm not even sure of that."

"Aye, he fought well," Idalkos said.

Praise from the veteran made Krispos glow. He also found he did not mind praise from Yphantes. Whether or not the man who had married Zoranne was jealous of Krispos, Krispos was no longer jealous of him. Zoranne remained special in his memory, but only because she had been his first. What he'd felt for her at fourteen seemed very far away after three years of growth and change.

Such thoughts fled as Krispos saw his father coming up with right hand clutched to left shoulder. Blood trickled between

Phostis' fingers and splashed his tunic. "Father!" Krispos exclaimed. "Are you—"

Phostis cut him off. "I'll live, boy. I've done worse to myself with a sickle more than once. I've said often enough that I'm not cut out for this soldiering business."

"You're alive. That's what counts," Idalkos said. "And while you may not want to soldier, Phostis, your boy here has the knack for it, I'd say. He sees what needs doing and he does it—and if it's giving an order, men listen to him. That's Phos' own gift, nothing else—I've seen officers without it. If ever he wanted to head to Videssos the city, the army'd be glad to have him."

"The city? Me?" Krispos had never even imagined traveling to the great imperial capital. Now he tasted the idea. After a moment, he shook his head. "I'd sooner farm. It's what I know. Besides, I don't fancy killing any more than my father does."

"Neither do I," Idalkos said. "That doesn't mean it isn't needful sometimes. And, like I told you, I think you'd make a good soldier."

"No, thanks. All I really want to make is a good crop of beans this year, so we don't go hungry when winter comes." Krispos spoke as firmly as he could, both to let Idalkos know he meant what he said and to reinforce that certainty in his own mind.

The veteran shrugged. "Have it your way. If you want to go on being a farmer, though, we'd best make sure these were the only Kubratoi operating around here. The first thing we'll do is strip the bodies." Some of the villagers had already started taking care of that. Idalkos went on, "The cuirasses and the bows are better than what we already have. The swords are more for fighting from horseback like the Kubratoi do than afoot, but we'll still be able to use 'em."

"Aye, but what about the wild men now?" Krispos demanded. "We were both worried they'd have a scout close to the village. If he got away and warned another, bigger band—"

"Then the swords and arrows we're gathering won't matter, because we don't have enough men to hold off a big, determined band. So if there is a scout, he'd best not get away." Idalkos cocked his head. "Well, brave captain Krispos, how would you go about making sure he doesn't?"

In a tone of voice only slightly different, the veteran's question would have been mockery. As it was, though, he seemed rather to be setting Krispos a problem, the way Varades sometimes had when he gave the youth a long, hard word to spell out. Krispos thought hard. "If most of us march down the road toward the village," he said at last, "anybody would be sure to notice us. A rider could get away easy enough by going wide around us, but he'd come back to the road after he did, to find out what had happened to his friends. So maybe we ought to set some archers in ambush just up ahead there, before the bugger could round that bend and see what we've done to the rest of the wild men."

"Maybe we should." Grinning, Idalkos gave Krispos a Videssian military salute, clenched fist over heart. He turned to Phostis. "Skotos take you, man, why couldn't you have raised a son who was discontented with following in his father's footsteps?"

"Because I raised one with sense instead," Krispos' father said. "Better to be turning up the ground than to have it tossed on top of you on account of you've been killed too young."

Krispos nodded vigorously. Idalkos sighed. "All right, all right. It's a good scheme, anyhow; I think it'll work." He started yelling to the villagers. A couple of them cut branches and vines to make travois on which to drag back their dead and the three or four men hurt too badly to walk. They left the horses of the Kubratoi for the ambush party to fetch back, and the wild men's corpses for ravens' meat.

When Krispos watched his plan unfold, he felt the same awe that seeing the seeds he had planted grow to maturity always gave him. Just as he'd guessed, a lone Kubrati was sitting on his horse a couple of miles closer to the village than his comrades had rested. The rider started violently at the sight of spear-waving Videssians bearing down on him. He kicked his horse to a trot, then to a gallop. The villagers gave chase, but could not catch him.

As Krispos had expected, the Kubrati rode back to the road. The youth and Idalkos grinned at each other as they watched the column of dust the wild man's horse kicked up fade in the distance. "That should do for him," Krispos said happily. "Now we can head for home."

They arrived not long after sunset—a little before the raiders would have hit the village if they still lived. In the fading light, Krispos saw women and children waiting anxiously outside their homes, wondering whether husbands, fathers, sons, and lovers would come back again.

As one, the returning men shouted, "Phos!" Not only was it a cry no Kubratoi would make, their loved ones recognized their voices. Shouting themselves, they rushed toward the victorious farmers. Some of their glad cries turned to wails as they saw not all the men had come home safe. For most of them, though, it was a time of joy.

Embracing his mother, Krispos noticed how far he had to stoop to kiss her. Stranger still was the kiss he got from Evdokia. In the passage from one day to the next, he'd paid scant heed to the way his sister had grown, but suddenly she felt like a woman in his arms. He needed a moment to realize she was as old now as Zoranne had been on that Midwinter's Day.

As if the thought of Zoranne were enough to conjure her up, he found himself kissing her next. Their embrace was awkward; he had to lean over her belly, now big with child, to reach her lips.

Close by the two of them, a woman shouted, "Where's my Hermon?"

"It's all right, Ormisda," Krispos told her. "He's one of the archers we left behind to trap the wild man we couldn't catch. Anyone you don't see here is waiting in that ambush."

"Oh, Phos be praised!" Ormisda said. She kissed Krispos, too, though she was close to three times his age. More people kissed him—and one another—over the next hour than he'd seen during half a dozen Midwinter's Day's rolled into one.

Then, in the middle of the celebration, the archers returned to the village. Though everyone fell on them with happy shouts— Ormisda almost smothered Hermon against her ample bosom— they hung back from fully joining the rest of the villagers. Krispos knew what that had to mean. "He got away," he said.

He knew it sounded like an accusation. So did the archers. They hung their heads. "We must have shot twenty arrows at him and his horse," one of them said defensively. "Some hit, too—the yells he let out had to be curses."

"He got away," Krispos repeated. It was the worst thing he could think of to say. No, not so; a moment later he found something worse yet: "He'll bring the rest of the Kubratoi down on us."

The celebration died very quickly after that.

The next five days passed in a blur of apprehension for Krispos. That was true of most of the villagers, but Krispos' dread had two causes. Like everyone else, he was sure the Kubratoi would exact a terrible revenge for the slaughter of their raiding party. But that, for him, was only secondary, for his father's wounded shoulder had gone bad.

Phostis, as was his way, tried to make light of the injury. But he could barely use his left arm and quickly came down with a fever. None of the poultices the village women applied to the wound did any good. Phostis had always been burly, but now, with shocking suddenness, the flesh seemed to melt from his bones.

Thus Krispos was almost relieved when, late that fifth afternoon, a lookout posted in a tall tree shouted, "Horsemen!" Like the rest of the men, he dashed for his weapons—against Kubratoi, at least, he could hit back. And in the heat of fighting, he would have no time to worry about his father.

The lookout shouted again. "Hundreds of horsemen!" His voice wobbled with fear. Women and children were already streaming into the forest, to hide as best they could. "Hundreds and hundreds!" the lookout cried.

Some of the farmers threw down spears and bows and bolted with the women. Krispos grabbed at one who ran in front of him, but Idalkos shook his head. "What's the use?" the veteran said. "If they outnumber us that bad, a few more on our side won't matter much. We can't win; all we can do is hurt the bastards as bad as we're able."

Krispos clutched his spear shaft so tight his knuckles whitened on it. Now he did not need the lookout to know the wild men were coming. He could hear the hooves of their horses, quiet now but growing louder with dreadful speed.

He set himself. *Take one out with the spear,* he thought, *then drag another one off his horse and stab him.* After that—if he still lived after that—he'd see what other damage he could do.

"Won't be long now, lads," Idalkos said, calm as if the villagers were drawn up for parade. "We'll yell 'Phos!' again, just like we did the first time, and pray for the good god to watch over us."

"Phos!" That was not one of the farmers standing in ragged line in front of their houses. It was the lookout. He sounded so wild and shrill that Krispos wondered if he had lost his mind. Then the man said, "They're not Kubratoi, they're Videssian troopers!"

For a moment, the villagers stared at one another, as if the lookout had shouted in a foreign tongue. Then they cheered louder than they had after they first beat the Kubratoi. Idalkos' voice rose above the rest. "Stankos!" he said. "Stankos brought us our soldiers back!"

"Stankos!" everyone shouted. "Hurrah for Stankos!" "Good old Stankos!"

Stankos, Krispos thought, was getting more praise jammed into a few minutes than he'd had in the past five years. Krispos shouted the farmer's name, too, over and over, till his throat turned raw. He had stared death in the face since the lookout called. Nothing could ever frighten him worse. Now he, also, knew what reprieve felt like.

Before long, the Videssian cavalrymen pounded into the village. Stankos was with them, riding a borrowed horse. Half a dozen farmers pulled him off the beast, as if he were a Kubrati. The pounding he got was almost as hard as if he had been.

Krispos quickly counted the troopers. As best he could tell, there were seventy-one of them. So much for the lookout's frightened *hundreds and hundreds*, he thought.

The horsemen's captain bemusedly watched the villagers caper about. "You don't seem to have much need for us," he remarked.

"No, sir." Idalkos stiffened to attention. "We thought we did, when we didn't know for sure how many Kubratoi were about. You gave us a bad turn there—our lookout mistook you for a band of the wild men."

"By the bodies, I saw you'd dealt with the ones you found," the captain said. "Far as we know, that's the lot of them. I'd say they were just out for a little thievery. There's no general invasion, or anything like that."

A small band operating on its own, Krispos thought. The day he first picked up a sword, that was what Varades had told him the peasants might be able to handle. The veteran had known what he was talking about.

The Videssian captain turned to a priest beside him. "Looks like we won't need you today, Gelasios, except maybe for a prayer of thanksgiving."

"Nor am I sorry," Gelasios answered. "I can heal wounded men, aye, but I also think on the suffering they endure before I come to them, so I am just as well pleased not to ply my trade."

"Sir!" Krispos said. He had to repeat himself before the priest looked his way. "You're a healer, holy sir?"

"What of it, young man?" Gelasios said. "Phos be praised, you seem hale enough."

"Not me," Krispos said impatiently. "My father. This way."

Without looking to see whether Gelasios followed, he hurried toward his house. When he threw open the door, a new smell came out with the usual odors of stale smoke and food, a sweetish, sickly smell that made his stomach want to turn over.

"Yes, I see," Gelasios murmured at Krispos' elbow. The priest's nostrils flared wide, as if to gauge from the scent of corruption how great a challenge he faced. He went inside, stooping a little to get through the doorway. Now it was Krispos' turn to follow him.

Gelasios stooped beside Phostis, who lay near the edge of the straw bedding. Bright with fever, Phostis' eyes stared through the priest. Krispos bit his lip. In those sunken eyes, in the way his father's skin clung tight to bones beneath it, he saw the outline of coming death.

If Gelasios saw it, too, he gave no sign. He pulled Phostis' tunic aside, peeled off the latest worthless poultice to examine the wound. With the poultice came a thick wave of that rotting smell. Krispos took an involuntary step backward, then checked, hating himself—what was he doing, retreating from his father?

"It's all right, lad," Gelasios said absently, the first sign since he'd come into the house that he remembered Krispos was with him. He forgot him again, an instant later, and seemed to forget Phostis, too. His eyes went upward, as if to see the sun through the thatched roof of the cottage. "We bless thee, Phos, Lord with the great and good mind," he intoned, "by thy grace our protector, watchful beforehand that the great test of life may be decided in our favor."

Krispos echoed his prayer. It was the only one he knew all the way through; everyone in the whole Empire, he supposed, had Phos' creed by heart.

Gelasios said the prayer again, and again, and again. The priest's breathing grew slow and deep and steady. His eyes slid shut, but Krispos was somehow sure he remained very much aware of self and surroundings. Then, without warning, Gelasios reached out and seized Phostis' wounded shoulder.

The priest's hands were not gentle. Krispos expected his father to shriek at that rough treatment, but Phostis lay still, locked in his fever dream. Though Gelasios no longer prayed aloud, his breathing kept the same rhythm he had established.

Krispos looked from the priest's set face to his hands, and to the wound beneath them. The hair on his arms and at the nape of his neck suddenly prickled with awe—as he watched, that gaping, pus-filled gash began to close.

When only a thin, pale scar remained, Gelasios lifted his hands away from Phostis' shoulder. The flow of healing that had passed from him to Krispos' father stopped with almost audible abruptness. Gelasios tried to rise; he staggered, as if he felt the force of that separation.

"Wine," he muttered hoarsely. "I am fordone."

Only then did Krispos realize how much energy the healing had drained from Gelasios. He knew he should rush to fulfill the priest's request, but he could not, not at once. He was looking at his father. Phostis' eyes met his, and there was reason in them. "Get him his wine, son," Phostis said, "and while you're at it, you might bring some for me."

"Yes, Father, of course. And I pray your pardon, holy sir." Krispos was glad for an excuse to rummage for clean cups and the best skin of wine in the house: it meant no one would have to see the tears on his face.

"Phos' blessings on you, lad," Gelasios said. Though the wine put some color back in his face, he still moved stiffly, as if he had aged twenty years in the few minutes he'd needed to heal Phostis. Seeing the concern on Krispos' face, he managed a wry chuckle: "I'm not quite so feeble as I appear—a meal and good night's sleep, and I'll be well enough. Even without, at need I could heal another man now, likely two, and take no lasting harm."

Too abashed to speak, Krispos only nodded. His father said, "I just praise Phos you were here to heal me, holy sir. I do thank you for it." He twisted his head so he could peer down at his shoulder and at the wound there that, by the look of it, could have been five years old. "Isn't that fine?" he said to no one in particular.

He stood, more smoothly than Gelasios had. They walked out into the sunlight together. The men of the village raised a cheer to see Phostis returned to health. Somebody called, "And Tatze would have been such a tempting widow, too!" They all laughed, Phostis louder than anyone.

Krispos came out behind the two older men. While most of the villagers were still making much of his father, Idalkos beckoned to him. The veteran had been talking with the commander of the Videssian cavalry force. "I've told this gentleman—his name is Manganes—something about you," he said to Krispos. "He says—"

"Let me put it to him myself," Manganes said crisply. "From what your fellow villager here says, Krispos—do I have your name right?—you sound like a soldier the imperial army could use. I'd even offer you, hmm, a five goldpiece enlistment bonus if you rode back to Imbros with us now."

Without hesitating, Krispos shook his head. "Here I stay, sir, all the more so since, by your kindness and Gelasios' healing magic, my father has been restored to me."

"As you wish, young man," Manganes said. He and Idalkos both sighed.

III

Krispos came back from the fields one hot, sticky summer afternoon to find his mother, his sisters, and most of the other village women gathered round a peddler who was showing off a fine collection of copper pots. "Aye, these'll last you a lifetime, ladies, may the ice take me if I lie," the fellow said. He whacked one with his walking stick. Several women jumped at the clatter. The peddler held up the pot. "See? Not a dent in it! Made to last, like I said. None of this cheap tinker's work you see too often these days. And they're not too dear, either. I ask only three in silver, the eighth part of a goldpiece—"

Krispos waved to Evdokia, but she did not notice him. She was as caught up as any of the others by the peddler's mesmerizing pitch. Krispos walked on, a trifle miffed. He still wasn't used to her being out of the house, though she'd married Domokos nearly a year ago. She was eighteen now, but unless he made a conscious effort not to, he still thought of her as a little girl.

Of course, he was twenty-one himself, and the older men in the village still called him "lad" a lot of the time. No one paid any attention to change until it hit him in the head, he thought, chuckling wryly.

"Dear ladies, these pots—" The peddler broke off with a squeak that was no part of his regular sales pitch. Beneath his tan, blood mounted to his cheeks. "Do excuse me, ladies, I pray." His walk toward the woods quickly turned into an undignified dash. The women clucked sympathetically. Krispos had all he could do not to guffaw.

The peddler emerged a few minutes later. He paused at the well to draw up the bucket and take a long drink. "Your pardon," he said as he came back to his pots. "I seem to have picked up a touch of the flux. Where was I, now?"

He went back to his spiel with almost as much verve as he'd shown before. Krispos stood around and listened. He didn't intend to sell pots, but he had some piglets he was fattening up to take to market at Imbros soon, and the peddler's technique was worth studying.

Not much later, though, the man had to interrupt himself again. This time he went for the woods at a dead run. He did not look happy when he returned; his face was nearer gray than red.

"Ladies, much as I enjoy telling you about my wares, I think the time has come to get down to selling, before I embarrass myself further," he said.

He looked unhappy again through the bargaining that followed. The breaks in his talk had weakened his hold on the village women, and they dickered harder than he would have liked. He was shaking his head as he loaded pots back onto his mule.

"Here, stay for supper with us," one of the women called. "You shouldn't set out on the road so downcast."

The peddler managed a smile and a low bow. "You're too kind to a traveling man. Thank you." Before he got his bowl of stew, though, he needed to rush off to relieve himself twice more.

"I do hope he's well," Tatze said that evening to Phostis and Krispos.

A scream jerked the village awake the next morning. Krispos came running out of his house spear in hand, wondering who'd set upon whom. The woman who had invited the trader to stay over stood by his bedroll, horror on her face. Along with several other men, Krispos ran toward her. Had the wretch repaid her kindness by trying to rape her?

She screamed again. Krispos noticed she was fully clothed. Then, as she had, he looked down at the bedroll. "Phos," he whispered. His stomach churned. He was glad it was empty; had he had breakfast, he would have lost it.

The peddler was dead. He looked shrunken in on himself,

and bruised; great violet blotches discolored his skin. From the way the blankets of the bedroll were drenched and stinking, he seemed to have voided all the moisture from his body in a dreadful fit of diarrhea.

"Magic," Tzykalas the cobbler said. "Evil magic." His hand made the sun-sign on his breast. Krispos nodded, and he was not the only one. He could imagine nothing natural that would result in such gruesome dissolution of a man.

"No, not magic," Varades said. The veteran's beard had been white for years, but Krispos had never thought of him as old till this moment. Now he not only looked his years, he sounded them, as well; his voice quivered as he went on, "This is worse than magic."

"What could be worse than magic?" three men asked at once.

"Cholera."

To Krispos it was only a word. By the way other villagers shook their heads, it meant little more to them. Varades filled them in. "I only saw it once, the good god be thanked, when we were campaigning against the Makurani in the west maybe thirty years ago, but that once was enough to last me a lifetime. It went through our army harder than any three battles—through the enemy the same way, I suppose, or they would've just walked over us."

Krispos looked from the veteran to the peddler's twisted, ruined corpse. He did not want to ask the next question: "It's . . . catching, then?"

"Aye." Varades seemed to pull himself together. "We burned the bodies of those that died of it. That slowed the spread, or we thought it did. I suppose we ought to do it for this poor bugger here. Something else we ought to do, too."

"What's that?" Krispos said.

"Fast as we can, ride to Imbros and fetch back a priest who knows healing. I think we're going to need one."

Smoke from the peddler's pyre rose to the sky. The villagers' prayers to Phos rose with it. As he had four years earlier when the Kubratoi came, Stankos set off for Imbros. This time, instead of a mule, he rode one of the horses captured from the wild men.

But for his being gone, and for the black, burned place on the village green, life went on as before. If other people worried every time they felt a call of nature, as Krispos did, they did not talk about it.

Five days, Krispos thought. Maybe a little less, because Stankos was on a horse now and could get to Imbros faster. Maybe a little more, because a priest might not ride back with the same grim urgency the Videssian troopers had shown—but Phos knew that urgency was real.

The healer-priest arrived on the morning of the sixth day after Stankos rode out of the village. He was three days behind the cholera. By the time he got there, the villagers had burned three more bodies, one the unfortunate woman who had asked the peddler to stay. More people were sick, diarrhea pouring out of them, their lips blue, their skin dry and cold. Some suffered from pain and cramps in their arms and legs, others did not. Out of all of them, though, flowed that endless stream of watery stool.

When he saw the victims who still lived, the priest made the sun-circle over his heart. "I had prayed your man here was wrong," he said, "but I see my prayer was not answered. In truth, this is cholera."

"Can you heal it?" Zoranne cried, fear and desperation in her voice—Yphantes lay in his own muck outside their cottage. "Oh, Phos, can you heal it?"

"For as long as the lord with the great and good mind gives me strength," the priest declared. Without stopping even to give his name, he hurried after her. The healthy villagers followed.

"He's called Mokios," Stankos said as he trooped along with the rest of them. "*Aii,* my arse is sore!" he added, rubbing the afflicted portion of his anatomy.

Mokios knelt beside Yphantes, who feebly tried to make the sun-sign when he recognized a priest. "Never mind that now," the priest said gently. He pushed aside the villager's befouled tunic, set hands on his belly. Then, as Gelasios had when healing Krispos' father, he recited Phos' creed over and over, focusing all his will and energy on the suffering man under his fingers.

Yphantes showed no external wound, as Phostis had. Thus the marvel of watching him grow well again was not there this time. Whether or not it was visible, though, Krispos could feel the current of healing pass from Mokios to the villager.

At last the priest took away his hands. He slumped back, weariness etching lines deep into his face. Yphantes sat up. His eyes were sunken but clear. "Water," he said hoarsely. "By the good god, I've never been so dry in my life."

"Aye, water." Mokios gasped. He sounded more worn than the man he had just healed.

Half a dozen villagers raced to be first to the well. Zoranne did not win the race, but the others gave way when she said, "Let me serve them. It is my right." With the pride of a queen, she drew up the dripping bucket, untied it, and carried it to her husband and Mokios. Between them, they all but drank it dry.

The priest was still wiping water from his mustache and beard with the sleeve of his blue robe when another woman tried to tug him to his feet. "Please, holy sir, come to my daughter," she got out through tears. "She barely breathes!"

Mokios heaved himself upright, grunting at the effort it took. He followed the woman. Again, the rest of the villagers followed him. Phostis touched Krispos on the shoulder. "Now we pray he can heal faster than we fall sick," he said softly.

Mokios succeeded again, though the second healing took longer than the first. When he was done, he lay full length on the ground, panting. "Look at the poor fellow," Krispos whispered to his father. "He needs someone to heal him now."

"Aye, but we need him worse," Phostis answered. He knelt and shook Mokios. "Please come, holy sir. We have others who will not see tomorrow without you."

"You are right," the priest said. Even so, he stayed down several more minutes and, when he did rise, he walked with the shambling gait of a man either drunk or in the last stages of exhaustion.

Krispos thought Mokios' next healing, of a small boy, would fail. How much, he wondered, could a man take out of himself before he had nothing left? Yet in the end Mokios somehow summoned up the strength to vanquish the child's disease. While the boy, with the resilience of the very young, got up and began to play, the healer-priest looked as if he had died in his place.

But others in the village were still sick. "We'll carry him if we have to," Phostis said, and carry him they did, on to Varades.

Again Mokios recited Phos' creed, though now in a voice as dry as the skins of the cholera victims he treated. The villagers prayed with him, both to lend him strength and to try to ease their own fears. He sank into the healing trance, placed his hands on the veteran's belly. They were filthy now, from the stools of the folk he had already cured.

Once more Krispos felt healing flow out of Mokios. This time, however, the priest slumped over in a faint before his task was done. He breathed, but the villagers could not bring him back to himself. Varades moaned and muttered and befouled himself yet again.

When they saw they could not rouse Mokios, the villagers put a blanket over him and let him rest. "In the morning, the good god willing, he'll be able to heal again," Phostis said.

By morning, though, Varades was dead.

Mokios finally roused when the sun was halfway up the sky. Videssian priests were enjoined to be frugal of food and drink, but he broke his fast with enough for three men. "Healers have dispensation," he mumbled round a chunk of honeycomb.

"Holy sir, so long as it gives you back the power to use your gift, no one would say a word if you ate five times as much," Krispos told him. Everyone who heard agreed loudly.

The priest healed two more, a man and a woman, that day. Toward sunset, he gamely tried again. As he had with Varades, though, he swooned away before the cure was complete. This time Krispos wondered if he'd killed himself until Idalkos found his pulse.

"Just what my father worried about," Krispos said. "So many of us are deathly ill that we're dragging Mokios down with us."

He'd hoped Idalkos might contradict him, but the veteran only nodded, saying, "Why don't you go on home and get away from the sickness for a while? You're lucky; none of your family seems to have come down with it."

Krispos made the sun-sign over his heart. A few minutes later, after seeing that Mokios was as comfortable on the ground as he could be, he took Idalkos' advice.

He frowned as he came up to his house. Being near the edge of the village, it was always fairly quiet. But he should have heard his father and mother talking inside, or perhaps Tatze teaching Kosta some trick of baking. Now he heard nothing. Nor was cooksmoke rising from the hole in the center of the roof.

All at once, his belly felt as if it had been pitched into a snowdrift. He ran for the door. As he jerked it open, out came the latrine stench with which he and the whole village had grown too horribly familiar over the last few days.

His father, his mother, his sister—they all lay on the floor. Phostis was most nearly conscious; he tried to wave his son away. Krispos paid him no heed. He dragged his father to the grass outside, then Tatze and Kosta. As he did, he wondered why he alone had been spared.

His legs ached fiercely when he bent to lift his mother, and when he went back for Kosta he found his arms so clenched with cramps that he could hardly hold her. But he thought nothing of it until suddenly, without willing it, he felt an overpowering urge to empty his bowels. He started for the bushes not far away, but fouled himself before he got to them. Then he realized he had not been spared after all.

He began to shout for help, stopped with the cry unuttered. Only the healer-priest could help him now, and he'd just left Mokios somewhere between sleep and death. If any of the villagers who were still healthy came, they would only further risk the disease. A moment later he vomited, then suffered another fit of diarrhea. With his guts knotted from end to end, he crawled back to his family. Perhaps their cases would be mild. Perhaps . . .

His fever was already climbing, so thought soon became impossible. He felt a raging thirst and managed to find a jar of wine in the house. It did nothing to ease him; before long, he threw it up.

He crawled outside again, shivering and stinking. The full moon shone down on him, as serene and beautiful as if no such thing as cholera existed. It was the last thing Krispos remembered seeing that night.

"Oh, Phos be praised," someone said, as if from very far away.

Krispos opened his eyes. He saw Mokios' anxious face peering down at him and, behind the priest, the rising sun. "No," he said. "It's still dark." Then the memory came crashing back. He tried to sit. Mokios' hands, still on him, held him down. "My family!" he gasped. "My father, my mother—"

The healer-priest's haggard face was somber. "Phos has called your mother to himself," he said. "Your father and sister live yet. May the good god grant them strength to endure until I recover enough to be of aid to them."

Then he did let Krispos sit. Krispos tried to weep for Tatze, but found the cholera had so drained his body that he could make no tears. Yphantes, now up and about, handed him a cup of water. He drank it while the priest drained another.

He had to force himself to look at Phostis and Kosta. Their eyes and cheeks were sunken, the skin on their hands and feet and faces tight and withered. Only their harsh breathing and the muck that kept flowing from them said they were not dead.

"Hurry, holy sir, I beg you," Krispos said to Mokios.

"I shall try, young man, truly I shall. But first, I pray—" He looked round for Yphantes. "—some food. Never have I drained myself so."

Yphantes fetched him bread and salt pork. He gobbled them down, asked for more. He had eaten like that since he'd entered the village, but was thinner now than when he'd come. His cheeks, Krispos thought dully, were almost as hollow as Phostis'.

Mokios wiped at his brow. "Warm today," he said.

To Krispos, the morning still felt cool. He only shrugged by way of answer; as, not long before, he had been in fever's arms, he did not trust his judgment. He looked from his father to his sister. How long could they keep life in them? "Please, holy sir, will it be soon?" he asked, his nails digging into his palms.

"As soon as I may," the healer-priest replied. "Would I were younger, and recovered more quickly. Gladly would I—"

Mokios paused to belch. Considering how much he had eaten, and how quickly, Krispos saw nothing out of the ordinary in that. Then the healer-priest broke wind, loudly—as poor Varades never would again, Krispos thought, mourning the veteran with the small part of him not in anguish for his family.

And then utter horror filled Mokios' thin, tired face. For a moment, Krispos did not understand; the stench of incontinence by his house—indeed, throughout the village—was so thick a new addition did not easily make itself known. But when the healer-priest's eyes went fearfully to the wet stain spreading on his robe, Krispos' followed.

"No," Mokios whispered.

"No," Krispos agreed, as if their denial were stronger than truth. But the priest had tended many victims of the cholera, had smeared himself with their muck, had worked himself almost to death healing them. So what was more likely than a yes, or than that *almost* being no almost at all?

Krispos saw one tiny chance. He seized Mokios by both shoulders; weak as he was, he was stronger than the healer-priest. "Holy sir," he said urgently, "holy sir, can you heal yourself?"

"Rarely, rarely does Phos grant such a gift," Mokios said, "and in any case, I have not yet the strength—"

"You must try!" Krispos said. "If you sicken and die, the village dies with you!"

"I will make the attempt." But Mokios' voice held no hope, and Krispos knew only his own fierce will pushed the priest on.

Mokios shut his eyes, the better to muster the concentration he needed to heal. His lips moved soundlessly; Krispos recited Phos' creed with him. His heart leaped when, even through fever, even through sickness, Mokios' features relaxed toward the healing trance.

The priest's hands moved toward his own traitorous belly. Just as he was about to begin, his head twisted. Pain replaced calm confidence on his face, and he puked up everything Yphantes had brought him. The spasms of vomiting went on and on, into the dry heaves. He also fouled himself again.

When at last he could speak, Mokios said, "Pray for me, young man, and for your family, also. It may well be that Phos will accomplish what I cannot; not all who take cholera perish of it." He made the sun-sign over his heart.

Krispos prayed as he had never prayed before. His sister died that afternoon, his father toward evening. By then, Mokios was unconscious. Some time that night, he died, too.

After what seemed forever but was less than a month, cholera at last left the village alone. Counting poor brave Mokios, thirty-nine people died, close to one inhabitant in six. Many of those who lived were too feeble to work for weeks thereafter. But the work did not go away because fewer hands were there to do it; harvest was coming.

Krispos worked in the fields, in the gardens, with the animals, every moment he could. Making his body stay busy helped keep his mind from his losses. He was not alone in his sudden devotion to toil, either; few families had not seen at least one death, and everyone had lost people counted dear.

But for Krispos, going home each night was a special torment. Too many memories lived in that empty house with him. He kept thinking he heard Phostis' voice, or Tatze's, or Kosta's. Whenever he looked up, ready to answer, he found himself alone. That was very bad.

He took to eating most of his meals with Evdokia and her husband, Domokos. Evdokia had stayed well; Domokos, though he'd taken cholera, had suffered only a relatively mild case—his survival proved it. When, soon after the end of the epidemic, Evdokia found she was pregnant, Krispos was doubly glad of that.

Some villagers chose wine as their anodyne instead of work; Krispos could not remember a time so full of drunken fights. "I can't really blame 'em," he said to Yphantes one day as they both swung hoes against the weeds that had flourished when the cholera made people neglect the fields, "but I do get tired of breaking up brawls."

"We should all be grateful you're here to break them up," Yphantes said. "With your size and the way you wrestle, nobody wants to argue with you when you tell 'em to stop. I'm just glad you're not one of the ones who like to throw their weight around to show how tough they are. You've got your father's head on your shoulders, Krispos, and that's good in a man so young."

Krispos stared down as he hacked at a stinging nettle. He did not want Yphantes to see the tears that came to him whenever he thought of his family, the tears he'd been too weak and too dry inside to shed the day they died.

When he could speak again, he changed the subject. "I wonder how good a crop we'll end up bringing in?"

No farmer could take that question less than seriously. Yphantes rubbed his chin, then straightened to look out across the fields that were now beginning to go from green to gold. "Not very good," he said reluctantly. "We didn't do all the cultivating we should have, and we won't have as many people to help in the harvest."

"Of course, we won't have as many people eating this winter, either," Krispos said.

"With the harvest I fear we'll have, that may be just as well," Yphantes answered.

Not since he was a boy in Kubrat had Krispos faced the prospect of hunger so far in advance. What with the rapacity of the

Kubratoi, every winter then had been hungry. Now, he thought, he would face starvation cheerfully if only he could starve along with his family.

He sighed. He did not have that choice. He lifted his hoe and attacked another weed.

"Uh-oh," Domokos whispered as the tax collector and his retinue came down the road toward the village. "He's a new one."

"Aye," Krispos whispered back, "and along with his clerks and his packhorses, he has soldiers with him, too."

He could not imagine two worse signs. The usual tax collector, one Zabdas, had been coming to the village for years; he could sometimes be reasoned with, which made him a prince among tax men. And soldiers generally meant the imperial government was going to ask for something more than the ordinary. This year, the village had less than the ordinary to give.

The closer the new tax collector got, the less Krispos liked his looks. He was thin and pinch-featured and wore a great many heavy rings. The way he studied the village and its fields reminded Krispos of a fence lizard studying a fly. Lizards, however, did not commonly bring archers to help them hunt.

There was no help for it. The tax collector set up shop in the middle of the village square. He sat in a folding chair beneath a canopy of scarlet cloth. Behind him, his soldiers set up the imperial icons: a portrait of the Avtokrator Anthimos and, to its left, a smaller image of his uncle Petronas.

It was a new picture of Anthimos this year, too, Krispos saw, showing the Emperor with a full man's beard and wearing the scarlet boots reserved for his high rank. Even so, his image looked no match for that of Petronas. The older man's face was hard, tough, able, with something about his eyes that seemed to say he could see behind him without turning his head. Petronas was no longer regent—Anthimos had come into his majority on his eighteenth birthday—but the continued presence of his image said he still ruled Videssos in all but name.

Along with the other villagers, Krispos bowed first to the icon of Anthimos, then to that of Petronas, and last to the fleshly representative of imperial might. The tax collector dipped his head a couple of inches in return. He drew a scroll from the small wooden case he had set beside his left foot, unrolled it, and began to read:

"Whereas, declares the Phos-guarded Avtokrator Anthimos, from the beginning of our reign we have taken a great deal of care and concern for the common good of affairs, we have been equally concerned to protect well the state which Phos the lord of the great and good mind has granted us. We have discovered that the public treasury suffers under many debts which weaken our might and make difficult the successful prosecution of our affairs. Even matters military have been damaged by our being at a loss for supplies, with the result that the state has been harmed by the boundless onslaughts of barbarians. According to our ability, we deem the situation worthy of needed correction . . .''

He went on in that vein for some time. Looking around, Krispos watched his neighbors' eyes glaze. The last time he'd heard rhetoric so turgid was when Iakovitzes ransomed the captive peasants from Kubrat. That speech, at least, had presaged a happy outcome. He doubted the same would be true of this one.

From the way the soldiers shifted their weight, as if to ready themselves for action, he knew when the tax man was about to come to the unpalatable meat of the business. It arrived a moment later: "Accordingly, all assessments for the present year and until the conclusion of the aforementioned emergency are hereby increased by one part in three, payment to be collected in gold or in kind at the times and locations sanctioned by long-established custom. So decrees the Phos-guarded Avtokrator Anthimos.''

The tax collector tied a scarlet ribbon round his proclamation and stowed it away in its case. *One part in three,* Krispos thought. *No wonder he has soldiers with him.* He waited for the rest of the villagers to join him in protest, but nobody spoke. Perhaps he was the only one who'd managed to follow the speech all the way through.

"Excellent sir,'' he said, and waited till the tax man's eyes swung his way. "Excellent . . .'' He waited again.

"My name is Malalas,'' the tax collector said grudgingly.

"Excellent Malalas, we can pay no extra tax this year,'' Krispos said. Once he found the boldness to speak, others nodded with him. He went on, "We would have trouble paying the usual tax. This has been a hard year for us, excellent sir.''

"Oh? What's your excuse?'' Malalas asked.

"We had sickness in the village, excellent sir—cholera. Many died, and others were left too weak to work for a long time. Our crop is small this year.''

At the mention of the dread word *cholera*, some clerks and a few soldiers stirred nervously. Malalas, however, amazed Krispos by bursting into laughter. "Nice try, bumpkin! Name a disease to excuse your own laziness, make it a nasty one so we'll be sure not to linger. You'd fool some with that, maybe, but not me. I've heard it before.''

"But it's the truth!" Krispos said, appalled. "Excellent sir, you've not seen us till now. Our old tax collector, Zabdas, would recognize how many faces he knew aren't here today, truly he would."

Malalas yawned. "A likely tale.''

"But it's the truth!" Krispos repeated. The villagers backed him up: "Aye, sir, it is!" "By Phos, we had many dead, a healer-priest among 'em—" "My wife—" "My father—" "My son—" "I could hardly walk for a month, let alone farm,''

The tax collector raised a hand. "This matters not at all.''

Krispos grew angry. "What do you mean, it doesn't matter?" He ducked under Malalas' canopy, stabbed a finger down at the register on the tax man's knees. "Varades is dead. Phostis—that's *my* father—is dead, and so are my mother and sister. Tzykalas' son of the same name is dead . . .'' He went through the whole melancholy list.

None of it moved Malalas a hairsbreadth. "As you say, young man, I am new here. For all I know—in fact, I think it likely—the people you name may be hiding in the woods, laughing up their sleeves. I've seen that happen before, believe you me.''

Krispos did believe him. Had he not ferreted out such cheats, he would not have been so arrogantly certain of what was happening here. Krispos wished those cheats down to Skotos' ice, for they'd made the tax man blind to any real problems a village might have.

"The full proportion named is due and shall be collected,'' Malalas went on. "Even if every word you say is true, taxes are assessed by village, not by individual. The fisc has need of what you produce, and what the fisc needs, it takes.'' He nodded back toward the waiting soldiers. "Pay peaceably, or it will be the worse for you.''

"Pay peaceably, *and* it will be the worse for us,'' Krispos said bitterly. Taxes were assessed collectively, he knew, to make sure villagers tolerated no shirkers among them and so they would have to make good the labor of anyone who left. To use the law to force them to make up for disaster was savagely unjust.

That did not stop Malalas. He announced the amount due from the village: so many goldpieces, or their equivalent in the crops just harvested, all of which were carefully and accurately listed in the register.

The villagers brought what they had set aside for the annual assessment. With much sweat and scraping, they had amassed an amount just short of what they'd paid the year before. Zabdas surely would have been satisfied. Malalas was not. "We'll have the rest of it now," he said.

Guarded by his soldiers, the clerks he'd brought along swarmed over the village like ants raiding a pot of lard. They opened storage pit after storage pit and shoveled the grain and beans and peas into leather sacks.

Krispos watched the systematic plundering. "You're worse thieves than the Kubratoi!" he shouted to Malalas.

The tax man spoiled it by taking it for a compliment. "My dear fellow, I should hope so. The barbarians have rapacity, aye, but no system. Do please note, however, that we are not arbitrary. We take no more than the Avtokrator Anthimos' law ordains."

"You please note, excellent sir—" Krispos made the title into a curse. "—that what the Avtokrator's law ordains will leave some of us to starve."

Malalas only shrugged. For a moment, red fury so filled Krispos that he almost shouted for the villagers to seize weapons and fall on the tax collector and his party. Even if they massacred them, though, what good would it do? It would only bring more imperial soldiers down on their heads, and those troops would be ready to kill, not merely to steal.

"Enough, there!" Malalas called at length, after one of his clerks came up to whisper in his ear. "No, we don't need that barley—fill in the pit again. Now let us be off. We have another of these miserable little hamlets to visit tomorrow."

He remounted. So did his clerks and the cavalrymen who had protected them. Their harness jingled as they rode out of the village. The inhabitants stared after them, then to the emptied storage pits.

For a long time, no one spoke. Then Domokos tried to put the best light he could on things: "Maybe if we're all very watchful, we can . . ." His voice trailed away. Not even he believed what he was saying.

Krispos trudged back to his house. He picked up a trowel, went around to the side of the house away from the square, bent down, and started digging. Finding what he was looking for took longer than he'd expected; after a dozen years, he'd forgotten exactly where he'd buried that lucky goldpiece. At last, though, it lay gleaming on his muddy palm.

He almost threw the coin away; at that moment, anything with an Avtokrator's face on it was hateful to him. Common sense, however, soon prevailed. "Might be a good while before I see another one of these," he muttered. He struck the goldpiece in the pouch he wore on his belt.

He went into his house again. From their places on the wall he took down spear and sword. The sword he belted on next to his pouch. The spear would also do for a staff. He went outside. Clouds were building in the north. The fall rains had not yet started, but they would soon. When the roads turned to mud, a staff would be handy.

He looked around. "Anything else I need?" he asked out loud. He ducked inside one last time, came out with half a loaf of bread. Then he walked back to the village square. Domokos and Evdokia were still standing there, along with several other people. They were talking about Malalas' visit, in the soft, stunned tones they would have used after a flood or other natural disaster.

Domokos raised an eyebrow when he saw the gear Krispos carried. "Going hunting?" he asked his brother-in-law.

"You might say so," Krispos answered. "Hunting something better than this, anyhow. If the Empire can rob us worse than the wild men ever did, what's the use of farming? A long time ago, I wondered what else I could do. I'm off for Videssos the city, to try to find out."

Evdokia took his arm. "Don't go!"

"Sister, I think I have to. You and Domokos have each other. Me—" He bit his lip. "I tear myself up inside every time I go home. You know why." He waited until Evdokia nodded. Her face was twisted, too. He went on, "Besides, I'll be one less mouth to feed here. That's bound to help—a little, anyhow."

"Will you soldier, then?" Domokos asked.

"Maybe." Krispos still did not like the idea. "If I can't find anything else, I guess I will."

Evdokia embraced him. "Phos guard you on the road and in the city." Krispos saw by how quickly she stopped arguing that she realized he was doing what he needed to do.

He hugged her, too, felt the swell of her growing belly against him. He clasped Domokos' hand. Then he walked away from them, away from everything he'd ever known, west toward the highway that led south to the city.

From the village to the imperial capital was a journey of about ten days for a man in good condition and serious about his walking. Krispos was both, but took three weeks to get there. He stopped to help gather beans for a day here, to cut timber for an afternoon there, for whatever other odd jobs he could find. He got to Videssos the city with food in his belly and some money in his pouch besides his goldpiece.

He had already seen marvels on his way south, for as the road neared the city it came down by the sea. He'd stopped and stared for long minutes at the sight of water that went on and on forever. But that was a natural wonder, and now he was come to one worked by man: the walls of Videssos.

He'd seen city walls before, at Imbros and at several towns he'd passed on his journey. They'd seemed splendid things then, huge and strong. Next to the walls he approached now, they were as toys, and toddlers' toys at that.

Before Videssos' outer wall was a broad, deep ditch. That outwall loomed, five or six times as tall as a man. Every fifty to a hundred yards stood square or hexagonal towers that were taller still. Krispos would have thought those works could hold out Skotos himself, let alone any mortal foe the city might face.

But behind that outer wall stood another, mightier yet. Its towers were sited between those of the outwall, so some tower bore directly on every inch of ground in front of the wall.

"Don't stand there gawking, you miserable bumpkin," someone called from behind Krispos. He turned and saw a gentleman with a fine hooded cloak to keep him dry. The rain had started the night before; long since soaked, Krispos had stopped caring about it.

His cheeks hot, he hurried toward the gate. That proved a marvel in itself, with valves of iron and bronze and wood thick as a man's body. Peering up as he walked under the outwall, he saw troopers looking down at him through iron gates. "What are they doing up there?'' he asked a guardsman who was keeping traffic moving smoothly through the gate.

The guard smiled. "Suppose you were an enemy and somehow you'd managed to batter down the outer door. How would you like to have boiling water or red-hot sand poured down on your head?''

"Not very much, thanks." Krispos shuddered.

The gate guard laughed. "Neither would I." He pointed to Krispos' spear. "Have you come to join up? You'll get better gear than that, I promise you.''

"I might, depending on what kind of other luck I find here," Krispos said.

By the way the gate guard nodded, Krispos was sure he'd heard those words or ones much like them many times. The fellow said, "They use the meadow south of here, down by the sea, for a practice field. If you do need to look for an officer, you can find one there.''

"Thanks. I'll remember," Krispos said. Everyone seemed to want to push him toward a soldier's life. He shook his head. He still did not want to be a soldier. Surely in a city as great as Videssos was said to be, a city as great as her walls proclaimed her to be, he would be able to find something, anything, else to do with his life. He walked on.

The valves of the inner wall's gates were even stouter than those of the outwall. As Krispos passed under the inner wall, he looked up and saw another set of murder-holes. Feeling quite the city sophisticate, he gave the soldiers over his head a friendly nod and kept going. A few more steps and he was truly inside Videssos the city.

Just as he had in front of the walls, he stopped in his tracks to stare. The only thing with which he could think to compare the view was the sea. Now, though, he gazed on a sea of buildings. He had never imagined houses and shops and golden-domed temples to Phos stretching as far as the eye could reach.

Again someone behind him shouted for him to get moving. He took a few steps, then a few more, and soon found himself walking through the streets of the city. He had no idea where he was going; for the moment, one place seemed as good as another. It was all equally strange, and all equally marvelous.

He flattened himself against the front of a shop to let a mule-drawn cart squeeze past. In his village, the driver would have been someone he knew. Even in Imbros, the fellow probably would have raised a finger to his forehead in thanks. Here, he paid Krispos no mind at all, though the squeaking wheels of his cart almost brushed the newcomer's tunic. By the set look on his face, he had someplace important to go and not enough time to get there.

That seemed to be a characteristic of the people on the streets. Living in the most splendid city in the world, they gave it even less notice than Krispos had the familiar houses of his village. They did not notice him, either, except when his slow walk exasperated them. Then they sidestepped and scooted past him with the adroitness, almost, of so many dancers.

Their talk, the snatches of it that he picked up over the squeal of axles, the banging of coppersmiths' hammers, and the patter of the rain, had the same quick, elusive quality to it as their walk. Sometimes he had to think to understand it, and some of what he heard eluded him altogether. It was Videssian, aye, but not the Videssian he had learned from his parents.

He wandered for a couple of hours. Once he found himself in a large square that he thought was called the Forum of the Ox. He did not see any oxen in it, though everything else in the world seemed to be for sale there.

"Fried squid!" a vendor shouted.

A twist of breeze brought the savory scent of hot olive oil, breading, and seafood to Krispos' nose. His stomach growled. Sightseeing, he realized suddenly, was hungry work. He wasn't sure what a squid was, but asked, "How much?"

"Three coppers apiece," the man answered.

Krispos still had some small change in his pouch from the last job he'd done before he got to the city. "Give me two."

The vendor plucked them from his brazier with a pair of tongs. "Mind your fingers, now, pal—they're hot," he said as he exchanged them for Krispos' coins.

Krispos almost dropped them, but not because they were hot. He shifted his spear to the crook of his elbow so he could point. "Can I eat these—these—" He did not even know the right word.

"The tentacles? Sure—a lot of people say they're the best part." The local gave him a knowing smile. "Not from around these parts, are you?"

"Er, no." Krispos lost himself in the crowd; he did not want the squid-seller watching while he nerved himself to eat what he'd bought. The meat inside the breadcrumbs proved white and chewy, without any pronounced flavor; the tentacles weren't much different, so far as he could tell, from the rest. He licked his fingers, flicked at his beard to dislodge stray crumbs, and walked on.

Darkness began to fall. Krispos knew just enough of cities to try to find an inn. At last he did. "How much for a meal and a room?" he asked the tall thin man who stood behind a row of wine and beer barrels that served as a bar.

"Five pieces of silver," the innkeeper said flatly.

Krispos flinched. Not counting his goldpiece, he did not have that much. No matter how he haggled, he could not bring the fellow down below three. "Can I sleep in the stables if I tend your animals or stand guard for you?" he asked.

The innkeeper shook his head. "Got a horseboy, got a bouncer."

"Why are you so dear?" Krispos said. "When I bought squid cheap this afternoon, I figured everything else'd be—how would you say it?—in proportion."

"Aye, squid and fish and clams are cheap enough," the innkeeper said. "If you just want a good fish stew, I'll give you a big bowl for five coppers. We have lots of fish here. How not? Videssos is the biggest port in the world. But we have lots of people, too, so space, now, space'll cost you."

"Oh." Krispos scratched his head. What the innkeeper said made a strange kind of sense, even if he was not used to thinking in those terms. "I'll take that bowl of stew, and thank you. But where am I supposed to sleep tonight? Even if it wasn't raining, I wouldn't want to do it on the streets."

"Don't blame you." The innkeeper nodded. "Likely you'd get robbed the first night—doesn't matter how sharp your spear is if you're not awake to use it. Armed that way, though, you could try the barracks."

"Not till I've tried everything else," Krispos said stubbornly. "If I sleep in the barracks once, I'll end up sleeping there for years. I just want a place to set my head till I find steady work."

"I see what you're saying." The innkeeper walked over to the fireplace, stirred the pot that hung over it with a wooden spoon. "Your best bet'd likely be a monastery. If you help with the chores, they'll house you for a while, and feed you, too. Not a nice stew like this—" He ladled out a large, steaming bowlful. "—but bread and cheese and beer, plenty to keep you from starving. Now let's see those coppers, if you please."

Krispos paid him. The stew was good. The innkeeper gave him a heel of bread to sop up the last of it. He wiped his mouth on his damp sleeve, waited until the innkeeper was done serving another customer. Then he said, "A monastery sounds like a good idea. Where would I find one?"

"There must be a dozen of 'em in the city." The innkeeper stopped to think. "The one dedicated to the holy Pelagios is closest, but it's small and hasn't the room to take in many off the street. Better you should try the monastery of the holy Skirios. They always have space for travelers."

"Thanks. I'll do that. How do I get there?" Krispos made the innkeeper repeat the directions several times; he wanted to be sure he had them straight. Once he was, he stood in front of the fire to soak up as much warmth as he could, then plunged into the night.

He soon regretted it. The directions might have served well enough by daylight. In the dark, with half the firepots that should have lit the streets doused by rain, he got hopelessly lost. The innkeeper's fire quickly became only a wistful memory.

Few people were out and about so late. Some traveled in large bands and carried torches to light their way. Others walked alone, in darkness. One of those followed Krispos for blocks and sank back into deeper shadow whenever Krispos turned to look his way. Farm boy or not, he could figure out what that meant. He lowered his spear and took a couple of steps toward the skulker. The next time he looked around, the fellow was gone.

The longer Krispos walked, the more he marveled at how many streets, and how many miles of streets, Videssos the city had. From the way his feet felt, he had tramped all of them and none twice, for nothing looked familiar. Had he stumbled on another inn, he would have spent his lucky goldpiece without a second thought.

Instead, far more by luck than design, he came upon a large low structure with several gates. All but one were barred and silent. Torches burned there, though, and a stout man in a blue robe stood in the gateway. He was armed with an even stouter cudgel, which he hefted when Krispos walked into the flickering circle of light the torches cast.

"What building is this?" he asked as he approached. He trailed his spear, to look as harmless as he could.

"This is the monastery that serves the memory of the holy

Skirios, may Phos hallow his soul for all eternity,'' the watchman replied.

"May he indeed!" Krispos said fervently. "And may I beg shelter of you for the night? I've wandered the streets searching for this monastery for—for—well, it seems like forever."

The monk at the gate smiled. "Not that long, I hope, though it is the sixth hour of the night. Aye, come in, stranger, and be welcome, so long as you come in peace." He eyed Krispos' spear and sword.

"By Phos, I do."

"Well enough," the watchman said. "Enter then, and rest. When morning comes, you can present yourself to our holy abbot Pyrrhos with the others who came in out of the rain this evening. He, or someone under him, will assign you some task for tomorrow—or perhaps for some time, if you need a longer time of shelter with us."

"Agreed," Krispos said at once. He started to walk past the monk, then paused. "Pyrrhos, you say? I knew a man by that name once." He frowned, trying to remember where or when, but gave it up with a shrug after a moment.

The monk also shrugged. "I've known two or three myself; it's a fairly common name."

"Aye, so it is." Krispos yawned. The monk pointed the way to the common room.

The abbot Pyrrhos was dreaming. It was one of those dreams where he knew he was dreaming but did not particularly want to break the mood by exerting his will. He was in a line of people coming before some judge, whether imperial or divine he could not say.

He could not hear the judgments the enthroned figure was passing on those in front of him, but he was not greatly concerned, either. He knew he had led a pious life, and his worldly sins were also small. Surely no harsh sentence could fall on him.

The line moved forward with dreamlike quickness. Only one woman stood between him and the judge. Then she, too, was gone. Had she walked away? Disappeared? Pyrrhos had not noticed, but that, too, was the way of dreams. The abbot bowed to the man—if it was a man—on the throne.

Eyes stern as those of Phos transfixed Pyrrhos. He bowed again and stayed bent at the waist. Almost he went to hands and knees and then to his belly, as if he stood before the Avtokrator. "Illustrious lord—" his dream-voice quavered.

"Silence, worm!" Now he could hear the judge's voice. It reverberated like a thunderclap in his head. "Do as I say and all will be well for Videssos; fail and all fails with you. Do you understand?"

"Aye, lord," dream-Pyrrhos said. "Speak, and I obey."

"Go then to the monastery common room. Go at once; do not wait for dawn. Call out the name Krispos, once, twice, three times. Give the man who answers every favor; treat him as if he were your own son. Get hence now, and do as I have ordained."

Pyrrhos woke to find himself safe in his own bed. A guttering lamp illuminated his chamber. Save for being larger and packed with books, it was like the cells in which his monks slept— unlike many abbots, he disdained personal comfort as a weakness.

"What a strange dream," he whispered. All the same, he did not get up. He yawned instead. Within minutes, he was asleep again.

He found himself before the enthroned judge once more. This time, he was at the head of the line. If he had thought those eyes stern before, they fairly blazed now. "Insolent wretch!" the judge cried. "Obey, or all totters around you. Summon the man Krispos from the common room, once, twice, three times. Give him the favor you would your own son. Waste no time in sottish slumber. This must be done! Now go!"

Pyrrhos woke with a violent start. Sweat beaded his forehead and his shaven crown. He still seemed to hear the last word of the judge's angry shout dinning in his ears. He started to get out of bed, then stopped. Anger of his own filled him. What business did a dream have, telling him what to do?

Deliberately he lay back down and composed himself for sleep. It came more slowly this time than before, but his disciplined mind enforced rest on him as if it were a program of exercise. His eyes sagged shut, his breathing grew soft and regular.

He felt a cold caress of terror—the judge was coming down from the throne, straight for him. He tried to run and could not. The judge seized him, lifting him as if he were light as a mouse. "Summon the man Krispos, fool!" he roared, and cast Pyrrhos from him. The abbot fell and fell and fell forever . . .

He woke up on the cold stone floor.

Trembling, Pyrrhos got to his feet. He was a bold man; even now, he started to return to his bed. But when he thought of the enthroned judge and those terrible eyes—and how they would look should he disobey yet again—boldness failed. He opened the door to his chamber and stepped out into the hallway.

Two monks returning to their cells from a late-night prayer vigil glanced up in surprise to see someone approaching them. As was his right, Pyrrhos stared through them as if they did not exist. They bowed their heads and, without a word, stood aside to let the abbot pass.

The door to the common room was barred on the side away from the men the monastery took in. Pyrrhos had second thoughts as he lifted the bar—but he had not fallen out of bed since he was a boy. He could not make himself believe he had fallen out of bed tonight. Shaking his head, he went into the common room.

As always, the smell hit him first, the smell of the poor, the hungry, the desperate, and the derelict of Videssos: unwashed humanity, stale wine, from somewhere the sharp tang of vomit. Tonight the rain added damp straw's mustiness and the oily lanolin reek of wet wool to the mix.

A man said something to himself as he turned over in his sleep. Others snored. One fellow sat against a wall, coughing the consumptive's endless racking bark. *I'm to pick one of these men to treat as my son?* the abbot thought. *One of* these*?*

It was either that or go back to bed. Pyrrhos got as far as putting his fingers on the door handle. He found he did not dare to work it. Sighing, he turned back. "Krispos?" he called softly.

A couple of men stirred. The consumptive's eyes, huge in his thin face, met the abbot's. He could not read the expression in them. No one answered him.

"Krispos?" he called again.

This time he spoke louder. Someone grumbled. Someone else sat up. Again, no one replied. Pyrrhos felt the heat of embarrassment rise to the top of his tonsured head. If nothing came of this night's folly, he would have some explaining to do, perhaps even—he shuddered at the thought—to the patriarch himself. He hated the idea of making himself vulnerable to Gnatios' mockery; the ecumenical patriarch of Videssos was far too secular to suit him. But Gnatios was Petronas' cousin, and so long as Petronas was the most powerful man in the Empire, his cousin would remain at the head of the ecclesiastical hierarchy.

One more fruitless call, the abbot thought, and his ordeal would be over. If Gnatios wanted to mock him for it, well, he had endured worse things in his service to Phos. That reflection steadied him, so his voice rang out loud and clear: "Krispos?"

Several men sat up now. A couple of them glared at Pyrrhos for interrupting their rest. He had already begun to turn to go back to his chamber when someone said, "Aye, holy sir, I'm Krispos. What do you want of me?"

It was a good question. The abbot would have been happier with a good answer for it.

Krispos sat in the monastery study while Pyrrhos bustled about lighting lamps. When that small, homely task was done, the abbot took a chair opposite him. The lamplight failed to fill his eyesockets or the hollows of his cheeks, leaving his face strange and not quite human as he studied Krispos.

"What am I to do with you, young man?" he said at last.

Krispos shook his head in bewilderment. "I couldn't begin to tell you, holy sir. You called, so I answered; that's all I know about it." He fought down a yawn. He would sooner have been back in the common room, asleep.

"Is it? Is it indeed?" The abbot leaned forward, voice tight with suppressed eagerness. It was as if he were trying to find out something from Krispos without letting on that he was trying to.

By that sign, Krispos knew him. He had been just so a dozen years before, asking questions about the goldpiece Omurtag had given Krispos—the same goldpiece, he realized, that he had in his pouch. Save for the passage of time, which sat lightly on it, Pyrrhos' gaunt, intent face was also the same.

"You were up on the platform with Iakovitzes and me," Krispos said.

The abbot frowned. "I crave pardon? What was that?"

"In Kubrat, when he ransomed us from the wild men," Krispos explained.

"I was?" Pyrrhos' gaze suddenly sharpened; Krispos saw that he remembered, too. "By the lord with the great and good mind, I *was*," the abbot said slowly. He drew the circular sun-sign on his breast. "You were but a boy then."

It sounded like an accusation. As if to remind himself it was true no more, Krispos touched the hilt of his sword. Thus reassured, he nodded.

"But boy no more," Pyrrhos said, agreeing with him. "Yet here we are, drawn back together once more." He made the sun-sign again, then said something completely obscure to Krispos: "No, Gnatios will not laugh."

"Holy sir?"

"Never mind." The abbot's attention might have wandered for a moment. Now it focused on Krispos again. "Tell me how you came from whatever village you lived in to Videssos the city."

Krispos did. Speaking of his parents' and sister's deaths brought back the pain, nearly as strong as if he felt it for the first time. He had to wait before he could go on. "And then, with the village still all in disarray, our taxes went up a third, I suppose to pay for some war at the other end of the Empire."

"More likely to pay for another—or another dozen—of Anthimos' extravagant follies." Pyrrhos' mouth set in a thin, hard line of disapproval. "Petronas lets him have his way in them, the better to keep the true reins of ruling in his own hands. Neither of them cares how they gain the gold to pay for such sport, so long as they do."

"As may be," Krispos said. "It's not why we were broken, but that we were broken that put me on my way here. Farmers have hard enough times worrying about nature. If the tax man wrecks us, too, we've got no hope at all. That's what it looked like to me, and that's why I left."

Pyrrhos nodded. "I've heard like tales before. Now, though, the question arises of what to do with you. Did you come to the city planning to use the weapons you carry?"

"Not if I can find anything else to do," Krispos said at once.

"Hmm." The abbot stroked his bushy beard. "You lived all your life till now on a farm, yes? How are you with horses?"

"I can manage, I expect," Krispos answered, "though I'm better with mules; I've had more to do with them, if you know what I mean. Mules I'm good with. Any other livestock, too, and I'm your man. Why do you want to know, holy sir?"

"Because I think that, as the flows of your life and mine have come together after so many years, it seems fitting for Iakovitzes' to be mingled with the stream once more, as well. And because I happen to know that Iakovitzes is constantly looking for new grooms to serve in his stables."

"Would he take me on, holy sir? Someone he's never—well,

just about never—seen before? If he would . . ." Krispos' eyes lit up. "If he would, I'd leap at the chance."

"He would, on my urging," Pyrrhos said. "We're cousins of sorts: his great-grandfather and my grandmother were brother and sister. He also owes me a few more favors than I owe him at the moment."

"If he would, if you would, I couldn't think of anything better." Krispos meant it; if he was going to work with animals, it would be almost as if he had the best of farm and city both. He hesitated, then asked a question he knew was dangerous: "But why do you want to do this for me, holy sir?"

Pyrrhos sketched the sun-sign. After a moment, Krispos realized that was all the answer he'd get. When the abbot spoke, it was of his cousin. "Understand, young man, you are altogether free to refuse this if you wish. Many would, without a second thought. I don't know if you recall, but Iakovitzes is a man of—how shall I say it?—uncertain temperament, perhaps."

Krispos smiled. He did remember.

The abbot smiled, too, but thinly. "That is one reason, of course, why he constantly seeks new grooms. Truly, I may be doing you no favor, though I pray to Phos that I am."

"Sounds to me like you are," Krispos said.

"I hope so." Pyrrhos made the sun-sign again, which puzzled Krispos. Pyrrhos hesitated, then went on, "In justice, there is one other thing of which I should warn you: Iakovitzes is said sometimes to seek, ah, services from his grooms other than caring for his beasts."

"Oh." That made Krispos hesitate, too. His memory of the way Iakovitzes had touched him was inextricably joined to the mortification he'd known on that Midwinter's Day when the villagers poked fun at him and Idalkos. "I don't have any leanings that way myself," he said carefully. "But if he pushes too hard, I suppose I can always quit—I'd be no worse off then than if I hadn't met you."

"What you say has a measure of truth in it," Pyrrhos said. "Very well, then, if it is your wish, I will take you to meet Iakovitzes."

"Let's go!" Krispos leaped to his feet.

The abbot stayed seated. "Not quite at this instant," he said, his voice dry. "Iakovitzes may occasionally go to bed in the ninth hour of the night, but I assure you he is not in the habit of rising at this time. If we went to his home now, we *would* be turned away from his door, most likely with dogs."

"I forgot what time it was," Krispos said sheepishly.

"Go back to the common room. Sleep the rest of the night there. When morning comes, we will visit my cousin, I promise you." Pyrrhos yawned. "I may even try for a little more sleep myself, assuming I don't get thrown out of bed again."

"Holy sir?" Krispos asked, but the abbot did not explain.

IV

Iakovitzes' house was large but, from the outside, not otherwise impressive. Only a few windows interrupted the long whitewashed front that faced the street. They were too narrow to let in any thief, no matter how young or skinny.

A second story stood above the first, and overhung it by three or four feet. In summer, that would have created shade; now, with the rain coming down again, it kept Krispos and Pyrrhos from getting any wetter as the abbot seized the horseshoe that served for a knocker and pounded it against Iakovitzes' stout front door.

A servant opened a little grillwork in the center of the door and peered through it. "Abbot Pyrrhos!" he said. Krispos heard him lift the bar. The door opened outward a moment later. "Come in, holy sir, and your friend as well."

Just inside the doorway lay a mat of woven straw. Pyrrhos stopped to wipe his muddy sandals on it before he walked down the hall. Admiring the wit of whoever had come up with such a useful device, Krispos imitated the abbot.

"Have you breakfasted, holy sir?" the servant asked.

"On monastery fare," Pyrrhos said. "That suits me well enough, but I daresay Krispos here would be grateful for a bit more. In any case, it is on his behalf that I have come to visit your master."

"I see. Krispos, you say his name is? Very well. Wait here, if you please. I'll have something sent him from the kitchen and will inform Iakovitzes directly."

"Thank you," Pyrrhos said. Krispos said nothing. He was

81

too busy staring. "Here"—Iakovitzes' waiting room—was the most magnificent place he had ever seen. The floor was a mosaic, a hunting scene with men spearing boars from horseback. Krispos had seen mosaic work once before, in the dome of Phos' temple at Imbros. Never in his wildest dreams had he imagined anyone save perhaps the Avtokrator possessing a mosaic of his own.

The waiting room opened onto a courtyard that seemed about the size of the village square Krispos had so recently left. In the center stood a horse, frozen in mid-rear. Krispos needed a moment to realize it was a statue. Around it were patterned rows of hedges and flowers, though most of the blooms had already fallen because the season was so late. A marble fountain plashed just outside the waiting room, as happily as if rain had never been invented.

"Here you are, sir." The view so enthralled Krispos that the young man at his elbow might have spoken two or three times before he noticed. When he turned with a stammered apology, the servant handed him a covered silver tray. "Lobster tail in cream sauce, with parsnips and squash. I hope that suits you, sir."

"What? Oh. Yes. Of course. Thank you." Noticing he was babbling, Krispos shut up. So far as he could remember, no one had ever called him "sir" before. Now this fellow had done it twice in about as many sentences.

When he lifted the lid, the delicious aroma that floated up from the tray drove such maunderings out of his mind. The lobster tasted even better than it smelled, which amazed him all over again. It was sweeter than pork and more delicate than veal, and he could only regret that it disappeared so fast. Iakovitzes' cook knew more about what to do with squash and parsnips than any of the village women had, too.

He had just set down the tray and was licking cream sauce off his mustache when Iakovitzes came into the waiting room. "Hello, Pyrrhos." He held out his hand for the abbot's clasp. "What brings you here so early, and who's this stalwart young chap you have with you?" His eyes walked up and down Krispos.

"You've met him before, cousin," Pyrrhos said.

"Have I? Then I'd best arrange a guardian to oversee my affairs, for my memory is plainly not what it was." Iakovitzes clapped a hand to his forehead in melodramatic despair. He waved Pyrrhos and Krispos to a couch and sat down himself in a chair close to Krispos. He pulled it closer yet. "Explain to me, then, if you would, my evident decline into senility."

Pyrrhos was either long used to Iakovitzes' histrionics or, perhaps more likely, without enough sense of humor to react much to them. "Krispos here was a great deal younger then," the abbot explained. "He was the boy who stood on the platform with you to seal one of your ransoming bargains with Omurtag."

"The more I forget about those beastly trips to Kubrat, the happier I'll be." Iakovitzes paused, stroking his carefully trimmed beard while he studied Krispos again. "By Phos, I do recall!" he said. "You were a pretty boy then, and you're quite the handsome youth now. By that proud nose of yours, I'd almost guess you were a Vaspurakaner, though if you're from the northern border I don't suppose that's likely."

"My father always said his side of the family had Vaspurakaner blood," Krispos said.

Iakovitzes nodded. "It could be so; 'princes' resettled there after some old war—or some old treachery. Whether or not, the look becomes you."

Krispos did not know how to answer that, so he kept quiet. Some of the village girls had praised his looks, but never a man before.

To his relief, Iakovitzes turned back to Pyrrhos. "You were about to tell me, I expect, how and why dear Krispos here comes to be in the city instead of back at his rustic village, and also how and why that pertains to me."

Krispos saw how his sharp eyes bored into the abbot's. He also noted that Iakovitzes was not going to say anything of consequence until he heard Pyrrhos' story. He thought better of him for it; whatever Iakovitzes' taste in pleasures, the man was no fool.

The abbot told the tale as Krispos had given it to him, then carried it forward. His explanation of how he had come to call for Krispos in the monastery was vague. Krispos had thought so the night before. Iakovitzes, however, was in a position to call Pyrrhos on it. "I don't follow you there," he said. "Back up and tell me just how that happened."

Pyrrhos looked harassed. "Only if I have your vow by the lord with the great and good mind to let the story go no further—and yours as well, Krispos." Krispos swore the oath; after a moment, Iakovitzes did, too. "Very well, then," the abbot said heavily. He told of his three dreams of the night before, and of ending up on the floor after the last one.

Silence filled the waiting room when he was done. Iakovitzes broke it, asking, "And you think this means—what?"

"I wish I knew," Pyrrhos burst out. He sounded as exasperated as he looked. "That it is a sending, I think no one could deny. But whether it is for good or evil, from Phos or Skotos or neither, I would not begin to guess. I can only say that in some way quite unapparent to me, Krispos here is more remarkable than he seems."

"He seems remarkable enough, though perhaps not in the way you mean," Iakovitzes said with a smile. "So you brought him to me, eh, cousin, to fulfill your dream's commandment to treat him like a son? I suppose I should be flattered—unless you think your dream does bode ill and are not letting on."

"No. No priest of Phos could do such a thing without yielding his soul to the certainty of Skotos' ice," Pyrrhos said.

Iakovitzes steepled his fingertips. "I suppose not." He turned his smile, charming and cynical at the same time, on Krispos. "So, young man, now that you are here—for good or ill—what would you?"

"I came to Videssos the city for work," Krispos said slowly. "The abbot tells me you're hiring grooms. I've lived on a farm all my life but for the last couple of weeks. You won't find many city-raised folk better with beasts than I am."

"There is probably a good deal of truth in that." Iakovitzes raised an eyebrow. "Did my cousin the most holy abbot—" He spoke with such fulsome sincerity that the praise sounded like sarcasm, "—also, ah, warn you that I sometimes seek more from my grooms than skill with animals alone?"

"Yes," Krispos said flatly, then kept still.

Finally, Iakovitzes prompted him: "And so?"

"Sir, if that's what you want from me, I expect you'll be able to find it elsewhere with less trouble. I do thank you for the breakfast, and for your time. Thank you as well, holy sir," Krispos added for Pyrrhos' benefit as he stood to go.

"Don't be hasty." Iakovitzes jumped to his feet, too. "I *do* need grooms, as a matter of fact. Suppose I take you on with no requirement past caring for the beasts, with room and board and—hmm—a goldpiece a week."

"You pay the others two," Pyrrhos said.

"Dear cousin, I thought you priests reckoned silence a virtue," Iakovitzes said. It was the sweetest snarl Krispos had heard. Iakovitzes turned back to him. "Very well, then, two goldpieces a week, though you lacked the wit to ask for them yourself."

"Just the beasts?" Krispos said.

"Just the beasts"—Iakovitzes sighed—"though you must not hold it against me if from time to time I try to find out whether you've changed your mind."

"Will *you* hold it against *me* if I keep saying no?"

Iakovitzes sighed again. "I suppose not."

"Then we've got ourselves a bargain." Krispos stuck out his hand. It almost swallowed Iakovitzes', though the smaller man's grip was surprisingly strong.

"Gomaris!" Iakovitzes shouted. The man who had let in Krispos and Pyrrhos appeared a moment later, panting a little. "Gomaris, Krispos will be one of the grooms from now on. Why don't you find him some clothes better than those rags he has on and then get him settled in with the rest of the lads?"

"Of course. Come along, Krispos, and welcome to the household." Gomaris waited till he was halfway down the hall, then added softly, "Whatever else it is around here, it's rarely dull."

"That," said Krispos, "I believe."

"Here comes the farm boy."

Krispos heard the whisper as he came into the stable. By the way Barses and Meletios sniggered at each other, he had been meant to hear. He scowled. They were both younger than he, but they were also from the city, and from families of more than a little wealth. So were most of Iakovitzes' grooms. They seemed to enjoy making Krispos' life miserable.

Barses took a shovel off the wall and thrust it at Krispos. "Here you are, farm boy. Since you've lived with manure all your life, you can clean out the stalls today. You're used to smelling like the hind end of a horse." His handsome face split in a wide, mocking grin.

"It's not my turn to shovel out today," Krispos said shortly.

"Oh, but we think you should do it anyway," Barses said. "Don't we, Meletios?" The other groom nodded. He was even handsomer than Barses; almost pretty, in fact.

"No," Krispos said.

Barses' eyes went wide in feigned surprise. "The farm boy grows insolent. I think we'll have to teach him a lesson."

"So we will," Meletios said. Smiling in anticipation, he stepped toward Krispos. "I wonder how fast farm boys learn. I've heard they're not too bright."

Krispos' frown deepened. He'd known for a week that the hazing he'd been sweating out would turn physical sooner or later. He'd thought he was ready—but two against one wasn't how he'd wanted it to happen. He held up a hand. "Wait!" he said in a high, alarmed voice. "I'll clean 'em. Give me the shovel."

Barses held it out. His face showed an interesting mix of amusement, triumph, and contempt. "You'd best do a good job, too, farm boy, or we'll make you lick up whatever you—"

Krispos snatched the shovel from his hands, whirled, and rammed the handle into the pit of Meletios' stomach. The groom closed up on himself like a bellows, gasping uselessly for air.

Krispos threw the shovel aside. "Come on!" he snarled at Barses. "Or aren't you as good with your hands as you are with your mouth?"

"You'll see, farm boy!" Barses sprang at him. He was strong and fearless and knew something of what he was doing, but he'd never been through anything like the course in nasty fighting Krispos had taken from Idalkos. In less than two minutes he was down in the straw beside Meletios, groaning and trying to hold his knee, his groin, his ribs, and a couple of dislocated fingers, all at the same time.

Krispos stood over the other two grooms, breathing hard. One of his eyes was half closed and a collarbone had gotten a fearful whack, but he'd dished out a lot more than he'd taken. He picked up the shovel and tossed it between Meletios and Barses. "You can shovel out for yourselves."

Meletios grabbed the shovel and started to swing it at Krispos' ankles. Krispos stamped on his hand. Meletios shrieked and let go. Krispos kicked him in the ribs with force nicely calculated to yield maximum hurt and minimum permanent damage. "Come to think of it, Meletios, you do the shoveling today. You just earned it."

Even through his pain, Meletios let out an indignant squawk and cast a look of appeal toward Barses.

The other groom was just sitting up. He shook his head, then grimaced as he regretted the motion. "I'm not going to argue with him, Meletios, and if you have any sense, you won't, either." He managed a lopsided grin. "Nobody with any sense is going to argue with Krispos, not after today."

The harassment did not disappear. With a dozen grooms ranging from their mid-teens up to Krispos' age, and all living in one another's pockets, that would hardly have been possible. But after Krispos dealt with Barses and Meletios, he was accepted as one of the group and got to hand it out as well as take it.

Not only that, he got himself listened to, where before the other grooms had paid no attention to what he thought. Thus when they wcrc hashing over the best way to treat a horse with a mild but stubborn fever, one of them turned to Krispos and asked, "What would you have done about this in that backwoods place you came from?"

"The green forage is all very well," he said after a little thought, "and the wet, sloppy food and gruel, but we always said there was nothing like beer to speed things along."

"Beer?" The grooms whopped.

Barses asked, "For us or the animal?"

Krispos laughed, too, but said, "For the animal. A bucket or three ought to do the job."

"He means it," Meletios said in surprise. He turned thoughtful. He was all business where horses were concerned. Iakovitzcs tolerated no groom who was not, whatever other charms he might have. In a musing tone, Meletios went on, "What say we try it? I don't see how it could do any harm."

So a couple of buckets of beer went into the horse's trough every morning, and if the grooms bought a bit more than the sick animal really needed, why, only they knew about that. And after a few days, the horse's condition did improve: his breathing slowed, his eyes brightened, and his skin and mouth lost the dry look and feel they'd had while he was ill.

"Well done," Barses said when the horse was clearly on the mend. "Next time I take a fever, you know what to do with me, though I'd sooner have wine, I think." Krispos threw a clod of dirt at him.

Iakovitzes had watched the treatment with as much interest as any of the grooms. When it succeeded, he handed Krispos a goldpiece. "And come sup with me this evening, if you care to," he said, his sharp voice as smooth as he could make it.

"Thank you very much, sir," Krispos said.

Meletios sulked for the rest of the day. Krispos finally asked him what was wrong. He glared. "If I told you I was jealous, you'd probably beat on me again."

"Jealous?" Krispos needed a few seconds to catch on. "Oh! Don't worry about that. I only fancy girls."

"So you say," Meletios answered darkly. "But Iakovitzes fancies you."

Krispos snorted and went back to work. Around sunset, he walked over to Iakovitzes' main house. This was the first meal he'd eaten there since his breakfast of lobster tail; the grooms had their own dining hall. Like as not, he thought, Meletios was fretting over nothing; if some big banquet was planned, Krispos might not even be at the same table as his master.

As soon as Gomaris led him to a chamber large enough only for two, Krispos knew Meletios had been right and he himself wrong. A small lamp on the table left most of the room in twilight. "Hello, Krispos," Iakovitzes said, rising to greet him. "Here, have some wine."

He poured with his own hand. Krispos was used to the rough vintages the villagers had made for themselves. What Iakovitzes gave him slid down his throat like a smooth whisper. He would have thought it mere grape juice but for the warmth it left in his middle.

"Another cup?" Iakovitzes asked solicitously. "I'd like the chance to toast you for your cleverness in dosing Stormbreeze. The beast seems in fine fettle again, thanks to you."

Iakovitzes raised his cup in salute. Krispos knew drinking too much with his master was not a good idea, but had no polite way to do anything else. The wine was so good, he scarcely felt guilty about soaking it up.

Gomaris fetched in supper, a platter of halibut grilled with garlic and leeks. The herbs' sharp flavors reminded Krispos of his home, but the only fish he'd had there was an occasional trout or carp taken from a stream, hardly worth mentioning beside a delicacy like this. "Delicious," he mumbled in one of the few moments when his mouth was not full.

"Glad you enjoy it," Iakovitzes said. "We have a proverb hereabouts: 'If you come to Videssos the city, eat fish.' At least this fish is to your liking."

After the fish came smoked partridges, one little bird apiece, and, after the partridges, plums and figs candied in honey. The grooms ate well enough, but not fare like this. Krispos knew he was stuffing himself. He found he did not care; after all, Iakovitzes had invited him here to eat.

His master rose to fill his cup again, then sent him a reproachful look when he saw its contents hardly touched. "Dear boy, you're not drinking. Does the vintage fail to suit you?"

"No, it's very good," Krispos said. "It's just that—" He groped for an excuse "—I don't want to get all sozzled and act the fool."

"A commendable attitude, but you needn't worry. I recognize that part of the pleasure of wine is not worrying so much over what one does. And pleasures, Krispos, do not come to us so often in this life that they are to be lightly despised." Remembering the troubles that had made him leave his village, Krispos found some truth in Iakovitzes' words. Iakovitzes went on, "For instance, I am sure, though you do not complain of it, that you must be worn from your toil with the horses. Let me soothe you if I can."

Before Krispos could reply, Iakovitzes hurried round behind his chair and began to massage his shoulders. He knew what he was about; Krispos felt the tension flowing out of him.

He also felt, though, the quivering eagerness Iakovitzes could not keep from his hands. He knew what that meant; he had known when he was nine years old. Not without some reluctance, he twisted in his seat so he faced Iakovitzes. "I said when you took me on that I didn't care for these games."

Iakovitzes kept his aplomb. "And I told you that wouldn't stop me from being interested. Were you like some I've known, I could offer you gold. Somehow, though, with you I don't think that would do much good. Or am I wrong?" he finished hopefully.

"You're not wrong," Krispos said at once.

"Too bad, too bad." The dim lamplight caught a spark of malice in Iakovitzes' eye. "Shall I turn you out on the street, then, for your obstinacy?"

"Whatever you like, of course." Krispos kept his voice as steady as he could. He refused to give his master such a hold on him.

Iakovitzes sighed. "That would be ungrateful of me, wouldn't it, after what you did for Stormbreeze? Have it as you wish, Krispos. But it's not as if I were offering you anything vile. Many enjoy it."

"I'm sure that's true, sir." Krispos thought of Meletios. "I just don't happen to be one of those folk."

"Too bad," Iakovitzes said. "Here, have some more wine anyhow. We might as well finish the jar."

"Why not?" Krispos drank another cup; it was too good to decline. Then he yawned and said, "It must be late. I'd best get back to my own chamber if I'm going to be worth anything in the morning."

"I suppose so," Iakovitzes said indifferently—one hour was as good as another to him. When he tried to kiss Krispos good night, Krispos thought he made his sidestep seem completely natural until he saw his master raise an ironic eyebrow.

After that, Krispos retreated in some haste. To his surprise, he found Barses and a couple of the other grooms waiting up for him. "Well?" Barses said.

"Well, what?" Krispos set himself. If Barses wanted revenge for their fight, he might get it. Three against one, in fact, just about guaranteed he would.

But that was not what Barses had in mind. "Well, you and Iakovitzes, of course. Did you? No shame to you if you did— the only reason I want to know is that I have a bet."

"Which way?"

"I won't tell you that. If you say it's none of my business, the bet waits until Iakovitzes makes things clear one way or the other. He will, you know."

Krispos was sure of that. The wine he'd drunk weakened whatever urge he had to keep the evening a secret. "No, we didn't," he said. "I like girls too well to be interested in the sports he enjoys."

Barses grinned and clapped him on the back, then turned to one of the other grooms with his palm up. "Pay me that gold-piece, Agrabast. I told you he wouldn't." Agrabast gave him the coin. "Next question," Barses said. "Did he toss you out for turning him down?"

"No. He thought about it, but he didn't."

"Good thing I didn't let you double the bet for that, Barses," Agrabast said. "Iakovitzes loves his beasts about as well as he loves his prick. He wouldn't throw away anybody who'd shown he knew something about horseleeching."

"I figured that out," Barses said. "I was hoping you hadn't."

"Well, to the ice with you," Agrabast retorted.

"To the ice with all of you, if you don't get out of my way

and let me have some sleep." Krispos started to push past the other grooms, then stopped and added, "Meletios can stop worrying now."

Everyone laughed. When the chuckles died down, though, Barses said, "You *are* from the country, Krispos; maybe we look at things a little different from you. I meant what I said before—there'd be no shame in saying yes to Iakovitzes, and Meletios isn't the only one of us who has."

"I never said he was," Krispos answered. "But as far as I can see, he's the only one who's put some worry into it. So now he can stop."

"That's fair enough, I suppose," Barses said judiciously.

"Whether it is or whether it's not, out of my way before I fall asleep where I'm standing." Krispos made as if to advance on the other grooms. Laughing again, they moved aside to let him by.

All winter long, Iakovitzes cast longing looks Krispos' way. All winter long, Krispos pretended he did not see them. He tended his master's horses. Iakovitzes usually took along a groom when he went to a feast, Krispos as often as anyone else. And when he feasted other nobles in turn, all the grooms attended so he could show them off.

At first, Krispos viewed the Empire's nobility with the same awe he had given Videssos the city when he was just arrived. His awe for the nobles soon wore off. He found they were men like any others, some clever, some plain, some downright stupid. As Barses said of one, "It's a good thing for him he inherited his money, because he'd never figure out how to make any on his own."

By contrast, the more Krispos explored the city, the more marvelous he found it. Every alleyway had something new: an apothecary's stall, perhaps, or a temple to Phos so small only a double handful of worshipers could use it.

Even streets he knew well gave him new people to see: swarthy Makuraners in caftans and felt pillbox hats, big blond Halogai gaping at Videssos just as he had, stocky Kubratoi in furs. Krispos kept his distance from them; he could not help wondering if any had been among the riders who'd kidnapped him and his family or plundered the village north of the mountains.

And there were the Videssians themselves, the people of the

city: brash, bumptious, loud, cynical, nothing like the farm folk among whom he'd grown up.

"To the ice with you, you blithering, bungling booby!" a shopkeeper shouted at an artisan one afternoon. "This pane of glass I ordered is half a foot too short!"

"Up yours, too, friend." The glassblower pulled out a scrap of parchment. "That's what I thought: seventeen by twenty-two. That's what you ordered, that's what I made. You can't measure, don't blame me." He was yelling, too. A crowd began to gather. People poked their heads out of windows to see what was going on.

The shopkeeper snatched the parchment out of his hand. "I didn't write this!"

"It didn't write itself, friend."

The glassblower tried to snatch it back. The shopkeeper jerked it away. They stood nose to nose, screaming at each other and waving their fists. "Shouldn't we get between them before they pull knives?" Krispos said to the man beside him.

"And wreck the show? Are you crazy?" By the fellow's tone, he thought Krispos was. After a moment, he grudgingly went on, "They won't go at it. They'll just yell till it's out of their systems, then go on about their business. You wait and see."

The local proved right. Krispos would have admitted it, but the man hadn't stayed to see the results of his prediction. After things calmed down, Krispos left, too, shaking his head. His home village hadn't been like this at all.

He was almost to Iakovitzes' house when he saw a pretty girl. She smiled when he caught her eye, strode up to him bold as brass. His home village hadn't been like that, either.

Then she said, "A piece of silver and I'm yours for the afternoon; three and I'm yours for the whole night, too." She ran her hand along his arm. Her nails and lips were painted the same shade of red.

"Sorry," Krispos answered. "I don't feel like paying for it."

She looked him up and down, then gave a regretful shrug. "No, I don't expect you'd need to very often. Too bad. I would've enjoyed it more with someone who didn't *have* to buy." But when she saw he meant his no, she walked on down the street, swinging her hips. Like most people in the city, she didn't waste time where she had no hope of profit.

Krispos turned his head and watched her till she rounded a corner. He decided not to go back to Iakovitzes' right away after all. It was too late for lunch, too early for supper or serious drinking. That meant a certain pert little barmaid he knew ought to be able to slip away for—for just long enough, he thought, grinning.

Snow gave way to sleet, which in turn yielded to rain. By the standards Krispos used to judge, Videssos the city had a mild winter. Even so, he was glad to see spring return. Iakovitzes' horses were, too. They cropped the tender new grass till their dung came thin and green. Shoveling it made Krispos less delighted with the season.

One fine morning when such shoveling was someone else's concern, he started out on an errand of his own—not the little barmaid, with whom he had broken up, but a more than reasonable substitute. He opened Iakovitzes' front door, then drew back in surprise. What looked like a parade was coming up to the house.

The city folk loved parades, so this one, not surprisingly, had a fair-size crowd around it. Krispos needed a moment to see that at its heart were bearers with—he counted quickly—eleven silk parasols. The Avtokrator of Videssos rated only one more.

As Krispos realized who Iakovitzes' visitor had to be, a gorgeously robed servitor detached himself from the head of the procession. He declared, "Forth comes his illustrious Highness the Sevastokrator Petronas to call upon your master Iakovitzes. Be so good, fellow, as to announce him."

Properly, that was Gomaris' job. Krispos fled without worrying about such niceties. If the Emperor's uncle wanted something done, niceties did not matter.

By luck, Iakovitzes was up and about and had even finished breakfast. He frowned when Krispos burst into the waiting room where he was having a second cup of wine. When Krispos gasped out the news, he frowned again, in a very different way.

"Oh, plague! This place looks like a sty. Well, it can't be helped, not if Petronas wants to show up before anyone's awake." Iakovitzes gulped his wine and fixed Krispos with a glare. "What are you doing just standing around? Go tell his illustrious Highness I'm delighted to receive him—and any other sweet lies you can think up on the way."

Krispos dashed back to the door, expecting to relay the polite message to the Sevastokrator's man. Instead, he almost ran head-on into Petronas himself. Petronas' robe, of crimson shot with

gold and silver thread, made his servant's shabby by comparison.

"Careful, there; don't hurt yourself," the Sevastokrator said,
chuckling, as Krispos almost fell over himself trying to stop,
bow, and go to his right knee all at once.

"H-highness," Krispos stammered. "My master is d-delighted
to receive you."

"Not this early, he isn't." Petronas' voice was dry.

From his perch on one knee, Krispos glanced up at the most
powerful man in the Empire of Videssos. The images he'd seen
back in his village hadn't suggested that the Sevastokrator owned
a sense of humor. They also made him out to be a few years
younger than he was; Krispos guessed he was past fifty rather
than nearing it. But his true features conveyed the same sense
of confident competence as had his portraits.

Now he reached out to tap Krispos on the shoulder. "Come
on, young fellow, take me to him. What's your name, anyhow?"

"Krispos, Highness," Krispos said as he got to his feet. "This
way, if you please."

Petronas fell into step with him. "Krispos, while I'm engaged
with your master, can you see to it that my retinue gets some
wine, and maybe cheese or bread, as well? Just standing there
and waiting for me to finish is boring duty for them."

"I'll take care of it," Krispos promised.

Iakovitzes, he saw as he led the Sevastokrator into the waiting
room, had slipped into a new robe himself. It was also crimson,
but not so deep and rich a shade as Petronas'. Moreover, while
Iakovitzes still wore sandals, Petronas had on a pair of black
boots with red trim. Only Anthimos was entitled to boots scarlet
from top to toe.

When Krispos stuck his head into the kitchen with word of
what Petronas wanted, the cook who had fixed Iakovitzes'
breakfast yelped in dismay. Then he started slicing onion rolls
and hard cheese like a man possessed. He shouted for someone
to give him a hand.

Krispos filled wine cups—cheap earthenware cups, not the
crystal and silver and gold from which Iakovitzes' fancy guests
drank—and set them on trays. Other servants whisked them away
to Petronas' men. Having done his duty, Krispos slipped out a
side door to go meet his girl.

"You're late," she said crossly.

"I'm sorry, Sirikia." He kissed her, to show how sorry he

was. "Just as I was leaving to see you, Petronas the Sevastokra-tor came to visit my master, and they needed my help for a little while." He hoped she would imagine more intimate help than standing in the kitchen pouring wine.

Evidently she did, for her annoyance vanished. "I met the Sevastokrator once," she told Krispos. She was just a seam-stress. Though he would not have said so out loud, he doubted her until she proudly explained: "On Midwinter's Day a couple of years ago, he pinched my bottom."

"Anything can happen on Midwinter's Day," he agreed so-berly. He smiled at her. "I thought Petronas was a man of good taste."

She thought that over for a moment, blinked, and threw her arms around his neck. "Oh, Krispos, you say the sweetest things!" The rest of the morning passed most enjoyably.

Gomaris spotted Krispos on his way back to the grooms' quarters that afternoon. "Not so fast," the steward said. "Iakovitzes wants to see you."

"Why? He knows this was my morning off."

"He didn't tell me why. He just told me to look out for you. Now I've found you. He's in the small waiting room—you know, the one next to his bedchamber."

Wondering what sort of trouble he was in, and hoping his master *did* remember he'd had the morning free, Krispos hur-ried to the waiting room. Iakovitzes was sitting behind a small table with several thick scrolls of parchment, looking for all the world like a tax collector. At the moment, his scowl made him look like a tax collector visiting a village badly in arrears.

"Oh, it's you," he said as Krispos walked in. "About time. Go pack."

Krispos gulped. "Sir?" Of all the things he'd expected, being so baldly ordered to hit the streets was the last. "What did I do, sir? Can I make amends for it?"

"What *are* you talking about?" Iakovitzes said peevishly. After a few seconds, his face cleared. "No, you don't know what I'm talking about. It seems there's some sort of squabble going on between our people and the Khatrishers over who owns a stretch of land between two little streams north of the town of Opsikion. The local eparch can't make the Khatrishers see sense—but then, trying to dicker with Khatrishers'd drive Skotos mad. Petronas doesn't want this mess blowing up into a border war. He's sending me to Opsikion to try to make sense of it."

The explanation left Krispos as confused as before. "What does that have to do with me packing?"

"You're coming with me."

Krispos opened his mouth, then closed it again when he discovered he had nothing worthwhile to say. This would be travel on far more comfortable terms than the slog from his village to Videssos the city. Once he got to Opsikion, he could also hope to learn a good deal about what Iakovitzes was doing and how he did it. The more he learned, he was discovering, the more possibilities opened up in his life.

On the other hand, Iakovitzes would surely use the trip as one long chance to try to get him into bed. He had trouble gauging just how big a nuisance that would be, or how annoyed Iakovitzes might get when he kept saying no.

An opportunity, a likelihood of trouble. As far as he could tell, they balanced. He certainly had no other good options, so he said, "Very well, excellent sir. I'll pack at once."

The road dipped one last time. Suddenly, instead of mountains and trees all around, Krispos saw ahead of him hills dipping swiftly toward the blue sea. Where land and water met stood Opsikion, its red tile roofs glowing in the sun. He reined in his horse to admire the view.

Iakovitzes came up beside him. He also stopped. "Well, that's very pretty, isn't it?" he said. He let go of the reins with his right hand. As if by accident, it fell on Krispos' thigh.

"Yes, it is," Krispos said, sighing. He dug his heels into his horse's flanks. It started forward, almost at a trot.

Also sighing, Iakovitzes followed. "You are the most stubborn man I've ever wanted," he said, his voice tight with irritation.

Krispos did not answer. If Iakovitzes wanted to see stubbornness, he thought, all he needed to do was peer at his reflection in a stream. In the month they'd taken to ride east from Videssos the city to Opsikion, he'd tried seducing Krispos every night and most afternoons. That he'd got nowhere did not stop him; neither did the several times he'd bedded other, more complacent, partners.

Iakovitzes pulled alongside again. "If I didn't find you so lovely, curse it, I'd break you for your obstinacy," he snapped. "Don't push me too far. I might anyhow."

Krispos had no doubt Iakovitzes meant what he said. As he

had before, he laughed. "I was a peasant taxed off my farm. How could you break me any lower than that?" As long as Iakovitzes knew he was not afraid of such threats, Krispos thought, the peppery little man would hesitate before he acted on them.

So it proved now. Iakovitzes fumed but subsided. They rode together toward Opsikion.

As they were in none-too-clean travelers' clothes, the gate guards paid no more attention to them than to anyone else. They waited while the guards poked swords into bales of wool a fuzzy-bearded Khatrisher merchant was bringing to town, making sure he wasn't smuggling anything inside them. The merchant's face was so perfectly innocent that Krispos suspected him on general principles.

Iakovitzes did not take kindly to waiting. "Here, you?" he called to one of the guards in peremptory tones. "Stop messing about with that fellow and see to us."

The guard set hands on hips and looked Iakovitzes over. "And why should I, small stuff?" Without waiting for a reply, he started to turn back to what he'd been doing.

"Because, you insolent, ill-smelling, pock-faced lout, I am the direct representative of his illustrious Highness the Sevastokrator Petronas and of his Imperial Majesty the Avtokrator Anthimos III, come to this miserable latrine trench of a town to settle matters your eparch has botched, bungled, and generally mishandled."

Iakovitzes bit off each word with savage relish. As he spoke, he unrolled and displayed the large parchment that proved he was what he claimed. It was daubed with seals in several colors of wax and bore the Avtokrator's signature in appallingly official scarlet ink.

The gate guard went from furious red to terrified white in the space of three heartbeats. "Sorry, Brison," he muttered to the wool merchant. "You've just got to hang on for a bit."

"Now there's a fine kettle of crabs," Brison said in a lisping accent. "Maybe I'll pass the time mixing my horses around so you won't be sure which ones you've checked." He grinned to see how the gate guard liked that idea.

"Oh, go to the ice," the harassed guard said. Brison laughed out loud. Ignoring him, the guard turned to Iakovitzes. "I—I crave pardon for my rough tongue, excellent sir. How may I help you?"

"Better." Iakovitzes nodded. "I won't ask for your name after all. Tell me how to reach the eparch's residence. Then you can go back to your petty games with this chap here. I suggest that while you're at it, you sword his beard as well as his wool."

Brison laughed again, quite merrily. The gate guard stuttered out directions. Iakovitzes rode past them. He kept his eyes straight ahead, not deigning to acknowledge either man any further. Krispos followed.

"I put that arrogant bastard in chain mail in his place nicely enough," Iakovitzes said once he and Krispos got into town, "but Khatrishers are too light-minded to notice when they've been insulted. Cheeky buggers, the lot of them." Failing to get under someone's skin always annoyed him. He swore softly as he rode down Opsikion's main street.

Krispos paid his master little attention; he was resigned to his bad temper. Opsikion interested him more. It was a little larger than Imbros; a year ago, he thought, it would have seemed enormous to him. After Videssos, it reminded him of a toy city, small but perfect. Even Phos' temple in the central square was modeled after the great High Temple of the capital.

The eparch's hall was across the square from the temple. Iakovitzes took out his frustration over leaving Brison in good spirits by baiting a clerk as mercilessly as he had the gate guard. His tactics were cruel, but also effective. Moments later, the clerk ushered him and Krispos into the eparch's office.

The local governor was a thin, sour-looking man named Sisinnios. "So you've come to dicker with the Khatrishers, have you?" he said when Iakovitzes presented his impressive scroll. "May you get more joy from it than I have. These days, my belly starts paining me the day before I talk with 'em and doesn't let up for three days afterward."

"What's the trouble, exactly?" Iakovitzes asked. "I presume we have documents to prove the land in question is ours by right?" Though he phrased it as a question, he spoke with the same certainty he would have used in reciting Phos' creed. Krispos sometimes thought nothing really existed in Videssos without out a document to show it was there.

When Sisinnios rolled his eyes, the dark bags under them made him look like a mournful hound. "Oh, we have documents," he agreed morosely. "Getting the Khatrishers to pay 'em any mind is something else again."

"*I'll* fix *that*," Iakovitzes promised. "Does this place boast a decent inn?"

"Bolkanes' is probably the best," Sisinnios said. "It's not far." He gave directions.

"Good. Krispos, go set us up with rooms there. Now, sir—" This he directed to Sisinnios, "—let's see these documents. And set me up a meeting with this Khatrisher who ignores them."

Bolkanes' inn proved good enough, and by the standards of Videssos the city absurdly cheap. Taking Iakovitzes literally, Krispos rented separate rooms for his master and himself. He knew Iakovitzes would be irked, but did not feel like guarding himself every minute of every night.

Indeed, Iakovitzes did grumble when he came to the inn a couple of hours later and discovered the arrangements Krispos had made. The grumble, though, was an abstracted one; most of his mind remained on the fat folder of documents he carried under one arm. He took negotiations seriously.

"You'll have to amuse yourself as best you can for a while, Krispos," he said as they sat down to a dinner of steamed prawns in mustard sauce. "Phos alone knows how long I'm liable to be closeted with this Lexo from Khatrish. If he's as bad as Sisinnios makes him out to be, maybe forever."

"If you please sir," Krispos said hesitantly, "may I join you at your talks?"

Iakovitzes paused with a prawn in mid-air. "Why on earth would you want to do that?" His eyes narrowed. No Videssian noble trusted what he did not understand.

"To learn what I can," Krispos answered. "Please remember, sir, I'm but a couple of seasons away from my village. Most of your other grooms know much more than I do, just because they've lived in Videssos the city all their lives. I ought to take whatever chances I have to pick up useful things to know."

"Hmm." That watchful expression did not leave Iakovitzes' face. "You're apt to be bored."

"If I am, I'll leave."

"Hmm," Iakovitzes said again, and then, "Well, why not? I'd thought you content with the horses, but if you think you're fit for more, no harm in your trying. Who can say? It may turn out to my advantage as well as yours." Now Iakovitzes looked calculating, a look Krispos knew well. One of the noble's eyebrows quirked upward as he went on, "I didn't bring you here with that in mind, however."

"I know." Krispos was beginning to learn to keep his own maneuvers hidden. Now his thoughts were that, if he made himself useful enough to Iakovitzes in other ways, the noble might give up on coaxing him into bed.

"We'll see how it goes," Iakovitzes said. "Sisinnios is setting up the meeting with the Khatrisher for around the third hour of the day tomorrow—halfway between sunrise and noon." He smiled a smile Krispos had seen even more often than his calculating look. "Reading by lamplight gives me a headache. I can think of a better way to spend the night . . ."

Krispos sighed. Iakovitzes hadn't given up yet.

Sisinnios said, "Excellency, I present to you Lexo, who represents Gumush the khagan of Khatrish. Lexo, here is the most eminent Iakovitzes from Videssos the city, and his spatharios Krispos."

The title the eparch gave Krispos was the vaguest one in the Videssian hierarchy; it literally meant "sword bearer," and by extension "aide." An Avtokrator's spatharios might be a very important man. A noble's spatharios was not. Krispos was grateful to hear it all the same. Sisinnios could have introduced him as a groom and let it go at that.

"And now, noble sirs, if you will excuse me, I have other business to which I must attend," the eparch said. He left a little more quickly than was polite, but with every sign of relief.

Lexo the Khatrisher was dressed in what would have been a stylish linen tunic but for the leaping stags and panthers embroidered over every inch of it. "I've heard of you, eminent sir," he told Iakovitzes, bowing in his seat. His beard and mustaches were so full and bushy that Krispos could hardly see his lips move. Among Videssians, such unkempt whiskers were only for priests.

"You have the advantage of me, sir." Iakovitzes would not let a foreigner outdo him in courtesy. "I am willing to assume, however, that any emissary of your khagan is sure to be a most able man."

"You are too gracious to someone you do not know," Lexo purred. His gaze swung to Krispos. "So, young fellow, you're Iakovitzes' spatharios, are you? Tell me, just where do you bear that sword of his?"

The Khatrisher's smile was bland. Even so, Krispos jerked as if stung. For a moment, all he could think of was wiping the floor with Lexo, who was more than twice his age and weighed more than he did though several inches shorter. But months of living with Iakovitzes had taught him the game was not always played with fists. Doing his best to pull his face straight, he answered, "Against his foes, and the Avtokrator's." He looked Lexo in the eye.

"Your sentiments do you credit, I'm sure," Lexo murmured. He turned back to Iakovitzes. "Well, eminent sir, how do you propose to settle what his excellency the good Sisinnios and I have been haggling over for months?"

"By looking at the facts instead of haggling." Iakovitzes leaned forward, discarding formal ways like a cast-off cloak. He touched the folder the eparch had given him. "The facts are here, you will agree. I have here copies of all documents pertaining to the border between Videssos and Khatrish for as long as your state has been such, rather than merely nomad bandits too ignorant to sign a treaty and too treacherous to honor one. The latter trait, I notice, you still display."

Krispos waited for Lexo to explode, but the envoy's smile did not waver. "I'd heard you were charming," he said evenly.

Just as he was armored against insult, so was Iakovitzes against irony. "I don't care what you've heard, sir. I've heard—these documents say, loud and clear—that the proper frontier between our lands is the Akkilaion River, not the Mnizou as you have claimed. How dare you contradict them?"

"Because the memories of my people are long," Lexo said. Iakovitzes snorted. Lexo took no notice, but went on, "Memories are like leaves, you know. They pile up in the forests of our minds, and we go scuffing through them."

Iakovitzes snorted again, louder. "Very pretty. I hadn't heard Gumush was sending out poets to speak for him these days. I'd have thought their disregard for the truth disqualified them."

"You flatter me for my poor words," Lexo said. "Should you desire true poetry, I will give you the tribal lays of my folk."

He began to declaim, partly in his lisping Videssian, more often in a speech that reminded Krispos of the one the Kubratoi used among themselves. He nodded, remembering that the ancestors of both Khatrishers and Kubratoi had come off the Pardrayan steppe long ago.

"I could go on for some while," Lexo said after going on for some while, "but I hope you get the gist: that the great raid of Balbad Badbal's son reached the Mnizou and drove all Videssians over it. Thus it is only just for Khatrish to claim the Mnizou as its southern boundary."

"Gumush's grandfather didn't, nor his father either," Iakovitzes replied, unmoved by his opponent's oratory. "If you stack the treaties they signed against your tribal lays, the treaties weigh heavier."

"How can any man presume to know where the balance between them lies, any more than a man can know the Balance between Phos and Skotos in the world?" Lexo said. "They both have weight; that is what Sisinnios would not see nor admit."

"Believe in the Balance and go to the ice, they teach us in Videssos," Iakovitzes said, "so I'll thank you not to drag your eastern heresy into a serious argument. Just as Phos *will* vanquish Skotos in the end, so *shall* our border be restored to its proper place, which is to say, the Akkilaion."

"Just as my doctrine is your heresy, the reverse also applies." Where his faith was questioned, Lexo lost his air of detached amusement. In a sharper voice than he'd used before, he went on, "I might also point out that the land between the Mnizou and the Akkilaion has quite as many Khatrishers herding as it does Videssians farming. The concept of the Balance seems relevant."

"Throw precedent into your cursed Balance," Iakovitzes suggested. "It will weigh down on the side of truth—the side of Videssos."

"The lay of Balbad Badbal's son, as I have *suggested*—" Irony again, this time laid on heavily enough to make Iakovitzes scowl "—is precedent older than any in that stack of moldering parchments in which you set your stock."

"That lay is a lie," Iakovitzes growled.

"Sir, it is not." Lexo met Iakovitzes' glare with his own. Had they been wearing swords, they might have used those, too.

In their duel, they'd so completely forgotten about Krispos that they both stared at him when he asked, "Is age the most important thing that goes into a precedent?"

"Yes," Lexo said in the same breath Iakovitzes used to say, "No."

"If it is," Krispos went on, "shouldn't Videssos claim all of Khatrish? The Empire ruled it long before the Khatrishers' forefathers arrived there."

"Not the same thing at all—" Lexo began, while Iakovitzes burst out, "By the good god, so we—" He, too, stopped before his sentence was done. Sheepishness did not suit his sharp-featured face, but it was there. "I think we've just been whirled round on ourselves," he said, much more quietly than he had been speaking.

"Perhaps we have," Lexo admitted. "Shall we thank your spatharios for the treatment?" He nodded to Krispos. "I must also crave your pardon, young sir. I see you do have some use beyond the ornamental."

"Why, so he does." Krispos would have been happier with Iakovitzes' agreement had his master sounded less surprised.

Lexo sighed. "If you set aside your folder there, eminent sir, I will sing you no more lays."

"Oh, very well." Iakovitzes seldom yielded anything with good grace. "Now, though, I have to find some other way to make you see that those herders you spoke of will have to fare north of the Akkilaion where they belong."

"I like that." Lexo's tone said he did not like it at all. "Why shouldn't your farmers be the ones to move?"

"Because nomads are nomads, of course. It's much harder to pack up good farmland and ride away with it."

The bargaining began again, in earnest this time, now that each man had seen he could not presume too far on the other. That first session yielded no agreement, nor did the second, nor the sixth. "We'll get our answer, though," Iakovitzes said one evening back at Bolkanes' inn. "I can feel it."

"I hope so." Krispos picked at the mutton in front of him—he was tired of fish.

Iakovitzes eyed him shrewdly. "So now you *are* bored, eh? Didn't I warn you would be?"

"Maybe I am, a little," Krispos said. "I didn't expect we would be here for weeks. I thought the Sevastokrator sent you here just because Sisinnios wasn't making any progress with Lexo."

"Petronas did, Sisinnios wasn't, and I am," Iakovitzes said. "These disputes take years to develop; they don't go away overnight. What, did you expect Lexo all of a sudden to break down and concede everything on account of the brilliance of my rhetoric?"

Krispos had to smile. "Put that way, no."

"Hrmmp. You might have said yes, to salve my self-respect. But schedules for how the Khatrishers withdraw, how much we pay them to go, and whether we pay the khagan or give the money direct to the herders who will be leaving—all such things have plenty of room in them for horse trading. That's what Lexo and I are doing now, seeing who ends up with a swaybacked old nag.''

"I guess so," Krispos said. "I'm afraid it's not very interesting to listen to, though."

"Go ahead and do something else for a while, then," Iakovitzes said. "I expected you to give up long before this. And you've even been useful in the dickering a couple of times, too, which I didn't expect at all. You've earned some time off."

So Krispos, instead of closeting himself with the diplomats, went wandering through Opsikion. After those of Videssos the city, its markets seemed small and for the most part dull. The only real bargains Krispos saw were fine furs from Agder, which lay in the far northeast, near the Haloga country. He had more money now than ever before, and less to spend it on, but he could not come close to affording a snow-leopard jacket. He came back to the furriers' stall several times, to peer and to wish.

He bought a coral pendant to take back to his seamstress friend. He almost paid for it with his lucky goldpiece. Since it had stopped being his only goldpiece, he'd kept it wrapped in a bit of cloth at the bottom of his pouch. Somehow it got loose. He noticed just in time to substitute another coin.

The jeweler weighed that one to make sure it was good. When he saw it was, he shrugged. "Gold is gold," he said as he gave Krispos his change.

"Sorry," Krispos said. "I just didn't want to part with that one."

"I've had other customers tell me the same thing," the jeweler said. "If you want to make sure you don't spend it by mistake, why not wear it on a chain around your neck? Wouldn't take me long to bore through it, and here's a very nice chain. Or if you'd rather have this one . . ."

Krispos came out of the shop with the lucky goldpiece bumping against his chest under his tunic. It felt odd there for the first few days. After that, he stopped noticing he was wearing it. He even slept with it on.

By that time, Iakovitzes had lost some of his earlier optimism. "That pox-brained Khatrisher is a serpent," he complained.

"Just when I think I have something settled, he throws a coil around it and drags it back into confusion."

"Do you want me to join you again?" Krispos asked.

"Eh? No, that's all right. Good of you to ask, though; you show more loyalty than most your age. You'd probably be more help if you spent the time praying for me. Phos may listen to you; that stubborn donkey of a Lexo surely won't."

Krispos knew his master was just grumbling. He went to the temple across from Sisinnios' residence just the same. Phos was the lord of the good; Videssos' case here, he was convinced, was good; how, then, could his god fail to heed him?

The crowd round the temple was thicker than he'd seen it before. When he asked a man why, the fellow chuckled and said, "Guess you're not from these parts. This is the festal day of the holy Abdaas, Opsikion's patron. We're all come to give thanks for his protection for another year."

"Oh." Along with everyone else—everyone in the whole town, he thought, as three people stepped on his toes, one after 9the other—Krispos filed into the temple.

He had worshiped at the High Temple in the capital several times. The sternly beautiful gaze of the mosaic image of Phos in the dome there never failed to fill him with awe. Opsikion was only a provincial town. As he was depicted here, the lord with the great and good mind looked more cross than majestic. Krispos did not much care. Phos was Phos, no matter what his image looked like.

Krispos feared, though, that he would have to pay homage to the good god standing up. The benches had all but filled by the time he got to them. The last few rows had some empty places, but the press of people swept him past them before he could claim one. He was still a villager at heart, he thought wryly; a born city man would have been quicker.

Too late—by now he was most of the way down toward the altar. With sinking hope, he peered around for some place, any place, to sit. The woman sitting by the aisle was also looking around, perhaps for a friend who was late. Their eyes met.

"Excuse me, my lady." Krispos looked away. He knew a noblewoman when he saw one, and knew better than to bother her by staring.

Thus he did not see her pupils swell till, like a cat's, each filled for a moment its whole iris, did not see her features go slack and far away in that same instant, took no notice of the word she whispered. Then she said something he could not ignore: "Would you care to sit here, eminent sir?"

"My lady?" he said foolishly.

"There's room by me, eminent sir, I think." The woman pushed at the youth next to her, a lad five or six years younger than Krispos: a nephew, maybe, he thought, for the boy resembled her. The push went down the row. By the time it reached the end, there was indeed room.

Krispos sat, gratefully. "Thank you very much, ah—" He stopped. She might—she probably would—think him forward if he asked her name.

But she did not. "I am Tanilis, eminent sir," she said, and modestly cast down her eyes. Before she did, though, he saw how large and dark they were. With them still lowered, she went on, "This is my son Mavros."

The youth and Krispos exchanged nods. Tanilis was older than he'd thought; at first glance, he'd guessed her age to be within a few years of his.

He was still not used to being called *sir. Eminent sir* was for the likes of Iakovitzes, not him: how could he become a noble? Why, then, had Tanilis used it? He started to tell her, as politely as he could, that she'd made a mistake, but the service began and robbed him of the chance.

Phos' creed, of course, he could have recited asleep or awake; it was engrained in him. The rest of the prayers and hymns were hardly less familiar. He went through them, rising and taking his seat at the proper times, most of his mind elsewhere. He barely remembered to ask Phos to help Iakovitzes in his talks with Lexo, which was why he had come to the temple in the first place.

Out of the corner of his eye, he kept watching Tanilis. Her profile was sculptured, elegant; no loose flesh hung under her chin. But, though arfully applied powder almost hid them, the beginnings of lines bracketed her mouth and met at the corners of her eyes. Here and there a white thread ran through her piled-up curls of jet. He supposed she might be old enough to have a son close to his age. She was beautiful, even so.

She seemed to take no notice of his inspection, giving herself wholly to the celebration of Phos' liturgy. Eventually Krispos had to do the same, for the hymns of praise for the holy Abdaas were Opsikion's own; he had not met them before. But even as he stumbled through them, he was aware of her beside him.

The worshipers spoke Phos' creed one last time. From his place at the altar, the local prelate lifted up his hands in blessing. "Go now, in peace and goodness," he declared. The service was over.

Krispos rose and stretched. Tanilis and her son also stood up. "Thanks again for making room for me," he told them, as he turned to go.

"The privilege was mine, eminent sir," Tanilis said. Her ornate gold earrings tinkled softly as he looked down to the floor.

"Why do you keep calling me that?" he snapped, irritation getting the better of his manners. "I'm just a groom, and glad to be one—otherwise I expect I'd be starving somewhere. Come to think of it, I've done that, too, once or twice. It doesn't make you eminent, believe me."

Before he was halfway through, he knew he ought to keep quiet. If he offended a powerful local noblewoman like Tanilis, even Iakovitzes' connections at the capital might not save him. The capital was too far away for them to do him much good here. Even as that thought ran through his mind, though, he kept on till he was done.

Tanilis raised her head to look at him again. He started to stutter out an apology, then stopped. The last time he had seen that almost blind stare of perfect concentration was on the face of the healer-priest Mokios.

This time he watched her eyes go huge and black, saw her expression turn fixed. Her lips parted. This time ice ran through him as he heard the word she whispered: "Majesty."

She slumped forward in a faint.

V

Krispos caught her before she hit her head on the
bench in front of her. "Oh, Phos!" her son Mavros said. He
rushed up to help take her weight. "Thanks for saving her there,
uh, Krispos. Come on, let's get her out of the temple. She should
be better soon."

He sounded so matter-of-fact that Krispos asked, "This has
happened before?"

"Yes." Mavros raised his voice to speak to the townsfolk who
came hurrying up after Tanilis fell. "My mother just got out of
her seat too quickly. Let us by, please, so we can get her to fresh
air. Let us by, please."

He had to repeat himself several times before people moved
aside. Even then, several women and a couple of men stayed
with him. Krispos wondered why he did not shoo them away
too, then realized they had to be part of Tanilis' retinue. They
helped clear a path so Krispos and Mavros could carry the noblewoman up the aisle.

Tanilis muttered and stirred when the sun hit her face, but did
not wake at once. Krispos and Mavros eased her to the ground.
The women stood over her, exclaiming.

One of the servants said to Mavros, "I wish we'd come from
the house in town today, young master. Then she could go in
the sedan chair."

"That would make fetching her home again easier, wouldn't
it? However . . ." Mavros shrugged whimsically. He turned to
Krispos. "My mother sometimes . . . sees things, and sees them
so strong she can't withstand the force of the vision. I've grown

108

used to it, watching it happen over the years, but I do wish she wouldn't always pick such awkward times and places. Of course, what I wish has very little to do with anything.'' He gave that shrug again.

"That's the way things often work." Krispos decided he thought well of Mavros. The youngster had not only kept his head coping with an awkward situation, but was even able to make light of it. From everything Krispos had ever seen, that was harder.

Mavros said, "Genzon, Naues, fetch the horses here from round the corner. The crowd's thinning out; you shouldn't have much trouble now."

"I'll go with them, if you like," Krispos said. "That way each man won't have to lead so many."

"Thanks, that's generous of you. Please, a moment first, though." Mavros took a couple of steps away from his retinue and motioned for Krispos to follow. In a low voice, he asked, "What did my mother say to you, there in the temple? Her back was to me; I didn't hear."

"Oh, that." Krispos scratched his head, looking embarrassed. "Do you know, in all the hubbub since, it's gone clean out of my mind."

He hurried after Genzon and Naues. He was unhappy about lying to Mavros, but he'd lied without hesitation. He needed to think much more about the unbelievably fascinating, unbelievably dangerous word Tanilis had spoken before he admitted to himself—let alone to anyone else—that he'd heard it.

Most of the horses the servants loosed from the hitching rail were ponies for Tanilis' female attendants. The four that were not were animals fine enough to have belonged in Iakovitzes' stables. Four—that meant Tanilis was no mean rider, then. Krispos found himself unsurprised. She was plainly a woman of many accomplishments.

She had managed to sit up by the time Krispos, Genzon, and Naues brought the horses back to the temple, but still did not seem fully aware of herself or her surroundings. Mavros clasped Krispos' hand. "Thank you again. I'm grateful for all your help."

"My pleasure." Krispos heard the dismissal in Mavros' voice. He dipped his head and went back to Bolkanes' inn.

Iakovitzes was not there; he was closeted with Lexo again. Krispos hoped his absentminded prayer had done his master some good. He went down to the taproom for some wine and for a chance to pick Bolkanes' brain.

Both came slower than he wanted. The inn was crowded with people celebrating the holy Abdaas' festal day less piously than those who had gone to the temple. The tables were all filled. Working his way up to the bar took patience, but patience Krispos had. "Red wine, please," he told Bolkanes.

The innkeeper dipped out a measure and filled an earthenware mug. Only when he slid it across the counter did he look up to see whom he was serving. "Oh, hello, Krispos," he said and then, to the next man who'd wormed his way forward, "What'll it be for you today, Rekilas?"

Having gained his spot at the bar, Krispos did not give it up. He waited while Bolkanes served two more men, then said, "I saw a truly striking noblewoman at the temple today. A man told me her name was—"

He broke off; someone had asked Bolkanes for a cup of something finer than he kept in the barrels at the bar, and the innkeeper had to hurry away to get what the fellow wanted. When he returned—and after he dealt with another customer—Krispos started to repeat himself, but Bolkanes had been listening, even if he was too busy to talk. He broke in: "That'd be Tanilis, I expect."

"Yes, that was the name," Krispos said. "Sounds like she's well known hereabouts."

"I should say so," Bolkanes agreed. "She has—hello, Zernes, more of the white for you? Coming right up." Zernes not only wanted more white wine but needed change from a goldpiece, and counted it three times once he got it. Half a dozen men were waiting by the time he got done. Eventually Bolkanes resumed. "Tanilis? Aye, she has huge tracts of land hereabouts. A good many said she'd lose everything, trying to run 'em herself after her husband—what was her husband's name, Apsyrtos?"

"Vledas, wasn't it?" Apsyrtos answered. "Let me have a cup of mead this time, will you?"

"You head'll hurt come morning, mixing 'em that way," Bolkanes warned, but he plied the dipper. When he was done, he turned back to Krispos. "Vledas, that was it. He died ten, twelve years ago now, it must be, and she's prospered since. Done well in good years and bad, they say, though naturally I couldn't testify to that. But her estates do keep growing. It's almost uncanny—just a woman, you know.''

"Mm-hmm," Krispos said, though he had the feeling Tanilis was just a woman in the same way that Videssos was just a city.

Iakovitzes came in a little later. His good nature, always unreliable, had vanished altogether by the time he worked his way to the bar through the press of holiday drinkers. "Just because a holy man once cured a horse of fleas is no reason to turn a town on its ear," he growled.

"Is that what the holy Abdaas did?" Krispos asked.

"How should I know? In a backwoods bastion like this, I doubt one would need do much more to be reckoned a miracle-worker." Iakovitzes gulped his wine, then slammed the mug down on the bar for a refill.

Krispos thought of Tanilis again. He'd seen more than horse-doctoring. He wondered how he could find out more about her. If she was as grand a noblewoman as Bolkanes made her out to be—and nothing Krispos had seen left him doubting it—he could not just go and seek a meeting with her. She'd slap him down for such presumption. Approaching through her son seemed a better bet. Mavros, on brief acquaintance, had the feel of being someone Krispos could like. Bolkanes might know the amusements the youth favored when he came into town. . . .

Iakovitzes had said something that Krispos missed in his musing. "I crave pardon."

His master frowned. "For all the attention you paid me there, I thought for a moment I was back talking with Lexo. He started in on his stinking tribal lays again today, the blackguard, until I asked him if he was willing to listen while I read to him from the histories of the reign of Stavrakios the Great. After that he came rather closer to reason, though not close enough. By Phos, I'll poison the bastard if his delays make me spend the winter in this miserable place."

A day before, Krispos would have agreed. After Videssos the city, Opsikion was small and backward and not very interesting—in a word, provincial. Now, with Tanilis' mystery before him, he hoped Iakovitzes would stay a while longer. "Drive him wild, Lexo," he whispered, too low for his master to hear.

Bolkanes was rolling a fresh barrel of wine from the top of the cellar stairs to the taproom when Krispos walked into the inn a couple of afternoons later. "Want some help with that?"

Krispos asked. Without waiting for an answer, he hurried forward.

"You would come in after I've done the hard part myself." Bolkanes wiped sweat from his forehead. "I can manage from here. Anyhow, a fellow's waiting for you at the bar. Been here an hour, maybe a bit longer."

"For me?" Krispos hadn't thought anyone in Opsikion knew him well enough to find him worth waiting for. He walked into the taproom. The tall, lanky man standing at the bar turned at the sound of his footsteps. "Naues!" Krispos said, then added with sudden doubt, "Or are you Genzon?"

Tanilis' servitor smiled. "I'm Genzon. I don't blame you for having to ask. Things were hurried and confused at the temple the other day."

"So they were." Krispos hesitated. "I hope your mistress is improved?"

"Yes, thank you." Genzon's prominent larynx bobbed as he swallowed the last of the wine in his cup. "She thanks you, also, for the care and concern you showed. To show her gratitude further, she bids you dine with her this evening, if you care to."

"She does?" Krispos blurted. Try as he would, he was still new to the notion of keeping thoughts to himself. He needed a moment to let urbanity return. "I'd be delighted. Can you give me a little while to change?"

"Certainly. What are a few more minutes, save a chance for another cup of wine?" Genzon nodded to Bolkanes, who, along with his tapman, was wrestling the new barrel into place under the bar.

Krispos told the innkeeper, "Please let Iakovitzes know I've been asked away for the evening." As soon as he was sure Bolkanes had heard, he walked over to the stairway. He would not run, not where Genzon could see him, but he bounded up the steps two at a time.

For once, he wished he could borrow Iakovitzes' clothes. He usually thought them gaudy, but now he wanted to put on something that would impress Tanilis. Since Iakovitzes was more than half a foot shorter than he was, and correspondingly narrower as well, borrowing a tunic was impractical. He threw on his own best one, of a sober dark blue, and a pair of breeches that matched it. He went downstairs so fast he had to grab at the railing to keep from landing on his head.

"Let me saddle my horse and I'll meet you out front," he

called to Genzon. Tanilis' man nodded. Krispos went out to the stables behind the inn. He quickly put the saddle on his horse, made sure the cinch was tight—he'd learned about that back at the village, fortunately, or Iakovitzes' grooms never would have let him live it down—mounted, and walked the horse up to the street.

Genzon came out a couple of minutes later. "Good-looking animal," he said as he swung himself aboard his own mount.

"My master knows horses," Krispos said.

"Yes, I can see that. Nice smooth gait, too." Genzon started to say something more, visibly decided not to. Krispos thought he could guess the question Genzon swallowed: Why was the groom being invited to dine with his mistress, and not the visiting noble from the capital? As he had only hopes and wild speculations himself, he did not want to try to answer that.

Genzon led him out of Opsikion by the south gate. The road soon twisted away from the sea and ran up into the hills. Krispos' horse did not falter at the steep stretches. Indeed, the beast seemed to relish the challenge. Have to give him more exercise, Krispos thought.

Some of the hillsides were terraced. Up on the slopes, Krispos saw peasants weeding crops and pruning vines. They were too wrapped up in their tasks to look down at him. Watching them sent a remembered ache through his shoulders. Farming was the longest, hardest work there was. Having lived the peasant's life for so many years, he knew how lucky he was to have escaped it.

He wondered how his sister and brother-in-law were doing. He supposed he was an uncle by now, and hoped Evdokia had come through childbirth safely.

"All this is Tanilis' land," Genzon remarked.

"Is it?" Krispos said politely. He wondered what the scores, what the hundreds of people who worked it thought of that. Did she protect her peasants from the state's demands, or impose her own alongside them?

He hoped she looked after the people under her control. But, as he could not have a year before, he also wondered whether nobles who too effectively shielded their peasants from the state were good for Videssos. If nobles turned into petty kings on their own domains, how could the central government hope to function? He shook his head, thankful the problem was Anthimos'—or perhaps Petronas'—and not his.

He and Genzon rode on for some time. The sun was falling toward the jagged western horizon when Genzon pointed, saying, "There is Tanilis' villa."

The building ahead was so large Krispos had taken it for a fortress. It was well sited for one, on top of a rise that commanded the surrounding countryside. But as Krispos drew near, he saw it was too lightly made, with too many windows and too many doors, to serve as a stronghold.

He wondered how many peasants had gone hungry because they were busy building it instead of working their fields, then wondered again if such a thought had ever crossed one of the owners' minds. He doubted it. No one who owned a home like this—it made Iakovitzes' house look like Krispos' old cottage by comparison—had ever been a peasant.

Someone came out of the villa. As Krispos got closer, he saw it was Mavros. Tanilis' son recognized him—or more likely Genzon—a moment later. He waved. Genzon and Krispos waved back. They urged their horses into a trot.

Mavros came down to meet them. "About time you turned up," he said, grinning. "Mother's starting to fret and the cook's getting nervous. Never mind. You're here now, and that's what counts."

Boys hurried up to take the newcomers' horses and lead them back to the stables. Krispos expected his mount would get better care here than at Bolkanes'. Not that he had anything against the innkeeper, but Tanilis did not have to worry about how every copper was spent.

"You can have the rest of the day off, Genzon," Mavros said. The retainer dipped his head in thanks. Mavros turned to Krispos as Genzon hurried off. "Now you on the other hand, sirrah, you are in my mother's clutches."

"Oh? Why?" Krispos had—and ruthlessly stifled—a sudden, hungry vision of Tanilis clutching him, and him clutching back.

"The ice take me if I can tell you." Mavros shrugged in cheerful incomprehension. Krispos wished he could stay so jolly in the face of the unknown. In the life he'd led, unknown and dangerous were the same word. To Mavros, raised lacking for nothing, the world seemed a sunnier place. He went on, "She'll explain in her own good time, I'm sure. Me, I expect it has to do with whatever she said at the temple the other day. What was that, anyhow?"

"Hasn't she told you?" Krispos asked, surprised.

"She doesn't remember, not exactly. Her—visions are like that sometimes." Mavros shrugged again. "Whatever it was, it was something strong. Some of the old servants say the place hasn't been turned upside down like this since the Avtokrator Sermeios dined here in my grandfather's time."

"Since an Avtokrator—" Krispos echoed weakly. He tried to laugh, but only managed a ghastly chuckle. "I'm no Avtokrator, believe me."

"I believe you," Mavros said at once, but not so it sounded like an insult. "You seem a good fellow, though. I think so myself, and my mother wouldn't have invited you here if she'd seen anything wicked, now would she?"

"No," Krispos said. That he was going to eat where an Avtokrator had dined was stirring enough—but after all, Petronas had broken bread at Iakovitzes' house, and he was Emperor in all but name. But that an imperial-size fuss was being made over *him*—he wanted another try at laughing over that. He was sure he could do a proper job the second time around.

Mavros said, "Come in, come in. The longer I leave you standing around here, the longer everyone inside stands around fussing. The cook'll stop palpitating every time anything gets near done, which will be a great relief to everyone."

Krispos made the sun-sign over his heart as he walked beneath the image of Phos that hung above the door. The floor of the entrance hall was gleaming marble. "Is that you, son?" Tanilis' voice floated down it as Mavros slammed the door. "Where can Krispos be?"

"With me, as a matter of fact," Mavros said. Krispos heard Tanilis exclaim. Mavros told him, "Come on, she's out in the garden."

Krispos got a brief glimpse into each room that opened on the hallway as he hurried after Mavros. What he saw reminded him of Iakovitzes' splendid furnishings, but showed better taste and more money. That enormous round table inlaid with gold and ivory . . . not even an Avtokrator would have felt ashamed to eat a meal from a table like that.

The garden was also larger and finer than Iakovitzes', although, to be just, Krispos had never seen his master's garden in full bloom. Tanilis extended a slim hand. Krispos bowed over it. Rings glinted on her fingers. "Thank you, my lady, for inviting me here," he said. "This is—marvelous."

"It pleases me that you so say so, eminent sir. Surely, though, you must have seen homes far finer in Videssos the city."

He noted the title by which she addressed him. *She might not remember everything*, he thought, *but she hasn't forgotten everything, either*. Then his attention came back to what she'd said. "In truth, no," he said slowly. "The wonder of Videssos the city isn't any one home in it, but that there are so many homes, so many people, all in the same place."

"A thoughtful answer," Tanilis said. "I've never seen the city."

"Nor I." Mavros' face lit. "I'd love to go there one day, though it's hard for me to imagine a city bigger than Opsikion."

Krispos smiled. No matter how rich and easy Mavros' life was, he knew some things Tanilis' son did not. "If Videssos the city were a wolf, it could swallow a mouse like Opsikion without even chewing," he said.

Mavros whistled, soft and low, and shook his head. "Hard to believe."

"From everything your father said, it's true," Tanilis said. "Vledas went to the city once, when he was not much older than you are now, and never stopped talking about it to the day he died."

"I don't remember," Mavros said wistfully. He would have been a small boy when Vledas died, Krispos realized. He was surprised to think himself luckier in any way than this rich youth, but he'd known his father until he was a man grown.

Had Phostis died while he was young, say in Kubrat, who would have been there to keep him from doing all sorts of stupid things later? Most likely he would have ended up marrying Zoranne and staying a farmer all his life. A good part of a year away from the ceaseless labor that was farming, he no longer thought it the only right and proper way to live.

"You will see Videssos one day, too, son." Tanilis' voice was hollow; her eyes did not quite focus on Mavros. Krispos felt the hair on his arms trying to prickle upright. The oracular tone faded as she went on, "But for now, a shorter journey. Shall we go inside and eat?"

The cook, a nervous little man named Evtykhes, stopped fidgeting and sighed with relief as he saw his charges sit down around a small table topped with mother-of-pearl—it shimmered and almost seemed to shift in the glow of the lamps other servants set out.

"Soup?" Evtykhes asked. At Tanilis' nod, he dashed back to the kitchen. A boy appeared with the steaming bowls so quickly that Krispos suspected the cook was trying to make sure everyone kept sitting.

Back in his village, Krispos would have lifted the soup bowl straight to his lips. In taverns and eateries in the city, he still did. But he had learned to use a spoon at Iakovitzes'. Since Tanilis and Mavros ate with theirs, he imitated them. By the time he got to the bottom of the bowl, the soup was cold. Maybe the nobles didn't mind that, but he did. His breath went out in a silent sigh.

He was more used to his fork and was reaching for it when he saw Tanilis and Mavros pick up asparagus with their fingers. He imitated them again. Manners were confusing things.

The food kept coming: broiled duck in a glaze of candied berries, mushrooms stuffed with turtle meat, pureed chestnuts, a salad of oranges and apples, and at last a roast kid with a sweet-and-sour sauce and chopped onions. Mavros and Krispos ate ravenously, the one because he was still growing, the other because he'd learned to do so whenever he got the chance as a hedge against the hunger that was sure to follow. Tanilis sampled a little of every course and sent warm praise back to the cook after each one.

"By the good god," she said, watching her son and Krispos devastate the plate of cheese and strawberries that appeared after the kid, "I could get fat just from being in the same room with the two of you."

"You'd have to blame Krispos, then," Mavros said—rather blurrily, as his mouth was full. "If it came from being in the same room with me, it would've happened long ago."

Krispos eyed Tanilis, who was so perfectly and elegantly shaped that she might have been turned on a lathe. The phrase fit in more ways than one, he thought, for she plainly maintained her figure with a craftsman's disciplined artifice. He told her, "I don't think Phos—or you—would allow such a mishap."

She looked down at her wine cup. "A compliment and a truth together—indeed, the good god aids a man who helps himself."

"Then he aids me now." Mavros popped the last strawberry into his mouth.

"Son, you are incorrigible," Tanilis said fondly.

"It does seem that way," Mavros agreed.

Krispos sipped his own wine: something thick and sweet now,

to complement the sharp taste of the cheese. He said, "Phos is the only one who knows why he does as he does. My lady, I hope you will be kind enough to tell me why you've been so good to me. I told you at the temple, I'm only a groom, and lucky to be that. I feel I'm taking advantage of you." *And if one day you feel the same way,* he did not add, *you could cause me untold grief.*

Tanilis waited until a servant left with the last plates. She got up and closed the door to the small dining chamber after the man departed. Only then did she answer, her voice low, "Tell me truly, Krispos, have you never wondered if you might one day be more than what you are now? Truly?"

Despite that double admonition, "No" was the first answer that rose to his lips. But before he spoke it aloud, he thought of Pyrrhos calling his name that rainy night in the monastery. A moment later, he remembered how both Pyrrhos and the Kubrati *enaree* had looked at him during the ceremony when Iakovitzes ransomed the stolen peasants. The word Tanilis had spoken in the temple also echoed in his head.

"I've . . . wondered," he said at last.

"And that you *should* wonder is plain to anyone who can . . . see as I do." Tanilis used the same sort of hesitation he had.

Mavros looked ready to burst from curiosity. "What *did* you say to him back in the temple?" he asked her. "I think you know again."

Instead of answering, she glanced toward Krispos. He hesitated, then gave his head a tiny shake. New-come from the farm though he might be, he knew that word was dangerous. Tanilis' nod of understanding was equally small. "I do, and you will, too, son," she said. "But not yet."

"Thank you so much," Mavros said. The words were sarcastic; the tone was not. Krispos decided Mavros was too good-natured ever to grow skilled at using the stinging wit Iakovitzes relished.

"Since you did see . . . what you saw, what do you want from me?" Krispos asked Tanilis.

"To profit from your rise, of course," she answered. He blinked; he had not expected her to be so direct. She went on, "For me, for my family, what we have now is as much as we ever will have. That, too, I have seen—unless we tie ourselves to one with higher hopes. That one, I think, is you."

Krispos looked around the room. He thought of the house of

which that rich room was a part, of the vast estates surrounding that house. *Why,* he wondered, *would anyone want more than this?* He still wanted more than he had, but he did not have much, and that at the whim of his bad-tempered master. If Tanilis would help him get more, he'd play along. If she thought him a hand-puppet to move only at her bidding, she might get a surprise one day.

He knew better than to say that aloud. "What do you want from me?" he repeated. "And how will you help in this . . . rise . . . you saw?"

"The first thing I want is that you not grow too confident in your rise," she warned. "Nothing seen ahead of time is definite. If you think a thing will come to pass without your working toward it, that is the surest way I know to make certain it will never be."

The night the Kubratoi swept down on his village had taught Krispos once and for all that nothing in life was definite. He nodded. "What else?"

"That you take Mavros back to Videssos the city with you and reckon him your younger brother henceforth," Tanilis said. "The connections he makes there will serve him and you for the rest of his life."

"Me? The city? Really?" Mavros threw back his head and yowled with delight.

"He's welcome to go to Videssos by me," Krispos said, "but I'm not the one who'd have to choose to take him along. Iakovitzes would." He glanced over at Tanilis' son and tried to see him through Iakovitzes' eyes. "It might not be hard to get my master to ask him to go back with us, but—" He stopped. He would not speak ill of Iakovitzes, not before these people he hardly knew.

"I know of his habits," Tanilis said. "To his credit, he does not pretend to be other than what he is. Mavros, I think, will be able to take care of himself, and he's as good with horses— your master's other passion, are they not?—as anyone his age near Opsikion."

"That will help," Krispos agreed. He chuckled—one more handsome youth for Meletios and some of the other grooms to worry about. Growing serious again, he went on, "Besides Mavros, how will you aid me?" He felt he was horse trading with Tanilis, the only trouble being that she promised delivery of most of the horse some years from now. He wanted to make as sure as possible of the part he could see now.

"Gold, counsel, loyalty until your death or mine," Tanilis said. "If you like, I will take oath by the lord with the great and good mind."

Krispos thought that over. "If your word is bad, will your oath make it better?"

Tanilis lowered her eyes. Her hair hid her face. Even so, Krispos felt he had passed a test.

Mavros said plaintively, "Will the two of you please quit making deep plans without me? If I'm suddenly to leave for Videssos the city, shouldn't I know why?"

"You might be safer if you didn't," Tanilis said. But she must have seen the justice of her son's protest, for she pointed at Krispos and whispered the word she had spoken to him inside the temple.

Mavros' eyes widened. "Him?" he squeaked. Krispos did not blame him for sounding amazed. He did not believe the prediction either, not down deep.

But Tanilis answered, "It may be so." If all she'd said tonight was true, she would try to help it be so. Was she, then, simply following the path she had seen or trying to force it into existence? Krispos went round that dizzy loop of thought two or three times before he gave it up. Tanilis went on, "None of us should say that word again, not until the proper time comes, if it ever does."

"You're right." Mavros shook his head in wonder and grinned at Krispos. "I always figured I'd need a miracle to get me to Videssos the city, but I didn't know what one looked like till now."

Krispos snorted. "I'm no miracle." But he found himself grinning back. Mavros would make him a lively brother. He turned to Tanilis. "My lady, may I beg an escort from you? Otherwise, in the dark, I'd need a miracle to get back to Opsikion, let alone the city."

"Stay the night," she said. "I expected you would; the servants have readied a chamber for you." She rose and walked over to the dining room's doors. The small noise of their opening summoned two men. She nodded to one. "Xystos, please lead the eminent sir to his bedchamber."

"Certainly." Xystos bowed, first to Tanilis, then to Krispos. "Come with me, eminent sir."

As Krispos started to follow the servant away, Tanilis said, "Since we are become partners in this enterprise, Krispos, take a partner's privilege and use my name."

"Thank you, uh, Tanilis," Krispos said. Her encouraging smile seemed to stay with him after he turned a corner behind Xystos.

The bedroom was larger than the one Krispos had at Bolkanes' inn. Xystos bowed again and shut the door behind him. Krispos used the chamber pot. He took off his clothes, blew out the lamp Xystos had left, and lay down on the bed. It was softer than any he'd known before—and this, he thought, was only a guest room.

Even in darkness, he did not fall asleep at once. With his mind's eye, he kept seeing the smile Tanilis had given him as he left the dining room. Maybe she would slip in here tonight, to seal with her body the strange bargain they had made. Or maybe she would send in a serving girl, just as a kindness to him. Or maybe . . .

Maybe I'm a fool, he told himself when he woke the next morning, still very much alone in bed. He used the chamber pot again, dressed, and ran fingers through his hair.

He was going to the door when someone tapped on it. "Oh, good, you're awake," Mavros said when he opened it a moment later. "If you don't mind breakfasting on hard rolls and smoked mutton, we can eat while we ride back to town."

"Good enough." Krispos thought of how often he'd gone out to work in the fields after breakfasting on nothing. He knew Mavros had never missed a meal. He kept quiet, not just for politeness' sake but also because he'd long since decided hunger held no inherent virtue—life was better with a full belly.

They washed down the rolls and mutton with a skin of wine. "That's a very nice animal you're riding," Krispos said after a while.

"Isn't he?" Mavros beamed. "I'm not small, but my weight doesn't faze him a bit, no even when I'm in mail shirt and helmet." He took the reins in his left hand so he could draw a knife and make cut-and-thrust motions as if it were a sword. "Maybe one of these days I'll ride him to war against Makuran or Kubrat—or even Khatrish, if your master's mission fails. Take that, vile barbarian!" He stabbed a bush by the side of the road.

Krispos smiled at his enthusiasm. "Real fighting's not as . . . neat as you make it out to be."

"You've fought, then?" At Krispos' nod, Mavros' eyes went big and round. "Tell me about it!"

Krispos tried to beg off, but Mavros kept urging him until he baldly recounted the villagers' massacre of the Kubrati raiders. "Just our good luck there was only the one little band," he finished. "If the riders a couple of days later had been wild men instead of Videssian cavalry, I wouldn't be here now to give you the tale."

"I've heard true warriors don't speak much of glory," Mavros said in a rather subdued voice.

"What they call glory, I think, is mostly the relief you feel after you've fought and lived through it without getting maimed. If you have."

"Hmm." Mavros rode on in silence for some time after that. Before he and Krispos got to Opsikion, though, he was slaying bushes again. Krispos did not try to dissuade him. He suspected Mavros would make a better soldier than he did himself—the young noble seemed inclined to plunge straight ahead without worrying about consequences, a martial trait if ever there was one.

They got to Opsikion a little before midmorning. Being with Mavros got Krispos through the south gate with respectful salutes from the guards. When they came to Bolkanes' inn, they found Iakovitzes just sitting down to breakfast—unlike most folk, he did not customarily rise at dawn.

He fixed Krispos with a glare. "Nice of you to recall who your master is." His eyes flicked to Mavros. Krispos watched his expression change. "Or have you been cavorting with this magnificent creature?"

"No," Krispos said resignedly. "Excellent sir, let me present Mavros to you. He is the son of the noblewoman Tanilis, and is interested in returning to Videssos with us when your mission is done. He'd make a fine groom, excellent sir; he knows horses."

"Tanilis' son, eh?" Iakovitzes rose to return Mavros' bow; he'd evidently learned who Tanilis was. But he went on, "When it comes to grooms for my stables, I don't care if he's the Avtokrator's son, not that Anthimos has one."

He shot several searching questions at Mavros, who answered them without undue trouble. Then he went outside to look over the youth's mount. When he came back, he was nodding. "You'll do, if you're the one who's been tending that animal."

"I am," Mavros said.

"Good, good. You'll definitely do. We may even get to leave before fall comes; Lexo may see reason after all. At least I'm beginning to hope so again." Iakovitzes looked almost cheerful for a moment as he sat down. Then he found something new to complain about. "Oh, a plague! My sausage is cold. Bolkanes!"

As the innkeeper hurried up, Mavros whispered to Krispos, "Is your master always like that?"

"Now that you mention it, yes," Krispos whispered back.

"I wonder if I want to see Videssos the city enough to work for him." But Mavros was joking. He raised his voice to a normal level. "I'm going to ride home now, but I'll be in town a lot. If I'm not, just send a messenger for me and I'll come ready to travel." Bowing again to Iakovitzes, he left the taproom.

Around a mouthful of fresh, steaming sausage, Iakovitzes said, "So now you're hobnobbing with young nobles, are you, Krispos? You're coming up a bit in your choice of friends."

"If I hadn't spent these last months with you, excellent sir, I wouldn't have had any idea how to act around him," Krispos said. Flattery that was also true, he'd found, worked best.

It worked now. Iakovitzes' gaze lost the piercing quality it had when he was suspicious about something. "Hrmp," he said, and went back to his breakfast.

Three days later, Mavros brought Krispos another dinner invitation. Krispos went out and bought a new tunic, a saffron-yellow one that went well with his olive skin. After he paid for it, he felt odd. It was the first time he'd got a shirt just for the sake of having something new.

Tanilis' admiring glance that evening made the purchase seem worthwhile. She was worth admiring herself, in a thin dress of white linen that emphasized how small her waist was. More gold shone on her wrists and around her neck.

"You are welcome, as always," she said, holding out her hand.

Krispos took it. "Thank you, my . . . Tanilis." His tongue slipped by accident, but he watched her eyes fall as she heard the last two words together. Maybe his hope of the previous visit had not been so foolish after all.

But if that was so, she gave no hint of it during dinner. Indeed,

she said very little. Mavros did most of the talking; he bubbled
with excitement at the prospect of heading west for the city.
"When will we leave?" he asked. "Do you know? How fare
Iakovitzes' talks with the Khatrisher?"

"Better, I think," Krispos said. "He's hardly swearing at all
when he gets back from the eparch's residence these days. With
him, that's a very good sign."

"I'll start packing, then."

"Go ahead, but don't pack anything you might want before
you go. He was like this once before, weeks ago, and then things
fell apart again." Krispos took a last luscious bite of blackberry
tart and turned to Tanilis. "I wish your cook could come with
me along with your son. I don't think I've ever eaten so well."

"I'll tell Evtykhes you said so," she said, smiling. "Your
praise will please him more than what he gets from us—you're
not obliged to say kind things to him for politeness' sake."

Krispos had not thought about that. The servants at Iakovitzes'
home were the only ones he'd known, and he was one among
them. For that matter, Iakovitzes did not say kind things to
anyone for politeness' sake. He used the rough edge of his
tongue, not the smooth, to keep his people in line.

Tanilis said, "Though I must keep Evtykhes, Krispos, you
will need more than you have if what we hope is to be accomplished. When you and Mavros do at last depart for the imperial
city, I will send gold with you."

"My lady—" This time Krispos deliberately used her title
rather than her name— "even with Mavros with me in Videssos,
what's to keep me from spending the gold just on women and
wine?"

"You are." Tanilis looked him full in the face. Those huge
dark eyes held his; he had the uneasy feeling she could peer
deeper into him than he could himself. Now he was the first to
lower his gaze.

Mavros rose. "I'm off. If I'm to be leaving soon, I have some
farewells to make."

Tanilis watched him go. "What was it you said about wine
and women?" she asked Krispos. "Most of his farewells will
be of that sort, I expect."

"He's coming into a man's years and a man's pleasures,"
Krispos replied from the peak of maturity that was twenty-two.

"So he is," Tanilis' voice was musing. Her eyes met Krispos
again, but she looked through him rather than into him, back

toward the past. "A man. How strange. I must have been about the age he is now when I bore him."

"Surely younger," Krispos said.

She laughed, without mirth but also without bitterness. "You are gallant, but I know the count of years. They are part of me; why should I deny them?"

Instead of answering, Krispos took a thoughtful sip from his wine cup. He'd made a mistake by breaking the rule of flattery he'd used on Iakovitzes. With someone like Tanilis, it did not do to make mistakes.

Before long, Krispos got up to go, saying, "Thank you again for inviting me here, and for the aid you promise, and for this second wonderful feast."

"Truly, if it does not unduly anger your master, you would be well advised to stay till morning," Tanilis said. "The ride back to Opsikion will be twice as long in the darkness, and there are brigands in the hills, try as we will to keep them down."

"Iakovitzes is angry most of the time, it seems. Unduly?" Krispos shrugged. "I expect I can talk him round. Thank you once more."

Tanilis called for Xystos. The servant took Krispos to the same guest chamber he had used before. That soft bed beckoned. He stripped off his clothes, slid under the single light blanket that was all he needed on a warm summer night, and fell asleep at once.

He was a sound sleeper, a legacy of the many years he had gone to bed every night too tired to wake to anything less than an earthquake. The first he knew of anyone else's being in the room was the bed shifting as the weight of another body settled onto it.

He jerked upright. "Wha—" he said muzzily.

Even the small, flickering flame of the lamp Tanilis held was enough to dazzle his sleep-dulled eyes. A secret smile tugged at the corners of her mouth. "I'm sorry," she said. "I didn't mean to startle you."

"It's—all right," he answered after a moment, when he had full control of himself. Still not altogether sure why she had come—and not daring to be wrong here, where his head might answer for it—he pulled the blanket up to cover more of himself.

That secret smile came out in the open. "Wise to be cautious. But never mind." Then her expression changed. "What is that coin you wear round your neck?'' she asked, her voice suddenly sharp and interested.

"This?" Krispos' hand closed over the goldpiece. "It's just for luck."

"For more than luck, I think," Tanilis said. "Please, if you would, tell me how you came by it."

He told her how Omurtag had given him the coin at the ransoming ceremony back when he was a boy. Her eyes glittered in the lamplight as she followed his account. When he thought he was done, she questioned him about the incident as closely as Iakovitzes had grilled Mavros on horses.

Prodded so, he recalled more than he'd imagined he could, even to things like the expression on the Kubrati *enaree*'s face. The more he answered, though, the more glumly certain he became that she'd forgotten why she'd come to his bedroom in the first place. *Too bad,* he thought. The lamp's warm light made her especially lovely.

But she certainly seemed indifferent to their both being on the same bed. When she could pick no more memories from him, she said, "No wonder I saw as I did. The seeds of what you may be were sown long ago; at last they have grown toward the light of day."

He shrugged. At the moment, he cared little for the nebulous future. He was too busy thinking about what he wished he was doing in the very immediate present.

"You're rather a young man still, though, and not much worried about such things," Tanilis said. He gulped, wondering if she could read his mind. Then he saw she was looking down at the thin blanket, which revealed his thoughts clearly enough. He felt himself flush, but the smile was back on her face. "I suppose that's as it should be," she said, and blew out the lamp.

For a whole series of reasons, the rest of the evening proved among the most educational of Krispos' life. Every woman he'd been with before Tanilis suddenly seemed a girl by comparison. They *were* girls, he realized: his age or younger, chosen for attractiveness, kept for enthusiasm. Now for the first time he learned what polished art could add.

Looking back the exhausted morning after, he supposed Tanilis had taken him through his paces like Iakovitzes steering a jumper around a course. Had she taught him anything else that way, he was sure he would have resented her. He still did, a little, but resentment had to fight hard against languor.

He'd wondered for some little while if art was all she brought to the game. She moved, she stroked, she lay back to receive his caresses in silence, a silence that persisted no matter what he did. And though all her ploys were far more than just enjoyable, he also thought they were rehearsed.

Then at last some of his own urgency reached her. Kindled, she was less perfectly skilled than she had been before. Feeling her quiver beneath him, hearing her breath catch, made him want to forget all that perfect skill had wrought.

He wondered if the quivers, if the gasps, were also products of her art. He shrugged as he fastened the bone catches of his tunic. Art that fine was indistinguishable from reality; it was as if an icon of Petronas could move and speak with the Sevastokrator's voice.

Later, as he walked down the hall behind a servant toward the small dining chamber for breakfast, he decided he was wrong. If he'd altogether failed to please her, he doubted she'd give herself to him again.

She waited for him in the dining room, her self-possession absolute as usual. "I trust you slept well," she said in a tone any polite hostess might have used. Before he could answer, she went on, "Do try some of the honey on your bread. It's clover and orange together, and very fine."

He dipped it from the pot and tried it. It was good. He tried—as best he could with men and women of her household bustling in and out—to learn how she felt about the night before. She was impervious. That seemed ominous.

Then Mavros came in, looking rather the worse for wear, and Krispos had to give up. Tanilis showed more interest in her son's boasting than she'd given to Krispos' discreet questions.

Only as Krispos was saying his farewells did she give him even the smallest reason for hope. "Feel free to invite yourself here next time; you need not wait upon a formal invitation."

"Thank you, Tanilis, I'll do that," he said, and watched her face closely. Had she shown any trace of disappointment, he would never have gone back to the villa again. She nodded and smiled instead.

He made himself wait four days before he rode back again. Evtykhes the cook hadn't had anything special planned but, like Iakovitzes' chef, he could make the ordinary interesting.

What happened later that night was even more interesting, and not even slightly ordinary. "Don't delay so long the next time,'' Tanilis said as she slid out of the guest room bed to return to her own chamber. ''Or did you think I was seeking to entrap you with my charms?''

Krispos shook his head. Tanilis slipped away without asking anything further of him. He was not nearly sure he had truthfully answered her last question; indeed, he hadn't trusted his voice not to give him away.

Even so, he knew he would come to the villa again, and in less than four days. Did that mean he was entrapped? Maybe it did, he thought wryly. He was sure he'd never found such tempting bait.

Iakovitzes looked up from his breakfast porridge as Krispos walked toward his table in Bolkanes' taproom. The noble's eyebrows rose. ''Good of you to join me,'' he said. ''Such rare signs give me hope you do still remember you work for me.''

Krispos felt his ears grow hot. He grunted—the safest response he could think of—and sat down.

Nothing was guaranteed safe with Iakovitzes. ''Much as I hate to disrupt the lecherous tenor of your ways,'' he went on, ''I fear your little arrangement with that laundress or whatever she is at Mavros' place will have to end.''

Krispos had found no way to keep people from knowing how often he rode out to Tanilis' villa. Those visits—and the overnight stays that went with them—had to set tongues wagging. To make sure they did not wag in the wrong—or rather, the right—direction, he'd let on that he was having an affair with one of the servant girls. Now he said, still cautiously, ''Oh? Why is that, excellent sir?''

''Because I've finally settled with that puff-adder of a Lexo, that's why.''

''Have you really?'' Krispos said in genuine surprise.

''Yes, I have really, and on more than decent terms. If you'd been around here as you were supposed to be instead of exercising your private parts, this might not have come as such a startling development to you.''

Krispos hung his head at the rebuke. The acid in Iakovitzes' voice made it sting more than it might have otherwise, but he knew it was deserved. He also knew a certain amount of relief. If Iakovitzes was heading back to Videssos the city, he would have to accompany the noble. Not even Tanilis could think differently. A more convenient end to their liaison was hard to imagine.

Iakovitzes went on, "Since you do get out to Mavros' villa, however, be so good as to let him know I shall be departing shortly. Why I don't leave you here and head back just with him I couldn't say, let me tell you."

At first, the scolding washed over Krispos. If Iakovitzes meant to fire him, he would have done it long since. And even if the noble did give him the boot, Tanilis would still back him—or would she? Krispos grew more sober as he pondered that. If his fortunes changed, her vision might, too.

He decided he ought to stay in Iakovitzes' good graces after all, or as many of them as he could keep without letting the noble seduce him. "What were the terms you finally agreed to with Lexo, excellent sir?" he asked.

"As if you care," Iakovitzes jeered, but he was too full of himself to resist bragging about what he'd done. "The Khatrishers will all pull back of the Akkilaion by the end of next year, and three parts in four of the indemnity we pay for their leaving will go straight to the herders who get displaced, not to Gumush the khagan. I had to pay Lexo a little extra on the side to get him to go along with that, but it's money well spent."

"I see what you're saying." Krispos nodded. "If the indemnity stays with the local Khatrishers, they'll end up spending most of it here in Opsikion, so in the long run it'll come back to the Empire."

"Maybe that's why I keep you around in spite of the all-too-numerous faults you insist on flaunting," Iakovitzes said: "for your peasant shrewdness. Even Lexo didn't pick up the full import of that clause, and he's been in the business of cheating Videssos a good many years now. Aye, I snuck it past him, I did, I did." Nothing put Iakovitzes in a better mood than gloating over how he'd outsmarted an opponent.

"When do you sign the pact?" Krispos asked.

"Already did it—signed and sealed. I have one copy up in my room, and Lexo's got the other one wherever he keeps it." Iakovitzes knocked back a large cup of wine. Only when he swayed as he got to his feet did Krispos realize it was not his first, or even his third; his speech was perfectly clear. As the noble headed for the door, he said over his shoulder, "Come to think of it, I'm going across the square to the eparch's residence and rub the Khatrisher's nose in the break he gave me. Want to tag along?''

''Are you sure that's wise, excellent sir?'' Krispos said, in lieu of publicly asking his master whether he'd lost his mind. If Iakovitzes angered Lexo enough—and he could do it if anyone could—what was to keep the Khatrisher from tearing up his signed and sealed copy and either starting the war Petronas did not want or at least forcing negotiations open again?

But Iakovitzes said, ''Let him wallow in his own stupidity.'' He went out the door almost at a run.

Krispos heard the rumble and jingle of an approaching heavy wagon without listening to it; it was just one of the noises that went with staying in a city. Then he heard someone shout, ''Watch out, you blood drunken twit! Look over this—'' That was harder to ignore; it came from right in front of the inn. At the cry of agony that followed hard on its heels, Krispos and everyone else in the taproom dashed out to see what had happened.

The wagon was full of blocks of gray limestone from one of the quarries in the hills back of Opsikion, and drawn by a team of six draft horses. Iakovitzes lay thrashing on the ground between the near wheeler and the wagon's right front wheel. Another yard forward and it would have rolled over his body.

Krispos ran forward and dragged his master away from the wagon. Iakovitzes shrieked again as he was moved. ''My leg!'' He clutched at it. ''My leg!''

The white-faced driver gabbled, ''Fool walked right in front of me. Right in front of me like I wasn't there, and this maybe the biggest, noisiest rig in town. Right in front of me! One of the horses must have stepped on him, or maybe more than one. Lucky I was fast on the brake, or all you could do with him is clean him off the cobbles. Right in front of me!''

A couple of passers-by confirmed that Iakovitzes had not noticed the wagon at all. ''Way he was going,'' one said, ''he wouldn't have noticed Phos coming down from heaven for him.'' A couple of more pious souls made the sun-sign over their hearts at the mention of the good god's name.

Krispos tugged up Iakovitzes' robe so he could see how badly the noble was hurt. The unnatural bend between knee and ankle of his master's left leg and the enormous black bruise that spread over the leg as he watched told him everything he needed to know. ''It's broken,'' he said.

"Of course it's broken, you wide-arsed imbecile!" Iakovitzes screamed, pain and fury making him even louder and shriller than usual. "You think I need you to tell me that?" The inventive curses that spewed from him in the next couple of minutes proved his wits were intact, even if he did have cuts over both eyes and a bruise on one cheek. He finally slowed down enough to snarl, "Why are all you incest-loving cretins just standing around gaping? Someone fetch me a healer-priest!"

One of the locals trotted away. Iakovitzes kept swearing; Krispos did not think he repeated himself once in the quarter of an hour till the priest arrived. Some of the onlookers who might normally have gone about their business stayed to listen instead.

"What happened here?" the healer-priest asked when he finally arrived.

Several people in the crowd started to explain as they stood aside to let the priest—Sabellios, his name was—pass. From the ground, Iakovitzes yelled, "I broke my miserable leg, that's what. Why don't you stop gabbing there and start healing?"

"He's like that, holy sir," Krispos whispered to Sabellios as the healer-priest crouched beside him.

"It's not easy to be happy with a broken leg," Sabellios observed. "Easy, sir, easy," he went on to Iakovitzes, for the noble gasped and swore anew as the healer-priest set his hands on either side of the fracture.

Like the other healers Krispos had seen, Sabellios spoke Phos' creed again and again as he sank into his trance. Then the words trailed away, leaving nothing between Sabellios' will and the injury he faced. Krispos muttered with awe as he watched the swelling around the broken bone recede and the purple-black bruise fade.

The healer-priest released his hold. He wiped sweat from his forehead with the sleeve of his blue robe. "I have done what I can," he said in the worn voice every healer used just after his work was done. Krispos noted the effort he needed to raise his head to look up at the spectators who still ringed him and Iakovitzes. "One of you should go and bring Ordanes the physician here. He has a gentler touch for setting bones than I do."

"Setting bones?" Iakovitzes hissed from between clenched teeth. "Aren't you going to heal the break?"

Sebellios stared at him. "Heal—a fracture?"

"Why not?" Iakovitzes said. "I had it done for me once in Videssos the city, after I took a fall when my cursed mount couldn't leap a stream during a hunt. Some blue-robe from the Sorcerers' Collegium did it for me—Heraklonas, I think his name was."

"You were most fortunate to be treated by such a master of the art, excellent sir," the healer-priest said. "As with most of my brethren, my power is over flesh, not bone, which I have neither the strength nor the knowledge to heal. Bone, you see, is partly dead, so it lacks the vitality upon which the healing gift draws. No one in Opsikion—perhaps no one in any city save Videssos—can heal a broken bone. I am sorry to have to be the one to tell you that."

"Then what am I supposed to do?" Iakovitzes howled, anger now overcoming pain.

"Fear not, sir," Sebellios said. "Ordanes is a skilled bone-setter, and I can abate any fever you might contract during the healing process. Surely in two or three months you will be walk-ing again and, if you exercise your leg once the splints come off, you may not even limp."

"Two or three months?" Iakovitzes rolled his eyes like a trapped animal. "How long before I can ride?"

Sebellios pursed his lips. "Somewhere near the same length of time, I should say. Controlling one's horse puts considerable strain on the lower leg, as you must know."

"Two or three months?" Iakovitzes repeated it unbelievingly. "You're saying it'll be winter by the time I'm up and about?"

"Well, yes, probably," Sebellios said. "What of it?"

"No ships in winter—too many storms. No good going over-land, either, or not much—snowdrifts piled twice as high as a man." Iakovitzes had been speaking softly, almost to himself. Now, suddenly, he screamed. *"You mean to tell me I'm stuck in this backwoods Phos-forsaken shitpot pesthole of an excuse for a town until spring?"*

"Hello, hello." A fat bald man pushed through the crowd and grinned down at Iakovitzes. "My, you sound cheerful to-day. Nothing like breaking a leg to do that to a man, is there?"

"I'd sooner break your neck," Iakovitzes snarled. "Which icepit did Skotos let you out of?"

"Name's Ordanes," the fat man answered calmly—he was, Krispos saw, one of the rare men Iakovitzes could not infuriate with a few ill-chosen words. "I'll set that leg for you, if you like—I expect you'll need it whole so as you can get back to cramming both feet into your face." As Iakovitzes gaped and spluttered, the physician went on, "I'll need a couple of stout souls here to help hold him down. He'll like this even less than he likes anything else."

"I'm one," Krispos said. "He's my master."

"Lucky you." Ordanes lowered his voice so Iakovitzes would not hear. "Hate to tell you this, young fellow, but you and your master are going to be stuck here a goodish while. That's what I heard him yelling about before, isn't it?"

Krispos nodded.

"If you're his man, you'll have to wait on him like he was a baby for a while, because for the first month or so he shouldn't even be out of bed, not if he expects those bones to heal straight. Think you're up to it? I don't envy you, and that's a fact."

The idea of waiting on Iakovitzes hand and foot for a solid month was more nearly appalling than appealing. All the same, Krispos said, "I'm up to it. He took me into his service from the streets of Videssos the city when I had nothing to my name but what I was wearing. I owe him more than a little for that; wouldn't do to repay him by running off when he really needs me."

"Hmm." Ordanes' eyes were tracked with red, half hidden in folds of fat, and very knowing. "Seems to me he's better served by his man than you are by your master, but that's none of my affair." The physician looked up at the crowd of spectators. "Come on, people, don't just stand there. Lend a hand, will you? Wouldn't you want somebody to help if it were *your* leg? You, there, and you there in the blue tunic."

As the men bent to hold Iakovitzes, Krispos realized one of his questions had just been answered for him. If he was not leaving Opsikion any time soon, he would see Tanilis again. . . . And again and again, he thought.

Iakovitzes hissed and then groaned as Ordanes set to work. Despite the noble's anguish, Krispos had all he could do to keep from giggling. Tanilis was a much more alluring prospect in bed than his master.

VI

THAT MONTH OF CONSTANT ATTENDANCE ON IAKOVITZES proved even more wearing than Ordanes had predicted. The physician had compared it to tending a baby. Babies only cried. Iakovitzes used his searing tongue to inform Krispos of all his whims and all Krispos' shortcomings.

By the noble's reckoning, Krispos had plenty of them. Iakovitzes blamed him when the water for sponge baths was too hot or too cold, when Bolkanes' kitchen came up with a meal Iakovitzes found inadequate, when the bedpan was not perfectly placed, and even when his healing leg itched, which it seemed to do most of the time.

As for that bedpan, sometimes Krispos felt like braining Iakovitzes with it. It was, however, his master's one significant advantage over a baby: Iakovitzes, at least, did not foul the bed. In a time that held few large advantages, Krispos cherished the small one.

One afternoon about three weeks after the noble got hurt, someone knocked on the door of his room. Krispos jumped. Few people had come to see Iakovitzes. Krispos opened the door with one hand on his knife. A good-looking youth stared at him with equal suspicion.

"It's all right, Krispos, Graptos," Iakovitzes called from his bed. "In fact, Krispos, it's better than all right. You can take the rest of the day off. I'll see you in the morning."

"Excellent sir?" Krispos said doubtfully.

"Bolkanes arranged this for me," Iakovitzes assured him. "After all, if I'm bedridden, I might as well *be* bed-ridden, if

134

you see what I mean. And since you're so tiresomely obstinate on the subject—"

Krispos waited to hear no more. He closed the door behind him and hurried down to the stables. If Iakovitzes was going to sport, so would he. The sun was still an hour away from setting when he got to Tanilis' villa.

He had to wait some little time before he saw her; she was settling a dispute between two peasants who dwelt on her land. Neither seemed displeased as they walked past Krispos. He was unsurprised; Tanilis had more than enough sense to dispense justice.

She smiled as Naues led Krispos into her study. "I wondered if I would see you again, after your master's accident," she said. In front of her steward, her voice was perfectly controlled.

"I wondered, too." Krispos also kept his tone casual. He was sure Tanilis would be able to find all the double meanings he put into his words and perhaps some he left out. He went on, "The excellent Iakovitzes seems to be in better spirits these days." He explained who was taking care of the noble, and in what ways.

Naues snorted; the tiny curl of Tanilis' lip looked like less but spoke more. Aloud, she said, "You are welcome here regardless of the circumstances. Mavros may be back for the evening meal, but then again he may not. Now that he is sure he won't be leaving for the city till spring, he gives all his time to one girl, knowing, I suppose, that afterward time and distance will fade the attachment."

Such cool, calculated good sense sounded more like Tanilis than young Mavros; for a moment Krispos was reminded of listening to his own father back in the days when Zoranne was all he'd thought of. He hoped Mavros was clever enough to recognize that his mother was cleverer still.

"Naues, are there any more out there who need me?" Tanilis asked. When her man shook his head, she told him, "Go and warn Evtykhes, then, that Krispos certainly will stay for supper, and that I do have some hope my son will appear, as well."

Mavros did come back to the villa. When he found Krispos there, he condescended to stay for dinner. "How'd you get loose?" he asked. "I thought Iakovitzes wanted you there every minute?" Krispos explained again. Mavros burst out laughing. "Good for the old bugger! He's feeling better, then?"

"Aye, but he's not up and about yet. And with the fall rains due any day now, it's just as he feared. He won't be riding back to the city till spring; he can't even hobble yet, let alone sit a horse."

"Too bad," Mavros said dolefully. "Here I've been champing at the bit for weeks, and now I'll have to wait for months. Such a long time." With a moody sigh, he raised his wine cup to his lips.

Tanilis said, "Be thankful you're young enough that a few months seem a long time to you. To me, next spring feels like the day after tomorrow."

"Well, not to me," Mavros said.

For the most part, Krispos agreed with Mavros; at twenty-two, he thought the world passed too slowly to suit him. Still, even slowness could have its advantages. He said, "From what I've heard, you've got a girl now, so just think of it as having a longer-seeming time to spend with her."

"I wish it were that easy," Mavros said, "but somehow when I'm with her the time flies by, so it never seems like enough no matter how long it is. Which reminds me." He finished his wine, rose, and sketched bows to Tanilis and Krispos. "I promised I'd meet her before the moon came up." Not quite trotting, he left the dining room.

"My poor, bereft son," Tanilis said dryly. "He hasn't set eyes on his beloved for, oh, several hours now. In a way, I suppose, I should be jealous, but he just makes me smile instead."

Krispos thoughtfully ate one of Evtykhes' lemon tarts. Tanilis hadn't told him anything he didn't already know; her practiced sensuality was worlds apart from Mavros' enthusiastic infatuation. Nevertheless, Krispos wished his lover had not made it so plain he was not her beloved.

But no matter what she did, she came to him that night. If she found what they did together distasteful, she hid it marvelously well. Afterward, Krispos leaned up on one elbow. "Why me?" he asked. Tanilis made a questioning noise. "Why me?" Krispos repeated. "Who you are and what you are, you could pick any man within a hundred miles of Opsikion, and he'd come running. So why did you pick me?"

"Because of your looks, your youth, your vigor. Because, having seen you, I could not help picking you."

The words were all Krispos could have hoped to hear. But he

also heard the faintest questioning tone in Tanilis' voice, as if she were offering him an explanation to see whether he'd accept it. Though he wanted to, he found he could not. He said, "You could find a dozen who outdo me on any of those at a glance—a hundred or a thousand with a little looking. I gather you haven't, which means you haven't answered me, either."

Now she sat up in bed. Krispos thought it was the first time she took him seriously for his own sake rather than as a cog in what she'd foreseen. After a short pause, she said slowly, "Because you don't take the easy way, but look to see what may lie behind it. That is rare at any age, doubly so at yours."

This time he felt she'd touched truth, but not given him the whole of it. "Why else?" he persisted.

He wondered if his drive to know would anger her, but soon saw it did not. If anything, it raised him in her estimation; when she replied, her voice had the no-nonsense tone of someone conducting serious business. "I'll not deny that the power implied by this—" She reached out to touch the goldpiece on its chain, "—has its own attraction. In and around Opsikion, I have done everything, become everything I could hope to do and become. To set up my own son in Videssos the city, to have a connection to one who may be . . . . what he may be: that could tempt me almost to anything. But only almost. Reckon me hard if you like, and calculating, and cunning, but you reckon me a whore at your peril." She did not sound businesslike then; she sounded dangerous.

Krispos nodded soberly. As with Iakovitzes, his chief shield against her was stubborn refusal to acknowledge that she could daunt him. "And so?" he asked.

The light from the single lamp in the bedchamber shifted shadows on her face to underscore her every change of expression. With that aid, Krispos saw he'd gained another point. "And so," she said, "I have no interest in men who seek to bed not me but my estates; nor in those who would reckon me only a prize possession, as if I were a hound; nor again in those who care just for my body and would not mind if Skotos dwelt behind my eyes. Do you see yourself in any of those groups?"

"No," Krispos said. "But in a way don't you fall into the first one, I mean with respect to me?"

Tanilis stared at him. "You dare—" He admired her for

the speed with which she checked herself. After a few seconds, she even laughed. "You have me, Krispos; by my own words I stand convicted. But here I am on the other end of the bargain; and I must say it looks different from how it seemed before."

To you, maybe, Krispos thought.

Tanilis went on, "A final reason I chose you, Krispos, at least after the first time, is that you learn quickly. One of the things you still need to know, though, is that sometimes you can ask too many questions."

She reached up and drew his face down to hers. But even as he responded to her teaching, he remained sure there was no such thing as asking too many questions. Finding the right way and time to ask them might be something else again, he admitted to himself. And this, he thought before all thought left him, was probably not it.

He woke the next morning to rain drumming on the roof. He knew that sound, though he was more used to the softer plashing of raindrops against thatch than the racket they made on tile. He hoped Tanilis' peasants were done with their harvest, then laughed at himself: they *were* done now, whether they wanted to be or not.

Tanilis, as was her way, had slipped off during the night. Sometimes he woke when she slid out of bed; more often, as last night, he did not. He wondered, not for the first time, if her servants knew they were lovers. If so, the cooks and stewards and serving maids gave no sign of it. He had learned from Iakovitzes' establishment, though, that being discreet was part of being a well-trained servant. And Tanilis tolerated no servant who was not.

He also wondered if Mavros knew. That, he doubted. Mavros was a good many things and would likely grow to become a good many more, but Krispos had trouble seeing him as discreet.

Her hair as perfectly in place as if he had never run his hands through it, Tanilis sat waiting for him in the small dining room. "You'll have a wet ride back to Opsikion, I fear," she said, waving him to the chair opposite her.

He shrugged. "I've been wet before."

"A good plate of boiled bacon should help keep you warm on the journey, if not dry."

"My lady is generous in all things," Krispos said. Tanilis' eyes lit as he dug in.

The road north had already begun to turn to glue. Krispos did not try to push his horse. If Iakovitzes could not figure out why he was late coming back to town, too bad for Iakovitzes.

Krispos wrung out his cloak in Bolkanes' front hall, then squelched up the stairs in wet boots to see how his master was doing. What he found in Iakovitzes' room startled him: the noble was on his feet, trying to stump around with two sticks. The only sign of Graptos was a lingering trace of perfume in the air.

"Hello, look what I can do!" Iakovitzes said, for once too pleased with himself to be snide.

"I've looked," Krispos said shortly. "Now will you please get back in bed where you belong? If you were a horse, excellent sir—" He'd learned the art of turning title to reproach. "—they'd have cut your throat for a broken leg and let it go at that. If you go and break it again from falling because you're on it too soon, do you think you deserve any better? Ordanes told you to stay flat at least another fortnight."

"Oh, bugger Ordanes," Iakovitzes said.

"Go ahead, but make him get on top."

The noble snorted. "No thank you."

Krispos went on more earnestly, "I can't give you orders, excellent sir, but I can ask if you'd treat one of your animals the way you're treating yourself. There's no point to it, the more so since with the fall rains starting you're not going anyplace anyhow."

"Mrmm," Iakovitzes said—a noise a long way from any sort of agreement, but one that, when the noble changed the subject, showed Krispos he had got through.

Iakovitzes continued to mend. Eventually, as Ordanes had predicted, he was able to move about with his sticks, lifting and planting them and his splinted leg so heavily that once people in the taproom directly below his chamber complained to Bolkanes about the racket he made. Since the innkeeper was getting, if not rich, then at least highly prosperous from his noble guest's protracted stay, he turned a deaf ear to the complaints.

By the time Iakovitzes could stump about the inn, the rains made sure he did not travel much farther. Outside large towns, Videssos had few paved roads; dirt was kinder to horses' hooves. The price of that kindness was several weeks of impassable soup each fall and spring. Iakovitzes cursed every day that dawned gray and wet, which meant he did a lot of cursing.

Krispos tried to rebuke him. "The rain's a blessing to farmers, excellent sir, and without farmers we'd all starve." The words were several seconds out of his mouth before he realized they were his father's.

"If you like farmers so bloody well, why did you ever leave that pissant village you sprang from?" Iakovitzes retorted. Krispos gave up on changing his master's attitude; trying to get Iakovitzes to stop cursing was like trying to fit the moon in a satchel. The noble's bad temper seemed as constant as the ever-shifting phases of the moon.

And soon enough, Krispos came to curse the fall rains, too. As Iakovitzes grew more able to care for himself, Krispos found himself with more free time. He wanted to spend as much time as he could with Tanilis, both for the sake of his body's pleasure and, increasingly, to explore the boundaries of their odd relationship. Riding even as far as her villa, though, was not to be undertaken lightly, not in the fall.

Thus he was overjoyed, one cold blustery day when the rain threatened to turn to sleet, to hear her say, "I think I will go into Opsikion soon, to spend the winter there. I have a house, you know, not far from Phos' temple."

"I'd forgotten," Krispos admitted. That night, in the privacy of the guest chamber, he said, "I hope I'll be able to see you more often if you come to town. This miserable weather—"

Tanilis nodded. "I expect you will."

"Did you—" Krispos paused, then plunged: "Did you decide to go into Opsikion partly on account of me?"

Her laugh was warm enough that, though he flushed, he did not flinch. "Don't flatter yourself too much, my—well, if I call you my dear, you *will* flatter yourself, won't you? In any case, I go into Opsikion every year about this time. Should anything important happen, I might not learn of it for weeks were I to stay here in the villa."

"Oh." Krispos thought for a moment. "Couldn't you stay here and foresee what you need to know?"

"The gift comes as it will, not as I will," Tanilis said. "Besides, I like to see new faces every so often. If I'd prayed at the chapel here, after all, instead of coming into Opsikion for the holy Abdaas' day, I'd not have met you. You might have stayed a groom forever."

Reminded of Iakovitzes' jibe, Krispos said, "It's an easier life than the one I had before I came to the city." He also thought, a little angrily, that he would have risen further even if Tanilis hadn't met him. That he kept to himself. Instead, he said, "If you come to Opsikion, you might want to bring that pretty little laundress of yours—Phronia's her name, isn't it?—along with you."

"Oh? And why is that?" Tanilis' voice held no expression whatever.

Krispos answered quickly, knowing he was on tricky ground. "Because I've spread the word around that she's the reason I come here so often. If she's in Opsikion, I'll have a better excuse to visit you there."

"Hmm. Put that way, yes." Tanilis' measuring gaze reminded Krispos of a hawk eyeing a rabbit from on high. "I would not advise you to use this story to deceive me while you carry on with Phronia. I would not advise that at all."

A chill ran down Krispos' spine, though he had no interest in Phronia past any young man's regard for a pretty girl. Since that was true, the chill soon faded. What remained was insight into how Tanilis thought. Krispos' imagination had not reached to concealing one falsehood within another, but Tanilis took the possibility for granted. That had to mean she'd seen it before, which in turn meant other people used such complex ploys. *Something else to look out for*, Krispos thought with a silent sigh.

"What was that for?" Tanilis asked.

Wishing she weren't so alert, he said, "Only that you've taught me many things."

"I've certainly intended to. If you would be more than a groom, you need to know more than a groom."

Krispos nodded before the full import of what she'd said sank in. Then he found himself wondering whether she'd warned him about Phronia just to show him how a double bluff worked. He thought about asking her but decided not to. She might not have meant that at all. He smiled ruefully. Whatever else she was doing, she was teaching him to distrust first impressions . . . and second . . . and third. . . . After a while, he supposed, reality might disappear altogether, and no one would notice it was gone.

He thought of how Iakovitzes and Lexo had gone back and forth, quarreling over what was thought to be true at least as much as over what was true. To prosper in Videssos the city, he might need every bit of what Tanilis taught.

Since Opsikion lay by the Sailors' Sea, Krispos thought winter would be gentler there. The winter wind, though, was not off the sea, but from the north and west; a breeze from his old home, but hardly a welcome one.

Eventually the sea froze, thick enough for a man to walk on, out to a distance of several miles from shore. Even the folk of Opsikion called that a hard winter. To Krispos it was appalling; he'd seen frozen rivers and ponds aplenty, but the notion that the sea could turn to ice made him wonder if the Balancer heretics from Khatrish might not have a point. The broad, frigid expanse seemed a chunk of Skotos' hell brought up to earth.

Yet the locals took the weather in stride. They told stories of the year an iceberg, perhaps storm-driven from Agder or the Haloga country, smashed half the docks before shattering against the town's seawall. And the eparch Sisinnios sent armed patrols onto the ice north of the city.

"What are you looking for, demons?" Krispos asked when he saw the guardsmen set out one morning. He laughed nervously. If the frozen sea was as much Skotos' country as it appeared, demons might indeed dwell there.

The patrol leader laughed, too. He thought Krispos had been joking. "Worse than demons," he said, and gave Krispos a moment to stew before he finished: "Khatrishers."

"In this weather?" Krispos wore a squirrelskin cap with earflaps. It was pulled down low on his forehead. A thick wool scarf covered his mouth and nose. The few square inches of skin between the one and the other had long since turned numb.

The patrol leader was similarly muffled. His breath made a steaming cloud around him. "Grab a spear and come see for yourself," he urged. "You're with the chap from the city, right? Well, you can tell him some of what we see around here."

"Why not?" A quick trip back to the armory gave Krispos a spear and a white-painted shield. Soon he was stumbling along the icy surface of the sea with the troopers. It was rougher, more irregular ice than he'd expected, almost as if the waves had frozen instead of breaking.

"Always keep two men in sight," said the patrol leader, whose name, Krispos learned, was Saborios. "You get lost out here by yourself—well, you're already on the ice, so where will your

soul end up?'' Krispos blew out a smoky sigh of relief to discover he was not the only one who had heretical thoughts.

The guardsmen paid attention to what they were doing, but it
was a routine attention, making sure they did nothing they knew
to be foolish. It left plenty of room for banter and horseplay.
Krispos trudged on grimly in the middle of the line. With neither
terrain nor risks familiar to him, he had all he could do just to
keep pace.

''Good thing it's not snowing,'' one of the troopers said. ''If
it was snowing, the Khatrishers could sneak an army past us
and we'd never know the difference.''

''We would when we got back,'' another answered. The first
guard chuckled.

Everything looked the same to Krispos; sky and frozen sea
and distant land all were shades of white and gray. Anything
colorful, he thought, should have been visible for miles. What
had not occurred to him was how uncolorful a smuggler could
become.

Had the trooper to Krispos' left not almost literally stumbled
over the man, they never would have spied him. Even then, had
he stayed still, he might have escaped notice: he wore white
foxskins and, when still, was invisible past twenty paces. But
he lost his head and tried to run. He was no better at it on the
slippery ice than his pursuers, who soon ran him down.

Saborios held out a hand to the Khatrisher, who had gone so
far as to daub white greasepaint on his beard and face. ''You
don't by any chance have your import license along, do you?''
the patrol leader asked pleasantly. The Khatrisher stood in glum
silence. ''No, eh?'' Saborios said, almost as if really surprised.
''Then let's have your goods.''

The smuggler reached under his jacket, drew out a leather
pouch.

The patrol leader opened it. ''Amber, is it? Very fine, too.
Did you give me all of it? Complete confiscation, you know, is
the penalty for unlicensed import.''

''That's everything, curse you,'' the Khatrisher said sullenly.

''Good.'' Saborios nodded his understanding. ''Then you
won't mind Domentzios and Bonosos stripping you. If they find
you've told the truth, they'll even give you back your clothes.''

Krispos was shivering in his furs. He wondered how long a
naked man would last on the ice. Not long enough to get off it
again, he was sure. He watched the smuggler make the same

unhappy calculation. The fellow took a pouch from each boot. The patrol leader pocketed them, then motioned forward the two troopers he had named. They were tugging off the Khatrisher's coat when he exclaimed, "Wait!"

The imperials looked to the patrol leader, who nodded. The smuggler shed his white fox cap. "I need my knife, all right?" he said. Saborios nodded again. The smuggler cut into the lining, extracted yet another pouch. He threw down the dagger. "Now you can search me."

The troopers did. They found nothing. Shivering and swearing, the Khatrisher dove back into his clothes. "You might have got that last one by us," Saborios remarked.

"That's what I thought," the smuggler said through chattering teeth. "Then I thought I might not have, too."

"Sensible," Saborios said. "Well, let's take you in. We've earned our pay for today, I think."

"What will you do with him?" Krispos asked as the patrol turned back toward Opsikion.

"Hold him for ransom," Saborios answered. "Nothing else we can do, now that I've seen he's smuggling amber. Gumush will pay to have him back, never fear." Krispos made a questioning noise. Saborios explained, "Amber's a royal monopoly in Khatrish. The khagan likes to see if he can avoid paying our tariffs every so often, that's all. This time he didn't, so we get some for free."

"Does he sneak in enough to make it worth his while?"

"That's a sharp question—I thought you were Iakovitzes' groom, not his bookkeeper. The only answer I know is, he must think so or he wouldn't keep doing it. But not this run, though." The patrol leader's eyes, almost the only part of his face visible, narrowed in satisfaction.

Iakovitzes howled with glee when Krispos told him the story that evening. They were sitting much closer than usual to Bolkanes' big fire; Krispos had a mug of hot spiced wine close at hand. He smiled gratefully when one of the barmaids refilled it. Iakovitzes said. "It'll serve Gumush right. Nothing I enjoy more than a thief having to pay for his own thievery."

"Won't he just raise the price later on to make up for it?" Krispos asked. "The legitimate price, I mean."

"Probably, probably," Iakovitzes admitted. "But what do I care? I don't much fancy amber. And no matter how hard he squeezes, the world doesn't hold enough gold for him to buy his way out of embarrassment.'' Contemplating someone else's discomfiture would put Iakovitzes in a good mood if anything would.

A couple of nights later, Tanilis proved coldly furious that the amber had been seized. ''I made the arrangements for it myself with Gumush,'' she said. ''Four parts in ten off the going rate here, which still allowed him a profit, seeing as the tariff is five parts in ten. He already has half the money, too. Do you suppose he'll send it back when he ransoms his courier?'' Her bitter laugh told how likely that was.

''But . . .'' Krispos scratched his head. ''The Avtokrator needs the money from the tariffs, to pay for soldiers and furs and roads and—''

''And courtesans and fine wines and fripperies,'' Tanilis finished for him; she sounded as scornful of Anthimos III as Pyrrhos had. ''But even if it were only as you say, I need money, too, for the good of my own estates. Why should I pay twice as much for amber as I need to for the sake of a handful of rich men in Videssos the city who do nothing for me?''

''Don't they?'' Krispos asked. ''Seems to me I wouldn't have come here with my master if the men in the city weren't worried about the border with Khatrish. Or are you such a queen here that your peasants would have fought off the nomad horsemen on their own?'' He recalled the Kubratoi descending on his vanished boyhood village as if it had happened only the day before.

Tanilis frowned. ''No, I am no queen, so what you say has some truth. But the Avtokrator and Sevastokrator chose peace with Khatrish for their own reasons, not mine.''

Remembering Petronas' ambitions against Makuran, Krispos knew she was right. But he said, ''It works out the same for you either way, doesn't it? If it does, you ought to be willing to pay for it.'' He and his fellow villagers had been willing to pay anything within reason to prevent another invasion from Kubrat. Only the Empire's demands reaching beyond reason had detached him from the land, and the rest of the villagers were there still.

''You speak well, and to the point,'' Tanilis said. ''I must confess, my loyalty is to my lands first, and to the Empire of Videssos only after that. What I say is true of most nobles, I think, almost all those away from Videssos the city. To us, the Empire seems more often to check our strength than to protect it, and so we evade demands from the capital as best we can.''

The more Krispos talked with Tanilis, the more complex his picture of the world grew. Back in his village, he'd thought of nobles as agents of the Empire and thanked Phos that the free-holders among whom he'd lived owed service to no lord. Yet Tanilis seemed no ally to the will of Videssos the city, but rather a rival. But she was no great friend of the peasants, either; she simply wanted to control them herself in place of the central government. Krispos tried to imagine how things looked from Petronas' perspective. Maybe one day he'd ask the Sevastokra-tor—after all, he'd met him. He laughed a little, amused at his own presumption.

"What do you find funny?" Tanilis asked.

Krispos' cheeks grew warm. Sometimes when he was with Tanilis, he felt he was a scroll she could unroll and read as she wished. Annoyed at himself for being so open, and sure he could not lie successfully, he explained.

She took him seriously. She always did; he had to give her that. Though he was certain he often seemed very young and raw to her, she went out of her way not to mock his enthusiasms, even if she let him see she did not share many of them. Even more than the sweet lure of her body, the respect she gave him made him want to spend time with her, in bed and out of it. He wondered if this was how love began.

The thought so startled him that he missed her reply. She saw that, too, and repeated herself: "If Petronas would tell you, I daresay you'd learn a great deal. A regent who can keep the reins of power even after his ward comes of age—and in such a way that the ward does not hate him—is a man to be reckoned with."

"I suppose so." Krispos knew he sounded abstracted and hoped Tanilis would not figure out why. Loving her could only complicate his life, the more so as he knew she did not love him.

Slow as the flow of syrup on ice, news dripped into Opsikion through the winter. Krispos heard of the death of khagan Omur-tag weeks after it happened; a son named Malomir ascended to the rule of Kubrat. In Thatagush, north and east of Khatrish, a band of Haloga raiders under a chief called Harvas Black-Robe sacked a whole string of towns and smashed the army that tried to drive them away. Some nobles promptly joined forces with the Halogai against their khagan. The King of Kings of Makuran sent a peace embassy to Videssos the city. Petronas sent it back.

"By the lord with the great and good mind, I gave Petronas what he wanted here," Iakovitzes said when that report reached him. "Now let's see what he does with it." His chuckle had a gloating tone to it. "Not as much as he wants, I'll wager."

"No?" Krispos helped his master out of a chair. The noble could walk with a stick these days, but he still limped badly; his left calf was only half as big around as his right. Krispos went on carefully, "The Sevastokrator strikes me as a man who generally gets what he wants."

"Oh, aye, he is. Here, I'm all right now. Thanks." Iakovitzes hissed as he put weight on his healing leg. Ordanes had given him a set of exercises to strengthen it. He swore through clenched teeth every time he began them, but never missed a day.

Now he took a couple of steps toward the stairway that led up to his room before he continued. "But what Petronas wants is to overthrow Makuran, and that won't happen. Stavrakios the Great couldn't do it, not when the Empire of Videssos ran all the way up to the border of the Haloga country. I suppose the Makurani Kings of Kings dream of worshiping their Four Prophets in the High Temple in Videssos the city, and that won't happen, either. If Petronas can bite off a chunk of Vaspurakan, he'll have done something worthwhile, at any rate. We can use the metals there and the men, even if they are heretics."

A guardsman coming off duty threw open the door to Bolkanes' taproom. Though he slammed it again right away, Krispos and Iakovitzes both shivered at the icy blast he let in. He stood in the front hall brushing snow off his clothes and out of his beard.

"Beastly weather," Iakovitzes said. "I could ride now, but what's the point? The odds are too good I'd end up a block of ice somewhere halfway between here and the city, and that would be a piteous waste. Come to think of it, you'd freeze, too."

"Thank you for thinking of me," Krispos said mildly.

Iakovitzes cocked an eyebrow. "You're getting better at that innocent-sounding comeback, aren't you? Do you practice in front of a mirror?"

"Er—no." Krispos knew his fencing with Tanilis helped sharpen both his wits and his wit. He hadn't realized anyone else would notice.

"Maybe it's the time you spend knocking around with Mavros,'' Iakovitzes said. Krispos blinked; his master's guess was good enough to startle him. Iakovitzes went on, "He has a noble's air to him, even if he is young.''

"I hadn't really noticed,'' Krispos said. "I suppose he gets it from his mother.''

"Maybe.'' As he did whenever a woman was mentioned, Iakovitzes sounded indifferent. He reached the stairway. "Give me your hand, will you, for the way up?'' Krispos complied. Chill or no, Iakovitzes was sweating by the time he got to the top of the stairs; his leg still did not take kindly to such work.

Krispos went through the usual small wrestling match he needed to get the noble to let go. "After a year with me, excellent sir, don't you believe I'm not interested?'' he asked.

"Oh, I believe it,'' Iakovitzes said. "I just don't take it seriously.'' Having had, if not Krispos, then at least the last word, he hobbled down the hall toward his room.

Rain pattered on the shutters of the bedroom window. "The second storm in a row with no snow in it,'' Tanilis said. "No sleet in this one either, or none to speak of. Winter is finally losing its grip.''

"So it is.'' Krispos kept his voice noncommittal. The imminent return of good weather meant too many different things now for him to be sure how he felt about it.

Tanilis sat up in bed and ran a hand through her hair. The gesture, artfully artless, made her bare breasts rise for Krispos' admiration. At the same time, though, she said, "When the rain finally stops, I will be going back to my villa. I don't think you would be wise to visit me there.''

Krispos had known she would tell him that, sooner or later. He'd thought he was ready. Actually hearing the words, though, was like taking a blow in the belly—no matter how braced he was, they still hurt. "So it's over,'' he said dully.

"This part of it,'' Tanilis agreed.

Again, he'd thought he could accept that, thought he could depart with Iakovitzes for Videssos the city without a backward glance. Had his master not broken his leg, that might well have been true. But wintering in Opsikion, passing so much more time with Tanilis, made it harder than he'd expected. All his carefully cultivated sangfroid deserted him. He clutched her to him. "I don't want to leave you!'' He groaned.

She yielded to his embrace, but her voice stayed detached,

logical. "What then? Would you turn aside from what I and others have seen for you, would you abandon this—" She touched the goldpiece Omurtag had given him. "—to stay in Opsikion? And if you would, would I look on you with anything but scorn because of it?"

"But I love you!" Krispos said.

Down deep, he'd always been sure telling her that would be a mistake. His instinct proved sound. She answered, "If you stayed here because of that, I surely could never love you. I am already fully myself, while you are still discovering what you can be. Nor in the long run would you be happy in Opsikion, for what would you be here? My plaything, maybe, granted a small respect reflected from the larger one I have earned, but laughed at behind people's hands. Is that the most you want for yourself, Krispos?"

"Your plaything?" That made him angry enough not to listen to the rest of what she said. He ran a rough hand along the supple curves of her body, ending at the edge of the neatly trimmed hair that covered her secret place. "Is that all this has meant? Is that all I've been to you?"

"You know better, or you should," Tanilis said calmly. "How could I deny you've pleased me? I would not want to deny it. But it is not enough. You deserve to be more than a bedwarmer, however fine a bedwarmer you are. And if you stayed with me, you would not find it easy to be anything else. Not only do I have far more experience and vastly greater wealth than you, I do not care to yield to anyone the power I've earned by my own efforts over the years. So what would that leave you?"

"I don't care," Krispos said. Though he sounded full of fierce conviction, even he knew that was not true.

So, obviously, did Tanilis. "Do you not? Very well, then, let us suppose you stay here and that you and I are wed, perhaps on the next feast day of the holy Abdaas. Come the morning after, what do you propose to say to your new stepson, Mavros?"

"My—" Krispos gulped. He had no trouble imagining Mavros his brother. But his stepson? He could not even make himself say the word. He started to laugh, instead, and poked Tanilis in the ribs. She was not usually ticklish, but he caught her by surprise. She yipped and wiggled away.

"Mavros my—" He tried again, but only ended up laughing harder. "Oh, a pestilence, Tanilis, you've made your point."

"Good. There's always hope for anyone who can see plain sense, even if I did have to bludgeon you to open your eyes." She turned her head.

"What is it?" Krispos asked.

"I was just listening. I don't think the rain will let up for a while yet." Now her hand wandered, came to rest. She smiled a catlike smile. "By the feel of things, neither will you. Shall we make the most of the time we have left?"

He did not answer, not with words, but he did not disagree.

"Let me give you a hand, excellent sir," Krispos said as a pair of stable boys led out his master's horse, his own, and their pack animals.

"Nonsense," Iakovitzes told him. "If I can't mount for myself, I surely won't be able to ride back to the city. And if I can't do that, I'm faced with two equally unpalatable alternatives: take up residence here, or throw myself off a promontory into the sea. On the whole, I believe I'd prefer throwing myself into the sea. That way I'd never have to find out what's become of my house while I've been gone." The noble gave a shudder of exquisite dread.

"When you wrote you'd been hurt, the Sevastokrator pledged to look after your affairs."

"So he did," Iakovitzes said with a skeptical grunt. "The only affairs Petronas cares anything about, though, are his own." He scowled at the boy who held his horse. "Back away, there. If I can't manage, high time I found out."

The stable boy retreated. Iakovitzes set his left foot in the stirrup, swung up and onto the horse's back. He winced as the newly healed leg took all his weight for a moment, but then he was mounted and grinning in triumph. He'd boarded the horse before, every day for the past week, but each time seemed a new adventure, both to him and to everyone watching.

"Now where's that Mavros?" he said. "I'm still not what you'd call comfortable up here. Anyone who thinks I'll waste time waiting that I could use riding will end up disappointed, I promise you that."

Krispos did not think Iakovitzes was speaking to him in particular; he sounded more as if he were warning the world at large. Krispos checked one last time to make sure all their gear was properly stowed on the packhorses' backs, then climbed onto his own beast.

Bolkanes came to bid his longtime guests farewell. He bowed to Iakovitzes. "A pleasure to serve you, eminent sir."

"I should hope so. I've made your fortune," Iakovitzes answered, gracious to the end.

As the innkeeper beat a hasty retreat, Mavros rode up on a big bay gelding. He looked very young and jaunty, with two pheasant plumes sticking up from his broad-brimmed hat and his right hand on the hilt of his sword. He waved to Krispos and dipped his head in Iakovitzes' direction. "You look like you were all set to take off without me."

"I was," Iakovitzes snapped.

If he thought to intimidate the youth, he failed. "Well, no need for that now, seeing as I'm here," Mavros said easily. He turned to Krispos. "My mother said to be sure to tell you goodbye from her. Now I've done it." *One more chore finished,* his attitude seemed to say.

"Ah. That's kind of her," Krispos said. Although he hadn't seen or heard from Tanilis in more than a month, she was in his thoughts every day, the memory of her as liable to sudden twinges as was Iakovitzes' leg. A limp in the heart, though, did not show on the outside.

"If you two are done nattering like washerwomen, shall we be off?" Iakovitzes said. Without waiting for an answer, he used knees and reins to urge his horse forward. Krispos and Mavros rode after him.

Opsikion's gate guards still had not learned to take any special notice of Iakovitzes, who, after all, had not come near the edge of the city since the summer before. But the feisty noble had no cause for complaint about the treatment he was afforded. Being with Mavros drew him such a flurry of salutes and guardsmen springing to attention that he said, not altogether in jest, "Anthimos should come here, to see what respect is."

"Oh, I expect he gets treated about as well in his hometown," Mavros said. Iakovitzes had to look at him sharply to catch the twinkle in his eye. The noble allowed himself a wintry chuckle, the most he usually gave wit not his own.

That chuckle, Krispos thought, was the only thing wintry about the day. It was mild and fair. New bright green covered the ground to either side of the road. Bees buzzed among fresh-sprouted flowers. The sweet, moist air was full of the songs of birds just returned from their winter stay in warmer climes.

Though the road climbed swiftly into the mountains, this near

Opsikion it remained wide and easy to travel, if not always straight. Krispos was startled when, with the sun still nearer noon than its setting, Iakovitzes reined in and said, "That's enough. We'll camp here till morning." But when he watched his master dismount, he hardly needed to hear the noble go on, "My thighs are as raw as a dockside whore's the night after the imperial fleet rows into port."

"No wonder, excellent sir," Krispos said. "Flat on your back as you were for so long, you've lost your hardening."

"I don't know about that," Mavros said. "I've had some lovely hardenings flat on my back."

Again, Iakovitzes' basilisk glare failed to wilt him. The noble finally grunted and hobbled off into the bushes, unbuttoning his fly as he went. Watching that slow, spraddling gait, Krispos whistled softly. "He is saddle-sore, isn't he? I guess he thought it couldn't happen to him."

"Aye, looks like he'll have to get used to it all over again. He won't be back from watering the grass right away, either." Mavros lowered his voice as he reached into a saddlebag. "Which means now is as good a time as any to pass this on to you from my mother. A parting gift, you might say. She told me not to give it to you when anyone else could see."

Krispos reached out to take the small wooden box Mavros held. He wondered what sort of last present Tanilis had for him and wondered even more, briefly alarmed, how much she'd told Mavros about what had passed between the two of them. Mavros as stepson, indeed, Krispos thought—she'd known how to cool him down, sure enough. *Maybe, though,* he said to himself, *it's like one of the romances minstrels sing, and she does love me but can't admit it except by giving me this token once I'm safely gone.*

The second the box was in his hand, its weight told him Tanilis' gift was the more pragmatic one she'd promised. "Gold?" he said.

"A pound and a half," Mavros agreed. "If you're going to be—what you're going to be—this will help. Money begets money, my mother says. And this will grow all the better since no one knows you have it."

A pound and a half of gold—the box fit easily in the palm of Krispos' hand. For Tanilis, it was not enough money to be missed. Krispos knew that if he were to desert his master and Mavros and make his way back to his village, he would be far and away the richest man there. He could go home as something close to a hero: the lad who'd made good in the big city.

But his village, he realized after a moment, was not home any more, not really. He could no more go back now than he could have stayed in Opsikion. For better or worse, he was caught up in the faster life of Videssos the city. After a taste of it, nothing less could satisfy him.

Rustlings from the bushes announced Iakovitzes' return. Krispos hastily stowed away the box of coins. With a hundred and eight goldpieces in his hands, he thought, he did not need to keep working for Iakovitzes anymore, either. But if he stayed on, he wouldn't have to start spending them. He didn't need to decide anything about that right away, not when he was only a short day's journey out of Opsikion.

"I may live," Iakovitzes said. He grimaced as he sat down on the ground and started pulling off his boots. "Eventually, I may even want to. What have we for supper?"

"About what you'd expect," Krispos answered. "Twice-baked bread, sausage, hard cheese, and onions. We have a couple of wineskins, but it's a ways to the next town, so we ought to go easy if we want to make it last. I hear a stream off that way—we'll have plenty of water to wash things down."

"Water. Twice-baked bread." The petulant set of Iakovitzes' mouth showed what he thought of that. "The next time Petronas wants me to go traveling for him, I'll ask if I can bring a chef along. He does, when he's out on campaign."

"There ought to be crawfish in the stream, and trout, too," Mavros said. "I have a couple of hooks. Shall I go see what I can come up with?"

"I'll start a fire," Krispos said. "Roast fish, crawfish baked in clay . . ." He glanced over to see how Iakovitzes liked the idea.

"Could be worse, I suppose," the noble said grudgingly. "See if you can find some early marjoram, too, why don't you, Mavros? It would add to the flavor."

"I'll do my best." Mavros rummaged through his gear till he found the hooks and some light line. "A chunk of sausage should be bait enough for the fish, but what do you suppose I should use to lure out the marjoram?"

Iakovitzes threw a boot at him.

One day when he was close to halfway back to the city, Krispos came across the little jet ornament he'd brought for Sirikia.

He stared at it; the seamstress hadn't crossed his mind in months. He hoped she'd found someone new. After Tanilis, going back to her would be like leaving Videssos for his farming village: possible, but not worth thinking about.

He was no monk on the journey westward; abstinence was not in his nature. But he had finally learned not to imagine himself in love each time his lust needed slaking. Mavros still sighed whenever he left behind another barmaid or dyeshop girl.

The travelers lay over in a town called Develtos to rest their horses. Iakovitzes surveyed the place with a jaundiced eye. His one-sentence verdict summed it up perfectly. "By the good god, it makes Opsikion look like a metropolis."

Mavros spluttered at that, but Krispos knew what his master meant. Develtos boasted a stout wall and had little else about which to boast. Seeing how small and gloomy a town the works protected, Krispos wondered why anyone had bothered to build them in the first place.

"The road does need strongpoints every so often," Iakovitzes told him when he said that aloud. The noble took another long look, sighed in despair. "But we'll have to make our own fun, that's for certain. Speaking of which . . ." His gaze traveled back to Krispos.

It was the groom's turn to sigh. Iakovitzes had not bothered him much since Mavros joined them. So far as Krispos knew, he hadn't made advances at Mavros, either. Had Krispos not seen a good-looking young stablehand a couple of towns back wearing one of the noble's rings the morning they set out, he would have wondered if Iakovitzes was fully healed. He'd enjoyed the peace while it lasted.

The inn Iakovitzes picked proved livelier than the rest of Develtos, whose people seemed as dour as the grim gray stone from which their wall and buildings were made. That was not the innkeeper's fault; he was as somber as any of his townsfolk. But a group of close to a dozen mother-of-pearl merchants from the eastern island of Kalavria made the place jolly in spite of its proprietor. Krispos had even met one or two of them back at Opsikion; they'd landed there before heading inland.

"Why didn't you just sail straight on to Videssos the city?" he asked one of the traders over a mug of wine.

"Bring mother-of-pearl to the city?" exclaimed the Kalavrian, a hook-nosed fellow named Stasios. "I might as well fetch milk to a cow. Videssos has more than it needs already. Here away from the sea, though, the stuff is rare and wonderful, and we get good prices."

"You know your business best," Krispos said. From the way the merchants were spending money, they'd done well so far.

The taproom grew gloomy as evening came on. The innkeeper waited longer than Krispos liked before lighting candles; likely he'd hoped his guests would go to bed when it got dark and save him the expense. But the Kalavrians were in no mood for sleep. They sang and drank and swapped stories with Krispos and his companions.

After a while, one of the traders took out a pair of dice. The tiny rattle they gave as he rolled them on the table to test his luck made Iakovitzes scramble to his feet. "I'm going upstairs," he told Krispos and Mavros, "and if the two of you have any sense you'll come with me. You start gambling with Kalavrians and you'll still be at it when the sun comes up again."

The merchants laughed. "So they know our reputation even in the city?" Stasios said. "I'd have bet they did."

"I know you would," Iakovitzes said. "You'd bloody well bet on anything. That's why I'm heading off to bed, to keep from having to stay up with you."

Mavros hesitated, then went upstairs with him. Krispos decided to stay and play. The stakes, he saw with some relief, were pieces of silver, not gold. "We're all friends," one of the traders said, noticing his glance at the money they'd got out. "There'd be no joy in breaking a man, especially since he'd have to stay with us till fall even so."

"Good enough," Krispos answered. Before long, the man to his left threw double sixes and lost the dice. They came to him. He rattled them in his hand, then sent them spinning across the tabletop. Twin ones stared up at the gamblers. "Phos' little suns!" Krispos said happily. He collected all the bets.

"Your first throw!" a Kalavrian said. "With luck like that, no wonder you wanted to stay down here. You knew you'd clean us out."

"They're your dice," Krispos retorted. "For all I knew, you'd loaded them."

"No, that'd be Rhangavve," Stasios said. "He's not with us this year—somebody back home on the island caught him at it and broke his arm for him. He's richer than any of us, though, the cheating bastard."

Krispos won a little, lost a little, won a little more. Eventually he found himself yawning and not being able to stop. He got up from the table. "That's enough for me," he said. "I want to be able to ride tomorrow without falling off my horse."

A couple of Kalavrians waved as he headed for the stairs. More had eyes only for the spinning bone cubes. Behind the bar, the innkeeper sat dozing. He jerked awake every so often. "Aren't you gents tired, too?" he asked plaintively, seeing Krispos leave. The traders laughed at him.

Krispos had just got to the head of the stairs when he saw someone quietly emerging from Iakovitzes' room. His hand dropped to the hilt of his sword. Then he relaxed. Though only a couple of tiny lamps lit the hall, he recognized Mavros. The youth leaned back into the doorway for a moment, murmured something Krispos could not hear, and went to his own room. It was farther down the hall than Iakovitzes', so he turned his back on Krispos and did not notice him.

Krispos frowned as he opened his door, then barred it behind him. He tried to tell himself what he'd seen didn't mean what he thought it did. He could not make himself believe it. He knew what a good-night kiss looked like, no matter who was giving it.

He asked himself what difference it made. Living in Iakovitzes' household had taught him that the grooms who let the noble take them to bed were not much different from the ones who declined, save in their choice of pleasures. If Mavros enjoyed what Iakovitzes offered, it was his business and none of Krispos'. It did not make him any less cheerful, clever, or enthusiastic.

That thought consoled Krispos long enough to let him undress and get into bed. Then he realized it was his business after all. Tanilis had charged him to treat Mavros as a younger brother. No matter how his perspective had changed, he knew it would not be easy if his younger brother acted as Mavros had.

He sighed. Here was something new and unwelcome to worry about. He had no idea what to say to Mavros or what to do if, as seemed likely, Mavros answered, "So what?" But he found he could not sleep until he promised himself he would say something.

Even getting the chance did not prove easy. Some of the Kalavrians were still gambling when he and Mavros came down for breakfast the next morning, and this was one conversation he did not want overheard.

For that matter, some of the Kalavrians were still gambling when Iakovitzes came down for breakfast quite a bit later. He rolled his eyes. "You'd bet on whether Phos or Skotos will triumph at the end of time," he said in disgust.

Stasios and a couple of others looked up from the dice. "You know, we just might," he said. Soon the bleary-eyed merchants started arguing theology as they played.

"Congratulations," Mavros told Iakovitzes.

"By the ice, what for?" Iakovitzes was listening to the Kalavrians as if he could not believe his ears.

With a sly grin, Mavros answered, "How many people can boast they've invented a new heresy before their morning porridge?"

Krispos swallowed wrong. Mavros pounded him on the back. Iakovitzes just scowled. Through the rest of the day, he remained as sour toward Mavros as he was with anyone else. Krispos began to wonder if he'd made a mistake. But no, he knew what he'd seen.

As the last of the all-night gamblers among the Kalavrians went upstairs, the traders who had gone to bed began drifting down once more. The game never stopped. Krispos fretted. Having to wait only made him more nervous about what he'd say to Mavros.

After checking the horses the next morning, Iakovitzes decided to ride on. "Another day wouldn't hurt the beasts, I suppose, but another day stuck in Develtos with those gambling maniacs would do me in," he said.

He was too good a horseman to push the pace with tired animals and rested them frequently. When he went off to answer nature's call at one of those stops, Krispos found himself with the opportunity he'd dreaded. "Mavros," he said quietly.

"What is it?" Mavros turned toward him. When he saw the expression on Krispos' face, his own grew more serious. "What is it?" he repeated in a different tone of voice.

Now that he was at the point, Krispos' carefully crafted speeches deserted him. "Did you end up in bed with Iakovitzes the other night?" he blurted.

"What if I did? Are you jealous?" Mavros looked at Krispos again. "No, you're not. What then? Why should you care?"

"Because I was bid to be your brother, remember? I never

had a brother before, only sisters, so I don't quite know how to do that. But I do know I wouldn't want any kin of mine sleeping with someone just to get in his good graces.''

If Mavros knew about him and Tanilis, Krispos realized as soon as the words were out of his mouth, he'd throw that right back at him, no matter how unfairly. But Mavros must not have. He said, "Why do I need to get in Iakovitzes' good graces? Aye, he lives at the capital, but I could buy and sell him. If he gives me too bad a time, I'd do it, too, and he knows it.''

Krispos started to answer, abruptly stopped. He'd judged Mavros' situation by his own, and only now did he see the two were not the same. Unlike him, Mavros had a perfectly satisfactory life to return to if the city did not suit him. With such independent means, though, why had he yielded to Iakovitzes? That was a question Krispos could ask, and did.

"To find out what it was like, why else?" Mavros said. "I've had plenty of girls, but I'd never tried it the other way round. From the way Iakovitzes talked it up, I thought I was missing something special.''

"Oh.'' The straightforward hedonism in the reply reminded Krispos of Tanilis. He needed a moment to get up the nerve to ask, "And what did you think?''

Mavros shrugged. "It was interesting to do once, but I wouldn't want to make a habit of it. As far as I'm concerned, girls are more fun.''

"Oh,'' Krispos said again. He felt foolish. "I guess I should have kept my big mouth shut.''

"Probably you should have.'' But Mavros seemed to reconsider. "No, I take that back. If we are to be brothers, then you have the right to speak to me when something troubles you— and the other way round, too, I suppose.''

"That's only fair,'' Krispos agreed. "This whole business takes some getting used to.''

"Things my mother arranges usually do,'' Mavros said cheerfully, "but they have a way of working out right in the end. And if this particular arrangement works out right in the end—'' He broke off. They were altogether alone except for Iakovitzes off somewhere in the bushes, but he was still wary of speaking about what Tanilis had seen. Krispos thought the better of him for it. He was a good deal more than wary himself.

"What were you two gossiping about?'' Iakovitzes asked when he came back a couple of minutes later.

"You, of course," Krispos said in his best innocent voice.

"A worthy topic indeed." Iakovitzes was noticeably smoother mounting than he had been back at Opsikion. He used his legs and the reins to get his horse moving once more. Krispos and Mavros followed him toward the city.

VII

"Hurry up, Krispos! Aren't you ready yet?" Iakovitzes said. "We don't want to be late, not to this affair."

"No, excellent sir," Krispos said. He had been ready for the best part of an hour. His master was the one who kept taking off one robe and putting on another, agonizing over how big a hoop to wear in his left ear and whether it should be gold or silver, bedeviling his servants about which scent to douse himself with. This once, Krispos did not blame Iakovitzes for fussiness. The Sevastokrator Petronas was giving the evening's feast.

"Come on, then," Iakovitzes said now. A moment later, almost as an afterthought, he added, "You look quite well tonight. I don't think I've seen that robe before."

"Thank you, excellent sir. No, I don't think you've seen it, either. I just bought it a couple of weeks ago."

The garment in question was dark blue, and of fine soft wool. Its sober hue and plain cut were suited to a man older and of higher station than Krispos. He'd used a few of Tanilis' goldpieces on clothes of that sort. One of these days, he might need to be taken seriously. Not looking like a groom could only help.

He rode half a pace behind Iakovitzes and to his master's left. Iakovitzes swore whenever cross traffic made them slow and grew livid to see how crowded the plaza of Palamas was. "Out of the way there, you blundering oaf!" he screamed when he got stuck behind a small man leading a large mule. "I have an appointment with the Sevastokrator."

160

Cheeky as most of the folk who called Videssos the city home, the fellow retorted, "I don't care if you've got an appointment with Phos, pal. I'm in front of you and that's how I like it."

After more curses, Iakovitzes and Krispos managed to swing around the muleteer. By then they were near the western edge of the plaza of Palamas, past the great amphitheater, past the red granite obelisk of the Milestone from which all distances in the Empire were reckoned.

"Here, you see, excellent sir, we're all right," Krispos said soothingly as traffic thinned out.

"I suppose so." Iakovitzes did not sound convinced, but Krispos knew he was grumbling only because he always grumbled. The western edge of the plaza bordered on the imperial palaces, and no one entered the palace district without business there. Soon Iakovitzes urged his horse up into a trot, and then into a canter.

"Where are we going?" Krispos asked, keeping pace.

"The Hall of the Nineteen Couches."

"The nineteen what?" Krispos wasn't sure he'd heard correctly.

"Couches," Iakovitzes repeated.

"Why do they call it that?"

"Because up until maybe a hundred years ago, people at fancy feasts ate while they reclined instead of sitting in chairs as we do now. Don't ask me why they did that, because I couldn't tell you—to make it easier for them to spill things on their robes, I suppose. Anyway, there haven't been any couches in there for a long time, but names have a way of sticking."

They swung round a decorative stand of willows. Krispos saw scores of torches blazing in front of a large square building, and people bustling around and going inside. "Is that it?"

"That's it." Iakovitzes gauged the number of horses and sedan chairs off to one side of the hall. "We're all right—not too early, but not late, either."

Grooms in matched silken finery led away his mount and Krispos'. Krispos followed his master up the low, broad stairs to the Hall of the Nineteen Couches. "Pretty stone," Krispos remarked as he got close enough to make out detail in the torchlight.

"Do you really think so?" Iakovitzes said. "The green veining in the white marble always reminds me of one of those crumbly cheeses that smell bad.''

"I hadn't thought of that,'' Krispos said, truthfully enough. He had to admit the comparison was apt. Even so, he would not have made it himself. Iakovitzes' jaundiced outlook made him take some strange views of the world.

A servitor in raiment even more splendid than the grooms' bowed low as Iakovitzes came to the entrance, then turned and loudly announced, "The excellent Iakovitzes!''

Thus introduced, Iakovitzes swaggered into the reception hall, as well as he could swagger with a limp that was still pronounced. Krispos, who was not nearly important enough to be worth introducing, followed his master inside.

"Iakovitzes!'' Petronas hurried up to clasp the noble's hand. "That was a fine piece of work you did for me in Opsikion. You have my gratitude.'' The Sevastokrator made no effort to keep his voice down. Heads turned to see whom he singled out for such public praise.

"Thank you, your Highness,'' Iakovitzes said, visibly preening.

"As I said, you're the one who has earned my thanks. Well done.'' Petronas started to walk away, stopped. "Krispos, isn't it?''

"Yes, your Imperial Highness,'' Krispos said, surprised and impressed the Sevastokrator remembered his name after one brief meeting almost a year before.

"Thought so.'' Petronas also seemed pleased with himself. He turned back to Iakovitzes. "Didn't you bring another lad with you from Opsikion, too? Mavros, was that the name? Tanilis' son, I mean.''

Iakovitzes nodded. "As a matter of fact, I did.''

"Thought so,'' Petronas repeated. "Bring him along one of these times when we're at a function together, if you could. I'd like to meet him. Besides which—'' The Sevastokrator's smile was cynical, ''—his mother's rich enough that I don't want to get her annoyed with me, and chatting him up can only help me with her.''

Petronas went off to greet other guests. Iakovitzes' gaze followed him. "He doesn't miss much,'' the noble mused, more to himself than to Krispos. "I wonder which of my people told him about Mavros.'' Whoever it was, Krispos did not envy him if his master found him out.

Still muttering to himself, Iakovitzes headed for the wine. He plucked a silver goblet from the bed of hoarded snow in which it rested, drained it and reached for another. Krispos took a goblet, too. He sipped from it as he walked over to a table piled high with appetizers. A couple of slices of boiled eggplant and some pickled anchovies took the edge off his appetite. He was careful not to eat too much; he wanted to be able to do justice to the supper that lay ahead.

"Your moderation does you credit, young man," someone said from behind him when he left the hors d'oeuvres after only a brief stay.

"Your pardon?" Krispos turned, swiftly added, "Holy sir. Most holy sir," he amended; the priest—or rather prelate—who'd spoken to him wore shimmering cloth-of-gold with Phos' sun picked out in blue silk on his left breast.

"Nothing, really," the ecclesiastic said. His sharp, foxy features reminded Krispos of Petronas', though they were less stern and heavy than the Sevastokrator's. He went on, "It's just that at an event like this, where gluttony is the rule, seeing anyone eschew it is a cause for wonderment and celebration."

Hoping he'd guessed right about what "eschew" meant, Krispos answered, "All I planned was to be a glutton a little later." He explained why he'd gone easy on the appetizers.

"Oh, dear." The prelate threw back his head and laughed. "Well, young sir, I appreciate your candor. That, believe me, is even rarer at these events than moderation. I don't believe I've seen you before?" He paused expectantly.

"My name is Krispos, most holy sir. I'm one of Iakovitzes' grooms."

"Pleased to meet you, Krispos. Since I see my blue boots haven't given me away, let me introduce myself, as well: I'm called Gnatios."

Just as only the Avtokrator wore all-red boots, only one priest had the privilege of wearing all-blue ones. Krispos realized with a start that he'd been making small talk with the ecumenical patriarch of the Empire of Videssos. "M-most holy sir," he stammered, bowing. Even as he bent his head, though, he felt a rush of pride—if only the villagers could see him now!

"No formality needed, not when I'm here to enjoy the good food, too," Gnatios said with an easy smile. Then those foxy features suddenly grew very sharp indeed. "Krispos? I've heard your name before after all, I think. Something to do with the abbot Pyrrhos, wasn't it?''

"The abbot was kind enough to find me my place with Iakovitzes, yes, most holy sir," Krispos said.

"That's all?" Gnatios persisted.

"What else could there be?" Krispos knew perfectly well what else; if Gnatios didn't, he was not about to reveal it for him.

"Who knows what else?" The patriarch's chuckle was thin. "Where Pyrrhos is involved, any sort of superstitious excess becomes not only possible but credible. Well, never mind, young man. Just because something is credible, that doesn't necessarily make it true. Not necessarily. A pleasant evening to you."

Gnatios' shaven skull gleamed in the torchlight like one of the gilded domes atop Phos' temple as he went on his way. Krispos took the rest of the wine in his cup at a gulp, then went over to the great basin of snow for another one. He was sweating in spite of the wine's chill. The patriarch, by the nature of his office, was the Avtokrator's man. Had he boasted to Gnatios instead of sensibly keeping his mouth shut . . . He wondered if he would even have got back to Iakovitzes' house safe and sound.

Little by little, the wine helped calm Krispos. Gnatios didn't seem to have taken seriously whatever tales he'd heard. Then a servant appeared at Krispos' elbow. "Are you Iakovitzes' groom?" he asked.

Krispos' heart jumped into his mouth. "Yes," he answered, readying himself to knock the man down and flee.

"Could you join your master, please?" the fellow said. "We'll be seating folk for dinner soon, and the two of you will be together."

"Oh. Of course." Krispos felt like giggling with relief as he scanned the Hall of the Nineteen Couches for Iakovitzes. He wished the noble were taller; he was hard to spot. Even though he had trouble seeing Iakovitzes, he soon heard him arguing with someone or other. He made his way over to him.

Servants carried away the tables of appetizers. Others brought out dining tables and chairs. Despite guests getting in their way, they moved with practiced efficiency. Faster than Krispos would have thought possible, the hall was ready and the servants began guiding diners to their seats.

"This way, excellent sir, if you please," a servitor murmured to Iakovitzes. He had to repeat himself several times; Iakovitzes was driving home a rhetorical point by jabbing a forefinger into the chest of a man who had been rash enough to disagree with him. The noble finally let himself listen. He and Krispos followed the servant, who said, "You have the honor of sitting at the Sevastokrator's table."

To Krispos, that said how much Petronas thought of the job Iakovitzes had done at Opsikion. Iakovitzes merely grunted, "I've had it before." His eyebrows rose as he neared the head table. "And up till now, I've never had to share it with barbarians, either."

Four Kubratoi, looking outlandish indeed in their shaggy furs, were already at the table. They'd quickly emptied one pitcher of wine and were shouting for another. The servant said, "They are an embassy from the new khagan Malomir and have ambassadors' privileges."

"Bah," was Iakovitzes' reply to that. "The one in the middle there, the big bruiser, you mean to tell me he's an ambassador? He looks more like a hired killer." Krispos had already noticed the man Iakovitzes meant. With his scarred, sullen face, wide shoulders, and enormous hands, he certainly resembled no diplomat Krispos had seen or imagined.

The servant answered, "As a properly accredited member of the party from Kubrat, he cannot be excluded from functions to which his comrades are invited." He lowered his voice. "I will say, however, that his principal area of prowess does appear to be wrestling, not reason."

Iakovitzes' expression was eloquent, but a second glance at the enormous Kubrati made him keep to himself whatever remarks he thought of making.

The servant seated him and Krispos well away from the Kubratoi, only a couple of places from Petronas. Krispos hoped the arrival of food would help quiet Malomir's envoys. It did help, but not much—it made them talk with their mouths full. Trays came and went, bearing soup, prawns, partridges, and lamb. After a while Krispos lost track of the number of courses he'd eaten. He only knew he was replete.

When the last candied apricots were gone, Petronas rose and lifted his goblet. "To the health and long life of his Imperial Majesty the Avtokrator of the Videssians, Anthimos III!" he declared. Everyone drank the toast. Petronas stayed on his feet. "And to the efforts of that clever and accomplished diplomat, the excellent noble Iakovitzes.'' Everyone drank again, this time with a spattering of polite applause.

Flushed with pleasure at being toasted next after the Emperor, Iakovitzes stood up. ''To his Imperial Highness the Sevastokrator Petronas!''

Petronas bowed as the toast was drunk. He caught the eye of one of the Kubrati envoys. ''To the long and peaceful reign of the great khagan Malomir, and to your own continued success, Gleb.''

Gleb stood. He raised his goblet. ''I drink also to the health of your Avtokrator,'' he said, his Videssian slow but clear, even polished.

''Didn't think he had manners enough for that,'' Iakovitzes said to Krispos. From the murmurs of pleasure that filled the hall, a good many other people were similarly surprised.

Gleb did not sit down. ''Since his Imperial Highness the Sevastokrator Petronas has only now deigned to notice my lord the khagan Malomir and me—'' Suddenly the Hall of the Nineteen Couches grew still; Krispos wondered whether Iakovitzes' joy was worth the slight the Kubrati plainly felt, ''—I now propose a toast to remind him of the might of Kubrat. Thus I drink to the strength of my comrade here, the famous and ferocious Beshev, who has beaten every Videssian he has faced.''

Gleb drank. So did the other Kubratoi. Most of the imperials in the hall kept their goblets in front of them.

''He goes too far!'' Iakovitzes did not bother to speak softly. ''I know Kubratoi are conceited and boastful, but this surpasses all due measure. He—''

Krispos made hushing motions. The famous and ferocious Beshev was climbing to his feet. As he rose, Krispos took his measure. He was surely very strong, but how much quickness did he have? By the way he moved, not a great deal. Indeed, if he was as slow as he seemed, Krispos wondered how he had won all his matches.

Beshev held his goblet high. His Videssian was much more strongly accented than Gleb's, but still understandable. ''I drink to the spirit of the brave Stylianos, whose neck I broke in our fight, and to the spirits of the other Videssians I will slay in wrestlings yet to come.''

He drained the goblet. With a satisfied smirk, Gleb drank, too. Petronas stared at the men from Kubrat, stony-faced. Angry shouts rang through the hall. None of them, though, Krispos

noted, came from anywhere close to Beshev. Not even Iakovitzes felt like affronting the Kubrati to his face.

Krispos turned to his master. "Let me take him on!"

"Eh? What?" Iakovitzes frowned. As comprehension
dawned, he looked to Beshev, back to Krispos, and slowly shook
his head. "No, Krispos. Bravely offered, but no. That barbarian
may be a musclebound hulk, but he knows what he's about. I
don't care to lose you for no good purpose." He put his hand
on Krispos' arm.

Krispos shook it off. "You wouldn't lose me to no good purpose," he said, angry now at Iakovitzes as well as the arrogant
Kubrati. "And I know what I'm about, too. If you doubt it,
remember how I handled Barses and Meletios a year and a half
ago. I learned wrestling back in my village, from a veteran of
the imperial army."

Iakovitzes looked at Beshev again. "That barbarian is as big
as Barses and Meletios put together," he said, but now his tone
was doubtful. "Are you really sure you can beat him?"

"Of course I'm not sure, but I think I have a chance. Do you
want this banquet remembered for your sake, or just as the time
when the Kubratoi bragged and got away with it?"

"Hmm." Iakovitzes plucked at the waxed ends of his mustache as he thought. With abrupt decision, he got to his feet.
"All right, you'll get your chance. Come on—let's talk to Petronas."

The Sevastokrator turned around in his chair as Iakovitzes and
Krispos came up behind him. "What is it?" he growled; Gleb
and Beshev had taken the joy out of the evening for him.

"I have here, lord, a man who, if you call on him, would
wrestle with this famous—" Iakovitzes loaded the word with
scorn, "—Kubrati. For his boasting is a great disgrace to us
Videssians; it would grow even worse if he returned to Kubrat
unbeaten."

"That is true enough. The Kubratoi are quite full of false
pretensions as it is," Petronas said. He studied Krispos with an
officer's experienced eye. "Maybe, just maybe," he said to himself, and slowly rose. He waited for silence, then lifted his goblet above his head. "I drink to the courage of the bold Krispos,
who will show Beshev the folly of his insolence."

The silence held a moment longer, then suddenly the Hall of
the Nineteen Couches was full of shouts: "Krispos!" "Kris-

pos!'' ''Hurrah for Krispos!'' ''Kill the barbarian!'' ''Flatten him!'' ''Stomp him!'' ''Beat him to a pulp!'' ''Krispos!''

The sound of his name loud in a hundred throats tingled through Krispos' veins like wine. He felt strong enough to beat a dozen Kubratoi at the same time, let alone the one he was about to face. He sent a challenging stare toward Beshev.

The look the wrestler gave back was so cold and empty that it froze Krispos' excitement. To Beshev, he was just another body to break. Without a word, the Kubrati got to his feet and began taking off his clothes.

Krispos pulled his robe over his head and tossed it aside. He took off his thin undertunic, leaving himself in linen drawers and sandals. He heard a woman sigh. That made him smile as he unbuckled the sandals.

The smile faded when he glanced over at Beshev. He was taller than the Kubrati, but he saw his foe outweighed him. And none of Beshev's bulk was fat; by the look of his huge, hard muscles, he might have been carved from stone.

Petronas had been shouting orders while Krispos and Beshev stripped. Servants scurried to shove tables aside and clear an open space in the center of the Hall of the Nineteen Couches. The two wrestlers walked toward it. Krispos studied the way Beshev moved. He still did not seem quick. *He'd better not be,* Krispos thought, *or he'll break my neck just like Stylianos'.*

He went through his own private wrestling match to put that thought down. Fear could cost him the fight, sure as his foe's strength. He took several deep breaths and concentrated on the feel of the cool, slick marble under his feet.

Slick . . . He turned back to Petronas. ''Highness, could you have them strew some sand out there? I wouldn't want this affair decided on a slip.'' *Especially not if I make it,* he thought.

The Sevastokrator looked a question at Beshev, who nodded. At Petronas' command, four servants hurried away. Both wrestlers stood around and waited until the men returned, lugging two large tubs of sand. They dumped it out and spread it about with brooms.

When they were done, Krispos and Beshev took their places at opposite ends of the cleared space. Beshev's great hands opened and closed as he stared. Krispos folded his arms across his chest and stared back, doing his best to look contemptuous.

"Are you both ready?" Petronas asked loudly. He swung down his arm. "Wrestle!"

The two men slid toward one another, each crouched low with arms outstretched. Krispos feinted at Beshev's leg. The Kubrati knocked his hand aside. That first touch warned Krispos Beshev was as strong as he looked.

They circled, eyes flicking to feet, to hands, and back to eyes again. Beshev sprang forward. He knew what he was about; nothing gave away the move before he made it. All the same, Krispos ducked under his grasping hands and spun behind him. He grabbed Beshev by the waist and tried to throw him down.

Beshev, though, was too squat and heavy to be thrown. He seized Krispos' forearms, then flung himself backward. Krispos twisted so they landed side by side instead of with Beshev on top. They grappled, broke away from each other, scrambled to their feet, and grappled again.

Beshev had an uncanny ability to slip holds. Every time Krispos thought he was about to throw his foe, the Kubrati managed to break free. It was almost as if his skin were oiled, though it did not feel slick to Krispos. He shook his head, baffled and frustrated. Beshev seemed to have tricks old Idalkos had never heard of.

Fortunately, the hulking Kubrati also found Krispos difficult. They stood panting and glaring at each other after a passage where Beshev somehow escaped from a wristlock Krispos knew he'd set well and truly, and where a moment later only a desperate jerk of his head kept Beshev from gouging out an eye.

The brief rest let Krispos notice the din that filled the Hall of the Nineteen Couches. While he fought, the crowd's yells had simply washed over him. Now he heard Iakovitzes screaming for him to maim Beshev; heard Petronas' calls of encouragement; heard dozens of people he did not know, all crying out for him. The shouts helped restore his spirits and made him eager once more.

No one shouted for Beshev. Gleb and the other Kubratoi stood at the edge of the cleared space and watched their man wrestle, but they did not cheer him on. Gleb's face was a mask of concentration; his hands, which he held in front of his chest, twitched and wiggled as if with a life of their own.

Somewhere long ago Krispos had seen hands jerk like that. He had no time to grope for the memory—Beshev thundered down on him like an avalanche. The Kubrati needed no cheers to spur him on. Krispos dove to one side; Beshev snagged him by an ankle and hauled him back.

Beshev was slow. But once he got a grip, that mattered less. Krispos kicked him in the ribs with his free leg. Beshev only grunted. He did not let go. And when Krispos tried to lay hold of the Kubrati's arm, his hands slid off it.

Since Krispos could not tear free, he went with Beshev's hold and let his foe pull him close. He butted the Kubrati under the chin. Beshev's head snapped back. His grip slackened, only for an instant, but long enough to let Krispos escape.

Panting, he scrambled to his feet. Beshev also rose. He must have bitten his tongue; blood ran into his beard from the corner of his mouth. He scowled at Krispos. From just behind him, so did Gleb. Gleb's hands were still twitching.

Whose hands had writhed so? Krispos shifted his weight, and remembered how it shifted at every step up on the hide platform during the ransom ceremony that had set him on the path to this moment. On the platform with him had been Iakovitzes, Pyrrhos, Omurtag—and Omurtag's *enaree*.

When the shaman checked the quality of Iakovitzes' gold, his hands had moved as Gleb's moved now. So Gleb was working some minor magic, was he? Krispos' lips skinned back from his teeth in a fierce grin. He would have bet all the gold Tanilis had given him that he knew just what kind. No wonder he hadn't been able to get a decent hold on Beshev all night long!

Krispos stopped, picking up a handful of the sand the servants had strewn about. With a shout, he rushed at Beshev. The Kubrati sprang forward, too. But Krispos was quicker. He twisted past Beshev and threw the sand full in Gleb's face.

Gleb screeched and whirled away, frantically knuckling his eyes. "Sorry. An accident," Krispos said, grinning still. He spun back toward Beshev.

The brief look of surprise and dismay on his foe's face told Krispos his guess had been good. Then Beshev's eyes grew cold once more. Even without sorcerous aid, he remained large, skilled, and immensely strong. The match still had a long way to go.

They grappled again. Krispos let out a whoop of glee. Now Beshev's skin was just skin—slick with sweat, yes, but not preternaturally so. When Krispos grabbed him, he stayed grabbed.

And when he hooked his leg behind Beshev's and pushed, Beshev went over it and down.

The Kubrati was a wrestler, though. He tried to twist while falling, as Krispos had before. Krispos sprang onto his back. Beshev levered himself up on his great arms. Krispos jerked them out from under him. Beshev went down flat on the sandy floor.

He tried to get up again. Krispos seized a great hank of greasy hair and slammed Beshev's face into the marble under the sand. Beshev groaned, then made one more effort to rise. Krispos smashed him down again. "For Stylianos!" he shouted. Beshev lay still.

Krispos climbed wearily to his feet. He felt the cheers of the crowd more than he heard them. Iakovitzes rushed up and kissed him, half on the cheek, half on the mouth. He did not even mind.

Something hit him in the heel. He whirled in shock—could Beshev want more? He was sure he'd battered the Kubrati into unconsciousness. But no, Beshev still had not moved. Instead, a goldpiece lay by Krispos' foot. A moment later, another one kicked up sand close by.

"Pick 'em up, fool!" Iakovitzes hissed. "They're throwing 'em for you."

Krispos started to bend down, then stopped. Was this how he wanted these nobles to remember him, scrambling for their coins like a dog chasing a thrown stick? He shook his head and straightened. "I fought for Videssos, not for gold," he said.

The cheers got louder. No one in the Hall of the Nineteen Couches knew why Krispos smiled so widely. Without the stake from Tanilis, he could never have afforded such a grand gesture.

He brushed at himself, knocking off as much sand as he could. "I'm going to put my robe back on," he said and walked out through the crowd. Men and women clasped his hands, touched him on the arm, and patted his back as he went by. Then they turned to jeer the Kubrati envoys who came into the open space to drag away their fallen champion.

The world briefly disappeared as Krispos pulled the robe on over his head. When he could see again, he found Petronas standing in front of him. He started to bow. The Sevastokrator raised a hand. "No formality needed, not after so handsome a victory," he said. "I hope you will not object if *I* choose to reward you, Krispos, so long as—" He let amusement touch his eyes, "—it is not in gold."

"How could I refuse?" Krispos said. "Wouldn't that be—what do they call it?—lèse majesty?"

"No, for I am not the Avtokrator, only his servant," Petronas said with a perfectly straight face. "But tell me, how were you able to overthrow the savage Kubrati who had beaten all our best?"

"He likely had some help from that Gleb." Krispos explained how he knew, or thought he knew, what Gleb had been up to. He went on, "So I figured I would see how well Beshev fought without him making those tiny little Kubrati-style passes, and the big fellow was a lot easier to handle after that."

Petronas scowled. "Gleb always fidgets that way when we're dickering, as well. Do you suppose he's trying to ensorcel *me*?"

"You'd be able to guess that better than I could," Krispos said. "Could it hurt, though, to have a wizard of your own there the next time you talk with him?"

"It could not hurt at all, and I will do it," Petronas declared. "By the lord with the great and good mind, I wondered why I said yes to some of those proposals the Kubrati set before me. Now perhaps I know, and now I have two reasons to reward you, for you have done me two services this night."

"I thank you." Krispos did bow this time, and deeply. As he straightened, his face bore a sly grin. "And I thank you."

Petronas started to answer, then checked himself. He gave Krispos a long, considering look. "So you have a working wit, do you, to go along with your strength? That's worth knowing." Before Krispos could reply, the Sevastokrator turned away from him and called to the servants. "Wine! Wine for everyone, and let no one's cup be empty the rest of the night! We have a victory to celebrate, and a victor. To Krispos!"

The Videssian lords and ladies rased goblets high. "To Krispos!"

Krispos plied the currycomb with a rhythm that matched the dull pounding in his head. The warm, smelly stuffiness of the stables did nothing to help his hangover, but for once he did not mind headache or sour stomach. They reminded him that, though he was back to the down-to-earth routine of his job, the night before had really happened.

Not far away, Mavros whistled while he plied the shovel. Krispos laughed softly. Anything more down-to-earth than shoveling horse manure was hard to image. "Mavros?" he said.

The shovel paused. "What is it?"

"How come a fancy young noble like you doesn't mind mucking out the stables? I've shoveled plenty, here and back in my village with the goats and cows and sheep and pigs, but I never enjoyed it."

"To the ice with goats and cows and sheep and pigs. These are horses," Mavros said, as if that explained everything.

Maybe it even did, Krispos thought. Iakovitzes didn't mind working up a sweat in the stables, but Krispos could not picture him having anything to do with a pigsty. He shook his head. To anyone farm-bred like him, livestock was livestock. Getting sentimental about it was a luxury he hadn't been able to afford.

Such mostly pointless musing helped him get through the quarter of an hour he needed to finish bringing the coat of the mare he was working on to an even glow. Satisfied at last, he patted her on the muzzle and went on to the next stall.

He'd just started in when he head someone come into the stable. "Krispos! Mavros!" Gomaris called.

"What?" Krispos said, curious. Iakovitzes' steward hardly ever came back where the grooms labored.

"The master wants the two of you, right now," Gomaris said.

Krispos looked at Mavros. They both shrugged. "Beats working," Mavros said. "But I hope he'll give me a few minutes to wash and change clothes." He held his nose. "I'm not what you call presentable."

"Right now," Gomaris repeated.

"Well, all right," Mavros said, shrugging again. "On his floors be it."

As Krispos followed Gomaris up to the house, he wondered what was going on. Something out of the ordinary, obviously. He didn't think he was in trouble, not if Iakovitzes wanted to see Mavros, too. Unless—had Iakovitzes learned more of his connection with Tanilis, or of what she'd seen? But how could he have, here in the city when he hadn't in Opsikion?

A gray-haired man Krispos had not met was waiting with Iakovitzes. "Here they are, Eroulos, in all their—" Iakovitzes paused for an ostentatious sniff, "—splendor." He turned to his grooms. "Eroulos is steward of the household of his Imperial Highness the Sevastokrator Petronas."

Krispos bowed low. "Excellent sir," he murmured.

Mavros bowed even lower. "How may we serve you, eminent sir?"

"You will not serve me, but rather the Sevastokrator," Eroulos answered at once. He was still straight and alert, with the competent air Krispos would have expected from one of Petronas' aides. He went on, "His Imperial Highness promised you a reward for your courage last night, Krispos. He has chosen to appoint you chief groom of his stables. You, Mavros, are bidden to come to the palaces, as well, out of the respect the Sevastokrator bears for your mother."

While Krispos and Mavros gaped, Iakovitzes said gruffly, "You should both know I wouldn't permit such a raid on my staff from anyone less than Petronas. Even from him, I resent it. That's a waste of time, though; what the Sevastokrator wants, he gets. So go on, and show him and his folk what kind of people come from this house." That was Iakovitzes to the core, Krispos thought: as kind a farewell as the noble had in him, mixed with bragging and self-promotion.

Then Krispos stopped worrying about what suddenly seemed the past. Going to the household of the Sevastokrator! He felt like shouting. He made himself stay calm. "Could we have a little time to pack our belongings?"

"And bathe?" Mavros added plaintively.

Eroulos unbent enough to smile. "I expect so. If I send a man for you tomorrow morning, will that be all right?"

"Yes, eminent sir."

"That would be fine, excellent sir."

"Until tomorrow, then." Eroulos rose, bowed to Iakovitzes. "Always a pleasure to see you, excellent sir." He nodded to Gomaris. "If you will be so kind as to show me out?"

When Eroulos had gone, Iakovitzes said, "I trust neither of you young gentlemen, now having risen higher, will forget whose house was his first in the city."

"Of course not," Krispos answered, while Mavros shook his head. Krispos heard something new in Iakovitzes' voice. All at once, his master—or rather, he thought dizzily, his former master—spoke to him as to a person of consequence instead of taking his obedience for granted. Iakovitzes never wasted respect where it was not needed. That he gave it now was Krispos' surest sign of what Eroulos' visit meant.

The news of that visit had reached the grooms' quarters by

the time Krispos and Mavros got back there. The other grooms waylaid them with a great jar of wine. Krispos did not start packing until late that night. He finished quickly—he did not have a lot to pack—and fell sideways across his bed.

"You can throw that sack onto one of my horses, if you like," Mavros said the next morning.

"They're loaded enough already, thanks. I can manage." But for the spear he'd brought to the city from his village, everything Krispos owned fit into a large knapsack. He paced back and forth with the sack slung over his shoulder. "So where is this man of Petronas'?"

"Probably in a tavern, drinking his breakfast. When you're the Sevastokrator's man, who this side of the Emperor is going to complain that you're late?"

"No one, I suppose." Krispos kept pacing.

The promised servant did show up a little later. "May I carry that for you?" he asked, pointing to Krispos' knapsack. He seemed surprised when Krispos turned him down. With a shrug, he said, "Follow me, then."

He led Krispos and Mavros through the plaza of Palamas and into the palace quarter. The palaces, Krispos discovered, were a secret city unto themselves, with rows of carefully planted trees screening buildings from one another. He soon found himself in a part of the quarter he had never seen before. "What's that building over there, the one by the cherry trees?" he asked.

"Nothing for the likes of you to worry about—or me, either, come to that," the fellow answered, grinning. "That's the Avtokrator's private residence, that is, and his Imperial Majesty has his own imperial servants, believe you me. They think they're better'n anyone else, too. Of course," he went on after a brief pause, "most of 'em are eunuchs, so I suppose they have to have something to be proud of."

"Eunuchs." Krispos wet his lips. He'd seen eunuchs a few times here in the city, plodding plumply about their errands. They made him shiver; more than once, unbuttoning his fly or pulling up his robe to relieve himself, he'd thanked Phos he was a whole man. "Why eunuchs?"

The Sevastokrator's man chuckled to hear such naïveté. "For one thing, they can't go plotting to make themselves Avtokrator—having no stones disbars 'em. For another, who better to trust to serve the Emperor's wife?"

"Nobody, I suppose." What the servant said made sense. All the same, Krispos fingered his thick, dark, curly beard, gladder than glad he could grow it.

The servitor led Mavros to a building not far from the Emperor's private chambers. "You'll be quartered here, with Petronas' other spatharioi. Find an empty suite and get yourself comfortable there."

"So I'm to be a spatharios, am I?" Mavros said. "Well, there are spatharioi and then there are spatharioi, if you know what I mean. Which sort does Petronas have in mind for me to be, useful or just decorative?"

"Whichever sort you make yourself into, I expect," the servant answered. "I'll tell you this, though, for whatever you think it's worth: Petronas isn't ashamed to get his own hands dirty when he needs to."

"Good. Neither am I." When Mavros grinned, he looked even younger than he really was. "And if you doubt me, ask your Eroulos how I smelled when he came to Iakovitzes' yesterday."

"Will I stay here, too?" Krispos asked.

"Eh? No. You come on with me," Petronas' man said.

With a quick wave to Mavros, Krispos obeyed. The servant took him to one of the larger and more splendid buildings in the palace complex. It made three sides of a square, closely enclosing a yard full of close-trimmed shrubberies.

"The Grand Courtroom," the servant explained. "His Imperial Highness the Sevastokrator lives here in the wing we're going toward so he can be right at hand if anything comes up that he needs to deal with."

"I see," Krispos said slowly. Anthimos' residence, on the other hand, was well away from the courtroom. Petronas, Krispos decided, missed very little. Then something else struck him. He stopped. "Wait. Are you saying the Sevastokrator wants me to live here, too?"

"Them's the orders I have." The servant gave an it's-not-my-problem shrug.

"This is finer than I expected," Krispos said as Petronas' man led him to the Grand Courtroom. He stopped the fellow again. "Where are the stables? If I'm going to be chief groom, don't you think I should know how to get to my work?"

"Maybe, and then maybe not." The servant looked him up and down. "Hope you don't mind my saying it, but you strike me as a trifle . . . raw . . . to be chief groom when some of the men in the stables have been there likely since before your father was born.''

"No doubt you're right, but that doesn't mean I can't put my hand to it. Or would Petronas want me to be a drone, any more than he would Mavros?''

Now the Sevastokrator's man stopped of his own accord. He looked at Krispos again, this time thoughtfully. "Mmm, maybe not, not if you don't care to be." He told Krispos how to get to the stables. "But first let's get you settled in here.''

Krispos could not argue with that. The servant led him up a stairway. A couple of armed guards in mail shirts leaned against the first doorway they passed. "This whole floor belongs to his Imperial Highness," the servitor explained. "You want the next one up.''

The story above the Sevastokrator's quarters was broken up into apartments. By the spacing of the doors, the one assigned to Krispos was among the smallest. All the same, it had both a living room and a bedroom. Though he did not say so, that enormously impressed Krispos. He'd never had more than one room to himself before.

The apartment also boasted both a large bureau and a closet. The storage space swallowed Krispos' knapsack-worth of belongings. He tossed his spear on the bed, locked the door behind him, and went down the stairs. The bright sun outside made him blink. He looked this way and that, trying to get his bearings. That long, low brick building behind the stand of willows should have been the stables, if he'd understood Petronas' man.

He walked toward the building. Soon both sound and smell told him he was right. The willows, though, had helped conceal the size of the stables. They dwarfed Iakovitzes' and Tanilis' put together. Someone saw Krispos coming and dashed into the building. He nodded to himself. He might have known that would happen.

By the time his feet crunched on the straw-strewn stable floor, the grooms and farriers and boys were gathered and waiting for him. He scanned their faces and saw resentment, fear, curiosity. "Believe me," he said, "my being here surprises me as much as it does you.''

That won him a couple of smiles, but most of the stable hands still stood quietly, arms folded across their chests, wanting to learn how he would go on. He thought for a moment. "I didn't ask for this job. It got handed to me, so I'm going to do it the best way I can. A good many of you know more about horses than I do. I wouldn't think of saying you don't. You all know more about the Sevastokrator's horses than I do. I hope you'll help me.''

"What if we don't care to?" growled one of the men, a tough-looking fellow a few years older than Krispos.

"If you go on doing what you're supposed to do, I don't mind," Krispos said. "That helps me, too. But if you try to make things hard for me on purpose, I won't like it—and neither will you." He pointed to a bruise under one eye. "You must have heard why Petronas took me into his service. After Beshev, I think I can handle myself with just about anybody. But I didn't come here to fight. I will if I have to, but I don't want to. I'd sooner work.''

Now he waited to see how the stable hands would respond. They muttered among themselves. The tough-looking groom took a step toward him. He set himself. A smaller, gray-bearded man put a hand on the groom's arm. "No, hold on, Onorios," he said. "He sounds fair enough. Let's find out if he means what he says.''

Onorios grunted. "All right, Stotzas, since it's you who's asking." He scowled at Krispos. "But what do you want to bet that inside a month's time he doesn't bother setting foot in here? He'll collect the pay you deserve more and he'll stay in the Grand Courtroom soaking up wine with the rest of that lot there.''

"I'll take that bet, Onorios," Krispos said sharply. "At the end of a month—or two, or three, if you'd rather—loser buys the winner all he can drink. What do you say?''

"By the good god, you're on." Onorios stuck out his hand. Krispos took it. They squeezed until they both winced. When they let go, each of them opened and closed his fist several times to work the blood back in.

Krispos said, "Stotzas, will you show me around, please?" If the senior groom was willing not to despise him on sight, he would do his best to stay on Stotzas' good side.

Stotzas showed him the Sevastokrator's parade horse. "Pretty, isn't he? Too bad he couldn't catch a tortoise with a ten-yard start." Then his war horse. "Stay away from his hooves—he's trained to lash out. Maybe you should start giving him apples, so he gets to know you." Then the beasts Petronas took hunting, mares, a couple of retired stallions and geldings, up-and-coming colts—so many animals in all that Krispos knew he would not be able to remember every one.

By the time the tour was nearly done, Stotzas and Krispos were at the far end of the stables, well away from the other hands. The graybeard gave Krispos a sidelong look. "Think you can handle it?" he asked, his voice sly.

"I'll try. What more can I say right now? I only wish you could tell me about the people the same way you did about the horses."

Stotzas' shoulders shook. After a moment, Krispos realized the groom was laughing. "Ah, so you're not just a young fool with more muscles than he needs. I hoped you weren't. Aye, the people'll drive you madder than the beasts any day, but if you keep 'em happy and keep 'em tending to their jobs, things'll run smooth enough. If you have that trick, sonny, you'll do right well for yourself."

"I hope I do." Krispos met Stotzas' eyes. "I hope you'll help me, too."

"Won't stand in your road, anyhow," Stotzas said after a brief, thoughtful pause. "Any youngster who admits he don't know everything there is to know is worth taking a chance on, you ask me. And you handled Onorios pretty well. Reckon he'll be buying you wine a month from now instead of the other way round."

"That he will," Krispos promised.

"Well, let's head back," Stotzas said. As they walked down the center aisle of the stable toward the knot of expectantly waiting hands, the senior groom raised his voice a little to ask, "So what do you think we ought to do about that hunter with the sore shins?"

"You've been resting him, you said, and putting cold compresses on his legs?" Krispos waited for Stotzas' nod, then went on, "He doesn't look too bad. If you keep up with what you're doing for a few more days, then start exercising him on soft ground, he should do all right."

Neither of them let on that they'd quietly talked about the horse's problem in front of its stall. Stotzas rubbed his chin, nodded sagely. "Good advice, sir. We'll take it, I expect." He turned to the crowd of stable hands. "He'll do."

Allies made life easier, Krispos thought.

* * *

For the next several weeks, Krispos spent most of his waking hours in the stables. He learned more about horsemanship than he'd ever known, and more about the sometimes related art of guiding men, as well. When he collected his bet from Onorios, he made a point of also buying wine for the burly groom. After they drank together, Onorios hurried to do whatever Krispos needed and did it gladly. Stotzas said nothing, but a glint of amusement showed in his eyes once in a while.

Because he was working so hard, Krispos needed a while to notice how his life had changed since he moved to his apartment in the Grand Courtroom. At Iakovitzes', he'd been a servant. Here he had servants of his own. His bed linen was always clean; his clothes seemed to wash themselves as if by magic and re-appear, spotless, in his closet.

He also learned that any small valuables he left out might disappear, as if by magic. He was glad he'd hidden Tanilis' gift behind a piece of molding he'd loosened. Every so often, he would move the small cabinet he'd put in front of the loose place and add more money to his store. He lived frugally. He was too busy to do anything else.

He was about to go to sleep one warm summer night when someone tapped on his door. He scratched his head. His ac-quaintance with the officials and courtiers who lived in the other apartments down this hall was nodding at best; he'd been at the stables too much to get to know them well. "Who is it?" he called.

"Eroulos."

"Oh!" Krispos had not seen Petronas' steward since the day he came to Iakovitzes' house for him. After hastily throwing his tunic back on, he unbarred the door. "Come in!"

"No, you come out with me," Eroulos said. "I am bidden to bring you downstairs to the Sevastokrator. His Imperial High-ness is entertaining . . . a guest. He would like to have him meet you."

"A guest?"

"You'll see for yourself soon enough. Come along, if you please."

Krispos followed Eroulos down the hall and down the stairs. Petronas' guards gave the steward and him a thorough patting down at the doorway to the Sevastokrator's suite. Krispos let himself be searched without complaint; after all, he had never passed through this entrance before. But he was surprised Eroulos got the same treatment. If Petronas did not trust his own steward, whom did he trust? *Maybe no one,* Krispos thought.

Finally, nodding, the guards stood aside. One of them opened the door. Eroulos waved Krispos in ahead of him. Krispos had wondered how the Sevastokrator lived. What he saw reminded him of Tanilis' villa: a mix of great wealth and quiet good taste.

An icon of Phos arrested his eye. Respect for both the good god and the artist made him sketch the sun-sign over his heart; he'd never seen Phos portrayed with such perfectly mingled sternness and kindness. Eroulos followed his gaze. "That is the image, they say, after which the Phos in the dome of the High Temple is modeled," the steward remarked.

"I can well believe it," Krispos said. Even after he'd walked by, he had the uneasy feeling the god in the icon was still looking at him.

"Here we are," Eroulos said at length, halting before a door inlaid with lacy vines of gold and ivory. He tapped at it. For a moment, the two voices coming through it did not pause. One was Petronas. The other sounded lighter, younger. Eroulos tapped again. "All right, all right," Petronas growled.

The steward swung the door open. It moved silently, on well-greased hinges. "Here is Krispos, your Highness."

"Good." The Sevastokrator turned to the man sitting across a small table from him. "Well, nephew, I suppose the argument can wait a few minutes before we pick it up again. You wanted to see the fellow who overthrew the famous Beshev and sent Gleb back to Kubrat less high and mighty than he came here. This is Krispos."

Petronas' nephew! Krispos bowed low before the younger man, then went to his knees and down flat on his belly. "Your Majesty," he whispered.

"Up, up! How can I shake your hand when you're lying there?" Anthimos III, Avtokrator of the Videssians, waited impatiently while Krispos scrambled to his feet. Then he did as he'd said, giving Krispos' hand several enthusiastic pumps. "Nothing could be more boring than listening to the Kubratoi going on about how wonderful they are. Thanks to you, we don't have to for a while. I am in your debt, which means, of course, that all Videssos is in your debt." He cocked his head and grinned at Krispos.

Krispos found himself grinning back; Anthimos' slightly lopsided smile was infectious. "Thank you, your Majesty," he said. For the moment, he was an awestruck peasant again. No matter what Tanilis might have foreseen, a big part of him had never really imagined he would feel the Emperor's flesh pressing his own, be close enough to smell wine on the Emperor's breath.

"Nephew, you might want to present Krispos with some tangible token of your gratitude," Petronas said smoothly.

"What? Oh. Yes, so I might. Here you are, Krispos." He chuckled as he pulled a golden chain from around his neck and put it over Krispos' head. "I do apologize. Having the imperial treasury to play with, I'm apt to forget that other people don't."

"You're very generous, your Majesty," Krispos said, feeling the weight of the metal on his shoulders. "A poor man could feed himself and his family for a long time with so much gold."

"Could he? Well, I hope you're not a poor man, Krispos, and that my uncle is doing a satisfactory job of feeding you."

"Krispos is making a valued place for himself here as chief groom," Petronas said. "He might have treated the post as a sinecure, and the same gratitude you feel toward him, nephew, would have compelled me to let him retain it all the same. But he has plunged in, instead; indeed, his working with such diligence is the chief reason I have not been able to present him to you before—I seldom find him away from the stables."

"Good for him," Anthimos said. "A spot of work never hurt anyone."

Krispos wondered what Anthimos knew about work—by the look of him, not much. Though his features proclaimed him Petronas' close kin, they lacked the hard purpose that informed the Sevastokrator's face. That was not just youth, either; had Anthimos been Petronas' age rather than Krispos', he still would have looked indolent. Krispos could not decide what to make of him. He'd never known anyone who could afford the luxury of indolence except Tanilis and Petronas, and they did not indulge it.

Petronas said, "Wine, Krispos?"

"Yes, thank you."

The Sevastokrator poured for him. "For me once more, as well, please," Anthimos said. Petronas handed him a cup, as well. He tossed the wine down and held out the cup for a refill. Petronas poured again, and then again a moment later. He took occasional sips from his own cup, as did Krispos. They did not come close to emptying theirs.

The next time the Avtokrator held out his cup to his uncle,

wine slopped over the rim and down onto his fingers when he pulled it back. He licked them off. "Sorry," he said with a slightly unfocused smile.

"No matter, your Majesty," his uncle answered. "Now, if we may pick up the discussion in which we were engaged when Krispos came in, I still respectfully urge you to set your signature to the order I sent you last week for the construction of two new fortresses in the far southwest."

"I don't know that I want to sign it." Anthimos stuck out his lower lip. "Skombros says they probably won't ever be needed, because the southwest is a very quiet frontier."

"Skombros!" Petronas lost some of the air of urbanity Krispos had always seen from him before. He did not try to hide his contempt as he went on, "Frankly, I can't imagine why you even think of listening to your vestiarios on these matters. What a eunuch chamberlain knows of the proper placement of fortresses would fit into the ballocks he does not have. By the good god, nephew, you'd be better advised asking Krispos here what he thinks of the whole business. At least he's seen more of the world than the inside of the palaces."

"All right, I will," Anthimos said. "What *do* you think of the whole business, Krispos?"

"Me?" Krispos almost spilled his own wine. Drinking with the Sevastokrator and Avtokrator made him feel proud and important. Getting into the middle of their argument was something else again, something terrifying. He was all too conscious of Petronas' gaze on him as he picked his words with the greatest of care. "In matters of war, I think I would sooner rely on a warrior's judgment."

"Do you recognize plain truth when you hear it, Anthimos?" Petronas demanded.

The Avtokrator rubbed his chin. The tip of his beard was waxed to a point. Sounding faintly surprised, he said, "Yes, that is sensible, isn't it? Very well, Uncle, I'll sign your precious order."

"You will? Excellent!" Petronas sprang to his feet and slapped Krispos on the back hard enough to stagger him. "There's another present you'll have from me, Krispos, and another one you've earned, too."

"Your Highness is very kind," Krispos said.

"I reward good service," Petronas said. "Don't forget that. I also reward the other kind, as it deserves. Don't forget that, either. Now run along, why don't you? You'll just be bored if you hang about longer.''

"Good to meet you, Krispos," Anthimos said as Krispos bowed his way out. Even half sozzled, the Avtokrator had a charming smile.

Petronas' voice came clearly through the door Krispos closed behind him: "There, you see, Anthimos? That groom has a better notion of what needs doing than your precious vestiarios." The Sevastokrator paused. His voice turned musing. "By Phos, so he does—"

"Here, I'll show you out," Eroulos said. Krispos jumped. He hadn't heard the steward come up behind him.

"The Emperor. You didn't tell me you were taking me to see the Emperor," Krispos said accusingly as Eroulos took him past the guards.

"I was told not to. The Sevastokrator wanted to see how you would react." Eroulos started up the stairs with Krispos. "Truly, though, you should not have been surprised. Petronas once ruled for the Avtokrator, and still rules—with him."

Krispos caught the tiny pause. *Through him*, Eroulos had started to say. But a man discreet enough to be the Sevastokrator's steward was too discreet to say such things aloud.

Something else turned Krispos' thoughts aside. "*Why* did he want to see how I'd react?"

"I do not presume to speak for his Imperial Highness," Eroulos answered discreetly. "Would you not think it wise, though, to learn what you can of the quality of men who serve you, not least those you appoint to responsible posts on brief acquaintance?"

That means me, Krispos realized. By then, he and Eroulos were at his door. He nodded thoughtfully as he went inside. Tanilis would have done the same sort of thing. And if Petronas thought like Tanilis—Krispos could find no higher compliment to pay the Sevastokrator's wits.

Tanilis would never have forgotten a promised reward. Nor did Petronas. More, he gave it to Krispos publicly, coming to the stables to present him with a dagger whose hilt was lavishly chased with rubies. "For your quick thinking the other night," he said in a voice that carried.

Krispos bowed low. "You honor me, Highness." Out of the corner of his eye, he saw Onorios suddenly become very busy with his scissors as he trimmed a horse's mane. Krispos smiled to himself.

"You deserve it," Petronas said. "You're doing well here, from all I've heard, and from what I've seen of the condition of my animals."

"It's not all my doing. You had fine horses and fine hands long before you ever noticed me—not that I'm not grateful you did, Highness," Krispos added quickly.

"I'm glad you noticed, and also that you have the sense to share the credit. I know I am not in the habit of employing fools, and I'm increasingly pleased to discover I have not broken my rule with you." Petronas glanced into a stall, smiled a little at what he saw, and took a few paces to the next one. "Come, Krispos, walk with me."

"Of course, Highness."

As Stotzas had a few weeks before, the Sevastokrator waited until he and Krispos were out of earshot of most of the stable hands. Then he said, "Tell me what you know of a body servant's tasks."

"Highness?" The question caught Krispos by surprise. He answered slowly, "Not much, though, come to think of it, I guess you'd say I was Iakovitzes' body servant for a while there in Opsikion when he was laid up with a broken leg. I sort of had to be."

"So you did," Petronas agreed. "That may suffice. Indeed, I think it would. As here, in the post I have in mind you would be involved in overseeing others as much as with actually serving."

"What post is that?" Krispos asked. "Not your steward, surely. Or are you angry at Eroulos for something I don't know about?" If the Sevastokrator was displeased with Eroulos, the gossip of his household had not heard of it. That was possible, Krispos supposed, but unlikely.

And Petronas shook his head. "No, Eroulos suits me right well. I was thinking of rather a grander place for you. How would you like to be Anthimos' vestiarios one day?"

Krispos said the first thing that popped into his head: "Doesn't the vestiarios have to be a eunuch?" He felt his testicles creep up toward his belly as he spoke the word; he had all he could do to keep from shaping his hands into a protective cup over his crotch.

"It's usual, but by no means mandatory. I daresay we can

manage to keep you entire.'' Petronas laughed, then went on, ''I'm sorry; I'd not seen you look frightened before. I want you to think on this, though, even if I cannot promise you the office soon—or at all.''

''*You* can't promise, Highness?'' Krispos said, startled at the admission. ''How could you lack the power? Aren't you both Sevastokrator and the Avtokrator's uncle? Wouldn't he heed you?''

''In this, perhaps not. His chamberlain also has his ear, you see, and so may not be easily displaced.'' Petronas took a slow, deep, angry breath. ''That cursed Skombros is sly as a fox, too. He plots to weaken me and aggrandize his own worthless relations. I would not be surprised to learn he dreams of putting one of them on the throne, the more so as the Avtokrator's lady, the empress Dara, has yet to conceive.''

''And so you want Anthimos to have a vestiarios loyal to you and without schemes of his own,'' Krispos said. ''Now I understand.''

''Yes, exactly so,'' Petronas said.

''Thank you for your trust in me.''

''I place no great trust in any man,'' the Sevastokrator answered, ''but in this I do trust: that having raised you, I can cast you down at need. Do you understand that, as well, Krispos?'' His voice, though still quiet, had gone hard as stone.

''Very well, Highness.''

''Good. I think the best way to do this—if, as I say, it can be done at all—is to place you in Anthimos' eye from time to time. You seem to think clearly, and to be able to put your thoughts into words that, although they lack polish, carry the ring of conviction. Living as he does among eunuchs, the Avtokrator is unused to plain ideas plainly stated, save perhaps from me. They may prove an exotic novelty, and Anthimos is ever one to be drawn to the new and exotic. Should he wish to see more of you, and then more again—well, that is as the good god wills.'' Petronas set a large, heavy hand on Krispos' shoulder. ''Shall we try? Is it a bargain?''

''Aye, Highness, it is,'' Krispos said.

''Good,'' Petronas repeated. ''We shall see what we shall see.'' He turned and tramped back toward the stable entrance without a backward glance.

More slowly, Krispos came after him. So the Sevastokrator

expected him to remain a pliant creature, did he, even after becoming vestiarios? Krispos had said he understood that. He'd said nothing about agreeing with it.

VIII

The hunters ambled along on their horses, laughing and chatting and passing wineskins back and forth. They sighed with relief as they rode under a stand of trees that shielded them from the pounding summer sun. "Who'll give us a song?" Anthimos called out.

Krispos thought of a tune he'd known back in his village. "There was a young pig who got caught in a fence," he began. "A silly young pig without any sense . . ." If the pig had no sense, neither did the men who tried various unlikely ways of getting it loose.

When he was through, the young nobles who filled the hunting party gave him a cheer. The song was new to them; they'd never had to worry about pigs themselves. Krispos knew he was no great minstrel, but he could carry a tune. Past that, no one much cared. The wineskins had gone back and forth a good many times.

One of the nobles cast a glance at the sun, which was well past noon. "Let's head back to the city, Majesty. We've not caught much today, and we've not much time to catch more."

"No, we haven't," Anthimos agreed petulantly. "I'll have to speak to my uncle about that. This park was supposed to have been restocked with game. Krispos, mention it to him when we return."

"I will, Majesty." But Krispos was willing to believe it had been restocked. The way the Avtokrator and his companions rode thundering through woods and meadow, no animals in their right minds would have come within miles of them.

Grumbling still, Anthimos swung his horse's head toward the west. The rest of the hunters followed. They grumbled, too, and loudly, when they rode back out into the sunshine.

All at once, the grumbles turned to shouts of delight—a stag sprang out of the brush almost in front of the hunters' faces and darted across the grass.

"After him!" Anthimos yelled. He dug spurs into his horse's flank. Someone loosed an arrow that flew nowhere near the fleeing stag.

None of the hunters—not even Krispos, who should have paused to wonder—bothered to ask himself why the stag had burst from cover so close to them. They were young enough, and maybe drunk enough, to think of it as the perfect ending the day deserved. They were altogether off guard, then, when the pack of wolves that had been chasing the stag ran onto the meadow right under their horses' hooves.

The horses screamed. Some of the men screamed, too, as their mounts leaped and reared and bucked and did their best to throw them off. The wolves yelped and snarled; they'd been intent on their quarry and were at least as taken aback as the hunters by the sudden encounter. The stag bounded into the woods and vanished.

Maybe only Krispos saw the stag go. His mount was a sturdy gelding, fast enough and strong enough, but with no pretense to fine breeding. Thus he was in the rear of the hunters' pack when they encountered the wolves, and on a beast that did not have to be coaxed out of hysteria if a leaf blew past its nose.

No one, of course, rode a higher-bred horse than Anthimos'. Iakovitzes could not have thrown a finer fit than that animal did. Anthimos was a fine rider, but fine riders fall, too. He landed heavily and lay on the ground, stunned. Some of the other hunters cried out in alarm, but most were too busy trying to control their own mounts and fight off the wolves that snapped at their horses' legs and bellies and hindquarters to come to the Emperor's aid.

A big wolf padded toward him. It drew back for a moment when he groaned and stirred, then came forward again. Its tongue lolled from its mouth, red as blood. *Ah, crippled prey,* that lupine smile seemed to say. *Easy meat.*

Krispos shouted at the wolf. In the din, the shout was one among many. He had a bow, but did not trust it; he was no horse-archer. He drew out an arrow and shot anyway. In a romance, his need would have made the shaft fly straight and true.

He missed. He came closer to hitting Anthimos than the wolf. Cursing, he grabbed the mace that swung from his belt for finishing off large game—in the unlikely event he ever killed any, he thought, disgusted with himself for his poor shooting.

He hurled the mace with all his strength. It spun through the air. The throw was not what he'd hoped, either—in his mind, he'd seen the spiky knob smashing in the wolf's skull. Instead, the wooden handle struck it a stinging blow on the nose.

That sufficed. The wolf yelped in startled pain and sat back on its haunches. Before it worked up the nerve to advance on the Avtokrator again, another hunter managed to get his horse between it and Anthimos. Iron-shod hooves flashed near its face. It snarled and ran off.

Someone who was a better archer than Krispos drove an arrow into another wolf's belly. The wounded animal's howls of pain made more of the pack take to their heels. A couple of wolves got all the way round the hunters and picked up the stag's scent again. They loped after it. As far as Krispos was concerned, they were welcome to it.

The hunters leaped off their horses and crowded round the fallen Emperor. They all yelled when, after a minute or two, he managed to sit. Rubbing his shoulder, he said, "I take it back. This preserve has quite enough game already."

Even the Avtokrator's feeblest jokes won laughter. "Are you all right, your Majesty?" Krispos asked along with everyone else.

"Let me find out." Anthimos climbed to his feet. His grin was shaky. "All in one piece. I didn't think I would be, not unless that cursed wolf was big enough to swallow me whole. It looked to have the mouth for the job."

He tried to bend down, grunted, and clutched his ribs. "Have to be careful there." A second, more cautious, try succeeded. When he straightened again, he was holding the mace. "Whose is this?"

Krispos had to give his fellow hunters credit. He'd thought some ready-for-aught would speak up at once and claim he'd saved the Avtokrator. Instead, they all looked at one another and waited. "Er, it's mine," Krispos said after a moment.

"Here, let me give it back to you, then," Anthimos said. "Believe me, I won't forget where it came from."

Krispos nodded. That was an answer Petronas might have given. If the Avtokrator had some of the same stuff in him as the Sevastokrator, Videssos might fare well even if something befell Anthimos' capable uncle.

"Let's head back toward the city," Anthimos said. "This time I really mean it." One of the young nobles had recaptured the Emperor's horse. He grimaced as he got into the saddle, but rode well enough.

All the same, the hunting party remained unusually subdued, even when they were back inside the palace quarter. They all knew they'd had a brush with disaster.

Krispos tried to imagine what Petronas would have done if they'd come back with the news that Anthimos had got himself killed in some fribbling hunting accident. Of course, the accident would have made the Sevastokrator Emperor of Videssos. But it would also have raised suspicions that it was no accident, that Petronas had somehow arranged it. Under such circumstances, would the Sevastokrator be better off rewarding the witnesses who established his own innocence or punishing them to show they should have protected Anthimos better?

Krispos found himself unsure of the answer and glad he did not have to find out.

As the hunting band broke up, a noble leaned over to Krispos and said quietly, "I think I'd give a couple of inches off my prong to have saved the Avtokrator the way you did."

Krispos looked the fellow over. He was scarcely out of his teens, yet he rode a fine horse that he surely owned, unlike Krispos' borrowed gelding. His shirt was silk, his riding breeches fine leather, and his spurs silver. His round, plump face said he'd never known a day's hunger. Even if he hadn't saved Anthimos, he was assured a more than comfortable life.

"I mean no disrespect, excellent sir, but I'm not sure the price you name is high enough," Krispos answered after a moment's pause. "I need the luck more than you do, you see, having started with so much less of it. Now if you'll excuse me, I have to get back to my master's stables."

The noble stared after him as he rode away. He suspected—no, he was certain—he should have held his tongue. He was already far better at that than most men his age. Now he saw he would have to grow better still.

* * *

"So when does the most holy Gnatios set the crown on your head?" Mavros asked when he saw Krispos coming out of Petronas' stables a couple of days after the hunt.

"Oh, shut up," Krispos told his adopted brother. He was not worried about Mavros' betraying him; he just wanted him off his back. Mavros' teasing was the most natural thing in the world. Though Krispos hadn't bragged about what he'd done, the story was all over the palaces.

"Shut up? This humble spatharios hears and obeys, glad only that your magnificence has deigned to grant him to boon of words." Mavros swept off his hat and folded himself like a clasp knife in an extravagant bow.

Krispos wanted to hit him. He found himself laughing instead. "Humble, my left one." He snorted. Mavros had trouble taking anything seriously; after a while, so did anyone who came near him.

"Your left one would look very fine in a dish of umbles," Mavros said.

"Someone ought to run a currycomb over your tongue," Krispos told him.

"Is this another of your innovations in equestrian care?" Mavros stuck out the organ in question and crossed his eyes to look down at it. "Yes, it does seem in need of grooming. Go ahead; see if you can put a nice sheen on its coat."

Krispos did hit him then, not too hard. They scuffled good-naturedly for a couple of minutes. Krispos finally got a hammerlock on Mavros. Mavros was whimpering, without much conviction, when Eroulos came up to the two of them. "If you're quite finished . . ." the steward said pointedly.

"What is it?" Krispos let go of Mavros, who somehow contrived to look innocent and rub his wrist at the same time.

The theatrics were wasted; Eroulos took no notice of him. He spoke to Krispos instead, "Go back to the Grand Courtroom at once. One of his Imperial Majesty's servants is waiting for you there."

"For me?" Krispos squeaked.

"I am not in the habit of repeating myself," Eroulos said. Krispos waited no longer. He dashed for the Grand Courtroom. Mavros might have waved good-bye. Krispos did not turn his head to see.

The guards outside Petronas' wing of the Grand Courtroom

swung down their spears when they saw someone running toward them. Recognizing Krispos, they relaxed. One of them pointed to a man leaning against the side of the building. "Here's the fellow been waiting for you."

"You are Krispos?" Anthimos' servitor was tall, thin, and erect, but his hairless cheeks and sexless voice proclaimed him a eunuch. "I was given to understand that you were the Sevastokrator's chief groom, not that you would stink of horses yourself." His own scent was of attar of roses.

"I work," Krispos said shortly.

The eunuch's sniff told what he thought of that. "In any event, I am commanded to bid you come to a festivity his Imperial Majesty will hold tomorrow evening. I shall return then to guide you. I most respectfully suggest that, no matter how virtuous you deem your labors, the odor of the stables would be out of place."

Krispos felt his cheeks heat. Biting back an angry retort, he nodded. The eunuch's bow was fluid perfection, or would have been had he not made it so deep as to suggest scorn rather than courtesy.

"You don't want to get into a meaner-than-thou contest with a eunuch," one of the guards remarked after the Avtokrator's servant was too far away to hear. "You'll regret it every time."

"You'd be mean, too, if you'd had that done to you," another guard said. All the troopers chuckled. Krispos also smiled, but he thought the guard was right. Having lost so much, eunuchs could hardly be blamed for getting their own back in whatever petty ways they could devise.

He knocked off a little early the next afternoon to go from the stables to a bathhouse; he would not give that supercilious eunuch another chance to sneer at him. He oiled himself, scraped his skin with a curved strigil, and paid a boy a copper to get the places he could not reach. The cold plunge and hot soak that followed left him clean and helped loosen tired, tight muscles. He was all but purring as he walked back to the Grand Courtroom.

This time he waited for the Avtokrator's eunuch to arrive. The eunuch gave a disapproving sniff; perhaps, Krispos thought, he was seeking the lingering aroma of horse. "Come along," he said, sounding no happier for failing to find it.

Krispos had never been to—had never even seen—the small building to which his guide led him. He was not surprised; the palace quarter held dozens of buildings, large and small, he'd never been to. Some of the large ones were barracks for the regiments of imperial guards. Some of the small ones held soldierly supplies. Others were buildings former Emperors had used, but that now stood empty, awaiting the pleasure of an Avtokrator yet to come. This one, secluded among willows and pear trees, looked to be where Anthimos himself awaited pleasure.

Krispos heard the music when he was still walking the winding path under the trees. Whoever was playing, he thought, had more enthusiasm than skill. Raucous voices accompanied the musicians. He needed a moment to recognize the tavern song they were roaring out. Only when they came to the refrain—"The wine gets drunk but you get drunker!"—was he sure. Loud applause followed.

"They seem to have started already," he remarked.

The eunuch shrugged. "It's early yet. They'll still have their clothes on, most of them."

"Oh." Krispos wondered whether he meant most of the revelers or most of their clothes. He supposed it was about the same either way.

By then they were at the door. A squad of guardsmen stood just outside, big blond Haloga mercenaries with axes. An amphora of wine almost as tall as they were stood beside them, its pointed end rammed into the ground. One of them saw Krispos looking at it. The northerner's wide, foolish grin said he'd already made use of the dipper that stuck out of the jug, and his drawling Haloga accent was not the only thing that thickened his speech. "A good duty here, yes it is."

Krispos wondered what Petronas would do if he caught one of his own guards drunk on duty. Nothing pleasant, he was certain. Then the eunuch took him inside, and all such musings were swept away.

"It's Krispos!" Anthimos exclaimed. He set down the flute he'd been playing—no wonder the music sounded ragged, Krispos thought—and rushed up to embrace the newcomer. "Let's have a cheer for Krispos!"

Everyone obediently cheered. Krispos recognized some of the young nobles with whom he'd hunted, and a few people who had been at some of the wilder feasts he'd gone to with Iakovitzes. Most of the folk here, though, were strange to him, and by the look of some of them, he would have been as glad to have them stay so.

Torches of spicy-smelling sandalwood lit the chamber. It was strewn with lilies and violets, roses and hyacinths, which added their sweet scents to the air. Many of the Emperor's guests were also drenched in perfume. Krispos admitted to himself that his eunuch guide had been right—the odor of horse did not belong here.

"Help yourself to anything," Anthimos said. "Later you can help yourself to anybody." Krispos laughed nervously, though he did not think the Avtokrator was joking.

He took a cup of wine and a puffy pastry that proved to be stuffed with forcemeat of lobster. As Petronas had in the Hall of the Nineteen Couches, a noble rose to give a toast. He had to wait a good deal longer for quiet than the Sevastokrator had. Getting some at last, he called, "Here's to Krispos, who saved his Majesty and saved our fun with him!"

This time the cheers were louder. No one here, Krispos thought, would be able to revel like this without Anthimos' largess. Had the wolf killed Anthimos, Petronas would surely have taken the throne for himself. After that, most of the people here tonight would have counted themselves lucky not to be whipped out of the city.

Anthimos set down his golden cup. "What goes in must come out," he declared. He picked up a chamber pot and turned his back on his guests. The chamber pot was also gold, decorated with fancy enamelwork. Krispos wondered how many like it the Avtokrator had. For golden chamber pots, he thought, he'd been taxed off his land.

The notion should have made him furious. It did anger him, but less than he would have thought possible. He tried to figure out why. At last he decided that Anthimos just was not the sort of young man who inspired fury. All he wanted to do was enjoy himself.

A very pretty girl put her hand on Krispos' chest. "Do you want to?" she asked, and waved to a mountain of pillows piled against one wall.

He stared at her. She was worth staring at. Her green silk gown was modestly cut, but thinned to transparency in startling places. But that was not why he gaped. His rustic standards had taken a beating since he came to Videssos. Several times he'd gone off with female entertainers after a feast, and once with the bored wife of one of the other guests. But "In front of everyone?" he blurted.

She laughed at him. "You're a new one here, aren't you?" She left without even giving him a chance to answer. He took another cup of wine and drank it quickly to calm his shaken nerves.

Before long, a couple did avail themselves of the pillows. Krispos found himself watching without having intended to. He tore his gaze away. A moment later, he found his eyes sliding that way again. Annoyed at himself, he turned his back on the whole wall.

Most of the revelers took no special notice of the entwined pair, by the way they went on about their business, they'd seen such displays often enough not to find them out of the ordinary. A few offered suggestions. One made the man pause in what he was doing long enough to say, "Try that yourself if you're so keen on it. I did once, and I hurt my back." Then he fell to once more, matter-of-fact as if he were laying bricks.

Not far from Anthimos sat one who did nothing but watch the sportive couple. The robes he wore were as rich as the Avtokrator's and probably cost a good deal more, for they needed to be larger to cover his bulk. His smooth, beardless face let Krispos count his chins. Another eunuch, he thought, and then, Well, let him watch—it's probably as close as he can come to the real thing.

Some of the entertainment was more nearly conventional. Real musicians took up the instruments Anthimos and his cronies had set down. Acrobats bounced among the guests and sometimes sprang over them. The only thing remarkable about the jugglers, aside from their skill, was that they were all women, all lovely, and all bare or nearly so.

Krispos admired the aplomb one of them showed when a man came up behind her and fondled her breast. The stream of fruit she kept in the air never wavered—until a very ripe peach landed *splat!* on the fellow's head. He swore and raised a fist to her, but the storm of laughter in the room made him lower it again, his dripping face like thunder.

"Zotikos draws the first chance of the evening!" Anthimos said loudly. More laughter came. Krispos joined in, though he wasn't quite sure what the Avtokrator meant. Anthimos went on, "Here, Skombros, go ahead and give him a real one."

The eunuch who had stared so avidly at the couple making

love now rose from his seat. So this was Petronas' rival, Krispos thought. Skombros walked over to a table and picked up a crystal bowl full of little golden balls. With great dignity, he carried it over to Zotikos, who was trying to comb peach fragments out of his hair and beard.

Krispos watched curiously. Zotikos took one of the balls from the bowl. He twisted it between his hands. It came open. He snatched out the little strip of parchment inside. When he scanned it, his face fell.

Skombros delicately plucked the parchment from his fingers. The eunuch's voice was loud, clear, and musical as a middle-range horn's as he read what was written there: "Ten dead dogs."

More howls of laughter, and some out and out howls. Servants brought Zotikos the dead animals and dropped them at his feet. He stared at them, at Skombros, and at the bare-breasted juggler who had started his humiliation for the evening. Then, cursing, he stormed out of the hall. A chorus of yips pursued him and sped him on his way. By the time he got to the door, he was running.

"He didn't seem to want his chance. What a pity," Anthimos said. The Emperor's smile was not altogether pleasant. "Let's let someone else have a go. I know! How about Krispos?"

Anger filled Krispos as Skombros approached. Was this his reward for rescuing Anthimos—a chance to be one of the butts for the Avtokrator's jokes? He wanted to kick the crystal bowl out of Skombros' hands. Instead, grim-faced, he drew out a ball and opened it. The parchment inside was folded.

Skombros watched, cool and contemptuous, as Krispos fumbled with it. "Do you read, groom?" he asked, not bothering to keep his voice down.

"I read, eunuch," Krispos snapped. Nothing whatever changed in Skombros' face, but Krispos knew he had made an enemy. He finally got the parchment open. "Ten—" His voice suddenly broke, as if he were a boy. "—ten pounds of silver."

"How fortunate of you," Skombros said tonelessly.

Anthimos rushed up and planted a wine-soaked kiss on Krispos' cheek. "Good for you!" he exclaimed. "I was hoping you'd get a good one!"

Krispos hadn't known there were any good ones. He stood, still dazed, as a servant brought him a fat, jingling sack. Only when he felt the weight of it in his hands did he believe the money was for him. Ten pounds of silver was close to half a pound of gold: thirty goldpieces, he worked out after a little thought.

To Tanilis, a pound and a half of gold—108 goldpieces—had been enough to set up Krispos as a man with some small wealth of his own. To Anthimos, thirty goldpieces—and belike three hundred, or three thousand—was a party favor. For the first time, Krispos understood the difference between the riches Tanilis' broad estates yielded and those available to a man with the whole Empire as his estates. No wonder Anthimos thought nothing of a chamber pot made of gold.

A couple of more chances were given out. One man found himself the proud possessor of ten pounds of feathers—a much larger sack than Krispos'. Another got ten free sessions at a fancy brothel. "You mean I have to pay if I want to go back a second night?" the braggart asked, whereupon the fellow who had won the feathers poured them over his head.

Ten pounds of feathers let loose seemed plenty to fill up the room. People flung them about as if they were snow. Servants did their best to get rid of the blizzard of fluff, but even their best took a while to do any good. While most of the servitors plied brooms and pillowcases, a few brought in the next courses of food.

Anthimos pulled a last bit of down from his beard and let it float away. He looked over toward the new trays. "Ah, beef ribs in fish sauce and garlic," he said. "My chef does them wonderfully well. They're far from a neat dish, but oh so tasty."

The ribs would be anything but neat, Krispos thought as he walked toward them—they were fairly swimming in the pungent fermented fish sauce—but they did smell good. One of the men with whom he'd hunted got to them first. The fellow picked up a rib and took a big bite.

The rib vanished. The young noble's teeth came together with a loud click. He'd drunk enough wine that he stared foolishly at his dripping but otherwise empty hand. Then his gaze swung to Krispos. "I did have one, didn't I?" He sounded anything but sure.

"I certainly thought you did," Krispos said. "Here, let me try." He took a rib off the tray. It felt solid and meaty in his hand. He lifted it to his mouth. As soon as he tried to bite it, it disappeared.

Some of the people watching made Phos' sun-sign. Others, wiser in the ways of Anthimos' feasts, looked to the Avtokrator.

A small-boy grin was on his face. "I told the cooks to make them rare, but not so rare as that," he said.

"I suppose you're going to say you told them to get the plaster goose livers you served last time well done," someone called out.

"Half a dozen of my friends broke teeth on those livers," the Emperor said. "This is a safer joke. Skombros thought of it."

The eunuch looked smug and, also pleased that Krispos had been one of the people his trick had deceived. Krispos stuck his fingers in his mouth to clean them of fish sauce and juice from the ribs. What he was able to taste was delicious. He thought how unfair it was for some sneaky bit of sorcery to deprive him of the tender meat.

He picked up another rib. "Some people," Skombros announced to no one in particular, "have more stubbornness than sense." The vestiarios settled back in his chair, perfectly content to let Krispos make as thorough a fool of himself as he wanted.

This time, though, Krispos did not try to take a bite off the rib. He'd already seen that doing that did not work—bringing his jaws together seemed to activate the spell. Instead, he picked up a knife from the serving table and sliced a long strip of meat off each side of the bone.

He raised one of the strips to his mouth. If the meat vanished despite his preparations, he knew he was going to look foolish. He bit into it, then grinned as he started to chew. He'd hoped cutting it off the bone would sever the spell that made it disappear.

Slowly and deliberately, he ate all the meat he'd sliced away. Then he dealt with another rib, put the meat he'd carved from it on a small plate, and carried the plate to Anthimos. "Would you like some, your Majesty? You were right; they are very tasty."

"Thank you, Krispos; don't mind if I do." Anthimos ate, then wiped his fingers. "So they are."

Krispos asked, "Do you think your esteemed—" Eunuchs had a special set of honorifics that applied to them alone. "—vestiarios would care for some?"

The Avtokrator glanced over to Skombros, who stared back stonily. Anthimos laughed. "No, he's a good fellow; but he has plenty of meat on his bones already." Krispos shrugged, bowed, and walked away, as if the matter were of no importance. He

could not think of a better way to twist the knife in Skombros'
huge belly.

After Krispos showed how to eat the ribs, they vanished into
the revelers rather than into thin air. Servants took away the
trays. A new set of minstrels circulated through the crowd. Another erotic troupe followed them, then a group of dancers replaced the horizontal cavorters. All the acts did what they did
very well. Krispos smiled to himself. Anthimos could afford the
best.

Skombros strode through the hall every so often with his crystal bowl of chances. He came nowhere near Krispos. A noble
who won ten pounds of gold took his stroke of luck with enough
equanimity to make Krispos sure he was already rich. Anthimos
confirmed that, saying "More money for slow horses and fast
women, eh, Sphrantzes?"

"Fast horses, I hope, Majesty," Sphrantzes said amid general
laughter.

"Why should you change now?" the Avtokrator asked.
Sphrantzes spread his hands, as if to admit defeat.

Someone else chose ten peacocks for himself. Krispos wondered what peacock tasted like. But the birds the servants chiv-
vied out were very much alive. They honked and squawked and
spread their gorgeous tails and generally made nuisances of
themselves. "What do I *do* with them?" wailed the winner,
who had one bird under each arm and was chasing a third.

"I haven't the foggiest notion," Anthimos replied with a blithe
wave of his hand. "That's why I put that chance in there—to
find out."

The man ended up departing with his two birds in the hand
and forgetting about the rest. After some commotion, revelers,
entertainers, and servants joined in shooing the other eight peacocks out the door. "Let the Halogai worry about them," somebody said, which struck Krispos as a good enough idea.

Once the peacocks departed—shouts from outside said the
imperial guards were having their own troubles with the bad-
tempered birds—the feast grew almost calm for a little while,
as if everyone needed some time to catch his breath. "Well,
how is he going to top that?" Krispos said to the man next to
him. They were standing by a bowl of sweetened gelatin and
candied fruit, but neither felt like eating; the gelatin had peacock
tracks.

"I don't know," the fellow answered, "but I expect he'll manage."

Krispos shook his head. Then Skombros went round with his bowl again. He stopped in front of the young man whose beef rib had vanished. "Would you care for a chance, excellent Pagras?"

"Huh?" By now, Pagras needed a moment to come out of his wine-soaked haze. He fumbled while he was getting the ball out of the bowl, and fumbled more in getting it open. He read the parchment; Krispos saw his lips move. But, instead of announcing what chance he'd chosen, he turned to Anthimos and said, "I don't believe it."

"Don't believe what, Pagras?" the Emperor asked.

"Ten thousand fleas," Pagras said, looking at the parchment again. "Not even you'd be crazy enough to get together ten thousand fleas."

At any other time, the noble might have lost his tongue for using it so freely. Anthimos, though, was drunk, too, and, as usual, a friendly drunk. "So you doubt me, eh?" was all he said. He pointed to the doorway from which a servant emerged with a large alabaster jar. "Behold: ten thousand fleas."

"Don't see any fleas. All I see is a damn *jar*." Pagras lurched over to the servant and snatched it out of his hands. He yanked off the lid and stared down into the jar for several horrified seconds.

"If you plan on counting them, Pagras, you'd better do it faster," Anthimos said.

Pagras did not count fleas. He tried to clap the lid back on, but the jar slipped through his clumsy fingers and smashed on the marble floor. Krispos thought of a good-sized pile of ground black pepper. But this pile moved and spread without any breeze to stir it. A man yelled; a woman squealed and clapped a hand to the back of her leg.

The revel broke up very quickly after that.

Krispos spent the next morning scratching. Working as he did in the stables, he got fleabites fairly often, but never so many all at once as after Anthimos' feast. And he'd been one of the lucky ones, not too close to the broken jar and not too far from the door. He wondered what poor Pagras looked like—raw meat, probably.

Petronas surprised him by dropping by not long before noon. A glance from the Sevastokrator sent stable hands scurrying out of earshot. "I understand my nephew had things hopping last night," Petronas said.

"That's one way to put it, yes, Highness," Krispos said.

Petronas allowed himself a brief snort of laughter before turning serious once more. "What did you think of the evening's festivities?" he asked.

"I've never seen anything like them," Krispos said truthfully. Petronas waited without saying anything. Seeing something more was expected of him, Krispos went on, "His Imperial Majesty knows how to have a good time. I enjoyed myself, up till the fleas."

"Good. Something's wrong with a man who can't enjoy himself. Still, I see you're here at work in the morning, too." Petronas' smile was twisted. "Aye, Anthimos knows how to have a good time. I sometimes think it's all he does know. But never mind that for now. I hear you also put a spike in Skombros' wheel."

"It wasn't so much." Krispos explained how he'd got round the spell on the disappearing ribs.

"I'd like to set a spell on Skombros that would make him disappear," the Sevastokrator said. "But making the fat maggot look foolish is even better than showing that he's wrong the way you did a few weeks ago. The worse he seems to my nephew, the sooner he won't be vestiarios any more. And when he's not—Anthimos heeds whichever ear is spoken into last. Things would go smoother if he heard the same thing with both of them."

"Your voice, in other words," Krispos said. Petronas nodded. Krispos considered before he went on, "I don't see any large troubles there, Highness. From everything I've seen, you're a man of good sense. If I thought you were wrong—"

"Yes, tell me what you would do if you thought I was wrong," Petronas interrupted. "Tell me what you would do if you, a peasant from the back of beyond jumped to head groom here only by my kindness, would do if you thought that I, a noble who has been general and statesman longer than you've been alive, was wrong. Tell me that most precisely, Krispos."

Refusing to show he was daunted had taken Krispos a long way with Iakovitzes and Tanilis. Holding that bold front against Petronas was harder. The weight of the Sevastokrator's office and the force of his own person fell on Krispos' shoulders like heavy stones. Almost, he bent beneath them. But at the last moment he found an answer that kept his pride and might not bring Petronas' wrath down upon him. "If I thought you were wrong, Highness, I would tell you first, in private if I could. You once told me Anthimos never hears any plain speaking. Do you?"

"Truth to tell, I wonder." Petronas gave that snort again. "Very well, there is something to what you say. Any officer who does not point out what he sees as error to his commander is derelict in duty. But one who disobeys after his commander makes up his mind . . ."

"I understand," Krispos said quickly.

"See that you do, lad. See that you do, and one day before too long maybe you'll stop smelling of horse manure and take on the scents of perfumes and powders instead. What do you say to that?"

"It's the best reason I've heard yet for wanting to stay in the stables."

This time Petronas' laughter came loud and booming. "You *were* born a peasant, weren't you? We'll see if we can't make a vestiarios of you all the same."

Krispos hunted with the Avtokrator, went to chariot races at the Amphitheater in the boxes reserved for Anthimos' close comrades, and attended the feasts to which he was invited. As summer moved toward fall, the invitations came more often. He always found himself among the earliest to leave the night-long revels, but he was one of the few at them who took their day work seriously.

Anthimos certainly did not. In all the time Krispos saw him, he gave scant heed to affairs of state. Depending on who had been at him last, he would say "Go see my uncle" or "Ask Skombros about that—can't you see I'm busy?" whenever a finance minister or diplomat did gain access to him and tried to get him to attend to business. Once, when a customs agent waylaid him outside the Amphitheater with a technical problem, he turned to Krispos and asked, "How would you deal with that?"

"Let me hear the whole thing over again," Krispos said. The customs man, glad for any audience, poured out his tale of woe. When he was done, Krispos said, "If I follow you rightly, you're saying that duties and road tolls at some border stations away from the sea or river transport should be lowered to increase trade through them."

"That's exactly right, excellent—Krispos, was it?" the customs agent said excitedly. "Because moving goods by land is so much more expensive than by water, many times they never go far from the sea. Lowering duties and road tolls would help counteract that."

Krispos thought of the Kalavrian merchants at Develtos and of the mother-of-pearl for which they had charged outrageous prices. He also thought of how seldom traders with even the most ordinary good had visited his village, of how many things he'd never seen till he came to Videssos the city. "Sounds good to me," he said.

"So ordered!" Anthimos declared. He took the parchment from which the customs agent had been citing figures and scrawled his signature at the bottom of it. The bureaucrat departed with a glad cry. Anthimos rubbed his hands together, pleased with himself. "There! That's taken care of."

His cronies applauded. Along with the rest of them, Krispos accompanied the Avtokrator to the next feast he'd laid on. He was troubled all through it. Problems like the one he'd handled today should have been studied, considered, not attacked on the spur of the moment—if they were attacked at all. More often than not, Anthimos did not care to bother.

He disapproved of the Emperor for his offhandedness about such concerns, but had trouble disliking him. Anthimos would have made a fine innkeeper, he thought—the young man had a gift for keeping everyone around him happy. Unfortunately, being Avtokrator of the Videssians required rather more than that.

Which did not stop Krispos from enjoying himself immensely whenever he was in Anthimos' company—the Emperor kept coming up with new ways to make his revels interesting. He had a whole series of feasts built around colors: one day everything was red, the next yellow, and the next blue. At that last feast, even the fish were cooked in blue sauce, so they looked as if they'd come straight from the sea.

The Avtokrator's chances were never the same twice, either. Remembering what had happened to Pagras, the poor fellow who picked for himself "seventeen wasps" did not dare open the jar that held them. Finally Anthimos, sounding for once most imperial, had to order him to break the seal. The wasps proved to be exquisite re-creations in gold, with emeralds for eyes and delicate filigree wings.

Krispos rarely drew a chance. Skombros kept the crystal bowl and its hollow golden balls away from him. That did not bother him. He was just glad the vestiarios did not try slipping poison into his soup. Perhaps Skombros feared Petronas' revenge. In any case, he made do with black looks from afar. Sometimes Krispos returned them. More often he pretended not to see, which seemed to irk Skombros more.

Such byplay went straight by Anthimos. After a while, though, he did notice that Krispos had not had his hand in the bowl for weeks. "Go on over to him, Skombros," he said one night. "Let's see how his luck is doing."

"His luck is good, in that he enjoys your Majesty's favor," Skombros said. Nevertheless, he took Krispos the crystal bowl, thrusting it almost into his face. "Here, groom."

"Thank you, esteemed sir." Anyone who had not seen Krispos and Skombros before would have reckoned his tone perfectly respectful. Almost hidden by fat, a muscle twitched near the eunuch's ear as he set his jaw.

Krispos twisted open a gold ball. This was Anthimos' day for the number forty-three. The chances had already allotted forty-three goldpieces to one man, forty-three yards of silk to another, forty-three parsnips to a third. "Forty-three pounds of lead," Krispos read.

Laughter erupted around him. "What a pity," Skombros said, just as if he meant it. A puffing servant brought out the worthless prize. The vestiarios went on, "I trust you will know what to do with it."

"As a matter of fact, I was thinking of giving it to you," Krispos said.

"A token of esteem? A crude joke, but then I would have expected no more from you." At last the eunuch let his scorn show.

"No, not at all, esteemed sir," Krispos answered smoothly. "I just thought you would be used to carrying around the extra weight."

Several people who heard Krispos took a step or two away from him, as if they'd just realized he carried a disease they might catch. He frowned, remembering his family and the all too real disease they'd taken. Skombros' anger, though, might be as dangerous as cholera. The vestiarios' face was red but otherwise impassive as he deliberately turned his broad back on Krispos.

Anthimos had been too far away to hear Skombros and Krispos sniping at each other, but the chamberlain's gesture of contempt was unmistakable. "Enough, the two of you," the Avtokrator said. "Enough, I say. I don't care to have two of my favorite people at odds, and I will not tolerate it. Do you understand me?"

"Yes, your Majesty," Krispos said.

"Majesty," Skombros said, "I promise I shall always give Krispos all the credit he deserves."

"Excellent." Anthimos beamed. Krispos knew the eunuch's words had been no apology. Skombros would never think he deserved any credit. But even Skombros' hatred did not trouble Krispos, not for the moment. The Emperor had called him and the vestiarios "two of my favorite people." While he loathed Skombros, for Anthimos to mention him in the same breath with the longtime chamberlain was progress indeed.

Slow and ponderous as a merchant ship under not enough sail, Skombros returned to his seat. He sank into it with a sigh of relief. His small, heavily lidded eyes sought Krispos. Krispos gave back a sunny smile and lifted his wine cup in salute. Without Skombros' rudeness, he might have needed much longer to be sure how Anthimos felt about him.

The eunuch's suspicious frown deepened. Krispos' smile got wider.

Mavros stamped snow from his boots. "Warmer in here," he said gratefully. "All these horses are almost as good as a fireplace. Better, if you intend to go anyplace; you can't ride a fireplace."

"No, and I can't fling you into a horse for your foolish jokes, either, however much I wish I could," Krispos answered. "Was making that one the only reason you came? If it was, you've done your damage, so good-bye."

"Harumph." Mavros drew himself up, a caricature of offended dignity. "Just for that, I will go, and keep my news to myself." He made as if to leave.

Krispos and several stable hands quickly called him back. "What news?" Krispos said. Even here in Videssos the city, at the Empire of Videssos' heart, news came slowly in winter and was always welcome. Everyone who'd heard Mavros hurried over to find out what he'd dug up.

"For one thing," he said, pleased at the size of his audience, "that band of Haloga mercenaries under Harvas Black-Robe—remember, Krispos, we heard about them last winter back in Opsikion?—has plundered its way straight across Thatagush and out onto the Pardrayan steppe."

"It'll plunder its way right on back, then," Stotzas predicted. "The steppe nomads don't have much worth stealing."

"Who cares what happens in Thatagush, anyway?" someone else said. "It's too far away to matter to anybody." Several other people spoke up in agreement. Though he did not argue out loud, Krispos shook his head. Having known only his own village for so long, he found he wanted to learn everything he could about the wider world.

"My other bit of gossip you already know, Krispos, if you were at his Majesty's feast the night before last," Mavros said.

Krispos shook his head again, this time more emphatically. "No, I missed that one. Every so often, I feel the need to sleep."

"You'll never succeed till you learn to rise above such weaknesses," Mavros said with an airy wave of his hand. "Well, this also has to do with a Haloga, or rather with a Halogaina."

"A Haloga woman?" Two or three stable hands said it together, sudden keen interest in their voices. The big blond northerners often came to Videssos to trade or to hire on as mercenaries, but they left their wives and daughters behind.

Krispos tried to imagine what a Halogaina would look like. "Tell me more," he said. Again, his was not the only voice.

"Eyes the color of a summer sky, I heard, and the palest pink tips, and her hair gilded above and below," Mavros said. *It would be, wouldn't it?* Krispos thought; that hadn't occurred to him. The stable hands murmured, each painting his own picture in his mind. Mavros went on, "You could hardly blame Anthimos for trying her on then and there."

The murmurs got louder. "I wouldn't blame him for keeping her for a week or a month or a year or—" Onorios was all but panting. He must have liked the picture his mind painted.

But Krispos and Mavros said "No" at the same time. They glanced at each other. Krispos dipped his head to Mavros, who, he knew, was better with words. "His Majesty," Mavros explained, "only sleeps with a pleasure girl once. Anything more, he reckons, would constitute infidelity to the Empress."

That got the yowls and whoops Krispos had known it would. "Give me fidelity like that, any day," Onorios said. "Give it to me twice a day," someone else said. "Three times!" another groom added.

"The lot of you remind me of the rich old man who married a young wife and promised to kill her with passion," Krispos said. "He had her once, then fell asleep and snored all night long. When he finally woke up, she looked over at him and said, 'Good morning, killer.' "

The stable hands hissed at him. Grinning, he added, "Besides, if we spent all our time in bed, we'd never get anything done, and Phos knows there's plenty to do here." The men hissed again, but started drifting off toward their tasks.

"Not getting anything done doesn't seem to worry his Majesty," Onorios said.

"Ah, but he has people to do things for him. Unless you hired a servant while I wasn't looking, you don't," Krispos said.

"Afraid not, worse luck." Onorios sadly clicked his tongue and went back to work.

"Look at this—this bloodsucking!" Petronas slammed a fist down on the pile of parchments in front of him. They were upside down to Krispos, but that did not matter because the Sevastokrator was in full cry. "Thirty-six hundred goldpieces—fifty *pounds* of gold!—that cursed leech of a Skombros has siphoned off for his worthless slug of a nephew Askyltos. And another twenty pounds for the worthless slug's stinking father Evmolpos. When I show these accounts to my nephew—"

"What do you think will happen?" Krispos asked eagerly. "Will he give Skombros the sack?"

But Petronas' rage collapsed into moroseness. "No, he'll just laugh, curse it. He already knows Skombros is a thief. He doesn't care. What he won't see is that the Skotos-loving wretch is setting up his own relations as great men. Dynasties have died that way."

"If his Majesty doesn't care whether Skombros steals, why do you keep shoving accounts in his face?" Krispos asked.

"To *make* him care, by Phos, before the fox he insists on thinking a lapdog sinks its teeth into him." The Sevastokrator heaved a sigh. "Making Anthimos care about anything save his own amusement is like pushing water uphill with a rake."

Petronas' loathing for his rival, Krispos thought, blinded him to any way of dealing with Skombros but the one that had already shown it did not work. "What would happen if Skombros didn't amuse him, or amused him in the wrong sort of way?" Krispos asked.

"What *are* you talking about?" Petronas demanded crossly.

For a moment, Krispos had no idea himself. One of the lessons he should have learned from Tanilis was keeping his mouth shut when he had nothing to say. He bent his head in humiliation. Humiliation . . . he remembered how he'd felt when he was just a youth, when a couple of village wits lampooned his wrestling in a Midwinter's Day skit. "How would Anthimos like the whole city laughing at his vestiarios? It's only a couple of weeks to Midwinter's Day, after all."

"What does that have to do with—" Petronas suddenly caught up with Krispos. "By the good god, so it is. So you want to make him look ridiculous, do you? Why not? He is." The Sevastokrator's eyes lit up. As soon as he saw his objective, he planned how to reach it with a soldier's directness. "Anthimos has charge of the Amphitheater skits. They entertain him, so he pays attention to them. All the same, I expect I can slide a new one into the list without his noticing. Have to give it an innocuous title so that even if he does spot it, he won't think anything of it. Have to find mimes who aren't already engaged. And costumes—curse it, can we get costumes made in time?"

"We have to figure out what the mimes are going to do, too," Krispos pointed out.

"Aye, that's true, though Phos knows there's plenty to say about the eunuch."

"Let me get Mavros," Krispos said. "He has an ear for scandal."

"Does he?" Petronas all but purred. "Yes, go fetch him—at once."

"Now this," Mavros said, "is what I call an Amphitheater." He craned his neck to peer around and up.

"Only trouble is, I feel like I'm at the bottom of a soup bowl full of people," Krispos answered. Fifty thousand, seventy, ninety—he was not sure how many people the enormous oval held. However many it was, they were all here today. No one wanted to miss the Midwinter's Day festivity.

"I'd sooner be at the bottom than the top," Mavros said. "Who has better seats than we do?" They were in the very first row, right by what was a racecourse most of the time but would serve as an open-air stage today.

"There's always the people on the spine." Krispos pointed to the raised area in the center of the track.

Mavros snorted. "You're never satisfied, are you?" The spine was reserved for the Avtokrator, the Sevastokrator, the patriarch, and the chief ministers of the Empire. Krispos saw Skombros there, not far from Anthimos; the vestiarios was conspicuous for his bulk and his beardless cheeks. The only men on the spine who were not high lords or prelates were the axe-toting Halogai of the imperial guard. Mavros nodded toward them. "See? They don't even get to sit down. Me, I'd rather be comfortable here."

"I suppose I would, too," Krispos said. "Even so—"

"Hush! They're starting."

Anthimos rose from his throne and strode over to a podium set in the very center of the spine. He silently stood there, waiting. Quiet spread through the Amphitheater as more and more people saw him. When all was still, he spoke:

"People of Videssos, today the sun turns in the sky again." A trick of acoustics carried his voice clearly to the uppermost rows of the Amphitheater, from which he seemed hardly more than a bright-colored speck in his imperial robes. He went on, "Once more Skotos has failed to drag us down into his eternal darkness. Let us thank Phos the Lord of the great and good mind for delivering us for another year, and let us celebrate that deliverance the whole day long. Let joy pour forth unconfined!"

The Amphitheater erupted in cheers. Anthimos staggered as he walked back to his high seat. Krispos wondered if the acoustical trick worked in reverse, if all the noise in the huge building focused where the Emperor had stood. That would be enough to stagger anyone. On the other hand, maybe Anthimos had just started drinking at dawn.

"Here we go," Mavros breathed. The first troupe of mimes, a group of men dressed as monks, emerged from the gate that normally let horses onto the track. From the way one of them made a point of holding his nose, the horses were still much in evidence.

The "monks" proceeded to do a number of most unmonastic things. The audience howled. On Midwinter's Day, nothing was sacred. Krispos peered across the track to the spine to see how Gnatios enjoyed watching his clerics lampooned. The patriarch was paying the skit no attention at all; he was leaning over to one side of his chair so he could talk with his cousin Petronas. He and the Sevastokrator smiled at some private joke.

When the first mime troupe left, another took its place. This one tried to exaggerate the excesses at one of Anthimos' revels. The people who filled the stands alternately gasped and whooped. Unlike his uncle and Gnatios, the Emperor watched attentively and howled laughter. Krispos chuckled, too, not least because much of what the mimes thought wild enough to put in their act was milder than things he'd really seen at Anthimos' feasts.

The next troupe came out in striped caftans and felt hats that looked like upside-down buckets. The make-believe Makuraners capered about. The people in the stands jeered and hissed. In his high seat on the spine, Petronas looked pleased with himself.

"Make the men from the west look like idiots and weaklings and everyone will be more willing to go to war with them," Mavros said. He guffawed as one of the mimes pretended to relieve himself into his hat.

"I suppose so," Krispos said. "But there are a fair number of people from Makuran here in the city, rug-dealers and ivory merchants and such. They're just . . . people. Half the folk in the Amphitheater must have dealt with them at one time or another. They know Makuraners aren't like this."

"I daresay they do, when they stop to think about it. How many people do you know who always take the time to stop and think, though?"

"Not many," Krispos admitted, a little sadly.

The pseudo-Makuraners fled in mock terror as the next troupe, whose members were dressed as Videssian soldiers, came out. That won a last laugh and a cheer at the same time. The "soldiers" quickly proved no more heroic than the Makuraners they replaced, which to Krispos' way of thinking weakened the message Petronas was trying to put across.

Act followed act, all competent, some very funny indeed. The city folk leaned back in their seats to enjoy the spectacle. Krispos enjoyed it, too, even while he wished the troupes were a little less polished. Back in his village, a big part of the fun had lain in taking part in the skits and poking fun at the ones that went wrong. Here no one save professionals took part and nothing went wrong.

When he grumbled about that, Mavros said, ''For hundreds of years, Emperors have been putting on spectacles and entertaining people in the capital, to keep them from thinking up ways to get into mischief for themselves. Save for riots, I don't think they know how to make their own entertainment any more.'' He leaned forward. ''See these dancers? They come on just before that troupe the Sevastokrator hired.''

The dancers came on, went off. Krispos paid scant attention to them. He found he was pounding his fist on his thigh as he waited for the next company. He made himself stop.

The mimes came onto the track a few at a time. Some were dressed as ordinary townsfolk, others, once more, as imperial troops. The townsfolk acted out chatting among themselves. The troops marched back and forth. Out came a tall fellow wearing the imperial raiment. The soldiers sprang to attention; the civilians flopped down in comically overdone prostrations.

A dozen parasol-bearers, the proper imperial number, followed the mime playing the Avtokrator. But it soon became obvious they were not attached to him, but rather to the figure who emerged after him. That man was in a fancy robe, too, but one padded out so that he looked even wider than he was tall. A low murmur of laughter ran through the Amphitheater as the audience recognized who he was supposed to be.

''How much did we have to pay that mime to get him to shave his beard?'' Krispos asked. ''He looks a lot more like Skombros without it.''

''He held out for two goldpieces,'' Mavros answered. ''I finally ended up paying him. You're right; it's worth it.''

''Aye, it is. You might also want to think about paying him for a holiday away from the city till his beard grows back again, at least if he wants to live to work next Midwinter's Day,'' Krispos said. After a moment's surprise, Mavros nodded.

Up on the spine, Petronas sat at ease, watching the mimes but still not seeming to pay any great attention to them. Krispos admired his coolness; no one would have guessed by looking at him that he'd had anything to do with this skit. Anthimos leaned forward to see better, curiosity on his face—whatever he'd been told about this troupe's performance, it was something different from this. And Skombros—Skombros' fleshy features were so still and hard, they might have been carved from granite.

The mock-Anthimos on the track walked around receiving the plaudits of his subjects. The parasol-bearers stayed with the pseudo-Skombros, who was also accompanied by a couple of disgusting hangers-on, one with gray hair, the other with black.

The actors playing citizens lined up to pay their taxes to the Emperor. He collected a sack of coins from each one, headed over to pay the soldiers. At last the mime-Skombros bestirred himself. He intercepted Anthimos, patted him on the back, put an arm around him, and distracted him enough to whisk the sacks away. The Avtokrator's befuddlement on discovering he had no money to give his troops won loud guffaws from the stands.

Meanwhile, the mime playing the vestiarios shared the sacks with his two slimy colleagues. They fondled the money with lascivious abandonment.

Almost as an afterthought, the pseudo-Skombros went back to the Emperor. After another round of the hail-fellow-well-met routine he had used before, he charmed the crown off Anthimos' head. The actor playing the Emperor did not seem to notice it was gone. Skombros took the crown over to his black-haired henchman, tried it on him. It was much too big; it hid half the fellow's face. With a shrug, as if to say "not yet," the vestiarios restored it to Anthimos.

The Amphitheater grew still during that last bit of business. Then, far up in the stands, someone shouted, "To the ice with Skombros!" That one thin cry unleashed a torrent of abuse against the eunuch.

Krispos and Mavros looked at each other and grinned. Over on the spine, Petronas kept up his pose of indifference. The real Skombros sat very still, refusing to notice any of the gibes hurled at him. He had nerve, Krispos thought grudgingly. Then Krispos' eyes slid to the man for whom the skit had been put on, the Avtokrator of the Videssians.

Anthimos rubbed his chin and stared thoughtfully from the departing troupe of mimes to Skombros and back again. "I hope he got it," Mavros said.

"He got it," Krispos said. "He may be foolish, but he's a long way from stupid. I just hope he takes notice of—hey!"

An apple flung by someone farther back in the crowd had caught Krispos in the shoulder. A cabbage whizzed by his head.

Another apple, thrown by someone with a mighty arm, splashed not far from Skombros' seat. "Dig up the vestiarios' bones!" a woman screeched—the Videssian call to riot. In a moment, the whole Amphitheater was screaming it.

Petronas stood and spoke to the commander of the Haloga guards. Pale winter sun glittered on the northerners' axeblades as they swung them up over their shoulders. The Halogai yelled together, a deep, wordless shout that cut through the cries from the stands like one of their axes cleaving flesh.

"Now for the interesting question," Mavros said. "Will that hold them, or will we have ourselves an uprising right now?"

Krispos gulped. When he put his plan to Petronas, he hadn't thought of that. Getting rid of Skombros was one thing; pulling Videssos the city down with the eunuch was something else again. Given the capital's volatile populace, the chance was real.

The Halogai shouted again, the threat in their voices plain as the snarl of a wolf. Another troop of northerners, axes at the ready, tramped out onto the track from under the Amphitheater.

"There are enough people here to swamp them," Krispos said nervously.

"I know." Mavros seemed to be enjoying himself. "But are there enough people here willing to get maimed doing it?"

There weren't. Insults continued to rain down on Skombros, but the missiles more tangible than insults stopped. Finally someone yelled, "Get the soldiers off the track! We want the mimes!" Soon everyone took up the cry: "We want the mimes! We want the mimes!"

This time Anthimos spoke to the Haloga commander. The warrior bowed. At his command, the northerners lowered their weapons. The newly emerged band of imperial guards marched back through the gate from which they had come. A moment later, a fresh troupe of mimes replaced them. Cheers filled the Amphitheater.

"Fickle buggers," Mavros said with a contemptuous jerk of his head. "Half an hour from now, half of them won't remember what they were screaming about."

"Maybe not," Krispos said, "but Skombros will, and so will Anthimos."

"That is the point, isn't it?" Mavros leaned back in his chair. "Let's see what antics this new bunch has in 'em, shall we?"

* * *

The throne in the Grand Courtroom belonged to Anthimos. Sitting in a raised chair in his own suite, dressed in his full Sevastokrator's regalia, Petronas looked quite imperial enough, Krispos thought from his place at his master's left.

He looked around. "This room is different somehow," he said.

"I've screened off that part of it." Petronas pointed. Sure enough, a wooden screen like the one that gave privacy to the imperial niche at the High Temple was in place.

The openings in the woodwork were so small that Krispos could not see what, if anything, lay behind it. He asked, "Why did you put the screen up?"

"Let's just say you're not the only one who ever comes up with bright ideas," the Sevastokrator said. Krispos shrugged. If Petronas didn't feel like explaining, he could hardly force him to.

Eroulos came in and bowed to Petronas. "His Majesty and the vestiarios are here, Highness."

"Show them in, by all means," the Sevastokrator said.

Petronas' efficient steward had already supplied Anthimos and Skombros with goblets. The Emperor lowered his to grin at Krispos as he and Petronas rose in greeting. Skombros' face was somber. Had he been less practiced at schooling his features, Krispos judged, he would have looked nervously from one of his foes to the other. As it was, his eyes flicked back and forth between them.

Petronas welcomed him affably enough, waved him to a seat beside Anthimos', which was even more splendid than the one in which Petronas sat—the Sevastokrator did not believe in giving unintentional offense. After Eroulos refilled Anthimos' wine cup, Petronas said, "And what can I do for you today, nephew and Majesty?"

Anthimos sipped, glanced from Petronas to Skombros, licked his lips, and took a hefty swig of wine. Thus fortified, he said, "My vestiarios here would like to, ah, try to repair any ill-feeling that may exist between the two of you. May he speak?"

"You are my Avtokrator," Petronas declared. "If it be your will that he speak to me, of course I shall hear him with all the attention he merits." He turned his head toward Skombros and waited expectantly.

"I thank you, your Imperial Highness. You are gracious to me," Skombros said, his sexless voice soft and persuasive. "As I seem somehow to have offended your Imperial Highness—and that was never my intent, for my concern, as yours, is solely for the comfort and especially for the glory of his Imperial Majesty whom we both serve—I thought it best at this time to offer my deepest and most sincere apologies for whatever I have done to disturb your Imperial Highness' tranquility and to tender my assurances that any such disturbance was purely inadvertent on my part and shall not be repeated."

He paused to take a deep breath. Krispos did not blame him; he could not have brought out such a long sentence to save his life. He doubted whether he could have written one so complex.

Petronas was more used to the grandiloquence of formal Videssian speech. Nodding to the vestiarios, he began, "Esteemed sir—"

From behind that newly installed screen, a soft chorus of female voices chanted, "You have five chins, and a lard belly below them." Krispos happened to be taking a sip of wine; he all but choked on it. But for the content of what that hidden chorus sang, its response was much like that of a temple choir to the prayers of a priest.

Skombros sat perfectly still, but could not help the flush that rose from his neck to the roots of his hair. Anthimos looked about in surprise, as if unsure where the chorus was or whether he'd truly heard it. And Petronas seemed to shake himself. "I'm sorry," he told Skombros. "I must have been woolgathering. What was it you wanted?"

The vestiarios tried again. "Your Imperial Highness, I ah, wanted to apologize for, ah, anything I may have done to, ah, offend you, and I certainly want to assure you I, ah, meant no harm." This time, Krispos noted, his delivery was less polished than before.

Petronas nodded. "Esteemed sir—"

"You have five chins, and a lard belly below them." The voices of the chorus rang out once more.

This time Krispos was ready for them and kept his face straight. Anthimos stared again, then giggled. Hearing that, Skombros seemed to wilt. Petronas prompted him, "You were saying?"

"Does it matter?" Skombros asked bleakly.

"Why, esteemed sir—"

The chorus took up where the Sevastokrator left off: "You have five chins, and a lard belly below them."

Anthimos giggled again, louder. Ignoring all courtly etiquette, Skombros heaved his bulk out of his chair and stalked toward the door. "Dear me," Petronas exclaimed as the eunuch slammed it behind him. "Do you think I said something wrong?"

IX

Mavros, as was his way, heard the news first. "Skombros resigned his position last night."

"What, the esteemed sir?" Krispos whistled the choral response.

"Aye, the very same." Mavros laughed—that story had spread through the palace complex like wildfire. "Not only that, he's had himself tonsured and fled into a monastery. So, they tell me, have his nephew Askyltos and his brother-in-law Evmolpos."

"If I were wearing their robes, I'd flee to a monastery, too," Krispos said. "Petronas respects the good god's followers, so he might leave them there and not take their heads now that their protector's fallen."

"So he might." Mavros sound regretful. Then he brightened. "Now that their protector's fallen, who's to be the new vestiarios?" Grinning, he pointed at Krispos.

"We'll see. It's the Avtokrator's choice, of course." For all his own good times with Anthimos, for all Petronas' urging, he knew the Emperor might just choose another eunuch as his new chamberlain. That would be easiest, and Anthimos liked doing things the easiest way.

But a couple of hours later, while Krispos was making sure the new horseshoes on Petronas' favorite hunter were firmly nailed in place, Onorios came up to him and said, "There's a eunuch outside who wants to talk with you."

"Thanks. I'll see him in a minute." Krispos had one more hoof to check. As he'd expected, the blacksmith had done a good job. Knowing was better than expecting, though. When he was through, he walked out to see the Emperor's servant.

It was the tall, thin eunuch who had taken Krispos to his first revel with Anthimos the summer before. Now the fellow made no snide remarks about the smell of the stables. Instead, he bowed low. "Krispos, his Imperial Majesty bids you join his household as vestiarios, head of his domestic staff."

"He honors me. Tell me your name, please, esteemed sir. If we are both of His Majesty's household, I should know you."

The eunuch straighted. "I am called Barsymes," he said with the first approval Krispos had heard from him. "Now if you will follow me, ah—" He stopped, frowning. "Should I call you 'esteemed sir' or 'eminent sir'? You are vestiarios, a post traditionally held by an esteemed sir, and yet you—" He hesitated again, "—you have a beard. The proper protocol is a puzzlement."

Krispos started to laugh, then realized he would be worrying about just such concerns himself in his new post. "Either way is all right with me, Barsymes," he said.

"I have it!" The eunuch looked as pleased as his doleful features would allow. "Now if you will come with me, esteemed and eminent sir . . ."

Krispos obediently followed. If Barsymes had found a formula that satisfied him, well and good. They scuffed through snow together for a while before Krispos said, "I hope you and your comrades will not be troubled, serving with . . . serving with someone who has a beard."

"It is the Avtokrator's will," Barsymes said, which was no answer at all. He walked on, not looking at Krispos. After a while, he decided to continue. "We do remember that you mocked Skombros for being a eunuch."

"Only when he mocked me first for being a groom," Krispos said.

"Yes, there is some truth in that," Barsymes said judiciously, "though by now you will have noted, esteemed and eminent sir, that your condition is rather easier to change than Skombros'." Being without any better reply, Krispos could only nod. He felt a little easier when Barsymes went on, half to himself, "Still, you may indeed be entitled to the benefit of the doubt."

They passed through a grove of cherry trees, bare-branched and skeletal with winter. Armed Halogai stood outside the entrance to the elegant little building in the center of the grove.

Krispos had seen some of them before, guarding Anthimos' revels. Most of them had been drunk then. Now they looked sober and reliable. He knew little of soldiers' ways, but the difference seemed remarkable.

As if reading his mind, Barsymes said, "Any guard who fails of alertness while protecting their Majesty's residence is forthwith banished back to Halogaland, forfeiting all pay and benefactions earned here."

"A good plan." Krispos wondered why it didn't hold wherever the Emperor was. Knowing Anthimos, probably because when he was having a good time, he wanted everyone else to have one, too.

The Halogai nodded to Barsymes and gave Krispos curious looks as he walked up the stairs with the eunuch. One of the guards said something in his own language. The others laughed. Krispos had no trouble imagining several rough jokes, most of them at his expense. He sighed. However much it meant to him, this business of taking over a eunuch's post brought complications.

His eyes needed a moment to adjust to the dimmer light inside the imperial residence, and a moment more to notice that what light there was came neither from torches nor, for the most part, from windows. Instead, panes of alabaster scraped to translucent thinness were set into the ceiling.

The pale, clear light that filtered through them displayed to best advantage the treasures set along both sides of the central hallway. Barsymes pointed to some of them as he led Krispos past. "Here is the battle helmet of a Makuraner King of Kings, taken centuries ago after a tremendous victory not far from Mashiz. . . . This is the chalice from which the assembled prelates of Phos drank together in ritual renunciation of Skotos at the great synod not long after the High Temple was built. . . . Here is a portrait of the Emperor Stavrakios, most often called the Conqueror. . . ."

The portrait drew Krispos' eye. Stavrakios wore the red boots, the imperial crown, and a gilded mail shirt, but he did not look like an Emperor to Krispos. He looked like a veteran underofficer about to give his troops a hard time for a sloppy piece of drill.

"Come along," Barsymes said when Krispos paused to study that tough face. He followed the eunuch down the hall, thinking that Anthimos did not look like his idea of an Emperor, either.

He laughed at himself. Maybe he just didn't know what an Emperor was supposed to look like.

Another eunuch heard Barsymes and Krispos coming and stuck his head out a doorway. "You have him, eh?" he said. "Very well. His Majesty will be glad to see him." If the eunuch himself was glad to see Krispos, he concealed it magnificently.

The fellow's head disappeared again. Krispos heard his voice, too low to make out words, then Anthimos', louder: "What's that, Tyrovitzes? He's here? Well, bring him in." Barsymes heard, also, and led Krispos forward.

Anthimos sat at a small table eating cakes. Krispos went down on his belly in a full proskynesis. "Your Imperial Majesty," he murmured.

"Get up, get up," the Emperor said impatiently. "The bowing and scraping can stop when you're in here. You're part of my household now. You didn't bow and scrape when you were in your parents' household, did you?"

"No, your Majesty," Krispos said. He wondered what his father would have made of having his household compared to the Avtokrator's. Most likely, Phostis would have laughed himself silly. That Anthimos could make the comparison only showed how little he realized what a special life he led.

The Emperor said, "Anything special you think you'll need, Krispos?"

"Having you remember I'm more used to tending horses than people would help a lot, your Majesty," Krispos answered. Anthimos stared at him, then let out a startled laugh. Krispos went on, "I'm sure your other servants will help me learn what I need to know as fast as I can."

Anthimos glanced toward Barsymes. "Of course, your Majesty," the eunuch said in his neutral voice.

"Good. That's settled, then," the Emperor said. Krispos hoped it was. Anthimos went on, "Take Krispos to his room, Barsymes. He can have the rest of today and tomorrow to move in; I expect the rest of you will be able to care for me and Dara till morning after next."

"We shall manage, your Majesty," Barsymes agreed. "Now if you will excuse us? This way, Krispos." As he led Krispos down the hall, he explained, "The vestiarios' bedchamber is next to that of the Avtokrator, so that he may most conveniently attend his master at any hour of the day or night." The eunuch opened a door. "You will stay here."

Krispos gasped. He'd never seen such a profusion of gold and fine silks. Petronas surely had more, but did not flaunt it so. And the featherbed in the center of the room looked thick enough to smother in.

"You will understand, I hope," Barsymes said, seeing his expression, "that Skombros, having no hope of progeny, saw no point in stinting his personal comfort. The failing is not unique to us eunuchs, but is perhaps more common among us."

"I suppose so," Krispos said, still stunned by the room's opulence. Near that fabulous featherbed, a little silver bell hung from a red cord that ran up into the ceiling and disappeared. He pointed to it. "What's that for?"

"The cord runs to the imperial bedchamber next door. When that bell rings, you must attend."

"All right." Krispos hesitated, then went on, "Thanks, Barsymes. You've helped." He held out his hand.

The eunuch took it. His palms were smooth, but his grip showed surprising strength. "Not all of us were enamored of Skombros," he remarked. "If you do not despise us for what we are, we may be able to work together well enough."

"I hope so." Krispos was not making idle chitchat; as at Petronas' stables, he knew he would fail if the people he was supposed to oversee turned against him. And eunuchs, unlike the straightforward stable hands, moved with proverbial guile; he was not sure he was ready to counter their machinations. With luck, he wouldn't have to.

He was relieved to escape the room that had been Skombros' and was now his, though he wondered how the ex-vestiarios enjoyed a bare monastery cell, so different from this splendor. The image of Stavrakios caught his eye again as he walked down the hall. Imagining what that warrior-Emperor would have said about Skombros' luxuries—or Anthimos'—gave him something to smile about while he went back to say good-bye to his friends and collect his belongings.

At the stables, after the inevitable round of congratulations and backslapping, he managed to get Stotzas off to one side for a few minutes. "Do you want my job now that I'm leaving?" he asked the senior groom. "The good god knows you're the best man with horses here, and I'd be pleased to speak with Petronas for you."

"You're a gentleman, lad, and I'm pleased you asked, but no thanks," Stotzas said. "You're right, it's the horses I fancy, and

I'd have less time for 'em if I had to worry about bossing the men around instead."

Krispos nodded. He'd thought Stotzas would say that, but he hadn't been sure; if the graybeard wanted the job, he deserved it. Since he didn't, Krispos had someone else in mind to recommend to the Sevastokrator.

When he got back to his apartment in the Grand Courtroom, he discovered he needed more than one duffel bag for what he had inside. He smiled to himself as he went back to the stables to borrow Petronas' brown gelding one last time. The horse snorted reproachfully as he loaded it with his worldly goods.

"Oh, hush," he told it. "Better your back than mine." The horse did not seem convinced, but let him lead it over to the imperial residence.

The bell beside Krispos' bed rang. At first, he tried to fit the sound into his dream. The bell kept ringing. He woke with a start. Anthimos was calling him!

He sprang out of bed naked, threw on a robe, shoved his feet into sandals, and dashed for the imperial bedchamber. "Your Majesty," he said, puffing. "How may I serve you?"

Wearing no more than Krispos had, Anthimos was sitting up in bed—a bed that looked comfortable enough, but not nearly so magnificent as the one Krispos had appropriated from Skombros. The Avtokrator grinned at his new vestiarios. "I'll have to get used to your appearing so quickly," he said, which eased Krispos' mind—he hadn't taken too long to wake, then. Anthimos went on, "Time to face the day."

"Certainly, your Majesty." The eunuchs had spent the previous afternoon talking themselves hoarse about the Emperor's routine. Krispos hoped he remembered it. Beside the bed stood a chamber pot; first things first, for Emperor as for peasant. Bowing, Krispos lifted it and handed it to Anthimos.

While the Avtokrator stood up and used it, Krispos got him clean drawers and a fresh robe. He helped Anthimos dress, then ceremoniously escorted him to a mirror of polished silver. Anthimos made a face at his reflection while Krispos combed his hair and beard. "Looks like me," the Emperor said when he was done. "Eyes aren't even too bloodshot—but then, I got to sleep early last night." He turned back to the bed. "Didn't I, Dara?"

"What's that?" Buried in blankets to the crown of her head, Anthimos' Empress sounded more than half asleep herself.

"Didn't I get to bed early last night?" the Avtokrator repeated. "I've even found an advantage to it—my eyes look much clearer than usual this morning."

Dara rolled over and sat up. Krispos did his best not to stare—like Anthimos, she slept nude. Then she noticed him, squeaked, and yanked the blankets up to her chin.

Anthimos laughed. "No need for such worries, my dear. This is Krispos, the new vestiarios."

Keeping his eyes on his own toes, Krispos said in his most formal voice, "I did not mean to startle you, your Majesty."

"It's—all right," Dara said after a moment. "Seeing the beard caught me by surprise, that's all. His Majesty said you were a whole man, but it must have slipped my mind. Go ahead with what you were doing; I'll summon a maidservant." She had a bellpull on her side of the bed, too, with a green cord. She held the blankets in place with one hand, reached out with the other.

Krispos fetched the Emperor's red boots from the closet and helped Anthimos into them. They were tight, and pulling them onto the imperial feet took some work. The maidservant came in while he was still fighting to get them on. She paid no attention to Krispos' beard. Indeed, with him bent down in front of the Emperor, she could hardly have noticed whether he had one—or whether he had horns and fangs, for that matter. She chose a gown from Dara's closet and whisked away the bedclothes so she could dress the empress.

Dara again glanced nervously toward Krispos, but relaxed when she saw him intent on his own duties. He did his best to take no special notice of her. If she had been easy in the presence of the former vestiarios, he did not want to rob her of that ease.

At the same time, even the brief, self-conscious glimpses he'd had of her showed she was a dazzling young woman. She was small and dark, with lustrous, almost blue-black hair that crackled as her maidservant brushed it. She had an aquiline profile, with high, sculptured cheekbones and a strong, rather pointed chin. Her body was as lovely as her face.

Krispos wondered why Anthimos, having such an Empress, also bedded any girl who caught his eye. Maybe Dara lacked passion, he thought. Or maybe Anthimos was like some of Petronas' stable hands, unable to pass up any opportunity he found.

And unlike them, he found plenty—few would say no to the Avtokrator of the Videssians.

Such wherefores were not his concern, though. Getting the Emperor's boots on was. Grunting with effort, he finally succeeded. "Good job," Anthimos said, laughing and patting him on the head. "From all I've heard, you had a tougher time wrestling with my boots than you did with that giant Kubrati."

"Different sort of wrestling, Majesty." Krispos had to remind himself what came next in the routine. "And now, with what would you and your lady care to break your fast?"

"A bloater for me," Anthimos said. "A bloater and wine. How about you, my dear?"

"Just porridge, I think," Dara said. Krispos' sympathies lay with her. Smoked and salted mackerel was all very well, but not his idea of breakfast food.

He carried the imperial couple's requests back to the kitchens and had a bowl of porridge himself while the cook fixed a tray. "The good god be thanked his Majesty's in a simple mood today," the fellow said as he poured wine from an amphora into a silver carafe. "Have you ever tried fixing shrimp and octopus stew while he's waiting? Or, worse, had to go running out to try to buy oranges out of season because it crossed his mind he wanted some?"

"Did you find any?" Krispos asked, intrigued.

"Aye, there's a shop or two that sells 'em preserved by magic, for those who have the urge and the money at the same time. Didn't cost me above twenty times what they usually run, and what sort of thanks did I get? Precious little, I'll tell you."

Carrying the tray to a dining hall not far from the imperial bedchamber, Krispos wondered if Anthimos had even known the fruit was out of season. When would he have occasion to learn? All he needed to do was ask for something to have it appear before him.

The Emperor devoured his bloater with lip-smacking gusto. "Now, my dear," he said to Dara, "why don't you go and tend to your embroidery for a while? Krispos and I have some serious business to discuss."

Krispos would have resented such a cavalier dismissal. Whatever Dara felt, she did not let it show. She rose, nodded to Anthimos, and left without a word. She took as much notice of Krispos as of the chair on which he sat.

"What business is there, your Majesty?" Krispos asked, curious and a little worried; none of the Emperor's eunuchs had warned him anything special was in the wind.

But Anthimos answered, "Why, we have to decide what the chances will be for tonight's festivities."

"Oh," Krispos said. Following the Emperor's pointing finger, he saw the ball-filled crystal bowl sitting on a shelf. He got it down, took apart the balls, and set their halves on the table between himself and Anthimos. "Where can I find pen and parchment, your Majesty?"

"Somewhere around here," Anthimos said vaguely. While Krispos poked through drawers in a sideboard, Anthimos continued, "I think the number tonight will be eleven, after the paired single pips on the dice when someone throws Phos' little suns. What goes well with eleven?"

Krispos found writing materials at last. "Eleven dice, your majesty, since the number is taken from gambling?"

"Excellent! I knew you were clever. What else?"

"How about—hmm—eleven mice?"

"So you want to rhyme tonight, do you? Well, why not? I expect the servants can find eleven mice by evening. What else?"

They came up with eleven pounds of ice, eleven grains of rice, eleven lice—"I *know* the servants can find those," Anthimos said—eleven drams of spice, eleven things nice, and eleven kinds of vice. "Both of those will send the winner to the stews," the Avtokrator declared.

"How about eleven gold*pice*?" Krispos suggested when their inspiration began to flag. "It's not a perfect rhyme—"

"It is if you write it that way," Anthimos said, so Krispos did.

"Your Majesty, could I get you to think on something else about these chances for a moment?" Krispos asked. At the Emperor's nod, he went on, "You might want to give them out to the entertainers along with your guests. They're not rich; think how overjoyed they'd be to pick one of the good chances."

Anthimos' answering smile was not altogether pleasant. "Yes, and think how downcast they'd be if they didn't. That could be amusing, too. We'll give it a try."

Krispos knew he hadn't got his way for the reason he wanted, but he'd got it. Some of the jugglers and musicians and courtesans would end up better off, and even the ones who came away from the chances disappointed would actually be in no worse state than before, he told himself.

"What's next?" the Avtokrator asked.

"I am given to understand a new Makuraner embassy has come to the city," Krispos said carefully. "If you cared to, I suppose you could meet the high ambassador."

Anthimos yawned. "Another time, perhaps. Petronas will tend to them. That's his proper function, seeing to such tiresome details."

"As you wish, your Majesty." Krispos did not press the issue. He'd done his best to make the meeting sound dull. He knew Petronas wanted to keep his own hands firmly on the Empire's relations with its neighbors.

Instead of meeting with the Makuraner high ambassador, Anthimos went to the Amphitheater. He ate the coarse, greasy food the vendors sold there; he drank rough wine from a cracked clay cup; he awarded five hundred goldpieces to a driver who'd brought his chariot from the back of the pack to first in the last couple of laps. The crowd cheered his generosity. It all worked well enough, Krispos thought; they had a symbol, Anthimos had fun, and Petronas had the government.

And what do I have? Krispos wondered. Part of the answer was plain enough: good food, good lodging, even the ear of the Avtokrator of the Videssians—for such matters as chances at revels, anyhow. All that was marvelously better than the nothing with which he'd arrived at Videssos the city a few years before.

He was discovering, though, that the more he had, the more he wanted. He'd read two or three chronicles of the Empire's past. None of them recorded the name of a single vestiarios.

A few days later, Anthimos went hunting. Krispos stayed behind. Running the imperial residence, even with the Emperor absent, was a full-time job. He was not unduly surprised when Eroulos came by a little before noon. This time Petronas' steward bowed to him. "His Imperial Highness the Sevastokrator would be pleased to take lunch with you, esteemed and eminent sir, your duties permitting."

"Of course." Krispos gave Eroulos a quizzical look. "So you've heard my new title?"

Eroulos sounded surprised that Krispos need ask. "It's my business to hear such things."

Petronas had heard it, too. "Ah, the esteemed and eminent vestiarios," he said, bowing back when Krispos went on one knee before him. "Here, have some wine. How fares my nephew?"

"Well enough, Highness," Krispos said. "He showed no great interest in making the acquaintance of the new envoy from Makuran."

"Just as well," Petronas said, scowling. "There will be war soon—if not this year, then the next. Probably next year. I'll have to take the field in person, and to do that, I need you solidly in place with Anthimos so he won't listen to too much nonsense while I'm away from the city in the westlands."

There lay the weakness in Petronas' position, Krispos thought: while he ruled, he was not Videssos' ruler. If Anthimos ever decided to take up the reins of power for himself, or if someone else steered him, the prestige that went with the imperial title might well make officials follow him rather than his uncle.

Krispos said, "I'm glad you place such confidence in me, Highness."

"We've discussed why I do." Petronas suavely changed the subject, "Anthimos' gain is my loss, I'm finding. The stable hands still do their individual work well enough, but there's less overall direction to things without you. I asked Stotzas if he wanted your job, but he turned me down flat."

"He did the same with me when I asked him if he wanted me to mention him to you." Krispos hesitated. "May I suggest someone else?"

"Why not? Whom do you have in mind?"

"How about Mavros? I know he's even younger than I am, but everyone likes him. And he wouldn't be slack; he takes horses seriously. He's more a real horseman than I, as a matter of fact. I got to the point where I knew what I was doing, but he comes by it naturally."

"Hmm." Petronas stroked his beard. At last he said, "You may have something there. He's likelier than anyone I'd thought of, at any rate. I'll see what Eroulos has to say; he's not Mavros' personal friend, as you are. If he thinks the youngster will answer, I may well give him a try. My thanks."

"I'm pleased to help, even if I'm not part of your household any more." Krispos doubted Eroulos would have anything bad to say about Mavros. All the same, he took note of Petronas' caution. Knowing Krispos' advice was not disinterested, the Sevastokrator would not move until he heard some that was.

Another bit of business worth remembering, Krispos thought. He wondered if he'd ever have a chance to use it.

The chance came sooner than he'd expected. A few days later, he received a letter from a certain Ypatios, asking if the two of them could meet to "discuss matters of mutual interest." Krispos had never heard of Ypatios. Some discreet inquiry among the eunuchs let him find out that the fellow headed a large trading house. Krispos arranged a meeting at the imperial residence on an afternoon when Anthimos was watching the chariots.

Barsymes ushered Ypatios into the antechamber where Krispos sat waiting. The man bowed. "A pleasure to make your acquaintance, esteemed sir," he began, and then stopped, seeming to notice Krispos' beard for the first time. "I meant no offense by that title, I want you to know. You are vestiarios, after all, but I see—"

"I'm usually styled 'esteemed and eminent.' " This routine, Krispos realized, was one he'd need to get used to.

Ypatios quickly recovered his poise. " 'Esteemed and eminent' it is. Very good." The merchant was about fifty, well fed and shrewd-looking. "As I said in my letter, esteemed and eminent sir, I believe we have interests in common."

"You said so," Krispos agreed. "You didn't say what they were, though."

"One can never tell who all reads a letter," Ypatios said. "Let me explain: my sons and I specialize in importing fine furs from the kingdom of Agder. For some time his Imperial Majesty, may his years be many, has had under consideration a law to lower the import duties upon such furs. His favorable action upon this law would, I'll not deny, work to our advantage."

"Would it?" Krispos steepled his fingertips. He began to see in which quarter the wind lay.

Ypatios nodded solemnly. "It would indeed. And my sons and I are prepared to be generous in our appreciation. As you are in such intimate contact with his Imperial Majesty, surely you might find occasion to suggest a course of action to him. Our own humble requests, expressed in written form, perhaps have not had the good fortune to come under his eyes."

"Maybe not," Krispos said. It occurred to him that even had Anthimos been the most conscientious ruler Videssos ever knew, he would have had trouble staying up with all the minutiae of the Empire. Since Anthimos was anything but, he undoubtedly had never seen the law he was supposed to be considering. Krispos went on, "Why are the duties against the furs so high now?"

Ypatios' lip curled in a fine round sneer. "Who can say why stupid laws remain in force? To make beggars of me and my family, I suspect." He did not look as if he'd be whining for crusts on a street corner any time soon. His next words confirmed that. "Still, I might see my way clear to investing twenty pieces of gold to repair the injustice presently on the books."

"I will be in touch with you" was all Krispos said. Ypatios' florid face fell. He bowed his way out. Krispos tugged at his beard and thought for a while. The gesture reminded him of Petronas. He decided to call on the Sevastokrator.

"And how may I help the esteemed and eminent sir this day?" Petronas asked. Krispos explained. Petronas said, "He only offered you twenty? Stick him for at least a pound of gold if you decide to do it. He may squeal a bit, but he can afford to pay you."

"Should I do it, though?" Krispos persisted.

"For things like that, make up your own mind, lad. I don't care one way or the other—too small to worry about. If you're not just out for the cash, maybe you *should* find out why the law is the way it is. That will give you a clue as to whether it needs changing."

Krispos did some digging, or tried to. Navigating the maze of Videssian bureaucracy proved anything but easy. The clerk of the courts referred him to the master of the archives. The master of the archives sent him to the office of the eparch of the city. The eparch of the city's adjutant tried to send him back to the clerk of the courts, at which point Krispos threw a tantrum. The adjutant had second thoughts and suggested he visit the customs commissioner.

The customs commissioner was not in his office and would not be back for a week; his wife had just had a baby. As Krispos grumpily turned to go, someone called, "Excellent sir! May I help you, excellent sir?"

Turning, Krispos found himself face to face with the customs agent whose scheme he'd urged on Anthimos outside the Amphitheater. "Maybe you can," he said, not bothering to correct the fellow's use of his title. "Here's what I need . . ."

"Yes, I can find that," the customs agent said when he was done. "A pleasure to be able to repay your kindness in some small way. Wait here if you would, excellent sir." He vanished into a room filled with boxes of scrolls. At last he reemerged, wiping dust from his hands and robe. "Sorry to be so long; things are in a frightful muddle back there. The law you mention turns out to have been promulgated to protect the livelihood of trappers and hunters who lived by the Astris River from competition from Agderian furs."

"By the Astris?" Krispos said. "But the Kubratoi have ruled the lands around there for hundreds of years."

"You know that, and I know that, but the law doesn't seem to have heard the news."

"It will," Krispos promised. "Thanks for your help."

"After what you did for me, excellent sir, it was my privilege."

Krispos went back to the imperial residence and scribbled a note to Ypatios. "Though your case has weight, it does not yet have enough weight to go forward." He was sure the merchant would be able to figure out that he was talking about the weight of coins.

Sure enough, when Ypatios met him again, the first thing he asked was, "Just how heavy does our case have to be?"

"A pound would do nicely," Krispos said, remembering Petronas' guess. He kept his voice bland, but waited nervously for Ypatios to scream at him.

The fur seller only sighed. "A pound it is, esteemed and eminent sir. You're still cheaper to do business with than Skombros was."

"Am I?" When Skombros became a priest, all his worldly possessions were forfeited to the imperial fisc. They would likely keep Anthimos in revels a good long time, Krispos thought, wondering just how many bribes the former vestiarios had taken.

After the gold changed hands, Krispos put the proposed change to Anthimos. "Why not?" the Avtokrator said. "Huzzah for cheaper furs!" Krispos produced the necessary document. Anthimos signed it with ink of imperial scarlet.

Krispos sent Petronas a dozen goldpieces. The Sevastokrator returned them with a note saying, "You need these more than I do, but I'll remember the thought." Since that was true, Krispos was glad to have them back. And since Petronas understood why he'd sent them, he got all the benefits of generosity without actually having to pay for it.

The singer opened the golden ball, read "Fourteen pieces of gold," screamed—right on key—and kissed Krispos on the mouth. He would have enjoyed the kiss more had the singer been a woman. Other than that, the performer's reaction left nothing to be desired. The fellow ran through the hall, musically shrieking at the top of his lungs.

Fourteen goldpieces was nothing worth shrieking about for most of Anthimos' guests. As Krispos had expected, seeing someone get so excited about what they thought of as so little amused them mightily. Moreover, what the singer now had wasn't so little for him at all.

Laughing at himself—he hadn't had to worry about kisses from men since he left Iakovitzes' service—Krispos took a long pull at his wine. He'd learned to nurse his cups at Anthimos' affairs. Tonight, though, he hadn't done as good a job as usual; he could feel his head starting to spin.

He picked his way through the crowd back to the Emperor. "May I be excused, your Majesty?"

Anthimos pouted. "So early?" It was somewhere near midnight.

"You have a midmorning meeting with Gnatios, if you'll remember, Majesty." Krispos grinned a wry grin. "And while *you* may be able to sleep until just before the time, or even to keep the most holy sir waiting, *I* have to be up early to make sure everything is as it should be."

"Oh, very well," Anthimos said grouchily. Then his eyes lit up. "Here, give me the bowl. I'll hand out chances myself for the rest of the evening." That was entertainment far less ribald than most of what he favored, but it was something new and therefore intriguing.

Krispos gladly surrendered the crystal bowl. The cool, sweet air of the spring night helped clear his head. The racket from the revel faded behind him as he walked to the imperial residence. The Haloga guards outside the entrance nodded as he went by them; they were long since used to him now.

He had just climbed into bed when the bell on the scarlet cord rang. He scowled as he scrambled into his robe in the dark; what was Anthimos doing back in his bedchamber already? The only thing he could think of was that the Emperor had sneaked after him to twit him for going to sleep so soon. That was the sort of thing Anthimos might do, but not when he'd been so excited about dealing out little gold balls.

Several lamps glowed in the imperial bedroom, but Anthimos

was not there. The Empress sat up in bed. "I can't seem to get to sleep tonight, Krispos," Dara said. "Could you please fetch me a cup of wine? My serving maids are all asleep, and I heard you just coming in. Do you mind?"

"Of course not, Majesty," Krispos said. He told the truth—a vestiarios had better not mind doing what the Empress of Videssos asked of him. "I'll be back directly."

He found a jar of wine in the dining room and poured a cup from it. "My thanks," Dara said when he brought it to her. She tossed it down almost as quickly as Anthimos might have. She was as bare as she'd been the morning Krispos first came into the imperial bedchamber, but did not bother to pull up the sheet; to her, he might as well have been a eunuch. Holding out the cup, she told him, "Fetch me another, please."

"Of course," he repeated.

She drained the cup a second time as fast as she had the first, set it down empty on the night table by the bed. "Tell me," she said, "do you expect his Imperial Majesty to return any time soon?"

"I don't know when his Majesty will come back," Krispos answered. "When I left the feast, he still seemed to be enjoying himself."

"Oh," Dara said tonelessly. "He usually returns not long after you do, I've noticed. Why not tonight?"

"Because I have to be up early tomorrow morning, to make sure everything is ready for his Majesty's meeting with the patriarch. His Majesty was kind enough to let me leave before him."

"Oh," Dara said again. Without warning, tears started streaming from her eyes. They ran down her cheeks and splashed on her uncovered breasts. That Krispos should see her upset bothered her more than him seeing her nude; she choked out, "Go away!"

He all but fled. One foot was already out in the hall when the Empress said, "No, wait. Come back, please."

Reluctantly he turned. He would sooner have faced a wolf alone and unarmed than the distraught Empress. But he did not dare disobey her, either. "What's wrong, your Majesty?" he asked in the same soft, calm tone he would have used to try to talk the wolf out of ripping his throat open.

Now she raised the sheet to her neck; if not as a man, she was aware of him as a person rather than a faceless servant.

"What's wrong?" she echoed bitterly. "What could possibly be wrong, with me trapped here in the imperial residence and my husband at hunts or the horse races by day and his cursed revels by night?"

"But—he is the Avtokrator," Krispos said.

"And so he can do just as he pleases. I know," Dara said. "Sometimes I think he is the only free man in all the Empire of Videssos. And I am his Empress. Am I free? Ha! A tradesman's wife has more freedom than I do, far more."

Krispos knew she was right. Except for rare ceremonial appearances in the Grand Courtroom, the Empress lived a sheltered, indeed a sequestered life, always screened away from the wider world by her maidservants and the palace eunuchs. As gently as he could, he said, "But surely you knew this would be so when you consented to be his Majesty's bride?"

"There wasn't much consent to it," Dara said. "Do you know what a bride show is, Krispos? I was one of a long line of pretty girls, and Anthimos happened to pick me. I was so surprised, I couldn't even talk. My father owns estates in the westlands, not far from the border with Makuran. He was thrilled—he'd have an Avtokrator for a grandson. But I—haven't even managed—to do that as I—should have." She started to cry again.

"You still have time," Krispos said. "You're younger than I am."

That distracted her, as he'd hoped it would. She gave him a sharp look, gauging his years. "Maybe a little," she said at last, not fully convinced.

"I'm certain you are. And surely his Majesty still—" He paused to make sure he used the right words, "—cares for you."

Dara understood. "Oh, aye, when he's here and not drunk asleep, or when he hasn't futtered himself out with one of his doxies—or with six of them." Fire flashed through her tears; Krispos saw she had a temper when she let it loose. Then her shoulders sagged and she bent her head. "But what's the use? I haven't given him a child, and if I don't he'll cast me out one of these days."

Again, Krispos knew she was right. Even Emperors like Anthimos, who worried about nothing, sooner or later worried about an heir. But Dara already felt far too hurt for him simply to agree with her. Instead, he said, "For all you know, you may be carrying the Avtokrator's son right now. I hope you are."

"I may be, but I don't think I am," Dara said. She studied

him, curiosity on her face. "You sound as if you mean it. Skombros said the same thing, but I was always sure he was lying."

"Skombros was ambitious for his own nephew," Krispos said. With that, he thought of his niece—no, nieces now, he'd heard—back in his own village. He sent gold every year to his sister Evdokia and Domokos. Now that he had more, he resolved to send more.

"Yes, he was," Dara said distantly. "I'm glad he's gone." After a little while, she went on, "If you fetched me one more cup of wine, I think I could sleep now, Krispos."

He brought the jar into the bedchamber. "If you find you need a bit more, your Majesty, here it is."

"Thank you, Krispos." She gave him the cup to fill. When he handed it back, her fingers closed over his for a moment. "Thank you, also, for listening to me. I think you're kind."

"I hope you do sleep, Majesty, and sleep well. Shall I blow out the lamps?"

"If you would. Leave the one on my night table burning, though, please. I'll tend to it when I'm ready." As Krispos bowed his way out of the bedchamber, Dara added, "I hope you sleep well, too."

Krispos bowed again. "Thank you for thinking of me, Majesty." He went back to his own room. Despite the wine he'd drunk at the Emperor's feast, he lay awake for a long time.

Anthimos rose from his chair. "Care to come for a stroll with me, Gnatios?"

Krispos felt like pounding his head against a wall. If the Avtokrator and the ecumenical patriarch were going out walking, then three parts in four of his preparations for this meeting had been wasted effort. More to the point, he could have slept an extra hour or two. A dull headache and scratchy eyes told him he should have.

Gnatios also rose. "Whatever your Majesty wishes."

Maybe, Krispos thought hopefully, he could doze for a bit while his master and the patriarch talked. Then Anthimos said, "You come along too, Krispos."

Thinking resentful thoughts, Krispos came. A couple of imperial guards attached themselves to the party as the Emperor and his companions walked outside.

Anthimos made cheerful small talk as he led his little party through the palace complex. Gnatios' replies were polite enough, but also increasingly curious, as if he were unsure where the Emperor was going, either in the stroll or the conversation. Krispos quietly fumed. If Anthimos was only going to burble on about the weather, why did he need to see the patriarch at all?

The Avtokrator finally stopped in front of a tumbledown building set apart from its nearest neighbors—not that any were very near—by a thick grove of dark-green cypresses. "I've decided to study sorcery," he declared. "After you left last night, Krispos, a mage worked such marvelous feats that I decided then and there to learn how they were done."

"I see," Krispos said. He did, too; it was just like Anthimos to seize on a momentary enthusiasm and ride it till he got bored.

Gnatios said, "Forgive me, your Majesty, but may I ask what your sudden interest in sorcery has to do with this elderly temple here?"

"You see what it is, then, or was? Good." Anthimos beamed. "Not all sorcery is easy or safe—you know that as well as I. What I propose to do, Gnatios, is knock the building down and replace it with a proper magical study. The site is ideal, you will agree, being isolated from the rest of the palaces."

"You want to tear the temple down?" the patriarch echoed.

"That's right. No one's used it for what must be decades. You should see the spiderwebs inside. Some of them could catch birds, I expect. It wouldn't be sacrilege or anything, really it wouldn't." The Emperor smiled his most engaging smile at Gnatios.

The ecumenical patriarch was more than twice his sovereign's age, and a good deal more than twice as serious as Anthimos. Nevertheless, the Emperor charmed him almost as if he were already using magic. Gnatios was shaking his head, but he answered, "Pyrrhos and his narrow-minded followers will rail at me, but technically, your Majesty, I suppose you are correct. Very well, I agree; you may demolish this unused temple to employ the area for your own purposes."

"Perhaps, your Majesty, you could have another temple built somewhere else in the city to make up for tearing down this one," Krispos put in.

"An excellent notion," Gnatios said. "Will you pledge to do that, your Majesty?"

"Oh, certainly," Anthimos said. "Krispos, see to it that the logothetes at the treasury know to set aside funds for a new temple. We'll knock down this old ruin one day next week, then. Gnatios, I want you to be here."

Gnatios ran a hand over his shaven head. "As you wish, your Majesty, but why am I required?"

";Why, to say a prayer while the temple gets demolished, of course." Anthimos flashed his charming smile again.

This time, it did not work. Gnatios slowly shook his head. "Your Majesty, I fear I cannot. There is in the liturgy a prayer for the construction of a temple, but we have not inherited from our forefathers a prayer over the demolition of a temple."

"Then invent one," Anthimos said. "You are a great scholar, Gnatios. Surely you can find words that will please the good god."

"How can he be pleased that one of his temples is destroyed?" the patriarch said. "Because the temple is old and has long stood vacant, he may tolerate it, but I dare not ask him to do more than that."

"Because this one is being torn down, he'll soon have a new one that won't be empty," Krispos said.

Gnatios gave him an unfriendly look. "I will joyfully pray at the erection of the new. I would do so in any event. But at the loss of a temple—no, I cannot pray over that."

"Maybe Pyrrhos would," Krispos said.

"No. Here we would agree . . . or would we?" Gnatios was as much politician as prelate. That undid him now. More to himself than to Krispos or Anthimos, he went on, "Who knows what Pyrrhos might do to gain imperial favor for his fanaticism?" After another pause, he said sourly, "Oh, very well, your Majesty, you shall have your prayer from me."

"Splendid," Anthimos said. "I knew I could rely on you, Gnatios."

The patriarch set his jaw and nodded. Happily clapping him on the shoulder, Anthimos started back to the imperial residence. Gnatios and Krispos trailed along behind the Emperor. Gnatios said softly, "I wish you would have kept your mouth shut, vestiarios."

"I serve my master," Krispos said. "If I can help him get what he wants, I will."

"He and I will both look like fools because of this ceremony he's asked for," Gnatios said. "Is that your idea of good service?"

Krispos thought Gnatios worried more about Gnatios than

about Anthimos, but all he said was, "His Majesty doesn't seem worried." Gnatios sniffed and stamped on ahead of him, blue boots scuffing flagstones.

A week later, a small crowd of priests and officials gathered for the function the Emperor had demanded. Petronas was not there; he was closeted with the Makuraner envoys. He had real work to do, Krispos thought.

Anthimos walked up and said, "Krispos, this chap with me is Trokoundos, the mage who will be instructing me. Trokoundos, this is my vestiarios, Krispos. If Trokoundos needs funds to secure apparatus or mystical goods, Krispos, make sure he has what he asks for."

"Very well, your Majesty." Krispos eyed Trokoundos with suspicion. *Someone else who wants a grip on the Emperor,* he thought indignantly. The anger that surged through him brought him up short; all at once, he understood how Petronas felt about his nephew.

Trokoundos looked straight back at Krispos, his eyes heavy-lidded and clever. "I will see you often, for I have much to teach his Majesty," he said. His voice was deep and rich. It did not suit his frame—he was only of medium height and on the thin side. He shaved his head like a priest, but wore a robe of a most unpriestly orange.

"A pleasure to meet you, mage." Krispos' cool voice gave his words the lie.

"And you, eu—" Trokoundos stopped short. He'd started the same rude rejoinder Krispos had used against Skombros, only to notice, too late, that it did not apply. "And you, vestiarios," he amended lamely.

Krispos smiled. He was glad to find the mage human enough to miss things. "My title is esteemed and eminent sir," he said, rubbing Trokoundos' nose in the mistake.

"Ah, here comes Gnatios," Anthimos said happily. Krispos and Trokoundos both turned to watch the patriarch approach.

Gnatios stopped in front of the Avtokrator and prostrated himself with grim dignity. "I have composed the prayer you required of me, your Majesty," he said as he rose.

"By all means say it, then, so the workmen may begin," the Emperor said.

Gnatios faced the temple to be torn down. He spat on the ground in rejection of Skotos, then raised his hands to the sky.

"Glory to Phos the long-suffering at all times," he declared, "now, forever, and through eons upon eons. So may it be."

"So may it be," the assembled dignitaries echoed. Their voices were less hearty than they might have been; Krispos was not the only one who glanced over to see how the Emperor would respond to a prayer that as much as said Phos had to be patient to put up with his whims.

The implied criticism sailed past him. He bowed to Gnatios. "Thank you, most holy sir. Just what the occasion demanded." Then he called, "Go to it, lads," to the band of workmen standing by the temple.

The workers attacked the dilapidated old building with picks and crowbars. The ceremony over, court officers and prelates began drifting away. Krispos started to follow Anthimos back to the imperial residence when Trokoundos put a hand on his arm. He pulled free. "What do you want?" he asked roughly.

"I need enough money to purchase several hundred sheets of parchment," the mage answered.

"What do you need with several hundred sheets of parchment?"

"I have no need of them," Trokoundos said. "His Majesty does. If he would be a mage, he first must need copy out in his own hand the spells he will thereafter employ." He set hands on hips, plainly expecting Krispos to say no—and ready to go to Anthimos with the tale.

But Krispos said, "Of course. I'll have the money sent to you straightaway."

"You will?" Trokoundos blinked. His belligerent air vanished.

"In fact," Krispos went on, "if you want to come to the residence with me, I'll give you the gold right now; I'll take it from the household chest."

"You will?" Trokoundos said again. Those heavy-lidded eyes widened. "Thank you very much. That's most gracious of you."

"I serve his Majesty," Krispos said, as he had to Gnatios. "How much do you think you'll need?" However much it was, he would cheerfully pay it. If Trokoundos was going to set Anthimos to transcribing several hundred pages' worth of magical spells, he thought, the Avtokrator would not stay interested in sorcery for long. And that suited Krispos just fine.

* * *

"Gnatios is not happy with you," Petronas said a couple of days later, when Krispos found a chance to tell him how the ceremony had gone.

"Why, Highness?" Krispos asked. "I didn't think it was a matter of any importance, especially since Anthimos is going to build another temple to take the place of the one that got knocked down."

"Put that way, you're right." Despite reassuring words, Petronas still studied Krispos through narrowed eyes. "My cousin the patriarch, though, is, shall we say, unused to being faced down in front of the Emperor and having to do something he did not care to do in consequence."

"I wasn't trying to embarrass him," Krispos protested.

"You succeeded nevertheless," Petronas said. "Well, let it go. I'll soothe Gnatios' ruffled feathers for him. I didn't think you were quite so good at getting folk—especially a strong-willed fellow like my cousin—to go along with you."

"Oh," Krispos said. "You wanted me to be vestiarios because you thought I'd be able to help get Anthimos to do what you wanted. Why are you angry if I can do the same thing with someone else for his Majesty?"

"I'm not angry. Merely . . . thoughtful," the Sevastokrator said.

Krispos sighed, but consoled himself by remembering that Petronas never had trusted him much. He didn't think this latest brush would hurt his standing with Anthimos' uncle.

Petronas went on, "What's this I hear about some wizard sucking up to the Emperor?"

"Oh, that. I think I took care of that." Krispos explained how he'd given Trokoundos exactly what he wanted.

The Sevastokrator laughed out loud. "You'd kill a cat by drowning it in cream. That's better than I would have done; I'd have just sent the beggar packing, which would have made Anthimos sulk. And I don't need him sulking right now."

"The talks with the Makuraners aren't going well?" Krispos asked.

"They're not the problem," Petronas said. "The Makuraners like talk as much as we Videssians, and that's saying something. I just need to keep them talking a while longer, till I'm ready to fight. But I don't like the rumbles I hear out of Kubrat. Malomir's stayed quiet ever since old Omurtag died. If he decided to start raiding us now, then the war with Makuran might have to wait, and I don't want it to wait. I've waited too long already." He pounded a fist down on the padded arm of his chair.

Krispos nodded. Thinking of nomad horsemen sweeping down from the north could make him shiver even now. And if Videssos' armies were fully engaged in the far west, raids from Kubrat could reach all the way down to the walls of Videssos the city. The capital had stood Kubrati siege a couple of times. He wondered if the frontier with Kubrat wasn't more important than the one with Makuran, which would stay peaceful for a while if Petronas didn't stir it up.

Was he right? He wasn't sure himself; as the Sevastokrator had warned him, he'd had no practice making that kind of judgment. Maybe it wouldn't matter either way; maybe the Kubratoi would let themselves be bought off, as they sometimes did. He hoped so. Things would be simpler that way.

The higher he'd risen, though, and the closer he'd come to real power, the more complicated things looked.

Anthimos kept at his magical studies with a persistence that startled Krispos. While his new sanctum rose from the ruins of the temple, he transcribed texts at the imperial residence. Krispos had to go over to the clerks who scribbled by the Grand Courtroom to find out how they got ink off their fingers. When he fetched back some small pumice stones, Anthimos praised him to the skies.

"That's plenty for today," the Emperor said one hot, muggy summer afternoon, coming out of his study wringing his writing hand. "All work makes a man dull. What do we have laid on for tonight?"

"The feast features a troupe that performs with large dogs and tiny ponies," Krispos answered.

"Does it? Well, that should give the servants something new to clean up." Anthimos started down the hall. "Which robe have you chosen for me?"

"The blue silk. It should be coolest in this weather. Excuse me, your Majesty," Krispos called to the Emperor's retreating back, "but I believe you've forgotten something."

Anthimos stopped. "What's that?"

"Your fingers are still stained. You forgot to pumice them. Do you want people to say the Avtokrator of the Videssians is his own secretary? Here, let me fetch you a stone."

Anthimos looked down at his right hand. "I did forget to

clean off, didn't I?'' Now it was his turn to make Krispos pause. "You needn't bring me the pumice stone. I can take care of this myself, I think.''

Intense concentration on his face, the Emperor spread the ink-stained fingers of his writing hand. He waved his left hand above it and raised his voice in a rhythmic chant. Suddenly he cried out and clenched both hands into fists. When he opened them, they were both clean.

Krispos made the sun-sign over his heart. "You did it!'' he exclaimed, then hoped he didn't sound as surprised as he felt.

"I certainly did,'' Anthimos said smugly. "A small application of the law of contagion, which states that objects once in contact may continue to influence one another. As that pumice had so often scoured my fingers, I simply re-created the cleansing action by magical means.''

"I didn't realize you could start working magic before you had all your spells copied out,'' Krispos said. "Do you want me to take the pumice stones back to the clerks I got them from?''

"No, not yet. For one thing—'' The Emperor grinned a small-boy grin, ''—Trokoundos doesn't know I *am* working magic. I don't think I'm supposed to be. For another, cleaning my hands that way was a lot harder than simply scraping off the ink. I wanted to show off for you, but it wore me out. And I don't want to be worn out, not when there will be so many interesting women at the revels tonight. There will be, won't there, Krispos?''

"Of course, your Majesty. I always try to please you that way.'' Once more, Krispos wondered why Anthimos couldn't give, if not all, at least most of his attention to Dara. If nothing else, he'd have a better chance of begetting a legitimate heir if he spent some time with his own wife. It was not as if she were undesirable, Krispos thought—quite the opposite, in fact.

Whatever Anthimos' newfound sorcerous talents, he could not read minds. At the moment, perhaps, that was just as well. The Avtokrator went on, "I can hardly wait to show off my magecraft at a feast. For that, though, I'll need something rather more impressive than cleaning my hands without pumice. I tried something once, and it didn't work.''

"You did?'' Now Krispos didn't care if he sounded appalled. A mage who botched a spell was apt to be in even more immediate need of an heir than an Avtokrator. "What did you do?"

Anthimos looked sheepish. "I tried giving wings to one of the little tortoises that crawl through the gardens. I thought it would be amusing, flying around inside the hall where I usually have my feasts. But I must have done something wrong, because I ended up with a pigeon with a shell. Promise me you won't tell Trokoundos?"

"You're lucky you didn't end up shifting the shell to your own foolish face," Krispos said sternly. Anthimos shifted from foot to foot like a schoolboy taking a scolding he knew he deserved. As had happened so often before, Krispos found he could not stay angry at him. Shaking his head, he went on, "All right, I won't tell Trokoundos if you promise me you'll stop mucking about with things you don't understand."

"I won't," Anthimos said. He had gone off to look at the robe he would wear to the evening's festivities before Krispos noticed he hadn't quite made a promise. Even if he had, Krispos doubted he would have taken it seriously enough to keep. Anthimos just did not believe anything bad could ever happen to him.

Krispos knew better. If growing up on a farm had done nothing else for him, it had done that.

X

THE BELL BESIDE KRISPOS' BED TINKLED SOFTLY. HE WOKE up muttering to himself. When Anthimos held a feast, he was expected to roister along with the Emperor—and the Emperor was better than he at doing without sleep. When Anthimos spent a night with Dara in the imperial residence, Krispos expected to have the chance to catch up on his rest.

Even as he slipped a robe over his head, he knew he was not being fair. Though he'd got into the habit of keeping a lamp burning all night long to help him dress quickly in case the Avtokrator needed him, Anthimos seldom called him after he'd gone to bed. But tonight, he thought grouchily, only went to show that seldom didn't mean never.

He walked out his door and four or five steps down the hall to the imperial bedchamber. That door was closed, but a light showed under it. He opened the door. Anthimos and Dara turned their heads toward him.

He stopped in his tracks and felt his face go flame-hot. "Y-your pardon, I pray," he stammered. "I thought the bell summoned me."

"Don't go away, at least not yet. I did call you," the Emperor said, calm as if he'd been interrupted playing draughts—or at one of his revels. After that first startled glance toward the door, Dara looked down at Anthimos. Her long dark hair, undone now, spilled over her shoulders and veiled her so that Krispos could not see her face. Anthimos brushed some of that shining hair away from his nose and went on, "Fetch me a little olive oil, if you please, Krispos; that's a good fellow."

"Yes, your Majesty," Krispos said woodenly. He hurried out of the bedchamber. Behind him, he heard Anthimos say, "Why did you slow down, my dear? That was nice, what you were doing."

He found a jar of oil faster than he really wanted to. In truth, he did not want to go back to the bedchamber at all. Seeming a eunuch around Dara had been simple at first, but less easy after that night when she first let him see her as a person rather than an Empress. Now . . . now he would have trouble not imagining his body in place of Anthimos' under hers.

As he went back down the hall, he wondered what she thought. Maybe she was used to this, as Anthimos was. In that case, she would also be used to taking no notice of what servants imagined. Probably just as well, he thought.

He paused in the doorway. "Took you long enough," Anthimos said. "Don't just stand there, bring the oil over to me. How do you expect me to get it when you're half a mile away?"

Krispos reluctantly approached. Dara's head was lowered; her hair hid her face from him again. He did not want to speak or force her to notice his presence any more than she had to. Without a word, he held out the jar to the Avtokrator.

Anthimos dipped his fingers into it. "You can set it on the night table now, Krispos, in case we want more later on." Krispos nodded, did as he was told, and got out, but not before he heard the tiny smooth sound of Anthimos' slickened fingers sliding over Dara's skin.

He threw himself back into bed with what he knew was altogether unnecessary violence, and lay awake for a long time, staring at the ceiling. The flickering shadows the lamp cast there all looked lewd. Eventually it began to rain. The soft patter of raindrops on roof tiles lulled him to sleep at last.

He jerked in dismay when the bell woke him the next morning; returning to the Emperor's chamber was the last thing he felt like doing. What he felt like doing, however, mattered not in the least to Anthimos. The bell rang again, louder and more insistently. Krispos pulled on a clean robe and went to do his master's bidding.

But for the jar of olive oil on the table by the bed, the previous night might not have happened. As far as Anthimos was concerned, it plainly hadn't. "Good day," he said. "Rain, I see. Do you think it's just a shower, or is the fall wet season coming early this year?"

"It'll hurt the harvest if it is," Krispos answered, relieved to be able to talk dispassionately. "Do you prefer the purple robe today, your majesty, or the leek green?"

"The green, I think." Anthimos got out of bed and gave an exaggerated shiver. "Brr! Fall certainly seems to be in the air. Good thing for the heating ducts this building boasts, or I'd have to start thinking about sleeping in clothes." He glanced over at Dara, who was still under the covers. "That would be no fun at all, would it, my dear?"

"Whatever you say." The Empress reached out a slim arm and tugged on the bellpull for a maidservant.

Anthimos sniffed. He let Krispos dress him and help him on with his boots. "I'm for breakfast," he announced. He looked over at Dara again and frowned. "Aren't you coming, slugabed?"

"Presently." The Empress' serving girl had come in, but she showed no sign of being ready to get up. "Why don't you start without me?"

"Oh, very well. Krispos, ask the cook if he has any squab in the larder. If he does, I'll have a couple, roasted, with a jar of that sweet golden Vaspurakaner wine that goes so well with them."

"I'll inquire, your Majesty."

The cook had squab. He grinned at Krispos. "With all the statues and towers in the city to draw pigeons, not likely I wouldn't. Roasted, you said his Majesty wants 'em? Roasted they'll be."

Krispos fetched Anthimos the little birds, along with bread, honey, and the wine he'd asked for. The Avtokrator ate with good appetite, then rose and said, "I'm off to be sorcerous." Dara and her maidservant came into the dining room just as he was going out. His voice echoed through the central hallway: "Tyrovitzes! Longinos! Fetch umbrellas, and smartly. I don't propose to swim to my little workshop."

The eunuchs' sandals slapped on the marble floor as they hurried to obey. Krispos asked Dara, "What would you care for this morning, your Majesty?"

"I'm not very hungry," she answered. "Some of this bread and honey should do well enough for me."

She only picked at it. "Can I get you anything else, your Majesty?" the serving maid asked. "You're not a bird, to stay alive on crumbs."

Dara looked at the crust she was holding, then set it down. "Maybe a muskmelon would suit me better, Verina—stewed, I think, not raw."

"I'll get one for you, Majesty." Verina stood up, impudently wrinkled her nose. "I'll spend the time it's stewing gossiping with the cook. Phestos knows everything that goes on here three days before it happens."

"Nice to think someone does." Dara listened to Verina's steps fading down the hall, then said quietly, "Krispos, I want you to know I did not expect An—his Majesty to summon you last night. If you were embarrassed, I can only say I'm sorry. I was, too."

"Oh." Krispos thought about that for a while, thought about how much he might safely say to even a contrite Empress. Finally he continued, "It was a little awkward, being treated as if I were only a—a convenience."

"That's well said." Dara's voice stayed low, but her eyes blazed. She clenched her hands together. "That's just how Anthimos treats everyone around him—as a convenience, a toy for his amusement, to be put back on the shelf to sit until he feels like playing with it again. And by the Lord with the great and good mind, Krispos, I am no toy and I am sick to death of being used as one."

"Oh," Krispos said again, in a different tone. When angry, Dara was indeed no toy; she reminded him of Tanilis, but a Tanilis young and unskilled. Nor did the memory of her anger sustain her once it was gone, as Tanilis' did. Tanilis never would have let the Emperor keep her in the background like this.

"It was bad enough with Skombros, those tiny eyes staring and staring from that fat face," Dara said, "but after a while I got used to him and even pitied him, for what could he do but stare?"

Krispos nodded; he remembered having the same thought, watching the former vestiarios at that first revel he'd been to.

Dara went on, "But better he should have done without the oil, Krispos, or gotten it himself, than to have you bring it, you who have no need of such spectacles, who are whole and in every way as a man should be—" She broke off abruptly and stared down at her hands.

"I knew before last night that your Majesty was beautiful," Krispos said softly. "Nothing I saw then makes me want to change my mind." He heard footfalls in the hall and raised his voice. "Here comes that melon. I hope you like it better than the bread and honey."

The Empress shot him a grateful look. "I think I will, thank you." Verina came in, uncovering the bowl in which the stewed muskmelon lay. "And thank you, Verina. That smells lovely."

"I hope it pleases you." The maidservant beamed as she watched her mistress eat the whole melon. "All a matter of finding out what you want, isn't it, your Majesty?"

"So it is, Verina. So it is," Dara said. She did not look at Krispos; she knew how tiny and fragile a bubble privacy was in the palaces. For his part, Krispos understood for a new reason why vestiarioi were traditionally eunuchs.

"Stand aside there, you lumbering blond barbarians, or I'll turn the lot of you into yellow eels!"

Krispos watched with amusement as the Halogai scrambled out of Trokoundos' way. Despite the mage's big, booming voice, the northerners were far more imposing men than he, all at least a head taller and twice as thick through the shoulders. But they did not care to find out whether he meant his words literally.

Trokoundos stamped up the broad steps. Water flew from puddles on them at every step. "You move, too," he snarled at Krispos.

"Wipe your boots on this rug here first," Krispos said. Glowering, Trokoundos obeyed. He trod so hard that Krispos suspected he wished he weren't stepping on mere carpet. "What's the trouble?" Krispos asked. "Shouldn't you be closeted with the Emperor?"

"He's given me the sack, that's what the trouble is," the mage said. "I just spent seventeen goldpieces on new gear, too, and I expect to get paid back. That's why I'm here."

"Of course, if you can show me receipts for what you bought," Krispos said.

Trokoundos rolled his eyes. "It would take a stronger wizard than I even dreamed of being to get money from anyone in the government without receipts—think I don't know that? Here you are." He pulled several folded pieces of parchment from the leather wallet he wore at his belt.

Krispos felt his lips move as he added up the sums. He checked himself, then said, "Seventeen it is. Come along with me; I'll pay you right now."

"Good," Trokoundos growled. "Then I'll never have to come

back here again, so I won't run the risk of bumping into his damnfoolness of a Majesty and telling him just exactly what I think of him."

Hearing a loud, unfamiliar voice coming down the hall, Barsymes peered out of a dining room to see who it was. Hearing what the loud, unfamiliar voice had to say about his lord and master, the eunuch squeaked and pulled his head back in.

Krispos opened a strongbox and counted out coins. Trokoundos snatched them from his hand. "Now I'm not out anything but my patience and my digestion," he said, putting them into his wallet one by one.

"May I ask what went wrong?" Krispos said. "From what his Majesty's been saying, he's felt he's made good progress."

"Oh, he has. He's a promising beginner, maybe even better than promising. He can be very quick when he wants to be, and he has a good head for remembering what he learns. But he wants everything at once."

That sounded like Anthimos, Krispos thought. He asked, "How so?"

"Now that he has some of the basics down, he wants to leap straight into major conjurations—blasting fires, demons, who knows what will cross his mind next? Whatever it is, it's sure to be something big enough and difficult enough to be dangerous if anything goes wrong. I told him as much. That's when he sacked me."

"Couldn't you have guided him through some of the things he wanted to do, repaired any mistakes he might have made?"

"No, for two reasons. For one, I wouldn't let any other apprentice ask that of me, and his Imperial Majesty Anthimos III is no Avtokrator of magic, just another 'prentice." Krispos dipped his head to Trokoundos, respecting him very much for that. The mage went on, "For another, I'm not sure I *could* repair some of the things he wants to try if he botches them as badly as a 'prentice can. To be frank with you, esteemed and eminent sir, I don't really care to find out, either."

"What happens if he goes on without you?" Krispos asked in some alarm. "Is he likely to kill himself and everyone for half a mile around?" If he was, then this would be one time for Petronas to clamp down hard on his nephew.

But Trokoundos shook his head. "I don't think there's much danger of that. You see, as soon as he leaves his little laboratory today, all his books of spells will go blank. He's not the first rich dilettante I've tried to teach. There is magic to reconstitute them, but it has to be performed by the owner of the books, and it's not easy to work. I don't think his Majesty's quite up to it, and I doubt he'd have the patience to retranscribe the texts by hand.''

"I didn't think he'd do it the first time," Krispos agreed. "So you've left him without magic? Won't he just find himself another mage?"

"Even if he does, he'll still have to start over from the beginning. But no, he's not altogether bereft—he'll still be able to use whatever he has memorized. Phos willing, that'll be enough to keep him happy."

Krispos considered, then slowly nodded. "I suspect it may. Most of what he wanted with it was to impress people at his feasts."

"I thought as much," Trokoundos said scornfully. "He doesn't have a bad head for it, or wouldn't, but there's no discipline to him. You can't succeed at anything unless you're willing to put in the hard work you need to learn your craft." He glanced at Krispos. "You know what I'm talking about, I think."

"I've done some wrestling," Krispos said.

"Then you know, all right." Trokoundos' gaze sharpened. "I remember—you're the one who beat that Kubrati, aren't you? You weren't vestiarios then. I might have connected the name with the story sooner if I hadn't seen you in your fancy robes all the time."

"No, I wasn't vestiarios, just a groom," Krispos said. He smiled, both at Trokoundos and at the way his fortunes had changed. "I didn't think I was *just* a groom then, if you know what I mean. I grew up on a farm, so anything else looked good by comparison."

"I've heard that said, yes." The mage studied Krispos; as he had sometimes with Tanilis, he got the odd feeling he was transparent to the man. "I'd teach you sorcery if you wanted me to. You'd do what was needed, I think, and not complain. But that isn't the craft you're learning, is it?"

"What do you mean?" Krispos asked. Trokoundos was already on his way out the door and did not answer. "Cursed wizards always want the last word," Krispos muttered to himself.

Anthimos was wild with fury when he discovered all his hard-won spells had disappeared. "I'll have that bastard's balls," he shouted, "and his ears and nose, too!"

Normally not a bloodthirsty soul, he went on about pincers and knives and red-hot needles until Krispos, worried that he might really mean it, tried to calm him by saying, "You're probably just as well rid of the mage. I don't think your uncle would like you studying anything as dangerous as sorcery."

"To the ice with my uncle, too!" Anthimos said. "He's not the Avtokrator, and I bloody well am!" But when he sent a squad of Halogai to arrest Trokoundos, sending a priest with them in case he resisted with magic, they found his house empty. "Knave must have fled to the hinterland," the Emperor declared with some satisfaction when they brought him the news. By then his usual good humor had returned. "I daresay that's worse punishment than any I could inflict."

"Aye, good riddance to bad rubbish," said Krispos, who had quietly sent word to Trokoundos to get out of the city for a while.

To Krispos' surprise and dismay, Anthimos did start recopying his tome of spells. He never quite quit transcribing, either, but before long the pace of his work slowed to a crawl. He turned one of his revels inside out with a spell that made cabbage intoxicating for a night and left wine mild as milk. "You see?" he triumphantly told Krispos the next morning. "I am a mage, even if that stinking Trokoundos tried to keep me from being one. Did you hear how they cheered me last night when the wizardry worked just as I said it would?"

"Yes, your Majesty," Krispos said. His stomach rumbled like distant thunder. He'd eaten too much cabbage the night before. Given a choice, he would far soon have got drunk on wine.

Had he got drunk on wine, he might have chewed cabbage leaves to ease his morning-after pains. He wondered if a cup of wine would cure a cabbage hangover. Laughing, he decided to find out.

Midwinter's Day came and went. One whole section of the Amphitheater was full of soldiers. As soon as the roads froze after the fall rains, Petronas had begun calling in levies from the eastern provinces for his war on Makuran. They made a raucous audience, drinking hard, then cheering and booing each skit as the fancy—or the wine—seized them.

The hangover that bedeviled Krispos the morning after Midwinter's Day had nothing to do with cabbage—and did not want to yield to it, either. The wines he drank now were smoother and sweeter than the ones he'd quaffed on holidays past, but that did not mean they were exempt from giving retribution.

Nor did it mean he wanted to go back to the rougher vintages he'd formerly known. Ypatios was far from the only prominent man willing, and eager, to pay for influence with the Emperor. Some he could not help; some he did not want to help. He refused their gold. What he took in from the rest made him well-to-do, even by the standards of Videssos the city.

He bought a horse. He took Mavros along when he went to the market not far from the Forum of the Ox. "Nice to know you have confidence in me," Mavros said. "Let's see what kind of horrible screw I can stick you with."

"I like that," Krispos said. "Is that your way of showing thanks for getting named chief groom?"

"Now that you mention it, yes. The job's too much like work; I liked lying around on my arse as a spatharios a lot better. If I weren't working with horses, I really would resent you."

"What would your mother say if she heard you talking so fondly of shirking?"

"What she usually says, I expect—stop complaining and get to it."

The first dealer they tried was a plump little man named Ibas whose eyes were so round and moist and trustworthy that Krispos grew wary at once. The horse trader bowed low, but not before he had checked the cut and fabric of their robes. "If you are seeking a riding animal, my masters, I can show you a magnificent gelding not above seven years old," he said.

"Yes, show us," Mavros said.

On seeing the animal, Krispos was encouraged. Magnificent was too fine a word for it, but he'd expected as much; sellers of horseflesh sucked in hyperbole with their mother's milk. But the horse's limbs were sound, its dark roan coat well tended and shining.

Mavros only grunted, "Let's see the teeth."

Nodding, Ibas walked with him up to the animal's head. "You see," he said while Mavros made his examination, "the four middle teeth in each jaw are nicely oval, and the mark—or cavity, as some call it—in the center of each tooth is quite as deep and dark as it should be."

"I see a horse with a mouth full of spit," Mavros complained.

He looked thoughtfully at the small gap between the horse's upper and lower incisors. "Perhaps we'll be back another day, master Ibas. Thank you for showing him to us." Politely but firmly, he steered Krispos toward another dealer.

"What was wrong with him?" Krispos asked. "I rather fancied his looks."

"Seven, Ibas claimed? That horse is twelve if he's a day. Good old master Ibas is what they call a prelate—he takes away his horse's sins, usually with a file. He has a nice touch; with the animal's mouth so wet, I couldn't quite be sure of the rasp marks. But if you file down a horse's front teeth to give them the proper shape for a young animal, they won't quite meet, because you haven't done anything to the teeth in the back of the horse's mouth. And if Ibas has one like that, he'll have half a dozen, so we don't want to do business with him."

"I'm glad you're with me," Krispos said. "I might have bought the beast, for I did like him."

"So would I, were he sold for what he was. But to try to knock five years off him—no. Don't look so glum, my friend. There's more horses to suit you than just that one. All we have to do is keep looking."

Look they did, all that day and part of the next. At length, with Mavros' approval this time, Krispos bought a bay gelding of about the same age as Ibas had claimed for the roan. "By the teeth, this one really is seven or eight," Mavros said. "Not a bad animal at all. He wouldn't be the worst-looking horse in Petronas' stable—a long way from the best, but not the worst either."

"The best-looking animal in that stable is Petronas' show horse, and I wouldn't race him against a donkey," Krispos said.

"Something to that, too." Mavros patted the bay's neck. "I hope he serves you well."

"So do I." Even if the gelding spent most of the time in the stable, as it might very well, Krispos was pleased just to have it. Owning a horse was another sign of how far he'd come. No one in his village had owned a horse till they beat the Kubratoi; afterward, the animals had been owned in common. In the city, he'd cared for other people's horses and borrowed them when he needed to ride.

Now he had one of his own, and the hands in the imperial stables could see to its day-to-day care. That wasn't the proper attitude for a noble, but he didn't care. Nobles tended animals because they wanted to, not because they had to. Having had to, he didn't want to, not any more.

"What will you call him?" Mavros asked.

"I hadn't thought." Krispos did. After a little while, he smiled. "I have it! The perfect name." Mavros waited expectantly. Krispos said, "I'll call him Progress."

Anthimos essayed a spell to keep snow off the path that led to the hall where he held his feasts. He only succeeded in turning the snow on the path bright blue. The miscarried magic left him undismayed. "I've always wanted to revel till everything turned blue," he said, "and here's my chance."

"As you say, your Majesty." Krispos sent men with shovels to clear the tinted snow from the path so the Emperor and his guests could get to their revel. He wondered if Anthimos had learned a spell to heat the hall; fireplaces only reached so far. He doubted it—a magic so practical was not one likely to have appealed to the Emperor, or to have stuck in his memory if he'd ever learned it.

The revel itself Krispos enjoyed, at least for a time. But a steady diet of such carouses had begun to pall for him. He looked round for Anthimos. The Emperor was enjoying the attentions of an astonishingly limber girl—one of the evening's acrobats, Krispos saw when she assumed a new position. There were times, Krispos had found out, when Anthimos did not mind being interrupted in such pursuits, but he did not think asking permission to leave was important enough to bother him over. He just handed the bowl of chances to another servitor, found his coat, and departed.

The moon shone through patchy clouds. In its pale light, the snow the Emperor had colored looked almost black, making a strange border to the path. When Krispos got back to the imperial residence, he found that the Haloga guards had another word for it. "Isn't that the stupidest-looking thing you ever saw?" one of them said, pointing.

Krispos looked back toward the feast-hall, at the long blackish ribbon against the proper white snow that had come drifting down from Phos' sky. "Now that you mention it, yes."

The Halogai laughed. One of them, a veteran who'd served the Emperor for years, thumped him on the back. "You all right, Krispos," he said in his northern accent. "We make jokes like that with Skombros, he tell Anthimos, maybe we all shipped back to Halogaland." The rest of the guardsmen nodded.

"Thank you, Vagn," Krispos said; praise from the big blond warriors always pleased him. "You'll go home one day, I suppose, but better it's when you want to."

Vagn thumped him again, this time almost hard enough to pitch him down the steps into the snow. "Aye, you understand honor," the Haloga boomed in delight. He swung up his axe in salute, then held the door wide, as he might have for Anthimos. "Go in, warm yourself."

Krispos was glad to take Vagn's advice. The heating ducts under the floor gave some relief from the chill outside, but when he got to his room he lit a brazier all the same. He warmed his hands over it, stayed close by the welcome heat until his ears and nose began to thaw. Just as he started to take off his coat, the bell by his bed rang.

This time he knew Anthimos had not followed him home. But by now he was used to late-night summonses from the Empress; every so often, she liked to talk with him. "Your Majesty," he said as he came into the imperial bedchamber.

Dara waved him to a chair by the side of the bed. She was sitting up, but on this cold night she'd drawn blankets and furs over her shoulders. Krispos left the door open. Sometimes maidservants or eunuchs up raiding the larder peered in at them. Once Anthimos had come in while he and Dara were talking about horses. That was a nervous moment for Krispos, but the Avtokrator, far from being angry, had flopped down on the other side of the bed and argued with them till dawn.

Before Krispos sat down, he asked, "May I bring you anything, Majesty?"

"No, I thank you, but not tonight. Is his Majesty on his way, too?"

Remembering how Anthimos had been engaged when he left, Krispos answered, "I don't think so."

Something in his voice must have told more than he'd intended. "Why? What was he doing?" Dara asked sharply. When he could not come up with a plausible lie on the spur of the moment, she said, "Never mind. I suspect I can figure it out for myself." She turned her head away from him for a moment. "I find I've changed my mind. I might like some wine after all. Bring the jar, not just a cup."

"Yes, your Majesty." Krispos hurried away.

When he came back, Dara said, "You may get another cup for yourself, if you care to."

"No, thank you. I had enough at—" Reminding Dara of the revel did not seem a good idea. "I've had enough," Krispos said, and let it go at that.

"Have you? How lucky you are." The Empress drank, wordlessly held out the cup to Krispos. He refilled it. She drank about half, then slammed the cup down so hard that wine splashed onto the night table. "What's the use? Sober or drunk, I still know."

Krispos found a rag and walked up to the night table to wipe away the spilled wine. "Know what, your Majesty?"

"What do you think, Krispos?" Dara said bitterly. "Shall I spell it out in words a child can understand? All right, if you want me to: know that my husband—the Avtokrator, his Majesty, whatever you want to call him—is out enjoying himself with . . . no, let's mince no words at all, shall we? . . . is out fornicating with some new harlot. Again. For, let me see, the third night this week, or is it the fourth? I do lose track sometimes. Or am I wrong, Krispos?" She looked up at him, her eyes brimming but her face tensed with the effort to hold back the tears. "Can you tell me I'm wrong?"

Now Krispos could not meet her gaze, nor answer in words. Facing the wall, he shook his head.

"So that is what I know," Dara said. "I've known it for years. By the Lord with the great and good mind, I've known it since a couple of days after they put the flower crowns of marriage on us in the High Temple. Most of the time, I manage not to think of it, but when I can't help it—" She stopped for most of a minute. "When I can't help it, it's very bad. And I don't know why."

"Your Majesty?" Krispos said.

"Why?" Dara repeated. "Why does he do it? He doesn't hate me. He's even kind to me, when he's here and when he remembers to be. So why, then, Krispos? Can you tell me?"

Krispos turned back toward her. "Your Majesty, if you'll forgive my speaking up so bold, I've wondered over that since the first morning I saw you."

She might not have heard him. "Can it be that he doesn't want me? Could I repel him so?" Suddenly she swept the coverings from the bed. Beneath them, as usual, she wore nothing. "Would I—do I—repel you, Krispos?"

"No, your Majesty." His throat was dry. He'd seen the Empress nude countless times. Now she was naked. He watched her nipples stiffen from the chill in the room—or for another reason. He spoke her name for the first time. "Oh, no, Dara," he breathed.

"Lies come easy, with words," she said softly. "Shut the doors; then we'll see."

He almost went through the doorway instead of merely to it. He knew she wanted him more for revenge on Anthimos than for himself. And if he was caught in her bed, he might stay on as vestiarios, but likely after he was made like the others who had held that office.

But he wanted her. He'd been uneasily aware of that for months, however hard he tried to suppress it even from himself. Anthimos, he thought, would be occupied for some time yet. A eunuch or maidservant coming by would think the Empress here alone—he hoped. He closed the doors.

Dara felt the danger, too. "Hurry!" She held out her arms to him.

Slipping out of his robe was the work of a moment. He got down on the bed beside her. She clutched him as if she were drowning at sea and he a floating spar. "Hurry," she said again, this time into his ear. He did his best to oblige.

He thought of the sea once more as he separated from her some time later—the stormy sea. His lips were bruised; he began to feel the scratches she'd clawed in his back. And he'd wondered if she was without passion! "His Majesty," he said sincerely, "is a fool."

"Why?" Dara asked.

"Why do you think?" He stroked her midnight hair. She purred and snuggled against him. But, reluctantly, he left the bed. "I'd better dress." He got into his robe as fast as he'd taken it off. Dara slid back under the covers. He opened the doors again, then loosed a great sigh of relief out into the empty hallway. "We got away with it."

"So we did." Dara's eyes shone. She gestured him back to the chair that was his correct place in this room. "I'm glad we did."

"Glad we got away with it?" Krispos' shudder was not altogether exaggerated. "If we hadn't . . ." He'd already thought once about the consequences of not getting away with it. Once was plenty.

Dara shook her head. "I'm glad we did . . . what we did."
She cocked her head and studied him. "You're different from
Anthimos." Her voice was low; no one coming down the hall
could have made out her words.

"Am I?" Krispos said, as neutral a response as he could find.
Silence stretched between them. Finally, because she seemed
to want him to, he asked, "How?"

"Everything he does, everything he has me do, is for his
pleasure first, mine only afterward, if at all," Dara said.

That sounded like Anthimos, Krispos thought. What had he
said to Dara, that night when he called Krispos while he was
making love with her? *"Why did you slow down? That was nice,
what you were doing."*

The Empress went on, "You, I think, were out to please . . .
me." She hesitated, as if she had trouble believing it.

"Well, of course." Pity filled Krispos. "The better for you,
the better for me, too."

"Anthimos doesn't think that way," Dara said. "I didn't know
anyone did. How could I? He's the only man I've ever been in
bed with till now. Till now," she repeated, half gloating over
doing once to the Emperor what he'd done so often to her, half
marveling at her own daring.

"I ought to go back to my chamber," Krispos said. Dara
nodded. He got up from the chair, went over to the bed, and
gave her a quick kiss. She smiled up at him, a lazy, happy smile.

"I may summon you again," she said when he was almost at
the door.

"Your Majesty, I hope you do," Krispos answered. They
both laughed.

The next thing I have to worry about, Krispos thought as he
climbed into his own bed, *is not giving myself away when I go
in there tomorrow morning.* He'd had practice in that kind of
discretion with Tanilis. He expected he could manage it again.
He hoped Dara could, too.

Anthimos noticed nothing out of the ordinary, so they must
have done well enough. Krispos looked forward to the next time
the little silver bell rang late at night.

Krispos bowed low. "Excellent sir, I hope you're well."

"Well enough, esteemed and eminent sir." Iakovitzes' answering bow was as deep as Krispos'. Afterward, the little noble
sank gratefully into a chair. "Well enough, though this cursed

leg will never be quite the same. But that's not what I came here to talk with you about.''

"I wouldn't have thought it was," Krispos agreed. He served Iakovitzes wine and prawns in a sauce of mustard and ginger. "What did you come to talk about, then?"

Before he answered, Iakovitzes made short work of the prawns. He wiped his lips and mustache on a square of linen. "I hear the war with Makuran will begin as soon as the spring rains stop." He waved a hand at the drops splashing against the windowpane.

"Excellent sir, that's hardly a secret," Krispos said. "The Sevastokrator's been mustering soldiers and supplies since last fall."

"I'm quite aware of it, thank you," Iakovitzes said, tart as usual. "What I'm also aware of, and what Petronas seems to be blithely ignoring, is that all the signs point to Malomir coming down out of Kubrat this spring, too. I've been in the Phosforsaken place enough times over the years to hear what goes on there."

"Petronas does worry about Kubrat," Krispos said slowly. "Truly he does. But he's been set on this war against Makuran for years, you know, and now that he's finally ready to get on with it, he doesn't want to listen to anything that might set it back again. Have you told him what you just told me?"

"Every word and more. It's just as you said—he doesn't want to listen. He thinks the screen on the frontier will hold the wild men, 'if they do attack,' he says." Iakovitzes raised an eyebrow. "They will."

"He raised the tribute we pay Kubrat last year, didn't he?" Krispos said, trying to find a hopeful sign. "That might keep Malomir quiet."

"His illustrious Highness may think so. But Malomir's no idiot. If you give him money, he'll take it. And when he decides to fight, he'll bloody well fight. Kubratoi like to fight, you know. You of all people should, eh?" Iakovitzes said. Troubled, Krispos nodded. Iakovitzes went on, "What we have in the north isn't enough to stop the wild men if they do come down in force. Everything I know makes me think they're going to. That could be most unpleasant."

"Yes." Krispos thought of his nieces carried off into captivity as he had been—if they were lucky. He thought of what could happen to them if they were unlucky . . . and to his sister, and to everyone in his old village, and to countless people he'd never heard of. "How can we get Petronas to hold up again and reinforce the north?"

"*I* can't. The good god knows I've tried. But you, esteemed and eminent sir, you have the ear of his Majesty. And if the Avtokrator gives an order, not even the Sevastokrator may disobey." Iakovitzes grinned craftily. "And since, by an accident of fate and former status about which I would not presume to bore you by reminding you of it, I enjoy the good fortune of your acquaintance . . ."

Krispos grinned back. "You thought you'd take advantage of it."

"Of course I did. That's what having friends in high places is for, after all."

"I'll see what I can do," Krispos promised.

"Good," Iakovitzes said. "I'd kiss you to show how pleased I am, but you'd probably go and use that notorious influence of yours to get me sent to the mines if I tried, so I'll just take my leave instead."

"You're incorrigible."

"By the good god, Krispos, I certainly hope so."

Krispos was laughing as he escorted his one-time master from the imperial residence. The laughter faded when Iakovitzes was no longer there to see. Apprehension replaced it. If he tried to stop the war with Makuran, Petronas would not be pleased with him. And no matter how much influence he had with the Emperor, the Sevastokrator was far more powerful than he, and he knew it.

"Your Imperial Highness," Krispos murmured, eyes on the ground as he went to one knee before Petronas.

The Sevastokrator frowned. "What's all this in aid of, Krispos? You haven't needed to be so formal with me for a long time, and you know it. That's all a waste of time, anyhow, and I have no time to waste right now, not if I'm going west once the rains ease up. So say what you have to say and have done."

"Yes, illustrious Highness," Krispos said. Petronas' frown deepened. Krispos took a deep breath before he went on, "Illustrious Highness, when you were gracious enough to help me become vestiarios, I promised I'd speak to you first over any doubts I had about what you were doing. I'm here today to keep that promise."

"Are you indeed?" Had Petronas been a lion, his tail would have lashed back and forth. "Very well, esteemed and eminent sir, you have my attention. Continue, by all means." Now he, too, was formal; dangerously so.

"Illustrious Highness, is it truly wise to use all the Empire's forces in your war against Makuran? Are you sure you've left behind enough to keep the northern frontier safe?" He explained Iakovitzes' concerns about what Malomir was going to do.

"I've heard this myself," Petronas said, when he was done. "It does not concern me."

"I think it should, though, your Imperial Highness," Krispos said when he was done. "Iakovitzes has had dealings with the Kubratoi for twenty years or so now. If anyone can divine what they plan, he's the man. And if he says they're likely to attack—would you risk the north for the sake of the west?"

"Given the choice, yes," Petronas said: "The westlands are richer and broader in extent than the country between here and the Kubrati border. But I say to you what I said to Iakovitzes—the choice does not arise. Malomir is being paid well to leave us at peace, and the border is not altogether denuded, as you seem to believe."

Krispos thought of the thousands of soldiers who funneled through Videssos the city on their way west. Those were the men whose presence made the Kubratoi stay in their own domain. Surely Malomir could not fail to notice they were gone.

When he said as much, Petronas answered, "You let that be my worry. I say to you that the Kubratoi will not attack. And if I am wrong and they do harass us, their bands will not be able to penetrate far past the frontier."

"I am reassured to hear you say it, illustrious Highness, but suppose you are mistaken?" Krispos persisted. "Could you stop fighting Makuran and send soldiers back to the north? That might not be easy."

"No, it might not," the Sevastokrator said. "But since it is not likely to become necessary, either, I do not intend to worry overmuch about it. And even if everything you describe should come to pass, ways remain of bringing the Kubratoi to heel, I assure you of that."

Krispos raised a skeptical eyebrow. "Would your Imperial Highness please explain them to me?"

"No, by the Lord with the great and good mind, I will not.

Listen to me, esteemed and eminent sir—'' Though never a servant, Petronas had learned the art of using titles to cut rather than praise. ''—and listen well: I need explain myself to no man in Videssos save only the Avtokrator himself. And I do not expect to have to do that in this case. Do I make myself quite clear, Krispos?''

''Aye, illustrious Highness.'' Petronas did not want him to raise the issue with Anthimos, Krispos thought. ''I will have to think on what to do, though.''

''Think carefully, Krispos.'' Now Petronas spoke in unmistakable warning. ''Think very carefully indeed, before you seek to measure your influence with his Majesty against mine. Think also on the fate of Skombros, and on whether you care to spend the rest of your days in the bare cell of a celibate monk. You would find that harder to endure than a eunuch does, I assure you, and yet it is the best fate to which you might aspire. Anger me sufficiently and you may know far worse. Remember it always.''

''Believe me, I will, illustrious Highness.'' Krispos rose to go. He did his best not to show how his heart pounded. ''But I will also remember what I think best for the Empire.'' He bowed his way out. If nothing else, he thought, this marked the first time he'd ever had the last word with Petronas.

Leaves glowed green under the spring sun's cheerful rays. The chatty trills of newly returned wagtails and chiffchaffs came through the open windows of the imperial residence along with the sunbeams and the sweet scent of the cherry blossoms now in riotous pink bloom all around the building.

Krispos fetched a tray of wine and sweet pastries in to Anthimos and Petronas, then contrived to hang about in the hallway outside the chamber where they were talking. He had a dust rag and every so often made a swipe at one of the antiquities there, but no one would have thought he was doing anything but eavesdropping.

The Avtokrator and Sevastokrator exchanged pleasantries before they got down to business. Krispos' dusting hand jerked when Petronas asked after Dara. ''She's quite well, thanks,'' Anthimos answered. ''She seems happy these days.''

''That's good,'' his uncle said. ''May she give you a son soon.''

As he cleaned the helmet of the long-ago King of Kings of

Makuran, Krispos thought with a small smile that the odds of Dara's conceiving had improved these days. She had called him back to her bed after that first time, again and again. They still had to be cautious, they took all the chances they could.

After more inconsequential talk, Anthimos said, "Uncle, may the good god grant you victory in your wars on Makuran, but are you certain you have left behind enough forces to hold back the Kubratoi if they attack?" Krispos stopped dusting altogether and craned his neck to make sure he heard Petronas' reply.

It took a while to come. At last the Sevastokrator said, "I do not think the Kubratoi will launch any serious assaults this year."

"But they've already begun, it seems to me." Anthimos rustled parchments. "See, here I have two reports that have just arrived, one from near Imbros, the other some distance farther east, of raids by the wild men, cattle and sheep stolen. I don't like such reports. They concern me." Under most circumstances, the young Emperor did not hear news of things that went wrong. Krispos, though, had made sure these reports came to his attention.

"Let me see them." Another pause, presumably while Petronas skimmed through the documents. The Sevastokrator snorted. "These are pinpricks, as you must see, Anthimos. The frontier guards drove off both bands without difficulty."

"But what if they grow worse?" Anthimos persisted. "The guards you've left behind would not be able to drive them off then." Krispos nodded to himself. He'd managed to get his own urgency through to the Emperor, sure enough.

"I consider that most unlikely, your Majesty," Petronas said.

"Uncle, I'm afraid I don't," Anthimos said. "If these attacks have begun already, they will only get larger. I really must insist that you strengthen the northern frontier with some of the troops you've shifted toward the westlands."

This time, Petronas was silent a long while. "Insist?" he said, as if he did not believe his ears. He repeated the word. "Insist, nephew?" Now he sounded as if he had caught Anthimos in an obvious error and was waiting for the Emperor to fix it.

But Anthimos, though his voice wobbled—Krispos knew his own would have wobbled, too, confronting Petronas' formidable presence—said, "Yes, I really must."

"Even if that means gutting the campaign against Makuran?" Petronas asked softly.

"Even then," Anthimos said, more firmly now. "After all, I am the Avtokrator."

"Certainly you are," Petronas said. "It's only that I'm surprised to find you taking so sudden an interest in the conduct of matters military. I'd thought I enjoyed your trust in such things." His voice was a finely tuned instrument, projecting now nothing but patience and reason.

"You do hold my trust. You know you do, Uncle," Anthimos said. Krispos feared he was weakening. But he went on, "In this particular case, though, I think your own eagerness for the fight makes you less cautious than you have been in the past."

"This is your final word, your Majesty?"

"It is." Anthimos could sound most imperial when he cared to, Krispos thought. He wondered if that would be enough for him to impose his will on the Sevastokrator.

It was, and then again it was not. After yet another long, thoughtful pause, Petronas said, "Your Majesty, you know your word is my command." Krispos knew what a lie that was; he wondered if Anthimos did. He got no chance to find out, for the Sevastokrator continued, "Perhaps, though, you will be gracious enough to let me propose a solution that permits me to keep the entire army, yet will confound the Kubratoi."

"Go ahead," Anthimos said cautiously, as if, like Krispos, he was wondering how Petronas proposed to accomplish the two goals that seemed incompatible.

"Thank you, Anthimos; I will. Perhaps you remember hearing of a Haloga mercenary band led by a northerner called Harvas Black-Robe."

"Well, yes, now that you mention it. They've been making mischief for a while in Khatrish, haven't they?"

"Thatagush actually, your Majesty. I've taken the liberty of inquiring of this Harvas what he would require to fall upon Kubrat instead. If his northerners do that, Malomir will be far too occupied with them to give us any trouble for some time to come, all without the use of a single good Videssian soldier. What say you to that?"

It was the Avtokrator's turn to hesitate. Out in the hall, Krispos kicked at the polished marble floor. Petronas had indeed had a scheme in reserve, and a good scheme to boot. Krispos learned what being outmaneuvered felt like.

"Uncle, I'll have to give that some thought," Anthimos said at last.

"Go ahead, but I hope you'll think quickly, for now that the weather is fine once more, every campaigning day lost counts against me," Petronas said.

"You'll know my decision tomorrow," the Avtokrator promised.

"Good enough," Petronas said jovially.

Krispos heard him set down his cup, then heard the chair shift under him as he got to his feet. He started to duck into another room—he did not want to face the Sevastokrator right now. But he was either too slow or too noisy, for Petronas came in after him. As protocol required, he went to one knee before the man with the second highest rank in the Empire of Videssos. "Your imperial Highness," he said, eyes on the ground.

"Look at me, esteemed and eminent sir," Petronas said. Unwillingly, Krispos obeyed. The Sevastokrator's face was hard and cold, his voice flat. "I did not intend throwing a fox out of the vestiarios' chamber only to replace him with a lion. I've warned you, not once but many times, that you would pay for disobeying me. All that remains is deciding how to punish you for your disobedience."

"I thought you were wrong to bare the border with Kubrat," Krispos said stubbornly. "I told you as much, and I still think so. I don't like your new plan much better. How much harm can a mercenary company do to a big country like Kubrat? Probably not enough to keep the wild men from going on with their raids against us."

"Thatagush is twice the size of Kubrat, and Harvas' raiders have kept it in chaos for years." Petronas nodded to Krispos. "That you don't grovel before me speaks well of you. Given age and experience, you could grow to be truly dangerous. I doubt you'll have the chance to gain them, though."

Krispos started to say that Anthimos would protect him against the Sevastokrator. He stopped—he knew better. The Sevastokrator's will was far stronger than his nephew's. One way or another, even if Anthimos ordered him not to, he would strike at Krispos. Anthimos might be sorry Krispos was gone, at least until he got used to the quiet, safe eunuch who would undoubtedly replace him. Dara would miss him more. But neither of them could keep Petronas from doing as he liked in the city.

Flight? If anyone in the Empire could track him down, Petronas could. Besides, he thought, what good was it to run away from the friends and allies he had? Getting rid of him might be harder here than on some lonely country road. Better to stay and do what he could. Now, still on that one knee, he met Petronas' eyes. "May I rise, your Highness?"

"Go ahead," Petronas said. "You'll fall again, soon enough."

Krispos did his best to talk Anthimos out of letting Petronas use Harvas Black-Robe's Halogai instead of Videssian troops against the Kubratoi. Anthimos listened and shook his head. "But why, your Majesty?" Krispos protested. "Even if the mercenaries do turn Kubrat topsy-turvy, Kubrati raiders will still wound your northern provinces."

Even being reminded by that "you" that the Empire was his personally did not change Anthimos' mind. "Maybe they will, but not that badly. Why should a little trouble on the frontier concern me? It can be set to rights later."

What was to Anthimos "a little trouble on the frontier" seemed a disaster in the making to Krispos. He wondered how the Avtokrator would have felt if he had a sister, nieces, a brother-in-law only too close to the wild men. But nothing that did not directly affect Anthimos was real to him.

With as much control as he could muster, Krispos said, "Your Majesty, truly the invasion you admit will happen could be stopped if we put our soldiers back where they belong. You know it's so."

"Maybe it is," Anthimos said. "But if I let Petronas go ahead, he'll be out of my hair for months. Think of the revels I could enjoy while he's not around." The Avtokrator leered in anticipation. Krispos tried to hide his disgust—was this the way an Emperor chose war or peace? Then Anthimos' face changed. All at once, he was as serious as Krispos had ever seen him. He went on quietly, "Besides, when it comes right down to it, I don't dare tell my uncle not to use the soldiers he's spent all this time mustering."

"Why not?" Krispos said. "Are you the Avtokrator or aren't you?"

"I am *now*," Anthimos answered, "and I'd like to keep being the Avtokrator a while longer, too, if you know what I mean. Suppose I order my uncle not to take his army to Makuran. Don't you think the first thing he'd use it for after that would be to throw me down? Then he'd march on Makuran anyway, and

I'd miss all those lovely revels I saw you sneering about a moment ago."

Abashed, Krispos hung his head. After a little thought, he realized Anthimos was right. He was surprised the Emperor could see so clearly. When Anthimos wanted to be, he was able enough. Trouble was, most of the time he didn't bother. Krispos mumbled, "Thank you for backing me as far as you did then, your Majesty."

"When I thought taking so many men west would pose a bad risk in the north, I was willing to argue with Petronas. But since he's managed to find a way to enjoy himself and have a good chance of checking the Kubratoi at the same time, why not let him have his fun? He doesn't begrudge me mine."

Krispos bowed. He knew he'd lost this duel with Petronas. "As your Majesty wishes, of course," he said, yielding as graciously as he could.

"That's a good fellow. I don't want to see you glooming about." Anthimos grinned at Krispos. "Especially since there's no need for gloom. A good carouse tonight to wash the taste of all this boring business we've had to do out of our mouths, and we'll both feel like new men." The grin got wider. "Or, if you feel like a woman instead, I expect that can be arranged."

Krispos did feel like a woman that evening, but not one of the complacent girls who enlivened the Avtokrator's feasts. He wished he could talk with Tanilis, to find out how badly she thought being bested by Petronas would hurt him. Since Tanilis was far away, Dara would do. Though he still thought her chief loyalty lay with Anthimos rather than with him—Anthimos was Avtokrator, and he was not—he was sure she preferred him to Anthimos' uncle.

But when, as he had a good many times before, he tried to leave the revel early, the Emperor would not let him. "I told you I didn't want you glooming about. I expect you to have a good time tonight." He pointed to a statuesque brunette. "She looks like she'd be a good time."

The woman Krispos wanted was back at the imperial residence. Telling the Emperor so seemed impractical. Krispos had taken a couple of girls at the revels, just so Anthimos would not notice anything out of the ordinary. But now he said, "I'm not in the mood for it this evening. I think I'll go over to the wine and drink for a while." Without a doubt, drinking fell within the Emperor's definition of a good time.

"*I* know what you need!" Anthimos exclaimed. He snatched the clear crystal bowl out of Krispos' hands. "Here, take a chance. You've been dealing them out for so long, you haven't been able to be on the grabbing end."

Obediently Krispos reached into the bowl and drew out a golden ball. He undid it, then unfolded the parchment inside. "Twenty-four pounds of horse manure," he read. Anthimos laughed so hard, he almost dropped the bowl. Grinning servants presented Krispos with his prize. He looked at the stinking brown mound and shook his head. "Well, it's been that kind of day."

The next day was no better. He had to greet Petronas when the Sevastokrator came to hear what Anthimos had decided. Then he had to endure Petronas' smirk of triumph after the Emperor's uncle emerged from being closeted with his nephew. "His Majesty is delighted that I set out for the westlands within the week," Petronas said.

Of course he is—this way you won't kill him and stick his head on the Milestone in the plaza of Palamas for the crowds to gape at, Krispos thought. Aloud he said, "May you triumph, your illustrious Highness."

"Oh, I shall," Petronas said. "First into Vaspurakan; the 'princes,' good soldiers all, will surely flock to me, for they follow Phos even if they are heretics, and will be glad to escape from the rule of those who worship the Four—false—Prophets. And then—on toward Mashiz!"

Krispos remembered what Iakovitzes had said about the centuries of inconclusive warfare between Videssos and Makuran. Petronas' planned trip to Mashiz would be quick and easy if his foes cooperated. If not, it was liable to take longer than the Sevastokrator expected. "May you triumph," he said again.

"What a smooth liar you've turned into, when you'd sooner see me ravens' meat. That's not likely, though, I'm afraid. No indeed. And in any event, as I told you before, your punishment awaits you. I don't think it will wait long enough for you to see me at all any more, let alone in my victorious return. A very good afternoon to you, esteemed and eminent sir." Petronas swaggered away.

Krispos stared at his retreating back. He sounded very sure of himself. What was he going to do, hire a band of bravoes to storm the imperial residence? Bravoes who tangled with the Emperor's Halogai would end up catmeat. And whatever Krispos ate, Anthimos ate, too. Unless Petronas wanted to be rid of his nephew along with Krispos, poison was unlikely, and he showed no sign of wanting to be rid of his nephew, not so long as he got his way.

What did that leave? Not much, Krispos thought, if I lay low until Petronas heads west. The Sevastokrator could hire assassins from afar, but Krispos did not greatly fear a lone assassin; he was a good enough man of his hands to hope to survive such an attack. Maybe Petronas was only trying to make him afraid and subservient once more—or maybe his anger would cool, away in the westlands. No, Krispos feared that was wishful thinking. Petronas was not the sort to forget an affront.

A few days later, troops under the Sevastokrator's command marched and rode down to the docks. Anthimos came to the docks, too, and made a fiercely martial speech. The soldiers cheered. Gnatios the patriarch prayed for the army's success. The soldiers cheered again. Then they lined up to be loaded onto ferries for the short journey over the Cattle-Crossing, the narrow strait that separated Videssos the city from the Empire's western provinces.

Krispos watched the tubby ferryboats waddle across the water to the westlands; watched them go aground; watched as, tiny in the distance, the warriors began to clamber down onto the beaches across from the city; saw the bright spring sunlight sparkling off someone's armor. That would be a general, he thought, maybe even Petronas himself. No matter how the Sevastokrator threatened, he was far less frightening on the other side of the Cattle-Crossing.

Anthimos must have been thinking the same thing. "Well," he said, turning at last to go back to the palaces, "the city is mine for a while, by Phos, with no one to tell me what I must or must not do."

"There's still me, your Majesty," Krispos said.

"Ah, but you do it in a pleasant tone of voice, and so I can ignore you if I care to," the Emperor said. "My uncle, now, I never could ignore, no matter how hard I tried." Krispos nodded, but wondered if Petronas would agree—the Sevastokrator seemed convinced his nephew ignored him all the time.

But having the wolf away from his door prompted Krispos to carouse with the best of them at the revel Anthimos put on that night "to celebrate the army's victory in advance," as the Avtokrator said. He was drinking wine from a large golden fruit bowl decorated with erotic reliefs when a Haloga guardsman came in and tapped him on the shoulder. "Somebody out there wants to see you," the northerner said.

Krispos stared at him. "Somebody out where?" he asked owlishly.

The Haloga stared back. "Out there," he said after a long pause. Krispos realized the guardsman was even drunker than he was.

"I'll come," Krispos said. He had almost got to the door when his sodden brain realized he was in no condition to fight off a toddler, let alone an assassin. He was about to turn around when the Haloga grabbed him by the arm and propelled him down the stairs—not, apparently, with malicious intent, but because the northerner needed help standing up himself.

"Krispos!" someone called from the darkness.

"Mavros!" He got free of the Haloga and stumbled toward his foster brother. "What are you doing here? I thought you were on the other side of the Cattle-Crossing with Petronas and the ret of his restinue—rest of his retinue," he corrected himself carefully.

"I was, and I will be again soon—I can't afford to be missed. I've got a little rowboat tied up at a quay not far from here. I had to come back across to warn you: Petronas has hired a mage. I came into his tent to ask him which horse he'd want tomorrow, and he and the wizard were talking about quietly getting rid of someone. They named no names while I was there, but I think it's you!"

XI

CERTAINTY WASHED THROUGH KRISPOS LIKE THE TIDE. "You're right. You have to be." Even drunk—perhaps more clearly because he was drunk—he could see that this was just how Petronas would deal with someone who had become inconvenient to him. It was neat and clean, with the Sevastokrator far away from any embarrassing questions, assuming they were ever asked.

"What are you going to do?" Mavros said.

The question snapped Krispos out of his rapt admiration for Petronas' cleverness. He tried to flog his slow wits forward. "Find a wizard of my own, I suppose," he said at last.

"That sounds well enough," Mavros agreed. "Whatever you do, do it quickly—I don't think Petronas will wait long, and the mage he was talking with seemed a proper ready-for-aught. Now I have to get back before I'm missed. The Lord with the great and good mind be with you." He stepped up, embraced Krispos, then hurried away.

Krispos watched him disappear into darkness and listened to his footfalls fade till they were gone. He thought how fortunate he was to have such a reliable friend in the Sevastokrator's household. Then he remembered what he had to do. "Wizard," he said aloud, as if to remind himself. Staggering slightly, he started out of the palace quarter.

He was almost to the plaza of Palamas before he consciously wondered where he was going. He only knew one sorcerer at all well, though. He was glad he hadn't been the one who'd antagonized Trokoundos. Otherwise, he thought, Anthimos' former tutor in magecraft would have been more likely to join Petronas' wizard than to help fend him off.

Trokoundos lived on a fashionable street not far from the palace quarter. Krispos pounded on his door, not caring that it was well past midnight. He kept pounding until Trokoundos opened it a crack. The mage held a lamp in one hand and a most unmystical short sword in the other. He lowered it when he recognized Krispos. "By Phos, esteemed and eminent sir, have you gone mad?"

"No," Krispos said. Trokoundos drew back from the wine fumes he exuded. He went on, "I'm in peril of my life. I need a wizard. I thought of you."

Trokoundos laughed. "Are you in such peril that it won't wait till morning?"

"Yes," Krispos said.

Trokoundos held the lamp high and peered at him. "You'd better come in," he said. As Krispos walked inside, the wizard turned his head and called, "I'm sorry, Phostina, but I'm afraid I have business." A woman's voice said something querulous. "Yes, I'll be as quiet as I can," Trokoundus promised. To Krispos, he explained, "My wife. Sit here, if you care to, and tell me of this peril of yours."

Krispos did. By the time he finished, Trokoundos was nodding and rubbing his chin in calculation. "You've made a powerful enemy, esteemed and eminent sir. Presumably he will have in his employment a powerful and dangerous mage. You know no more than you are to be assailed?"

"No," Krispos said, "and I'm lucky to know that."

"So you are, so you are, but it will make my task more difficult, for I will be unable to ward against any specific spells, but will have to try to protect you from all magics. Such a stretching will naturally weaken my own efforts, but I will do what I may. Honor will not let me do less, not after your gracious warning of his Majesty's wrath. Come along to my study, if you please."

The chamber where Trokoundos worked his magics was one part library, one part jeweler's stall, one part herbarium, and one part zoo. It smelled close and moist and rather fetid; Krispos' stomach flipflopped. Holding down his gorge with grim determination, he sat across from Trokoundos while the wizard consulted his books.

Trokoundos slammed a codex shut, rolled up a scroll, tied it with a ribbon, and put it back in its pigeonhole. "Since I do not know what form the attack upon you will take, I will use all three kingdoms—animal, vegetable, and mineral—in your defense." He went over to a large covered bowl and lifted the lid. "Here is a snail fed on oregano, a sovereign against poisonings and other noxiousnesses of all sorts. Eat it, if you would."

Krispos gulped. "I'd sooner have it broiled, with butter and garlic."

"No doubt, but prepared thus its virtue aims only at the tongue. Do as I say now: crack the shell and peel it, as if it were a hard-cooked egg, then swallow the creature down."

Trying not to think about what he was doing, Krispos obeyed. The snail was cold and wet on his tongue. He gulped convulsively before he could notice what it tasted like. Gagging, he wondered whether it would still protect him if he threw it up again.

"Very good," Trokoundos said, ignoring his distress. "Now then, the juice of the narcissus or asphodel will also aid you. Here is some, mixed with honey to make it palatable." Krispos got it down. After the snail, it was palatable. Trokoundos went on, "I will also wrap a dried asphodel in clean linen and give it to you. Carry it next to your skin; it will repel demons and other evil spirits."

"May the good god grant it be so," Krispos said. When Trokoundos gave him the plant, he tucked it under his tunic.

"Mineral, mineral, mineral," Trokoundos muttered. He snapped his fingers. "The very thing!" He rummaged among the stones on a table by his desk, held up a dark-brown one. "Here I have chalcedony, which, if pierced by an emery stone and hung round the neck, is proof against all fantastical illusions and protects the body against one's adversaries and their evil machinations. This is known as the counsel of chalcedony. Now where did that emery go?" He rummaged some more, until he finally found the hard stone he sought.

He clamped the chalcedony to the table and began to bore through it with the pointed end of the emery stone. As he worked, he chanted a wordless little song. "The power we seek lies within the chalcedony itself," the mage explained. "My chant is but to hasten the process that would otherwise be boring in two senses of the word. Ahh, here we are!" He worked a bit longer to enlarge the hole he had made, then held out the chalcedony to Krispos. "Have you a chain on which to wear it?"

"Yes." Krispos drew the chain on which he kept the gold-piece Omurtag had given him up over his head.

Trokoundos stared at the coin as it gleamed in the lamplight. "My, my," he said slowly. "What company my little stone will keep." He seemed about to ask Krispos about the goldpiece, then shook his head. "No time for my curiosity now. May the stone, the plant, and the snail keep you safe, that's all."

"Thank you." Krispos put the stone onto the chain, closed the catch, and slid the chain back onto his neck. "Now then, what do I owe you for your services?"

"Not a copper, seeing as I'd likely not be here to render those services had you not warned me the city would be unhealthy for a few weeks. No, I insist—this won't bankrupt me, I assure you."

"Thank you," Krispos repeated, bowing. "I had better get back to the imperial residence." He turned to go, then had another thought. "Not that I fail to trust your charms, but can I do anything to make them work even better?" He hoped the question would not offend Trokoundos.

Evidently it didn't, for the mage answered promptly. "Pray. The Lord with the great and good mind opposes all wicked efforts, and may well hear your sincere words and grant you his protection. Having a priest pray for you may also do some good; as Phos' holy men are sworn against evil, the good god naturally holds them in high regard."

"I'll do both those things," Krispos promised. As soon as he could he thought with wine-fueled intensity, he'd see Gnatios and ask for his prayers; who could be holier than the ecumenical patriarch?

"Good. I will pray for you as well," Trokoundos said. He yawned enormously. Whether that was a real yawn or a hint, Krispos knew it was time to go. He thanked the wizard one last time and took his leave. Dawn had already begun to pink the eastern sky. Krispos murmured two prayers to Phos, one for his own safety and the other that Anthimos would sleep late.

"You were a busy lad last night," Anthimos said roguishly as Krispos held up a robe for his approval. The Emperor had slept late, but not late enough. Krispos' head ached. Anthimos went on, "You weren't in your chamber when I got back. Did you go off with one of the wenches? Was she good?"

Without looking her way, Krispos sensed Dara listening

closely for his reply. "Not a wench, your Majesty," he said. "An old friend came to pay me a bet he owed, and afterward he and I went off and did a little more drinking."

"You should have told me before you left," the Emperor said. "Come to that, you could have brought your friend in. Who knows? He might have livened things up."

"Yes, your Majesty. Sorry, your Majesty." Krispos robed Anthimos, then went to the closet to get his master's red boots.

As he turned, he got a brief glimpse of Dara. He hoped that "he and I" had eased her mind. It had the advantage of being at least partly true; if she checked, she was sure to find someone who had seen him with Mavros. He hoped she would. If she thought he was betraying her, she had only to speak to Anthimos to destroy him. He did not like being so vulnerable to her. Maybe he should have worried more about that *before* he got into bed with her, he thought. Now was far too late.

Anthimos went off to the Amphitheater as soon as he had finished breakfast. Krispos stayed behind at the imperial residence for a little while, then headed for the patriarch's mansion. Gnatios was domiciled in the northern part of Videssos the city, in the shadow of the High Temple.

"You are . . . ?" a lesser priest haughtily asked at the door, looking down his nose at Krispos.

"I am the vestiarios to his Imperial Majesty Anthimos III, Avtokrator of the Videssians. I would have speech with the ec- umenical patriarch, at once." He folded his arms and waited. He hoped he sounded arrogant rather than anxious; only Pe- tronas and his mage knew when they would unleash their as- sault. He might need Gnatios' prayers right away.

He must have hit the proper tone—the priest deflated. "Yes, uh, esteemed, uh, eminent sir—"

"Esteemed *and* eminent," Krispos snapped.

"Yes, yes, of course; my apologies. The most holy sir is in his study. Come this way, please." Chattering nervously and bowing every few steps, the priest led him through the mansion. The artworks on the walls and set into niches were as fine as those in the imperial residence, but Krispos hardly noticed them. He followed close on his guide's heels, wishing the fellow would move faster.

Gnatios looked up frowning from the codex on his desk. "Curse it, Badourios, I told you I did not wish to be disturbed this morning." Then he saw who was behind the lesser priest and rose smoothly from his chair. "Of course I am always glad to make an exception for you, Krispos. Sit here, if you care to. Will you take wine?"

"No thank you, most holy sir," Krispos said, having mercy on his hangover. "May I ask for privacy, though?"

"You have only to reach behind you and close that stout door there," Gnatios said. Krispos did as he suggested. The patriarch leaned forward over the desk between them. "You've roused my curiosity, esteemed and eminent sir. Now, privately, what do you require?"

"Your prayers, most holy sir, for I have discovered that I am in danger of magical attack." As he started to explain to Gnatios, he realized that coming here was a mistake, a large mistake. His stomach knotted from something other than his hangover. Not only did the patriarch belong to Petronas' faction, he was the Sevastokrator's cousin. Krispos could not even tell him who had brought news of his danger for that might put Mavros at risk. Thus he knew his story limped as it came out.

Gnatios gave no sign of noticing. "Of course I shall pray for you, esteemed and eminent sir," he said fulsomely. "If you will give me the name of the man who so bravely brought word of this plot against you, I will pray for him as well. His courage should not go unrewarded."

The words were right. The tone was sincere—a little too sincere. Suddenly Krispos was certain that if he let Mavros' name slip out, the patriarch would get it to Petronas as fast as he could.

And so he answered, "Most holy sir, I fear I don't know her— uh, his—name. He came to me because, he said, he could not bear to see his master treat me unjustly. I don't even know who her—*his*—master is." With luck, those pretended slips would keep Gnatios from guessing how much Krispos knew and how he knew it.

"You will be in my thoughts and prayers for some time to come," the patriarch said.

Yes, but how? Krispos wondered. "Thank you, holy sir. You're very kind," he said. He bowed his way out, pondering what to do next. Ducking into a wineshop a few doors down the street from the patriarchal mansion let him ponder sitting down. He suspected Gnatios' prayers would not be for his continued good health. Who, then, could intercede with Phos for him?

While he sat and thought about that, a priest rushed past the wineshop. So close to the High Temple, blue robes were as common as fleas, but the fellow looked familiar. After a moment, Krispos recognized him: Badourios, Gnatios' doorkeeper. Where was he going in such a hurry? After tossing a couple of coppers on the table for the rather stale cake he'd eaten, Krispos slipped after him to find out.

Badourios was easy to follow; he did not seem to imagine he could be pursued. His destination soon became obvious: the harbor. Which meant, Krispos was sure, that as soon as he got over the Cattle-Crossing, Petronas would know his plans were no longer hidden from their intended victim.

And that, in turn, meant Krispos surely had very little time. It also meant everything he'd suspected about Gnatios was true, and then some. But that, for now, was a side issue. Through his robe, Krispos touched the chalcedony amulet Trokoundos had given him. The mage had as much as said the amulet, the asphodel, and the raw snail were not enough by themselves to ward him fully.

He started back toward the High Temple, intending to ask the first priest he saw to beseech Phos to protect him. Most blue-robes were fine men; he was willing to gamble on one chosen at random. Then he had a better idea. The abbot Pyrrhos had touched his life twice already. And not only was Pyrrhos notably holy, he was also bound to treat Krispos like his own son. Krispos turned, angry at himself for not having thought of Pyrrhos sooner. The monastery dedicated to the memory of the holy Skirios was—*that* way. Krispos headed for it faster than Badourios had gone to the harbor.

The gatekeeper made him wait outside the monastery. "The brethren just began their noontime prayers. They may not be disturbed for any reason."

Krispos drummed his fingers on the wall until the monks began filing out of the temple on the monastery grounds. The gatekeeper stood aside to let him pass. Their shaven heads and identical robes gave the monks no small uniformity, but Pyrrhos' tall, lean, erect figure stood out among them.

"Holy sir! Abbot Pyrrhos!" Krispos called. All the while, he kept expecting the spell from Petronas' mage to smash him down in the dust. The delay forced while the monks prayed might have given the wizard enough time to smite.

Pyrrhos turned, taking in Krispos' fine robe, so different from the plain blue wool he wore. Scorn sparked in the abbot's eyes. Then he recognized Krispos. His face changed—a little. "I have not seen you in some while," he said. "I gathered the loose life in the palaces was more to your liking than that which we live here."

Krispos felt himself flush, the more so because what Pyrrhos said held much truth. He said, "Holy sir, I need your aid," and waited to see what the abbot would do. If Pyrrhos only wanted to rant at him, he would go find another priest, and quickly.

But the abbot checked himself. Krispos saw he had not forgotten that strange night when Krispos first came to the monastery of the holy Skirios. "Phos bids us aid all men, that they may come to know the good," Pyrrhos said slowly. "Come to my study; tell me of your need."

"Thank you, holy sir," Krispos breathed. He followed the abbot through the narrow, dimly lit corridors of the monastery. He'd walked this way once before, he realized, but he had been too bemused then to make special note of his surroundings.

The study he remembered. Like Pyrrhos, it was spare and hard and served its purpose without superfluity. The abbot waved Krispos to an unpadded stool, perched on another, and leaned forward like a bearded bird of prey. "What is this aid you say you require? I would have thought you likelier to go to Gnatios these days, as he reckons most sins but a small matter."

Pyrrhos was not a man to make things easy, Krispos thought. But when he answered, "Gnatios would not help me, for the person from whom I need aid is the Sevastokrator Petronas." He knew he'd captured the abbot's attention.

"How did you fall foul of Petronas?" Pyrrhos asked. "Did you presume to suggest to the Emperor that his time might be better spent in attending to the duties of the state than in the wantonness and depravity in which, with his uncle's connivance, he currently wallows?"

"Something like that," Krispos said; he had indeed tried to get Anthimos to do more toward running the Empire. "And because of it, holy sir, the Sevastokrator, though now out of the city on campaign, seeks to slay me with sorcery. I've been told the prayers of a priest might help blunt the magic's power. Will you pray for my protection, holy sir?"

"By the good god, I will!" Pyrrhos sprang to his feet and caught Krispos by the arm. "Come to the altar with me, Krispos, and offer up your prayers as well."

The altar of the monastery temple was not of silver and gold and ivory and gems like the one in the High Temple. It was plain wood, as befitted the simplicity of monastic life. Pyrrhos and Krispos spat on the floor in front of it in ritual rejection of the dark god Skotos, Phos' eternal rival. Then they raised their hands to the heavens and spoke the creed together: "We bless thee, Phos, Lord with the great and good mind, by thy grace our protector, watchful beforehand that the great test of life may be decided in our favor."

Krispos prayed on in silence. Pyrrhos, more used to ordering his thoughts aloud, kept speaking after the creed was done: "Phos, I beseech you to protect this upright young man from the evil that approaches him. May he walk safe and righteous through it, as he has walked safe through the iniquity of the palaces. I pray for him as I would pray for my own son." His eyes met Krispos' for a moment. Yes, he remembered that first night Krispos had come to the monastery.

"Will your prayer save me, holy sir?" Krispos asked when the abbot lowered his arms.

"That is as Phos wills," Pyrrhos answered, "and depends on what your future is meant to be—also, I'll not deny, on the power of the sorcery sent against you. Though Phos will vanquish Skotos in the end, the dark god still ranges free in the world. I have prayed. Within me, I pray yet. May that suffice, that and whatever other wardings you have."

Pyrrhos was narrow, but he was also straight: he would not promise what he could not deliver. At any other time, Krispos would have had only approbation for that. Now, he thought, a reassuring lie might have felt very good. He thanked the abbot, dropped a goldpiece into the monastery poorbox, and started back to the palaces.

He spent the rest of the day in annoyed suspense. If the wizard was going to strike, he wished the fellow would *strike* and have done. Wondering whether he could withstand the attack seemed harder than waiting for it to come.

As he was carrying dinner in for Anthimos and Dara that evening, he got his wish. And, as is often the way of such things, he regretted ever making it. He was just lowering a wide silver tray from his shoulder to the table at which the Emperor and Empress sat when the strength suddenly flowed from his body like wine pouring from a jug. All at once, the tray seemed to weigh tons. Despite his desperate grip, it crashed to the floor.

Anthimos and Dara both jumped; the Empress let out a

squeak. "That wasn't very good, Krispos," Anthimos said, laying a finger by the side of his nose. "Even if you think the meal is bad, you should give us the chance to fling it about."

Krispos tried to answer, but only a croak came from his mouth; he was not strong enough to force his tongue to shape words. As Dara began to ask, "Are you all right?" his legs gave out from under him and he slid bonelessly down into the messy ruins of the dinner he had brought.

By luck, he landed with his head to one side. That let him keep breathing. Had he fallen face down in spilled soup or gravy, he surely would have drowned, for he could not have shifted to clear the muck from his mouth and nose.

He heard Dara scream. He could not see her; his eyes pointed in the wrong direction and he could not move them. Each breath was a separate struggle for air. His heart stuttered, uncertain in his chest.

Anthimos stooped beside him and rolled him onto his back. Breathing grew a precious trifle easier. "What's wrong, Krispos?" the Emperor demanded, staring down at him. Fetched by the racket of the dropped tray and by Dara's scream, servants rushed into the dining room. "He's had some sort of fit, poor beggar," Anthimos told them.

Barsymes said, "Let's get him to his bed. Here, Tyrovitzes, help me move him out of this muck." Grunting, the two eunuchs pulled Krispos away from the spilled food. Barsymes clicked tongue between teeth. "On second thought, we'd better clean him up before we put him into bed. We'll just take him out to the hallway first." As if he were a sack of lentils, they dragged him away from the table and out of the dining room.

"Put him down a moment," Tyrovitzes said. Barsymes helped ease Krispos to the marble flooring. Tyrovitzes went back into the dining room. "Your Majesties, I am sorry for the disturbance. Someone will be along directly, I assure you, to clean up what was unfortunately spilled and to serve you a fresh meal."

Had he been able to, Krispos would have snickered. *So sorry the vestiarios turned to a puddle of mush right before your eyes, your Majesties. A fresh meal will be along directly, so don't worry about it.* But had someone else been stricken in the same way, he knew he also would have tried to keep things running smoothly. That was how life worked in the palaces.

"Krispos, can you hear me? Can you understand me?" Barsymes asked. Though the answer to both was yes, Krispos could not give it. He could only stare up at Barsymes. The eunuch's smooth face lengthened in thought. "If you do understand, can you blink your eyes?"

The effort was like lifting a boulder as big as he was, but Krispos managed to close his eyelids. The world went frighteningly dark. Sweat burst out on his face as he fought to open his eyes again. At last he succeeded. He felt as worn as if a hundred harvests had all been pressed into one day.

"He has his wits, then," Tyrovitzes said.

"Yes." Barsymes laid a cool hand on Krispos' forehead. "No fever, I'd say. The good god willing, we don't have to fear catching—whatever this is." The chamberlain undid Krispos' robe and eased his arms out of it as if he were a doll. "Fetch water and towels, if you would, Tyrovitzes. We'll wash him and put him to bed and see if he gets better."

"Aye, what else can we do?" Tyrovitzes' sandals flapped down the hall.

Barsymes squatted on his heels, studying Krispos. Watching him in return, Krispos realized how helpless he was. Any small remembered slight, any resentment the eunuch still felt at being passed over for a whole man, and Petronas' magic would prevail even if it had not—quite—killed him outright.

Tyrovitzes came back, setting a bucket next to Krispos' head. Without a word, the two eunuchs set to work. The water was chilly. Krispos found himself shivering. Movements not under his conscious control seemed to function, after a fashion. But that blink had been plenty to exhaust him; he could not have raised a finger to save his soul from Skotos' ice.

The eunuchs hauled him down the corridor to the chamber that had once been Skombros'. "One, two—" Barsymes said. At "three," he and Tyrovitzes lifted Krispos and put him on the bed.

Krispos stared up at the ceiling; he had no other choice. If this was what the Sevastokrator's magic had done to him while he was warded, he wondered what would have become of him without protection. About the same thing, he supposed, that happened to a bull when the fellow at the slaughterhouse hit it between the eyes with his hammer. He would have dropped down dead, and that would have been that.

Barsymes came back a little later with a wide, flat pan. As gently as he could, he worked it under Krispos' buttocks. "You won't want to soil the sheets,'' he observed. Krispos did his best to put a thank-you look on his blank face. That hadn't occurred to him. A lot about being completely unable to care for himself hadn't occurred to him. Over the dreadfully long, dreadfully slow course of that summer and fall, he found out about all of them.

The palace eunuchs kept him alive. They cared for members of the imperial family at all phases of life. Sometimes they treated Krispos like an infant, sometimes like a senile old man. Longinos held him upright while Barsymes massaged his throat to get him to swallow broth, a spoonful at a time. He watched himself grow thinner day by day.

Physicians poked and prodded him and went away shaking their heads. Anthimos ordered a healer-priest to come see him. The priest fell into a trance, but woke from it baffled and defeated. ''I am sorry, your Majesty, but the illness has no cause upon which my talent can light,'' he told the Avtokrator.

That was only a few days after Krispos was stricken. For those first few days, and for a while afterward, Anthimos was constantly in his chamber, constantly making suggestions to the eunuchs about his care. Some of the suggestions were good ones; he urged the eunuchs to roll Krispos from side to side periodically to slow the start of bedsores. But when Krispos showed no signs of leaping to his feet and getting on with his duties as if nothing had happened, the Emperor began to lose interest not so much in him but in his case, and came to see him less and less often.

Although he did not leap to his feet, ever so slowly Krispos did begin to mend. Had he stayed as weak and limp as he was when the magic laid him low, he likely would have died, of slow starvation or from fluid puddling in his flaccid lungs. The milestones he reached were small ones, at first so small he scarcely noticed them himself, for who pays attention to being able to blink, or to cough? From blinking and coughing, though, he progressed to swallowing on his own, and then, later still, to chewing soft food.

He still could not speak. That required control more delicate than his muscles could yet achieve. Being able to smile again, and to frown, seemed as valuable to him. Babies used no more to let people know how they felt.

Krispos especially valued the return of expressiveness to his face when Dara visited him. She did not go into his chamber often, certainly not as often as Anthimos had after he was laid low. But where Anthimos lost interest in him because his condition changed so slowly, Dara kept coming back.

Once in a while she would take a bowl and spoon from one of the eunuchs, prop Krispos up with pillows, and feed him a meal. Barsymes, Tyrovitzes, Longinos, and the rest of the chamberlains were gentler and neater than she was. Krispos did not care. He was part of their duty; she helped him only because she wanted to. Being able to smile back at her let her know he understood that.

Though he could not answer, she talked at him while she visited. He picked up palace gossip, and snatches of what went on in the wider world, as well. Petronas, he learned, was advancing in Makuraner-held Vaspurakan, but slowly. The breakthrough, the advance on Mashiz of which the Sevastokrator dreamed, was nowhere in sight. Some of his generals had started to grumble. He'd even sent one packing—a certain Mammianos now found himself commanding the western coastal lowlands, a rich province but one peaceful for so long as to be a graveyard for a fighting soldier.

If Petronas himself never came back from his western campaign, Krispos would not have shed a tear—had his condition allowed it, he might have danced around the room. He did hope Mavros was all right.

Krispos was less delighted to learn that Petronas' plan for handling Kubrat looked to be working exactly as the Sevastokrator had predicted. Harvas Black-Robe's Haloga mercenaries, falling on the Kubratoi from the north, left them too distracted to launch any large raids against the Empire.

"They say Malomir may even lose his throne," Dara told Krispos one warm summer evening. Wanting to hear more, he widened his eyes and did his best to look attentive. But instead of going on about the affairs of the Kubratoi, Dara looked out toward the hallway. "Quiet tonight," she said. Mixed anger and hurt showed in her eyes, a blend Krispos had seen there before. "Why shouldn't it be quiet? Anthimos has been out carousing since a little past noon, and the good god alone knows when he'll decide to honor us by coming back. So a great many folk, I have no doubt, have gone off to pursue their own pleasures."

The Empress' laugh was full of self-mockery. "And with you in this state, Krispos, I can't even do that, can I? I find I've missed you, more than I thought I would. Don't you wish we could . . ." Dara's voice sank to a throaty whisper as she described what she wished they could do. Either her imagination was very fertile, or she'd been thinking for a long time.

Krispos felt heat rise in him that had nothing to do with the weather. Something else also rose; those parts of him not under full conscious control had always been less subject to Petronas' magic than the rest.

Dara saw what her words had done. After another quick glance to the door, she reached out and stroked him through the bed-clothes. "What a shame to waste it," she said. She stood up, hurried out of the room.

When she came back, she blew out the lamps. She went out-side again, looked in, and nodded. "Dark enough," Krispos heard her say. She walked over to the bed and drew back the covers. "The door to my bedchamber is closed," she murmured to Krispos. "Anyone will think I'm there. And no one can see in here from the hallway. So, if we're quiet . . ."

She slipped off her drawers. She did not get out of her gown, but hiked it up so she could lower herself onto Krispos. She moved slowly, to keep the bed from creaking. Even so, he knew he would explode too soon to please her. Nothing he could do about that, though, he thought through building ecstasy.

Suddenly Dara froze, stifling a gasp that had nothing to do with passion. Krispos heard sandals in the hallway. Tyrovitzes walked past the door. Dara started to slide away, but the move-ment made the bedframe start to groan. She froze again. Kris-pos could not move at all, but felt himself shrinking inside her as fear overpowered lust.

The eunuch did not even glance in, but kept walking. Dara and Krispos stayed motionless until he came back, crunching on an apple. Once more, he paid no attention to the dark door-way. The sound of his footsteps and his chewing faded.

When everything was quiet again, Dara did get off the bed. She covered Krispos once more. Linen rustled against her skin as she slid her drawers up her legs. "I'm sorry," she whispered. "That was a bad idea." She slipped away. This time, she did not return.

Too late, Krispos was aroused again, with nothing whatever he could do about it. A bad idea indeed, he thought, more than a little annoyed. It had left everyone unsatisfied.

Summer wore on. One morning, Krispos woke up on his stomach. For a moment, he thought nothing of it. Then he realized he had rolled over in his sleep. He tried to roll back again and succeeded after an effort that left him panting.

Not long after that, his speech returned, first as a hoarse whisper, then, little by little, tones that sounded more as he remembered he should. As control slowly returned to his arms and legs, he sat up in bed and then, wobbly as any toddler, stood on his own two feet.

That made Anthimos notice him again. "Splendid," the Avtokrator said. "Good to see you on the mend. I look forward to having you serve me again."

"I look forward to it, too, your Majesty," Krispos said, and found himself meaning it. After months of forced inactivity, he would have looked forward to a long, hot stint in the fields. *No*, he thought; *maybe to a* short *stint*. He did look forward to returning to the imperial bedchamber, both when Anthimos was occupying it and even more when he wasn't.

He found himself weak and clumsy as a pup. He began to exercise. At first, the least labor was plenty to wear him out. His strength slowly returned. A few weeks before the fall rains came, he went back to work. He bought handsome presents for the chamberlains who had cared for him so well and so long.

"This was not necessary," Barsymes said as he unwrapped a heavy gold chain. "The relief of having you on duty once more and no longer needing to try to keep up with his Majesty at those feasts of his . . ." The eunuch shook his head. But his long face, usually sour, wore a small, grudging smile. Krispos decided he had spent his money wisely.

He soon reconnected himself to the tendrils of the grapevine. He hardly needed to, for the first piece of news that came in was on everyone's lips: not only had Harvas Black-Robe's Halogai smashed the Kubratoi again, they had seized Pliskavos, the capital and the only real city Kubrat boasted. "By sorcery, I hear they took it," Longinos said, lowering his voice at the word and sketching the sun-sign over his heart.

The bare mention of magic was enough to make Krispos shudder. All the same, he shook his head. "Sorcery doesn't work well in battle," he said. "Everyone is too keyed up for it to stick, or so I've been told."

"And I," Longinos agreed. "But I also know that my sources in the north do not lie."

The palace eunuchs heard everything, and usually knew truth

from rumor. Krispos scratched his head and worried a little. He sent a note to Iakovitzes. If anyone really knew what was happening north of the Paristrian mountains, the little noble was the man.

The next day, one of Iakovitzes' retainers brought an answering note: "Everything's gone to the ice up there. Harvas is a worse murderer than any of the khagans ever dreamed of being. Maybe he is a wizard, too. I can't think of any other way for him to have won so quickly and easily."

Krispos worried a little more, but only for a couple of days. Then he found something more important to worry about. A messenger sailed into Videssos the city from the westlands with word that Petronas was on his way home.

That news dismayed Anthimos, too. "He'll be impossible," the Emperor said, pacing back and forth the next morning while Krispos tried to dress him. "Impossible, I tell you. He's fought Makuran all summer long and he hasn't gained two towns worth having. He'll be humiliated and he'll take it out on me."

On you? Krispos thought. But he held his tongue. Since he recovered enough to talk, he'd told no one the Sevastokrator was to blame for his collapse. He had no proof save Mavros' word, and Mavros was with Petronas in the west. But he exercised harder than ever and began working with his sword again.

Petronas' imminent return made Anthimos start an incessant round of revels, as if he feared he would never get another chance once his uncle was back. Krispos' lingering weakness gave him the perfect excuse not to accompany his master to his carousings. As he'd hoped, the silver bell in his chamber sometimes rang even when the Avtokrator was away from the imperial residence.

After that dangerous fiasco while he'd been recovering, Dara took fewer chances. Her summonses most often came well after midnight, when the rest of the household could be counted on to be asleep. Sometimes, though, she called him openly in the early evening, just for the sake of talk. He did not mind; on the contrary. He'd learned from Tanilis that talk was intercourse, too.

"What do you think it will be like, having Petronas back again?" Dara said on one of those early visits, a few days before the Sevastokrator was due.

"Perhaps I'm not the one to ask," Krispos answered cautiously. "You know he and I didn't agree about his campaign. I will say that the Empire doesn't seem to have fallen apart while he was gone." That was as far as he was willing to go. He did not know how the Empress felt about Petronas.

He found out. "I wish the Makurani had slain him," she said. "He's done everything he could to keep Anthimos first a boy and then a voluptuary, so he can go on holding all the power in the Empire in his own fists."

Since that was inarguably true, and since Petronas had got Krispos the post of vestiarios the better to control the Emperor, he kept quiet.

Sighing, Dara went on, "I hoped that with Petronas away from the city, Anthimos might come into his own and act as an Avtokrator should. But he hasn't, has he?" She sadly shook her head. "I suppose I shouldn't have expected it. By now he is as his uncle made him."

"He's afraid of the Sevastokrator, too," Krispos said. "That's one of the reasons he let Petronas go fight in the westlands, for fear he'd have used his army here in the city if he were thwarted."

"I knew that," Dara said. "I didn't know anyone else did. I think he was right to be afraid. If Petronas seized the throne, what would become of Anthimos, or me—or you, come to that?"

"Nothing good," Krispos answered. Dara was not made for convent life—the best she could hope for—and Anthimos even less for the monastery. Krispos knew he himself would not be lucky enough to have a monastic cell saved for him. He continued, "But Anthimos has the power to override anything the Sevastokrator does, if only he can find the will to use it."

"If only." A world of cynical doubt lay behind Dara's words.

"But he almost did, this past spring," Krispos said, not thinking until later how odd it was for him to be defending his lover's husband to her. "Then Petronas came up with using Harvas' brigands against Kubrat, and that gave Anthimos an excuse for backing down, so he did. But I don't think he would have, otherwise."

"What do you think would have happened then?"

"Ask the Lord with the great and good mind, not me. Anthimos is Avtokrator, aye, but Petronas had brought all those troops into the city. They might have obeyed Anthimos and, then again, they might not. The only soldiers I'm sure are loyal to him are the Halogai in the guards regiment, and they wouldn't have been enough by themselves. Maybe it's just as well he changed his mind."

"Yielding once makes yielding the next time easier." Dara turned her head to make an automatic scan of the doorway. Mischief sparked in her eyes; her voice dropped. "As I should know, and you, as well."

Krispos was glad enough to change the subject. Smiling with her, he said, "Aye, your Majesty, and I'm glad that's so." But he knew that was not what Dara had meant at first, and knew she'd been right.

He wondered what Anthimos would require to stiffen his back so he would not yield to Petronas in a pinch. The threat of something worse happening if he yielded than if he didn't, Krispos supposed, or else a feeling that he could get away with defying his uncle. Unfortunately, Krispos had no idea where Anthimos could come up with either of those.

If Petronas was not returning from Makuran in triumph, he did his best to make sure the people of Videssos did not know it. He paraded two regiments of tough-looking troops from the Silver Gate up Middle Street to the palace quarter, with carts carrying booty and a few dejected Makuraner prisoners stumbling along in chains between mounted companies of his men. He himself headed to procession on his splendid but otherwise useless show horse.

As the soldiers tramped through the city, a herald cried out, "Glory to his illustrious Highness the Sevastokrator Petronas, the pale death of the Makurani! Phos' sun shines through him, the conqueror of Artaz and Hanzith, of Fis and Bardaa and Thelaw!"

"Glory!" shouted the soldiers. By the way they yelled and the herald proclaimed the names of the places Petronas had captured, anyone who did not know better would have taken them for great cities rather than Vaspurakaner hamlets that, all added together, might have produced a town not much smaller than, say, Imbros or Opsikion.

And, while Phos' sun may have shone through Petronas, it could not penetrate the thick gray clouds that overhung Videssos the city. Rain drenched the Sevastokrator's parade. Some Videssians stood under umbrellas and awnings and colonnades to cheer Petronas' troopers. More stayed indoors.

Krispos wore a wide-brimmed hat of woven straw to keep off the worst of the rain as he watched Petronas dismiss his soldiers to their barracks once they had traversed the plaza of Palamas and gotten out of the public eye. Then the Sevastokrator, cold water dripping from his beard, booted his horse into a slow trot—the only kind the animal possessed—and rode for his lodging in the building that housed the Grand Courtroom.

Anthimos received Petronas the next day. At Krispos' suggestion, he did so in the Grand Courtroom. Seated on the throne, decked in the full gorgeous imperial regalia, with chamberlains and courtiers and Haloga guardsmen formed up on all sides, the Avtokrator stared, still-faced, as Petronas walked up the long aisle toward him.

As custom required, Petronas halted about ten feet from the base of the throne. He went to his knees and then to his belly in full proskynesis before his nephew. As he started to go down, he spied Krispos, who was standing to the Emperor's right. His eyes widened, very slightly. Krispos' lips curved open in a show of teeth that was not a smile.

Petronas kept control of his voice. "Majesty," he said, face to the marble floor.

"Arise," Anthimos answered, a beat later than he might have: a subtle hint that Petronas did not enjoy his full favor, but one no courtier would fail to notice.

Petronas could not have failed to notice either, but gave no sign as he got to his feet. Nor did he give any sign that he had failed to accomplish all he'd hoped in the west. "Your Majesty, a promising start has been achieved against the vain followers of the Four Prophets," he declared. "When weather permits us to resume the campaign next spring, even grander triumphs will surely follow."

Standing close by Anthimos, Krispos stiffened. He had not thought the Sevastokrator would so boldly try to brazen out his failure and go on as if nothing had happened. The whispers that ran through the Grand Courtroom, soft as summer breeze through leaves, said the same. But while Anthimos sat on the imperial throne, Petronas had in truth controlled the Empire for well over a decade. How would the Avtokrator respond now?

Not even Krispos knew. The ancient formality of the court kept his head still, but his eyes slid toward Anthimos. Again the Emperor hesitated, this time, Krispos was sure, not to make a point but because he was uncertain what to say. At last he replied, "Next year's campaigning season is still a long way away. Between now and then, we shall decide the proper course to take."

Petronas bowed. "As your Majesty wishes, of course." Krispos felt like cheering. For all his encouragement, and for all that he knew Dara had given, even getting Anthimos to temporize was a victory.

The rest of the court sensed that, too. Those soft whispers began again. Petronas withdrew from before the imperial throne, bowing every few paces until he had retreated far enough to turn and march away. But as he strode from the Grand Courtroom, he did not have the air of a defeated man.

Krispos shook his head. "Please give my regrets to his Imperial Highness, excellent Eroulos. I was ill almost all summer, and I fear I am too feeble to travel to the Sevastokrator's lodgings." That was the politest way he could find to say he did not trust Petronas enough to visit him.

"I will pass your words on to my master," Eroulos said gravely. Krispos wondered what part Petronas' steward had played in the sorcerous attempt on his life. He liked Eroulos, and thought Eroulos liked him. But Eroulos was Petronas' man, loyal to the Sevastokrator. Faction made friendship difficult.

Petronas did not deign to come to the imperial residence to visit Krispos. He was frequently there nonetheless, trying to talk his nephew round to letting him continue his war against Makuran. Whenever he saw Krispos, he stared through him as if he did not exist.

Despite all Krispos' urging, he could tell Anthimos was wavering. Anthimos was far more used to listening to Petronas than to Krispos . . . and Petronas commanded his armies. Glumly, Krispos braced himself for another defeat, and wondered if he would keep his post.

Then, much delayed on account of the vile winter weather, word reached Videssos the city from what had been the frontier with Kubrat. Bands of Harvas Black-Robe's Halogai had crossed the border in several places, looted villages on Videssian soil, massacred their inhabitants, and withdrawn.

Krispos made sure Anthimos read through the reports, which described the slaughter of the villagers in lurid detail. "This is dreadful!" the Emperor exclaimed, sounding more than a little sickened. He shoved the parchments aside.

"So it is, your Majesty," Krispos said. "These northerners seem even more vicious than the Kubratoi."

"They certainly do." With a sort of horrid fascination, Anthimos picked up the reports and read them again. He shuddered and threw them down. "By the sound of things, they might have been doing Skotos' work."

Krispos nodded. "That's well put, your Majesty. They do seem to be killing just for the sport of it, don't they? And remember, if you will, whose advice caused you to make those butchers the neighbors of the Empire. Also remember who wants you to go right on ignoring them so he can keep up his pointless war with Makuran."

"We'll have to find you a wife one day, Krispos," Anthimos said with a dry chuckle. "That was one of the smoothest 'I told you so's' I've ever heard." Krispos dutifully smiled, thinking it was not in the Avtokrator to stay serious about anything for long.

But Anthimos was serious. The next day, Petronas came to talk about the campaign he planned in the west. Anthimos wordlessly handed him the dispatches from the northern frontier. "Unfortunate, aye, but what of them?" Petronas said when he was done reading. "By the nature of things, we'll always have barbarians on that border, and barbarians, being barbarians, will probe at us from time to time."

"Exactly so," Anthimos said. "And when they probe, they should run up against soldiers, not find all of them away in the west. Uncle, I forbid you to attack Makuran until these new barbarians of yours learn we will respond to their raids and can keep them in check."

Out in the corridor, Krispos whistled a long, low, quiet note. That was stronger language than he'd ever expected Anthimos to use to Petronas. He plied his dust rag with new enthusiasm.

"You forbid me, your Majesty?" Petronas' voice held a tone Krispos had heard there before, of grown man talking to beardless youth.

Usually Anthimos either did not catch it or paid it no mind. This time, it must have rankled. "Yes, by the good god, I forbid you, Uncle," he snapped back. "I am the Avtokrator, and I have spoken. Do you propose to disobey my express command?"

Krispos waited for Petronas to try to jolly him round, as he had so often. But the Sevastokrator only said, "I will always obey you, Majesty, for as long as you are Emperor." The feet of his chair scraped on polished marble as he rose. "Now if you will excuse me, I have other business to attend to."

Petronas walked past Krispos as if he were not there; had he stood in the middle of the corridor, he suspected the Sevasto-krator would have walked over him rather than swerve aside. A couple of minutes later, Anthimos came out of the room where he'd met with Petronas. In a most unimperial gesture, he wiped his forehead with his sleeve.

"Whew!" he said. "Standing up to my uncle is bloody hard work, but by Phos, I did it! He said he'd obey." He sounded proud of himself. Krispos did not blame him.

Being who he was, Anthimos celebrated what he saw as his triumph over Petronas with a jar of wine, and then with another one. Thus fortified, he headed off for an evening of revels, dragging Krispos along.

Krispos did not want to revel. The more he listened to Petronas' words in his mind, the less they seemed a promise to obey. He had no trouble escaping the carouse; for one of the rare times since Krispos had known him, Anthimos drank him-self insensible. Krispos ducked out of the feast and hurried back to the imperial residence.

Seeing a light under the closed door of the bedchamber the Emperor and Empress used, he softly tapped at the door. Dara opened it a moment later. She smiled. "You grow bold," she said. "Good." She pressed herself against him and tilted her face up for a kiss.

He gladly gave it, but then stepped away from her. "Tell me what you think of this," he said, and repeated Anthimos' con-versation with Petronas as exactly as he could.

By the time he was done, Dara's expression had gone from lickerish to worried. "He'll obey as long as Anthimos is Em-peror, he said? What happens if Anthimos isn't Emperor any more?"

"That's just what I thought," Krispos said. "I wanted to be sure I wasn't imagining things. If Petronas wants to overthrow the Avtokrator, it shouldn't be hard for him. Most of the soldiers and almost all the high officers look to him, not to Anthimos. Till now, though, he hasn't wanted to."

"Why should he have bothered?" Dara said. "Anthimos was always pliant enough to suit him—till now, as you say. How are we going to stop him?" Her worry was fast becoming fear.

"We have to convince Anthimos that his uncle hasn't meekly backed down," Krispos said. "We ought to be able to manage that, the more so since I'm sure it's true. And if we do—" He paused, thinking hard. "How does this sound . . . ?"

Frowning, Dara listened to what he proposed. At one point, she raised a hand to stop him. "Not Gnatios," she said.

"No, by the good god, and I'm twice an idiot now for thinking of him," Krispos exclaimed, mentally kicking himself. Dara looked a question at him, but he did not explain. Instead, he went on, "I keep forgetting that even holy men have politics. The abbot Pyrrhos would serve as well, then, and he'd leap at the chance." He finished setting forth his scheme.

"Maybe," Dara said. "Maybe. And maybe, right now, looks better than any other chance we have. Let's try it."

"How may I serve you, your Majesty?" Petronas asked off-handedly. His indifference, Krispos thought, was enough by itself to damn him and confirm all suspicions. If the Sevastokrator no longer cared what Anthimos did, that could only be because he was preparing to dispense with him.

"Uncle, I think I may have been hasty the other day," Anthimos said. Dara had suggested that he sound nervous; he was having no trouble following the suggestion.

"You certainly were," Petronas rumbled. No, no sign of give there, Krispos thought. The Sevastokrator went on, "That's what you get for heeding the rascal who keeps pretending to dust outside there." Krispos felt his ears blaze. So he hadn't gone unnoticed, then. Even so, he did not stop listening.

"Er, yes," Anthimos said—nervously. "Well, I hope I can make amends."

"It's rather late for that," Petronas said. Krispos shivered. He only hoped he and Dara were not too late to save Anthimos' crown.

"I know I have a lot to make amends for," the Emperor said. "Not just for ordering you to stand down the other day, but for all you've done for me and for the Empire as regent when my father died and also since I've come of age. I want to reward you as you deserve, so, if it please you, I'd like to proclaim you co-Avtokrator before the whole court three days from now. Having done so much of the work for so long, you deserve your full share of the title."

Petronas stayed quiet so long that Krispos felt his hands curl into tight fists, then his nails biting into his palms. The Sevastokrator could seize the full imperial power for himself—would he be content with the offer of part of it, legally given? He asked,

"If I am to rule alongside you, Anthimos, does that mean you'll no longer try to meddle in the army and its business?"

"Uncle, you know more of such things than I do," Anthimos said.

"You'd best believe I do," Petronas growled. "High time you remembered it, too. Now the question is, do you mean all you say? I know how to find out, by the Lord with the great and good mind. I'll say yes to you, lad—if you cast that treacherous scoundrel of a Krispos from the palaces."

"The moment I set the crown on your head, uncle, Krispos will be cast not only from the palaces but from the city," Anthimos promised. Krispos and Dara had planned to have the Emperor tell Petronas just that. The risk remained that Anthimos would do exactly as he'd promised. If he feared Petronas more than he trusted his wife, his chamberlain, and his own abilities, he might pay the price for what he reckoned security.

"Hate to wait that long," Petronas said; then, at last, "Oh, very well, nephew, keep him another three days if it makes you happy. We have ourselves a bargain." The Sevastokrator got to his feet and triumphantly strode out of the chamber in which he had talked with Anthimos. Seeing Krispos outside, he spoke to him for the first time since he'd returned from the west: "Three days, wretch. Start packing."

His head lowered, Krispos dusted the gilded frame of an icon of Phos. He did not reply. Petronas laughed at his dismay and strutted past him down the corridor.

Fine snow fell outside the Grand Courtroom as the grandees and high ministers of the Empire gathered to see Petronas exalted. Inside, heat ducts that ran under the floor from a roaring furnace kept the throne room warm.

When all the officials and nobles were in their places, Krispos nodded to the captain of Anthimos' Haloga bodyguards. The captain nodded to his men. Axes held at present-arms before them, they slow-marched out in double row to form an aisle down the center of the hall, through which the Avtokrator and his party would advance. Their gilded chain mail glittered in the torchlight.

Once that aisle was made, Anthimos, Dara, Pyrrhos, and Krispos walked along it toward the throne—no, thrones now, Krispos saw, for a second high seat had been placed beside the first; if there were to be co-Avtokrators, each required his own place of honor. A crown lay on that second seat.

Silks rustled as courtiers prostrated themselves when Anthimos passed them. As they rose, the nobles whispered among themselves. "Where's Gnatios?" Krispos heard one say to the fellow beside him. "Ought to have the patriarch here to crown a new Emperor."

"He's down with the flux, poor chap," the other grandee answered. "Pyrrhos is a very holy man in his own right. The good god won't mind."

Everyone at the patriarchal mansion was down with the flux, Krispos thought. Considering the number of goldpieces he'd spent to make sure a particular potion got into the mansion's kitchen, he was not surprised. Poor Gnatios and his clerical colleagues would be dashing to the outhouse for the next several days.

Anthimos climbed the three steps to the thrones and seated himself in the one that had always been his. Dara stood at his right hand on the highest step, Pyrrhos in the center of the lowest step. Krispos was also to the Emperor's right, but off the steps altogether. He had helped plan the spectacle that was to come, but it was Anthimos' to play out.

The Avtokrator sat unmoving, staring without expression back toward the entrance to the Grand Courtroom. Beside and in front of him, Dara and Pyrrhos might also have been statues. Krispos wanted to fidget. With an effort, he controlled himself.

Petronas came into the Grand Courtroom. His robe, of scarlet silk encrusted with gold and gems, was identical to Anthimos'. Only his bare head declared that he was not yet Avtokrator. Marching with military precision, he approached the thrones. A tiny frown crossed his face when he saw Krispos, but then his eyes went back to the crown waiting for him on the throne that was to be his. He looked at Krispos again and smiled, unpleasantly.

Then, for the last time, he performed the proskynesis before his nephew. He rose and bowed to Anthimos as to an equal. "Majesty," he said. His voice was strong and proud.

"Majesty," Anthimos echoed. Some of the courtiers started whispering again, thinking that the formal recognition of Petronas' elevation. But Anthimos went on in a musing tone, "Majesty is the word we use to denote the sovereign of the state, the power that is his, a signpost of the imperial office, if you will, rather like the red boots only the Avtokrator is privileged to wear.''

Petronas gravely nodded. Krispos watched him go from attention to at ease. If Anthimos was going to make a speech before he got around to the coronation, Petronas would endure it in dignified comfort.

And Anthimos was going to make a speech. He continued, ''The Empire, of course, is indivisible. Ought not its sovereignty and the acknowledgment of that sovereignty to be the same? Many would say no, for Videssos has known co-Avtokrators before; the creation of another would be no innovation on the ancient customs of our state.''

Petronas nodded once more, this time, Krispos thought, with a trace of smugness. Anthimos was still speaking. ''And yet, those former Avtokrators surely each had reasons they reckoned pressing when they invested their colleagues with a share of the imperial dignity: perhaps to give a son or other chosen successor a taste of responsibility before the passing of the senior partner.

''My uncle Petronas, who stands before me now, is, as you all know, already familiar with the power inherent in the throne,'' Anthimos said. Petronas nodded yet again. His nephew went on, ''Indeed, for many years the administration of the state and of its armies was entrusted to him. At first this was because of my youth, later not least on account of his own desire to continue what he had begun.''

Petronas stood patiently, waiting for Anthimos to come to the point. Now Anthimos did: ''In his control of the armies, my uncle has fought against our ancient foe Makuran. Having failed to win any victories to speak of in his first year, he seeks a second year of campaigning, and this at a time when other barbarians, brought near our northern frontier at his urging, now threaten us.''

The smile suddenly faded from Petronas' face. Anthimos took no notice, continuing, ''When I urged him to consider this, he held it to be of scant import, and as much as told me he would use his influence over our soldiery to topple me from my throne if I failed to do as he wished.'' Anthimos raised his voice, called to the Halogai in the Grand Courtroom, ''Soldiers of Videssos, who is your Avtokrator, Anthimos or Petronas?''

''Anthimos!'' the northerners cried, so loud that echoes rang from the walls and high ceilings. ''Anthimos!''

The Emperor rose from his throne. ''Then seize this traitor

here, who sought to terrify me into granting him a share of the imperial power to which he has no right!''

"Why, you—" Petronas sprang toward his nephew. Dara screamed, throwing herself in front of Anthimos. Before Petronas could reach the steps that led up to the throne, though, Krispos grappled with him, holding him in place until three Halogai, axes upraised, came clattering from their posts nearest the imperial seat.

"Yield or die!" one shouted to Petronas, who was still struggling against Krispos' greater strength. All the rest of the imperial guards also held their axes above their heads, ready to loose massacre in the Grand Courtroom if any of Petronas' backers among the Empire's assembled nobles and commanders sought to rescue the Sevastokrator. No one did.

Krispos thought Petronas' fury so great he would die before he gave up. But the Sevastokrator was a veteran soldier, long used to calculating the odds of success in battle. Although hatred burned in his eyes, he checked himself, stepped back from Krispos, and bent his head to the big blond axemen. "I yield," he choked out.

"You'd better, Uncle," Anthimos said, sitting once more. "By the good god, I'd sooner see Krispos here on the throne than you." From her place just below him, Dara nodded vigorously. He went on, "And since you have yielded, you must be placed in circumstances where you can no longer threaten us. Will you now willingly surrender up your hair and join the brotherhood of monks at a monastery of our choosing, there to spend the rest of your days in contemplation of the Lord with the great and good mind?"

"Willingly?" By now Petronas had enough aplomb back to raise an ironic eyebrow. "Aye, considering the alternative, I'll abandon my hair willingly enough. Better to have my hair trimmed than my neck."

"Pyrrhos?" Anthimos said.

"With pleasure, your Majesty." The abbot stepped down onto the floor of the Grand Courtroom. In the pouch on his belt he carried scissors and a glitteringly sharp razor. He bowed to Petronas and held up a copy of Phos' scriptures. Formality kept from his voice any gloating he might have felt as he said, "Petronas, behold the law under which you shall live if you choose. If in your heart you feel you can observe it, enter the monastic life; if not, speak now."

Petronas took no offense at being addressed so simply—if he was to become a monk, the titles he had enjoyed were no longer his. He did permit himself one meaningful glance at the axemen around him, then replied, "I shall observe it."

"Shall you truly?"

"I shall truly."

"Truly?"

"Truly."

After Petronas affirmed his pledge for the third time, Pyrrhos bowed again and said, "Then lower your proud head, Petronas, and yield your hair in token of submission to Phos, the Lord with the great and good mind." Petronas obeyed. Graying hair fell to the marble floor as the abbot plied his scissors. When he had it cropped short, he switched to the razor.

The crown Petronas had expected to wear lay on a large cushion of scarlet satin. After Pyrrhos was done shaving Petronas' head, he climbed the steps to that second throne and lifted the cushion. Beneath it, folded flat, was a robe of coarse blue wool. The abbot took it and returned to Petronas.

"The garment you now wear does not suit the station in life you will have henceforth," he said. "Strip it off, and those red boots as well, that you may don the robe of monastic purity."

Again Petronas did as he was told, unhooking the fastenings that held the imperial raiment closed. With a fine shrug of indifference, he let the magnificent robe fall to the floor, then yanked off the imperial boots. His undertunic and drawers were of smooth, glistening silk. He stood easily, waiting for Pyrrhos to proceed. Defeated or not, Krispos thought, he had style.

Pyrrhos frowned to see Petronas' rich undergarments. "Those will also be taken from you when we reach the monastery," he said. "They are far too fine for the simple life the brethren live."

"You may take them now, for all I care," Petronas said, shrugging again.

Krispos was sure he'd hoped to embarrass Pyrrhos. He succeeded, too; the abbot went red to the top of his shaven pate. Recovering, he answered, "As I said, that may wait until you join your fellow monks." He held out the blue robe to Petronas. "Put this on, if you please." While Petronas slipped on the monastic robe, Pyrrhos intoned, "As the garment of Phos' blue covers your body, so may his righteousness enfold your heart and preserve it from all evil."

"So may it be," Petronas said. He traced the circular sun-sign over his heart. So did everyone in the Grand Courtroom, save only the heathen Halogai. Krispos did not feel hypocritical as he silently prayed that the man who till moments before had been Sevastokrator would make a good monk. Like all his countrymen, he took his faith seriously—and better for Petronas, he thought, to end up in a monastic cell than to spill his blood on the polished marble in front of the throne.

"It is accomplished, Brother Petronas," Pyrrhos said. "Come with me now to the monastery of the holy Sirikios, that you may make the acquaintance of your comrades in Phos' service." He began to lead the new monk out of the Grand Courtroom.

"Holy sir, a moment, if you please," Anthimos said from his throne. Pyrrhos looked back at the Avtokrator with obedience but no great liking: he had worked with Anthimos to bring down Petronas, but felt even more scorn for the younger man's way of life than for the elder's. Nonetheless he waited as Anthimos went on, "You might be well advised to have Vagn, Hjalborn, and Narvikka there accompany you to the monastery, lest Brother Petronas, ah, suddenly repent of his decision to serve the good god."

Dara had been proudly watching Anthimos since the drama in the throne room began, as if she had trouble believing he could face down his uncle and was overjoyed to be proven wrong. Now, hearing her husband speak such plain good sense, the Empress brought her hands together in a small, involuntary clap of delight. Krispos wished she would look at him that way.

He fought down a stab of jealousy. Anthimos, this time, was right. That made jealousy unimportant. When Pyrrhos hesitated, Krispos put in, "Were things different, Petronas himself would tell you that was a good idea, holy sir."

"You've learned well, and may the ice take you," Petronas said. Then, surprisingly, he laughed. "I probably would, at that."

Pyrrhos nodded. "Very well. Such untimely repentance would be a great sin, and sin we must always struggle against. Let it be as you say, your Majesty." Along with his new monk and the three broad, burly Haloga warriors, the abbot withdrew from the imperial presence.

"Anthimos, thou conquerest!" one of the courtiers shouted— the ancient Videssian cry of approval for an Avtokrator. In an instant, the Grand Courtroom was full of uproar, with everyone trying to outyell his neighbor to show his loyalty to the newly independent ruler: "Anthimos!" "Thou conquerest, Anthimos!" "Thou conquerest!" "Anthimos!"

Beaming, the Emperor drank in the praise. Krispos knew much of it was insincere, made by men still loyal to Petronas but too wise in the ways of survival at the imperial court to show it. He made a mental note to ask Anthimos to post Halogai around the monastery of the holy Sirikios to supplement Pyrrhos' club-wielding monks. But that could wait; for the moment, like Anthimos, Krispos was content to enjoy the triumph he'd helped create.

At last the Avtokrator raised a hand. Anthimos said, "As the first decree of this new phase of my reign, I command all of you here to go forth and live joyfully for the rest of your lives!"

Laughter and cheers rang through the Grand Courtroom. Krispos joined them. All the same, he was thinking Anthimos would need a more serious program than that if he intended to rule as well as reign. Krispos smiled a little. That program would have to come from someone. Why not him?

XII

"WHAT IS YOUR WILL, YOUR MAJESTY?" KRISPOS ASKED. "Shall we continue your uncle's war against Makuran on the smaller scale we'll have to use because we've shifted men back to the north, or shall we make peace and withdraw from the few towns Petronas took?"

"Don't bother me right now, Krispos." Anthimos had his nose in a scroll. Had the scroll been too far away for Krispos to read, he would have been impressed with the Emperor's industry, for it was a listing of property that looked much like a tax document. But Krispos knew it listed the wines in Petronas' cellars, which had fallen to Anthimos along with the rest of his uncle's vast holdings.

Krispos persisted. "Your Majesty, spring is hard upon us." He gestured to the open window, which let in a mild, sweet-smelling breeze and showed brilliant sunshine outside. "If you don't want to meet the envoy the King of Kings has sent us, what shall I tell him?"

"Tell him to go to the ice," Anthimos snapped. "Tell him whatever you bloody well please. This catalogue says Petronas had five amphorae of golden Vaspurakaner wine, and my cellarers have only been able to find three. I wonder where he hid the other two." The Avtokrator brightened. "I know! I'll cast a spell of finding to sniff them out."

Krispos gave up. "Very well your Majesty." He'd hoped to guide Anthimos. Like Petronas, he was discovering guiding was not enough most of the time. If anything needed doing, he had to do it. And so, while the Avtokrator busied himself with his spell of finding, Krispos bowed to Chihor-Vshnasp, the Makuraner ambassador.

Chihor-Vshnasp bowed back, less deeply. That was not an insult. Like most of his countrymen, Chihor-Vshnasp wore a bucket-shaped felt hat that was liable to fall off if he bent too far. "I hope his Imperial Majesty recovers from his indisposition soon," he said in excellent Videssian.

"So do I," Krispos said, continuing the polite fiction he knew Chihor-Vshnasp knew to be a polite fiction. "Meanwhile, maybe you and I can see how close we get to settling things for his approval."

"Shall we try that, esteemed and eminent sir?" Chihor-Vshnasp's knowledge of Videssian usages seemed flawless. Thoughtfully studying Krispos, he went on, "Such was the custom of the former Sevastokrator Petronas." It was as smooth a way as Krispos could imagine of asking him whether he in effect filled Petronas' place.

"I think the Avtokrator will ratify whatever we do," he answered.

"So." Chihor-Vshnasp drew the first sound of the word out into a hiss. "It is as I had been led to believe. Let us discuss these matters, then." He looked Krispos full in the face. His large, dark eyes were limpid, innocent, trusting as a child. They reminded Krispos of the eyes of Ibas, the horse trader who doctored the teeth of the beasts he sold.

Chihor-Vshnasp dickered like a horse trader, too. That made life difficult for Krispos, who wanted to abandon Petronas' war on Makuran; because of what he'd known growing up on both sides of the northern frontier and because of the unknown quantity Harvas Black-Robe's mercenaries represented, he thought the danger there more pressing than the one in the west.

But Krispos also feared just walking away from Petronas' war. Some disgruntled general would surely rise in rebellion if he tried. The high officers in the Videssian army had all resworn their oaths to Anthimos after Petronas fell, but if one rose, Krispos wondered whether the rest would resist him or join his revolt. He did not want to have to find out.

And so, remembering how Iakovitzes had gone round and round with Lexo the Khatrisher, he sparred with Chihor-Vshnasp. At last they settled. Videssos kept the small towns of Artaz and Hanzith, and the valley in which they lay. Vaspurakaners from the regions round the other towns Petronas had taken were to be allowed to move freely into Videssian territory, but Makuran would reoccupy those areas.

After Krispos swore by Phos and Chihor-Vshnasp by his people's Four Prophets to present to their sovereigns the terms on which they'd agreed, the Makuraner smiled a slightly triumphant smile and said, "Few from Fis and Thelaw and Bardaa will go over to you, you know. We saw that in the fighting last year—they loathe Videssos more for being heretic than Makuran for being heathen, and so did little to aid you."

"I know. I read the dispatches, too," Krispos said calmly.

Chihor-Vshnasp pursed his lips. "Interesting. You bargained long and hard for the sake of a concession you admit to be meaningless."

"It isn't meaningless," Krispos said, "not when I can present it to his Majesty and the court as a victory."

"So." Chihor-Vshnasp hissed again. "I have word, then, to take to his puissant Majesty Nakhorgan, King of Kings, pious, beneficent, to whom the God and his Prophets Four have granted many years and wide domains: that his brother in might Anthimos remains ably served by his advisors, even if the names change."

"You flatter me." Krispos tried not to show the pleasure he felt.

"Of course I do." Chihor-Vshnasp was in his mid-forties, not his late twenties. The look he gave Krispos was another act of flattery, for it seemed to imply that the two of them were equal in experience. Then he smiled. "That you notice says I have good reason to."

Krispos bowed in his chair toward the Makuraner envoy. He lifted his cup of wine. "Shall we drink to our success?"

Chihor-Vshnasp raised his cup, too. "By all means."

"By the good god!" Mavros exclaimed, staring wide-eyed at a troupe of young, comely acrobats who formed a pyramid with some most unconventional joinings. "I've never seen anything like *that* before!"

"His Majesty's revels are like no others," Krispos agreed. He'd invited his foster brother to the feast—Mavros was part of Anthimos' household these days. All of Petronas' men, all of Petronas' vast properties were forfeit to the Avtokrator when the Sevastokrator fell, just as Skombros' had been before. Anthimos had his own head groom, but Mavros' new post as that man's aide carried no small weight of responsbility.

And now, without warning, his eyes lit with a gleam Krispos had seen there before, but never so brightly. He turned and hurried off. "Where are you going?" Krispos called after him. He did not answer, but disappeared into the night. Krispos wondered if watching the acrobats had stirred him so much he had to go find some companionship. If that was what Mavros wanted, Krispos thought, he was foolish to leave. The women right here were more attractive than any he was likely to find elsewhere in the city—and Anthimos did not bid any likely to say no to come to his feasts. Krispos shrugged. He knew he didn't think things through all the time, however hard he tried. No reason Mavros should, either.

A man came out with a pandoura, struck a ringing chord, and began to sing a bawdy wedding song. Another fellow accompanied him with a set of pipes. The loud, cheerful music worked the same magic in the palace complex as in any peasant village throughout the Empire. It pulled people off couches and away from plates piled high with sea urchins and tuna, asparagus and cakes. It made them want to dance. As at any village wedding throughout the Empire, they formed rings and capered round and round, drowning out the singer as they roared along with his song.

The Halogai might have shouted outside. If they did, no one ever heard them. The first Krispos knew of Mavros' return was when a woman facing the entrance screamed. Others, some men among them, screamed, to. Pandoura and pipes played on for another few notes, then raggedly fell silent.

"Hello, your Majesty," Mavros said, spotting Anthimos in one of the suddenly halted rings. "I thought it was a shame for your friend here to be missing all the fun." He clucked to the horse he was riding—one of Anthimos' favorites—and touched its flanks with his heels. Hooves clattering on the smooth stone floor, the horse advanced through the revelers toward the tables piled high with food.

"Don't just stand there, Krispos," Mavros called. "Feed this good fellow a strawberry or six."

Krispos felt like throwing something at Mavros for involving him in this mad jape. Reluctantly he stepped toward the tables. Refusing, he thought, would only look worse. He picked up the bowl of strawberries. Amid vast silence, the snuffling of the horse as it ate was the only sound.

Then Anthimos laughed. All at once, everyone else was laughing, too: whatever the Emperor thought funny could not be an outrage. "Why didn't you bring a mare in season?" Anthimos called. "Then he could share all the pleasures we do."

"Maybe next time, your Majesty," Mavros said, his face perfectly straight.

"Yes, well, all right," Anthimos said. "Pity there's no entertainment that really could amuse him."

"Oh, I wouldn't say that, your Majesty," Mavros answered blithely. "After all, he has us to watch—and if we aren't funny, what is?"

Anthimos laughed again. As far as he was concerned, Mavros' headlong style of wit was a great success. Thinking about it, though, Krispos wondered if his foster brother hadn't been telling the exact and literal truth.

The Emperor said, "One reward we can give him—if he's finished with those strawberries there, why don't you fill that bowl up with wine? Here, you can use this jar if you care to." Nodding, Mavros took the jar to which Anthimos had pointed. He brought it back to where the horse stood patiently waiting, upended over the bowl that still held a few mashed strawberries. The thick wine poured out, yellow as a Haloga's hair.

"Your Majesty!" Krispos exclaimed. "Is that jar from one of the missing amphorae from Petronas' cellars?"

"As a matter of fact, it is." Anthimos looked smug. "I was hoping you'd notice. The spell I employed worked rather well, wouldn't you say? It took my men right to the missing jars."

"Good for you." Krispos eyed the Avtokrator with more respect than he was used to giving him. Anthimos had stuck with his magic and worked to regain it with greater persistence than he devoted to anything else save the pleasures of the flesh. As far as Krispos could tell, he still botched conjurations every so often, but none—yet—in a way that had endangered him. If only he gave as much attention to the broader concerns of the Empire, Krispos thought. Whenever he wanted to be, he was plenty capable. Too often, he did not care to bother.

Krispos wondered how often he'd had that identical thought. Enough times, he was sure, that if he had a goldpiece for each one, the pen-pushers in the imperial treasury could lower the taxes on every farm in Videssos.

They wouldn't, of course; whenever new money came along, Anthimos always invented a new way to spend it. As now: the thought had hardly crossed Krispos' mind before the Avtokrator sidled up to him and said, "You know, I think I'm going to have a pool dug beside this hall, so I can stock it with minnows."

"Minnows, your Majesty?" If Anthimos had conceived a passion for fishing, he'd done it without Krispos' noticing. "Trout would give you better sport, I'd think."

"Not that sort of minnows." Anthimos looked exasperated at Krispos' lack of imagination. He glanced toward a couple of the courtesans in the crowded room. "*That* sort of minnows. Don't you think they could be very amusing, nibbling around the way minnows do, in lovely cool water on a hot summer evening?"

"I suppose they might," Krispos said, "if you—and they— don't mind being mosquito food while you're sporting." Mosquitoes and gnats and biting insects of all sorts flourished in the humid heat of the city's summer.

The Emperor's face fell, but only for a moment. "I could hold the bugs at bay with magic."

"Your Majesty, if a bug-repelling spell were easy, everyone would use it instead of mosquito netting."

"Maybe I'll devise an easy one, then," Anthimos said.

Maybe he would, too, Krispos thought. Even if the Emperor no longer had a tutor, he was turning into a magician of sorts. Krispos had no interest whatever in becoming a wizard. He was, however, a solidly practical man. He said, "Even without sorcery, you could put a tent of mosquito netting over and around your pool."

"By the good god, so I could." Anthimos grinned and clapped Krispos on the back. He talked for the next half hour about the pool and the entertainments he envisioned there. Krispos listened, enthralled. Anthimos was a voluptuary's voluptuary; he took—and communicated—pleasure in talking about pleasure.

After a while, the thought of the pleasure he would enjoy later roused him to pursue some immediately. He beckoned to one of the tarts in the hall and took her over to an unoccupied portion of the pile of pillows. He'd hardly begun when he got a new idea. "Let's make a pyramid of our own," he called to the other couples and groups there. "Do you think we could?"

They tried. Shaking his head, Krispos watched. It wasn't nearly so fine as the acrobats' pyramid, but everybody in it seemed to be having a good time. That was Anthimos, through and through.

"Minnows," Dara hissed.

Krispos had never heard the name of a small, nondescript fish used as a swear word before, and needed a moment to understand. Then he asked, "How did you hear about *that*?"

"Anthimos told me last night, of course," the Empress answered through clenched teeth. "He likes to tell me about his little schemes, and he was so excited over this one that he told me *all* about it." She glared at Krispos. "Why didn't you stop him?"

"Why didn't I what?" He stared at her. Anthimos was out carousing, but the hour was still early and the door from the imperial bedchamber to the hall wide open. Whatever got said had to be said in a tone of voice that would attract no notice from anyone walking down the corridor. Remembering that helped Krispos hold his temper. "How was I supposed to stop him? He's the Avtokrator; he can do what he likes. And don't you think he'd wonder why I tried to talk him out of it? What reason could I give him?"

"That that cursed pool—may Skotos' ice cover it all year around—is just another way, and a particularly vile one, for him to be unfaithful to me."

"How am I supposed to tell him that? If I sound like a priest, he's more likely to shave my head and put me in a blue robe than to listen to me. And besides . . ." He paused to make sure no one was outside to hear, then went on, "Besides, things being as they are, I'm hardly the one to tell him anything of the kind."

"But he listens to you," Dara said. "He listens to you more than to anyone else these days. If you can't get him to pay heed, no one can. I know it's not fair to ask you—"

"You don't begin to." Krispos had thought defending Anthimos to Dara was curious. Now she wanted him to get Anthimos to be more faithful to her so she would have less time and less desire to give to him because she would be giving more to her husband. He had not been trained in fancy logic at the Sorcerers'

Collegium, but he knew a muddle when he stepped into one. He also knew that explaining it to her would be worse than a waste of time—it would make her furious.

Sighing, he tried another tack. "He listens to me when he feels like it. Even on the business of the Empire, that's not nearly all the time. When it comes to . . . things he really likes, he pays attention only to himself. You know that, Dara." He still spoke her name but seldom. When he did, it was a way to emphasize that what he said was important.

"Yes, I do know," she said in a low voice. "That's so even now that Petronas is locked up for good. All Anthimos cares about is doing just what he wants." Her eyes lifted and caught Krispos'. She had a way of doing that which made it next to impossible for him to tell her no. "At least try to get him to set his hand to the Empire. If he doesn't, who will?"

"I've tried before, but if you'll remember, I was the one who ended up hashing things out with Chihor-Vshnasp."

"Try again," Dara said, those eyes meltingly soft. "For me."

"All right, I'll try," Krispos said with no great optimism. Again he thought how strange it was for Dara to use her lover to improve her husband. He wondered just what that meant— probably that Anthimos was more important to her than he was. Whatever his flaws, the Avtokrator was handsome and affable— and without him, Dara would be only a westlands noble's daughter, not the Empress of Videssos. Having gained so much status through his connections to others, Krispos understood how she could fear losing hers if the person from whom it derived was cast down.

She smiled at him, differently from a moment before. "Thank you, Krispos. That will be all for now, I think." Now she spoke as Empress to vestiarios. He rose, bowed, and left her chamber, angry at her for changing moods so abruptly but unable to show it.

Having nothing better to do, he went to bed. Some time in the middle of the night, the small silver bell in his bedchamber rang. He wondered whether Anthimos was summoning him, or Dara. Either way, he thought grouchily as he dressed and tried to rub the sleep from his eyes, he would have to please and obey.

It was Dara; the Emperor was still out roistering. Even the comfort of her body, though, could not completely make up for the way she'd treated him earlier. As he had with Tanilis, he wanted to be more than a bedwarmer for her. That she sometimes remembered him as a person only made it worse when she forgot. One day, he thought, he'd have to talk with her about that—if only he could figure out how.

Krispos carried the last of the breakfast dishes to the kitchens on a tray, then went back to the dining room, where Anthimos was leaning back in his chair and working lazily on his first morning cup of wine. He'd learned the Avtokrator was more willing to conduct business now than at any other time of day. Whether "more willing" really meant "willing" varied from day to day. *I'll see,* Krispos thought.

"Your Majesty?" he said.

"Eh? What is it?" Anthimos sounded either peevish or a trifle the worse for wear. The latter, Krispos judged: the Emperor did not bounce back from his debauches quite as readily these days as he had when Krispos first became vestiarios. That was hardly surprising. Someone with a less resilient constitution might well have been dead by now if he abused himself as Anthimos did.

All that was beside the point—the Avtokrator in a bad mood was less likely to want to listen to anything that had to do with imperial administration. Nonetheless, Krispos had promised Dara he'd try—and if Anthimos was going to keep other people from becoming Emperor, he'd just have to handle the job himself. Krispos said, "Your Majesty, the grand logothete of the treasury has asked me to bring certain matters to your attention."

Sure enough, Anthimos' smile, lively enough a moment before, became fixed on his face. "I'm not really much interested right at the moment in what the grand logothete is worrying about."

"He thinks it important, your Majesty. After listening to him, so do I," Krispos said.

Anthimos finished his cup of wine. His mobile features assumed a martyred expression. "Go on, then, if you must."

"Thank you, your Majesty. The logothete's complaint is that nobles in some of the provinces more remote from Videssos the city are collecting taxes from the peasants on their lands but not turning the money over to the treasury. Some of the nobles are also buying up peasant holdings next to their lands, so that their estates grow and those of the free peasants who make up the backbone of the army suffer.''

"That doesn't sound very good," the Emperor said. The trouble was, he didn't sound very interested.

"The grand logothete wants you to put out a law that would stop the nobles from getting away with it, with punishments harsh enough to make even the hardest thief think twice before he tries cheating the fisc. The logothete thinks it's urgent, your Majesty, and it's costing you money you could be using to enjoy yourself. He's written a draft of the law, and he wants you to review it—''

"When I have the time," Anthimos said, which meant somewhere between *later* and *never*. He peered down into his empty cup, held it out to Krispos. "Fill this up again for me, will you? That's a good fellow."

Krispos filled the cup. "Your Majesty, the grand logothete gave me his draft. I have it here. I can show it to you—''

"When I have the time, I said."

"When will that be, your Majesty? This afternoon? Tomorrow? Next month? Three years from now?" Krispos felt his temper slipping. He knew it was dangerous, but could not help it. Part of it was pent-up frustration over Anthimos' refusal to do anything that didn't gratify him right then and there. He'd been trying to change that ever since he became vestiarios. More irritation sprang from the anger he hadn't been able to let out at Dara the night before.

"You want to give me this stupid law your boring bureaucrat dreamed up?" Anthimos was angry, too, scowling at Krispos; not even Petronas had spoken to him like that. Breathing hard, he went on, "Bring it to me now, this instant. I'll show you what I think of it, by Phos."

In his relief, Krispos heard the Emperor's words without paying attention to the way he said them. "Thank you, your Majesty. I'll fetch it right away." He hurried to his chamber and brought Anthimos the parchment. "Here you are, your Majesty."

The Avtokrator unrolled the document and gave it one quick, disdainful glance. He ripped it in half, then in quarters, then in eighths. Then, with more methodical care than he ever gave to government, he tore each part into a multitude of tiny pieces and flung them about the room, until it looked as though a sudden interior blizzard had struck.

"*There's* what I think of this stupid law!" he shouted.

"Why, you—" Of itself, Krispos' fist clenched and drew back. Had Anthimos been any other man in all the Empire save who he was, that fist would have crashed into his nastily grinning face. A cold, clear sense of self-preservation made Krispos think twice. Very carefully, as if it belonged to someone else, he lowered his hand and made it open. Even more carefully, he said, "Your Majesty, that was foolish."

"And so? What are you going to do about it?" Before Krispos could answer, Anthimos went on, "I'll tell you what: quick now, get broom and dustpan and sweep up every one of these miserable little pieces and dump 'em in the privy. That's just where they belong."

Krispos stared at him. "Move, curse you," Anthimos said. "I command it." Even if he would not act like an Emperor, he sounded like one. Krispos had to obey. Hating himself and Anthimos both, he swept the floor clean. The Avtokrator stood over him, making sure he found every scrap of parchment. When he was finally satisfied, he said, "Now go get rid of them."

Normally Krispos took no notice of the privies' stench; stench and privies went together. This time, though, he was on business different from the usual, and the sharp reek bit into his nostrils. As the torn-up pieces of law fluttered downward to their end, he thought that Anthimos would have done the same thing to the whole Empire, were it small enough to take in his two hands and tear.

Krispos was stubborn. All through his life, that had served him well. Now he brought his stubbornness to bear on Anthimos. Whenever laws were proposed or other matters came up that required a decision from the Emperor, he kept on presenting them to Anthimos, in the hope that he could wear him down and gradually accustom him to performing his duties.

But Anthimos proved just as mulish as he was. The Avtokrator quit paying day-to-day affairs even the smallest amount of attention he had once given them. He ripped no more edicts to shreds, but he did not sign them or affix the imperial seal to them, either.

Krispos took to saying, "Thank you, your Majesty," at the end of each day's undone business.

Sarcasm rolled off Anthimos like water from a goose's feathers. "My pleasure," he'd answer day by day. The response made Krispos want to grind his teeth—it kept reminding him of all that Anthimos really cared about.

Yet Anthimos could work hard when he wanted to. That irked Krispos more than anything. He watched the Avtokrator patiently studying magic on his own because it interested him; he'd always known how much ingenuity Anthimos put into his revels. He could have been a capable Emperor. That, worse luck, did not interest him.

Krispos regretted trying to get him to handle routine matters when something came up that was not routine. Urgent dispatches from the northern frontier told of fresh raids of Harvas Black-Robe's Halogai. Though Anthimos had strengthened the border after forcing Petronas into the monastery, the raiding bands coming south were too large and too fierce for the frontier troops to handle.

Anthimos refused to commit more soldiers. "But your Majesty," Krispos protested, "this is the border because of which you toppled your uncle when he would not protect it."

"That was part of the reason, aye." Anthimos gave Krispos a measuring stare. "Another part was that he wouldn't leave me alone. You seem to have forgotten that—you've grown almost as tiresome as he was."

The warning there was unmistakable. The troops did not go north. Krispos sent a message by imperial courier to the village where he'd grown up, urging his brother-in-law Domokos to bring Evdokia and their children down to Videssos the city.

A little more than a week later, a worn-looking courier brought his blowing horse up to the imperial residence and delivered Domokos' reply. " 'We'll stay here,' he told the rider who spoke with him, esteemed and eminent sir," the fellow said, consulting a scrap of parchment. " 'We're already too beholden to you,' he said, and, 'We don't care to depend on your charity when we can make a go of things where we are.' That's what he said, just as the other courier wrote it down."

"Thank you," Krispos said abstractedly, respecting his brother-in-law's pride and cursing him for being an obstinate fool at the same time. Meanwhile, the courier stood waiting.

After a moment, Krispos realized why. He gave the man a gold-piece. The courier saluted in delight and hurried away.

Krispos decided that if he could not go through Anthimos to protect the farmers near the northern border, he would have to go around him. He spoke with Dara. She agreed. They asked to meet with Ouittios, one of the generals who had served under Petronas.

To their dismay, Ouittios refused to come. "He will not see you, except at the Avtokrator's express command," the general's adjutant reported. "If you will forgive his frankness, and me for relaying it, he fears being entrapped into what will later be called treason, as Petronas was."

Krispos scowled when he heard that, but had to admit it made sense from Ouittios' point of view. A couple of other attempted contacts proved similarly abortive. "This desperately needs doing, and I can't get it done," Krispos complained to Mavros after yet another high-ranking soldier refused to have anything to do with him.

"If you like, I think I can put you in touch with Agapetos," Mavros said. "He has lands around Opsikion. He used to know my father; my mother would speak of him from time to time. Do you want me to try?"

"Yes, by the good god, and quick as you can," Krispos said.

With Mavros as go-between, Agapetos agreed to come to the imperial residence and listen to Krispos and Dara. Even so, the general's hard, square face was full of suspicion as he eased himself down into a chair. Suspicion turned to surprise when he found out why he'd been summoned. "You want me to go up there and fight?" he said, scratching an old scar on his cheek. "I figured you were out to disband troops, not put them to proper use. So did everybody, after what happened with Petronas. Why this sneaking around behind his Majesty's back?"

"Because I put his back up, that's why. He just won't take care of things in the north, since I'm the one who argued too hard that he ought to," Krispos answered. "I'd sooner wait till he comes round on his own, but I don't think we have the time. Do you?"

"No," Agapetos answered at once. "I know we don't. I'm only surprised you do, too. After what befell the Sevastokrator, like I said before, if you'll excuse me for speaking out so plainly, I would've figured you to be out to weaken the army more, not give it useful work to do."

"Petronas did not fall because he was a soldier," Dara said. "He fell because he was a rebellious soldier, one who valued his own wishes above those of his overlord. Surely the same is not true of you, excellent sir?"

Agapetos' chuckle was more grim than amused. "If it were, your Majesty, do you think I'd be dunce enough to admit it? All right, though, I take your point. But what happens to me when the Avtokrator finds out I've obeyed the two of you rather than him?"

"If you win, how can he blame you?" Krispos asked. "Even if he tries, we and your success will both shield you from him. And if you lose, you may well end up dead, in which case you'll worry about Phos' wrath, not Anthimos'."

"For all those fancy robes, you think like a soldier," Agapetos said. "All right, we'll try it your way. Anthimos said he wouldn't mind having you as Emperor, didn't he? I can see why. And I wouldn't mind having a go at the Halogai, truth to tell. Those axes the imperial guardsmen carry are fearsome enough, aye, but how would they fare against cavalry that knows something of discipline? It will be interesting to find out, yes it will."

Krispos could see him planning his new campaign, as if he were a carpenter picturing a new chair in his mind before he built it. "How many men will you take?" he asked.

"My whole army," Agapetos answered. "Say, seventy-five hundred troopers. That's plenty and then some to control raiding bands like the ones I expect we'll be seeing. The only time you need more is if you try to do something really enormous, the way Petronas did last year against Makuran. And look what that got him—no headway to speak of, and a blue robe and a cell at the end of it."

"His ambition earned him that, excellent Agapetos," Dara said. "I already asked you once if you had that kind of ambition, and you said no. You should be safe enough then, not so?"

The general said, "I expect you're right. Besides, from everything I've heard, this is something that needs taking care of, the sooner the better. If I set out inside the next ten days, will that suit you?"

Krispos and Dara looked at each other. Krispos had hoped for something more rousing, perhaps a cry of, *I'll ride for the frontier before the sun sets!* But he had seen enough since he came to the capital to understand that large organizations usually moved slower than small ones. "It will do," he said. Dara nodded.

"Well, with your leave, I'll be off, then," Agapetos said, rising from his chair. "I've a deal to make ready before we ride out." He dipped his head to Krispos, bowed deeply to Dara, and stamped away.

"I hope he'll serve," Krispos said when the general was gone. "From everything Harvas has done, he's a soldier who fights hard and moves fast. I just hope Agapetos understands that."

"The Halogai are foot soldiers," Dara said. "How can they move faster than our horsemen? More likely they'll flee at word of Agapetos' approach."

"You're probably right," Krispos said. He could not help thinking, though, that Harvas Black-Robe's Halogai had already beaten the Kubratoi, and the Kubratoi raised no mean cavalry, even if, as Agapetos had said, they lacked discipline.

He made himself shake off his worries. He'd done the best he could to protect the northern frontier. He'd certainly done more than Anthimos had. If Agapetos' army did not suffice, then Videssos would have a full-sized war on its hands. Not even Anthimos could ignore that—he hoped.

Krispos got more and more used to working around Anthimos rather than through him. Petronas had managed for years. But Petronas had been Sevastokrator, of the imperial family and with prestige almost imperial—sometimes more imperial than Anthimos'. Because he was only vestiarios, Krispos had to work harder to convince people to see things his way.

Having Dara with him when he saw Agapetos had helped persuade the general to go along. Sometimes, though, Krispos needed to beard officials in their own lairs. Much as he wanted to, he could not bring the Empress along.

"You have my sincere apologies, esteemed and eminent sir, but without his Imperial Majesty's seal or signature I cannot implement this new law on codicils to bequests," declared a certain Iavdas, one of the aides to the logothete of the treasury.

Krispos stared. "But you're the one who asked for it. I have your memorandum here." He waved the parchment at Iavdas. "It's a good law, a fair law. It should go into effect."

"I quite agree, but for it to do so, seal or signature must be affixed. That, too, is the law, and I dare not disobey it."

"His Majesty isn't signing or sealing much these days," Krispos said slowly. The more he urged Anthimos to do, the less the Emperor did, a defense of principle that would have been admirable had the principle defended been more noble than Anthimos' right to absolute laziness. "I assure you, though, that I do have the authority to tell you to go ahead with this."

"Unfortunately, I must disagree." Like most treasury officials Krispos had met, Iavdas owned a relentlessly literal mind. He went on, "I must follow the letter of the law, not the spirit, for spirit, by its nature, is subject to diverse interpretations. Without formal imperial approval, I cannot proceed."

Krispos almost told him to go to the ice. He bit back his anger. How could he get Iavdas to do what even Iavdas admitted needed doing? "Suppose we don't call this a new law?" he said after some thought. "Suppose we just call it an amendment to a law that's already there. Would my say-so be enough then?"

Iavdas' eyes got a faraway look. "I suppose it would be technically accurate to term this a correction of an ambiguity in the existing law. It was not framed so, but it could be reworked to appear as a revised chapter of the present code on codicils. And for a mere revision, no, seal and signature are not required." He beamed at Krispos. "Thank you, esteemed and eminent sir. An ingenious solution to a complex problem, and one that evades not only the defects in current legislation but also those posed by the Avtokrator's obstinacy."

"Er—yes." Krispos beat a hasty retreat. Talking with high functionaries reminded him of the limits of his own education. He could read and write, add and subtract, but he still felt at sea when people larded their talk with big words for no better reason than to hear them roll off their lips. Why, he wondered, couldn't they say what they meant and have done? He did understand that Iavdas liked his plan. That would do.

But, as he complained to Dara when she called him to her bedchamber some time past midnight, "We shouldn't have to go through this rigmarole every time we need to get something done. I can't always come up with ways of getting around Anthimos, and because I can't, things don't happen. If only Anthimos would—" He broke off. Lying in Anthimos' bed with Anthimos' Empress, he did not want to talk about the Avtokrator. Sometimes, though, like tonight, he got too frustrated with Anthimos to stop himself.

Dara put the palm of her hand on his bare chest, felt his heartbeat slow toward normal after their coupling. Smiling, she said, "If he hadn't neglected me, we wouldn't have happened. Still, I know what you mean. Just as you did, I hoped he'd rule for himself once his uncle was gone. Now—"

"Now he's so annoyed with me for trying to get him to rule that he won't even see to the little he did before." *You were the one who made me keep pushing at him, too,* he thought. He kept that to himself. Dara had been doing her best for her husband and the Empire. Had Anthimos responded, all would have been well.

"Never mind Anthimos now," Dara whispered, perhaps feeling some of the same awkwardness he had. She held him to her. "Do you think we can try again if we hurry?"

Krispos did his best to oblige. One did not say no, not to the Empress. Then he got out of bed and into his clothes. *Which turns me from lover back to vestiarios,* he thought with a touch of irritation. He slipped from the imperial bedchamber, shutting the doors behind him. He started to go back to his own room, then changed his mind and decided to have a snack first. He walked down the hall to the larder.

He was coming back, munching on a roll sticky with honey, when he saw a disembodied head floating toward him. His mouth dropped opened; a bit of roll fell out and landed on the floor with a wet smack. He needed a moment to gain enough control of himself to do anything more than stand, stare, and gurgle. In that moment of terror, before he could scream and flee, he recognized the head. It was Anthimos'.

The head recognized him, too. Winking, it spoke. Krispos frowned, tried to read its silent lips. "You'd eat better than that if you were with me," he thought it said.

"I s-suppose I would, your Majesty," he got out. If Anthimos could work magic this potent while at a revel, he was turning into a very impressive sorcerer indeed, Krispos thought. Aloud, he added, "You almost scared me to death."

The Emperor's head grinned. As he looked at it, he realized it was not physically there; he could see through it. That made it a trifle easier to take—he did not have to imagine an acephalous Anthimos lying on a couch among his cronies. He tried to smile back.

Grinning still, the Avtokrator—or as much of him as was present—moved past Krispos. The head came to the door of the imperial bedchamber. Krispos expected it to drift through the wood. Had it come a few minutes earlier—he shivered. He knew what it would have seen.

But instead of sailing ghostlike through the closed doors, the Emperor's projected head fetched up against them with a bump that was immaterial but nonetheless seemed to hurt, judging by the expression the slightly misty face wore and the words it was mouthing.

Krispos fought to keep his own face straight; Anthimos might be turning into a powerful mage, but he was still a careless one. "Would you like me to open it for you, your Majesty?" he asked politely.

"Piss off," Anthimos' head snarled. An instant later, it vanished.

Krispos leaned against the wall and let out a long, slow sigh. He suddenly realized his right hand was sticky—he'd squeezed that honeyed bun to pieces without even remembering he had it. He threw away what was left and went back to the larder for some water to wash his fingers. He did not take another bun. He'd lost his appetite.

One of the Halogai standing guard outside the imperial residence turned and spotted Krispos in the hallway. "Someone out here to see you," he called.

"Thanks, Narvikka. I'll be there in a minute." Krispos put away the armful of newly washed robes he was carrying, then went out onto the steps with the guardsmen. He blinked several times, trying to get his eyes used to the bright afternoon sunshine outside.

He did not recognize the worn-looking man who sat waiting for him on a worn-looking horse. "I'm Krispos," he said. "What can I do for you?"

The worn-looking man touched a finger to the brim of his straw traveler's hat. "My name's Bassos, esteemed and eminent sir. I'm an imperial courier. I'm afraid I have bad news for you."

"Go ahead. Give it to me." Krispos held his voice steady, wondering what had gone wrong now. His imagination painted plenty of possibilities; earthquake, pestilence, famine, rebellion, even invasion from Makuran in spite of the peace he thought he'd patched together.

But Bassos had meant bad news for *him*, not for the Empire. "Esteemed and eminent sir, the gold you sent up to your sister and brother-in-law . . ." The courier licked his lips, trying to figure out how to go on. At last he did, baldly: "Well, sir, we couldn't deliver that gold, on account of there wasn't much left of the village there after these new stinking barbarians we're mixed up with went through it. I'm sorry, esteemed and eminent sir."

Krispos heard himself say "Thank you" as if from very far away. Bassos pressed a leather pouch into his hands and made him count the goldpieces inside and sign a receipt. The Emperor's vestiarios was too prominent to be cheated. The courier remounted and rode away. Krispos stood on the steps looking after him. Evdokia, Domokos, two little girls he had never seen . . . He never would see them now.

Narvikka walked over to him, setting a large hand on his shoulder. "Their time came as it was fated to come, so grieve not for them," the Haloga said. "If the gods willed it, they took foes with them to serve them forever in the world to come. May it be so."

"May it be so," Krispos agreed. He had never had any use for the northerners' wild gods and fatalistic view of the world, but suddenly he very much wanted his family to have servants in the afterlife, servants they had slain with their own hands. That would be only just, and if justice was hard to come by in this world, he could hope for it in the next.

But was their time fated? Had Domokos been less proud . . . had Petronas not made his too-clever bargain with Harvas . . . had Anthimos listened and sent troops north in good time—had Anthimos listened even once, curse him. . . .

Thinking of the Emperor's failing filled Krispos with pure and frightening rage. His fists clenched. Only then did he notice he was holding the gold-filled leather pouch. He gave it to Narvikka, saying "Take it. I never want to see these coins again."

"I take it, I share them with the rest of the lads here." The Haloga nodded at the rest of his squad of guardsmen, who were watching him and Krispos. "Each of us, he takes a piece of your ill luck for himself."

"However you like," Krispos said mechanically. Much as he wanted not to, part of him responded to the Haloga's gesture. He found himself saying "My thanks. That's kind of you, to do such a thing for me."

Narvikka's massive shoulders moved up and down inside his mail shirt. "We would do it for each other, we will do it for a friend." As if Krispos were a child, the big northerner turned him round and gave him a light shove toward the imperial residence. "Is wine inside. You drink to remember them or to forget, whichever suits."

"My thanks," Krispos said again. Given a sense of purpose, his feet made for the larder without much conscious thought.

Before he got there, Barsymes came out of one of the other rooms that opened onto the corridor and saw him. The eunuch stared; later, remembering that look, Krispos wondered what expression his face had borne. Barsymes seemed to wrestle with courtesy, then spoke, "Your pardon, Krispos, but is something amiss?"

"You might say so," Krispos answered harshly. "Back at the village where I grew up, my sister, her husband, my nieces— Harvas Black-Robe's Halogai hit the place." He stopped, unable to go on.

To his amazement, he saw Barsymes' eyes fill with tears. "I grieve with you," the chamberlain said. "The loss of young kin is always hard. We eunuchs, perhaps, know that better than most; as we have no hope of progeny for ourselves, our siblings' children become doubly dear to us."

"I understand." As he never had before, Krispos wondered how eunuchs carried on through all the years after they were mutilated. A warrior should envy the courage that required, he thought, but most would only grow angry at being compared to a half-man.

Thinking of Barsymes' plight helped him grapple with his own. The eunuch said, "If you wish to leave off your duties the rest of the day, my colleagues and I will assume them. Under the circumstances, the Avtokrator cannot object—"

"Under the circumstances, I don't give a fart whether the Emperor objects," Krispos snapped. He watched Barsymes gape. "Never mind. I'm sorry. You don't know all the circumstances. Thank you for your offer. By your leave, I'll take advantage of it."

Barsymes bowed. "Of course," he said, but his face was still shocked and disapproving.

"I *am* sorry," Krispos repeated. "I shouldn't have lashed out at you. None of this is your fault."

"Very well," Barsymes said stiffly. Krispos kept apologizing until he saw the chamberlain truly relent. Barsymes awkwardly patted him on the shoulder and suggested, "Perhaps you should take a cup of wine, to help ease the shock to your spirit."

When Haloga and eunuch gave the same advice, Krispos thought, it had to be good. He drank one cup quickly, a second more slowly, then started to pour a third. He stopped. He had intended to drink to forget, but remembering suddenly seemed the better choice. He corked the jar and put it back on the shelf.

Outside, shadows were getting longer. The wine mounted from Krispos' stomach to his head. He yawned. *If I'm not going to attend their Majesties, I may as well sleep,* he thought. *Phos willing, all this will seem farther away when I wake up.*

He walked to his chamber. The wine and the muggy summer heat of Videssos the city left him covered with sweat. *Too warm to sleep in clothes,* he decided. He pulled his robe off over his head, though it did its best to stick to him.

He still wore the chain that held the chalcedony amulet Trokoundos had given him and his lucky goldpiece. He took off the chain, held the goldpiece in his hand, and looked at it a long time. The past couple of years, he'd thought little of what the coin might mean; in spite of being—perhaps because of being— so close to the imperial power, he hadn't contemplated taking it for himself.

Yet if Anthimos knew no rule save caprice, what then? Had the Emperor done his job as he should, Evdokia, Domokos, and their children would be fine today. Fury filled Krispos again— had Anthimos only paid attention to him, all would have been well. But the Avtokrator not only refused to rule, he refused to let anyone do it for him. That courted disaster, and had brought it to Krispos' family.

And so, the coin. Krispos wished he knew what message was locked inside it along with the gold. He did know he was no assassin. If the only way he could take the throne was by murdering Anthimos, he thought, Anthimos would stay Avtokrator till he died of old age. *To say nothing of the fact that the Halogai would chop to dogmeat anyone who assailed the Emperor,* the pragmatic side of his mind added.

Staring at the goldpiece told him nothing. He put the chain back around his neck and flopped heavily onto the soft bed that had once been Skombros'. After a while, he slept.

The silver bell woke him the next morning. He did not think much about it. It was part of his routine. He dressed, put on sandals, and went into the imperial bedchamber. Only when he saw Anthimos smiling from the bed he shared with Dara did memories of the day before come crashing back.

Krispos had to turn away for a moment, to make sure his features would be composed when he turned back to the Emperor. "Your Majesty," he said, voice expressionless.

Dara spoke before her husband. "I was saddened last night to hear of your loss, Krispos."

He could tell her sympathy was real, and warmed a little to it. Bowing, he said, "Thank you, your Majesty. You're gracious to think of me." They had played the game of passing messages back and forth under Anthimos' nose before. She nodded very slightly, to show she understood.

The Emperor nodded, too. "I'm sorry, also, Krispos. Most unfortunate. A pity you didn't have your—brother-in-law, was it?—come south to the city before the raiders struck."

"I tried to get him to come, your Majesty. He didn't wish to." After two polite, quiet sentences, Krispos found his voice rising toward a shout. "It's an even bigger pity you didn't see fit to guard the frontier properly. Then he could have lived his life as he wanted to, without having to fear raiders out of the north."

Anthimos' eyebrows shot up. "See here, sirrah, don't take that tone with me."

"By the good god, it's about time someone did!" Krispos yelled. He didn't remember losing his temper, but it was lost sure enough, lost past finding. "About time someone took a boot to your backside, too, for always putting your prick and your belly ahead of your empire."

"You be still this instant!" Anthimos shouted, loud as Krispos. Careless of his nakedness, the Avtokrator sprang out of bed and went nose to nose with his vestiarios. He shook a finger in Krispos' face. "Shut up, I tell you!"

"You're not man enough to make me," Krispos said, breathing heavily. "For a copper, I'd break you over my knee."

"Go ahead," Anthimos said. "Touch me, just once. Touch the Emperor. We'll see how long the torturers can keep you alive after you do. Weeks, I'd wager."

Krispos spat between Anthimos' feet, as if in rejection of Skotos. "You shield yourself behind your office whenever you choose to. Why don't you use it?"

Anthimos went white. "Remember Petronas," he said in a

ghastly whisper. "By the good god, you may end up envying him if you don't curb your tongue."

"I remember Petronas well enough," Krispos shot back. "I daresay the Empire would have been better off if he'd managed to cast you down from your throne. He—"

The Avtokrator's hands writhed in furious passes. Suddenly Krispos found he could not speak; he had no voice, nor would his lips form words. "Are you quite through?" Anthimos asked. Krispos felt that he could nod. He refused to. Anthimos' smile was as vicious as any with which Petronas had ever favored Krispos. "I suggest you admit you are finished—or do you care to find out how you'd relish being without breath as well as speech?"

Krispos had no doubt the Emperor meant what he said, nor that he could do what he threatened. He nodded.

"Is that yes, you are through?" Anthimos asked. Krispos nodded again. The Emperor moved his left hand, muttering something under his breath. He said, "Your speech is restored. I suggest, however—no, I order—that you do not use it in my presence now. Get out."

Krispos turned to leave, shaking from a mixture of rage and fright he'd never felt before. He hadn't thought he could ever grow truly angry at Anthimos; the Emperor's good nature had always left him proof against full-blown fury. But even less had he imagined Anthimos as a figure of fear. A figure of fun, certainly, but never fear. Not till now. The Emperor had never shown he'd learned enough wizardry to be frightening till now.

At the door, Krispos almost bumped into a knot of eunuchs and maidservants who had gathered to listen, wide-eyed, to his shouting match with Anthimos. They scattered before him as if he had something catching. So he did, he thought: the Avtokrator's disfavor was a disease that could kill.

He stamped back to his chamber and slammed the door behind him. He hit the wall a good solid whack, hard enough to send pain shooting up his arm. Then he used his restored voice to shout several very rude words. He was not sure whether he cursed the Emperor or his own foolish rashness. Either or both, he decided; he did no good either way.

That cold-blooded realization finally ended his fit of temper. He sat down at the edge of his bed and put his head in his hands. If he did not mean to strike at the Avtokrator, he should have kept his mouth shut. And he did not see how he could strike, not if he hoped to live afterward. "Stupid," he said. He meant it for a viler curse than any he'd used before.

Having been stupid, he had nothing left but to make the best of his stupidity. He came out of his room a few minutes later and went about his business—his business that did not directly concern Anthimos—as normally as he could. The rest of the servitors spoke to him in hushed voices, but they spoke to him. If he heard the whispers that followed him through the imperial residence, he could pretend he did not.

For all his outward show of calm, he jumped when, early that afternoon, Longinos said, "His Majesty wants to see you. He's in the bedchamber."

After a moment to gather himself, he nodded to the eunuch and walked slowly down the corridor. He could feel Longinos' eyes on his back. He wondered who all waited in the imperial bedchamber. In his minds' eye he saw a masked, grinning torturer, dressed in crimson leather so as not to show the stains of his trade.

He had to will his finger first to touch and then to work the latch he'd gladly opened so many times late at night. Eyes on the floor, he went in. Going against the Kubratoi, spear in hand, had been easier—he'd thought that would be grand and glorious, till the fighting started.

Anthimos was alone; Krispos saw only the one pair of red boots. He took his courage in both hands and looked at the Avtokrator's face. Indignation ousted fright. Anthimos was smiling at him, as cheerfully as if nothing had happened in the morning.

"Your Majesty?" he said, much more than the simple question in his voice.

"Hello, Krispos," the Emperor said. "I was just wondering, have the silk weavers delivered the new robe they've been promising for so long? If it's here at last, I'd like to show it off at the revel tonight."

"As a matter of fact, your Majesty, it got here a couple of hours ago," Krispos said, almost giddy with relief. He went to the closet, got out the robe, and held it in front of himself so the Emperor could see it.

"Oh, yes, that's very fine." Anthimos came up to run his fingers over the smooth, glistening fabric. He sighed. "All the poets claim women have skin soft as silk. If only they truly felt like this!" After a moment, he went on, "I will wear this to-night, Krispos. Make sure it's ready for me."

"Certainly, your Majesty." Krispos hung up the robe. Nodding, Anthimos started to leave. "Your Majesty?" Krispos called after him.

The Avtokrator stopped. "What is it?"

"Is that *all*?" Krispos blurted.

Anthimos eyes widened, either from guilelessness or an all but perfect simulation of it. "Of course that's all, dear fellow. What else could there possible be?"

"Nothing. Nothing at all," Krispos said quickly. He'd known the Emperor's temper was mercurial, but he'd never expected it to cool so quickly. If it had, he was not about to risk rekindling it. Nodding again, Anthimos hustled out. Krispos followed, shaking his head. So much luck seemed too good to be true.

XIII

"YOU'RE NOT MISSING A HEAD OR ANY OTHER VITAL APpendage, I see," Mavros said, waving to Krispos as he climbed the steps to the imperial residence. "From all the gossip I've heard the last couple of days, that's Phos' own special miracle. And miracles, my friend, deserve to be celebrated." He held up a large jar of wine.

The Haloga guards at the top of the stairs laughed. So did Krispos. "You couldn't have timed it better, Mavros. His Majesty just took off for a carouse, which means we should have the rest of the night to ourselves."

"If you find a few cups, Krispos, we can share some of this with the guardsmen here," Mavros said. "If his Majesty's not here to guard, surely their bold captain can't object to their having a taste."

Krispos looked questioningly, the other Halogai longingly, toward the officer, a middle-aged warrior named Thvari. He stroked his straw-yellow beard as he considered. "Vun cup vill do no harm," he said at last, his northern accent thick and slow. The guards cheered. Krispos hurried to get cups while Mavros drew a dagger, sliced through the pitch that glued the wine jar's cork in place, then stabbed the cork and drew it out.

Once in Krispos' chamber, Mavros poured hefty dollops for himself and Krispos. He lifted his silver goblet in salute. "To Krispos, for being intact!" he declared.

"That's a toast I'll gladly drink." Krispos sipped at the wine. Its vintage was as fine as any Anthimos owned; when Mavros bought, he did not stint. His robe was dark-green wool soft as duckdown, his neckcloth transparent silk dyed just the right shade of orange to complement the robe.

Now he raised a quizzical eyebrow. "And here's the really interesting question: *why* are you still intact, after calling Anthimos everything from a murderous cannibal to someone who commits unnatural acts with pigs?"

"I never called him *that*," Krispos said, blinking. He knew what rumor could do with words, but listening to it have its way with *his* words was doubly unnerving. He drank more wine.

"Never called him which?" Mavros asked with a wicked grin.

"Oh, keep still." Krispos emptied his cup and put it down on the arm of his chair. He stared at it for a few seconds, then said, "Truth is, may the ice take me if I know why Anthimos hasn't come down on me. I just thank Phos he hasn't. Maybe down deep he really is just a good-natured soul."

"Maybe." Mavros did not sound as though he believed it. "More likely, he was still so drunk in the morning that he'd forgotten by afternoon."

"I'd like to think so, but he wasn't," Krispos said. "He wasn't drunk at all. I can tell."

"Aye, you've seen him drunk often enough, haven't you?" Mavros said.

"Who, me?" Krispos laughed. "Yes, a time or twelve, now that you mention it. I remember the time he—" He stopped in surprise. The little silver bell by his bed was ringing. The scarlet cord on which it hung jerked up and down. Whoever was pulling it was pulling hard.

Mavros eyed the bell curiously. "I thought you said his Majesty was gone."

"He is." Krispos frowned. Had Anthimos come back for some reason? No. He would have heard the Emperor go by. He did not think Dara was summoning him; he'd let her know he had a friend coming by tonight. Surely she'd not be so indiscreet. But that left—no one. Krispos got up. "Excuse me. I think I'd better find out what's going on."

Mavros' smile was sly. "More of this good wine for me, then."

Snorting, Krispos hurried into the imperial bedchamber. It was Dara who waited for him there. Fright filled her face. "By the good god, what's wrong?" Krispos demanded. "Have we been discovered?"

"Worse," Dara said. He stared at her—he could not imagine anything worse. She started to explain, "When Anthimos left tonight, he didn't go carousing."

"How is that worse?" he broke in. "I'd think you'd be glad."

"Will you listen to me?" she said fiercely. "He didn't go carousing because he went to that little sanctum of his that used to be a shrine. He's going to work magic there, magic to kill you."

"That's crazy. If he wants me dead, all he has to do is tell one of the Halogai to swing his axe," Krispos said. But he realized it wasn't crazy, not to Anthimos. Where was the fun in a simple execution? The Emperor would enjoy putting Krispos to death by sorcery ever so much more. Something else struck him. "Why are you telling me this?"

"What do you mean, why? So you can stop him, of course." Dara needed a moment to see that the question went deeper. She took a deep breath, looked away from Krispos, let it out, and looked back. "Why? Because . . ." She stopped again, visibly willed herself to continue. "Because if I am to be Empress of Videssos, I would sooner be your Empress than his."

His eyes met hers. Those words, he knew, were irrevocable. She nodded, her resolve firming as she saw he understood.

"Strange," he said. "I always thought you preferred him."

"If you're that big a fool, maybe I've picked the wrong man after all." Dara slipped into his arms for a brief embrace. Drawing back, she said, "No time for more, not now. When you return . . ."

She let the words hang. It was his turn to nod. When he came back, they would need each other, she him to keep what she already had, he her to add legitimacy to what he'd gained. When he came back . . . "What will you do if Anthimos walks into this chamber instead of me?"

"Go on, as best I can," she said at once. He grimaced, nodding again. Tanilis would have said the same thing, for the same reason: ambition bound the two of them as much as affection. She went on, "But I will pray to Phos that it be you. Go now, and may the Lord with the great and good mind go with you."

"I'll get my sword," Krispos said. Dara bit her lip—that brought home what she was setting in motion. But she did not say no. Too late for that, he thought. She made a little pushing gesture, urging him out of the room. He hurried away.

As he trotted the few steps back to his own chamber, he felt his lucky goldpiece bounce on its chain. Soon enough, he thought, he'd find out whether the coin held true prophecy or only delusion. He remembered the last time he'd really looked at the goldpiece, and remembered thinking he would never try to get rid of Anthimos. But if the Avtokrator was trying to get rid of him . . . Waiting quietly to be killed was for sheep, not men.

All that ran through his head before he got to his own doorway. Mavros raised his cup in salute when he came in, then stared when, instead of sitting down, he started buckling on his sword belt. "What in the world—" Mavros began.

"Treason," Krispos answered, which shut his foster brother's mouth with a snap. "Or it'll be treason if I fail. Anthimos is planning to kill me by sorcery tonight. I don't intend to let him. Are you with me, or will you denounce me to the Halogai?"

Mavros gaped at him. "I'm with you, of course. But by the good god, how did you find out? You told me he was going carousing tonight, not magicking."

"The Empress warned me just now," Krispos said in a flat voice.

"*Did* she?" Mavros looked at Krispos as if he'd never seen him before, then started to laugh. "You haven't told me everything you've been up to, have you?"

Krispos felt his cheeks grow hot. "No. I never told anyone. It's not the sort of secret to spread around, you know, not if—"

"Not if you want to live to go on keeping it," Mavros finished for him. "No, you're right."

"Come on then," Krispos said. "We've no time to lose."

The Halogai guarding the doorway to the imperial residence chuckled when Krispos came out wearing his sword. "You drink a little wine, you go into the city looking for somet'ing to fight, eh?" one of them said. "You should have been born a northern man."

Krispos chuckled, too, but his heart sank within him. As soon as he and Mavros were far enough away from the entrance for the guards not to hear, he said, "We have gone looking for something to fight. How many Halogai will the Emperor have with him?"

The night was dark. He could not see Mavros' expression change, but he heard his breath catch. "If it's more than one, we're in trouble. Armored, swinging those axes of theirs—"

"I know." Krispos shook his head, but continued, "I'm going on anyway. Maybe I can talk my way past 'em, however many there are. I'm his Majesty's vestiarios, after all. And if I can't, I'd sooner die fighting than whichever nasty way Anthimos has worked out for me. If you don't want to come along, the good god knows I can't blame you."

"I am your brother," Mavros said, stiffening with offended dignity.

Krispos clasped his shoulder. "You are indeed."

They hurried on, making and discarding plans. Before long, the gloomy grove of cypresses surrounding the Emperor's sanctum loomed before them. The path wound through it. The dark trees' spicy odor filled Krispos' nostrils.

As they were about to emerge from the cypresses, a red-orange flash of light, bright as lightning, burst from the windows and open doorways of the building ahead. Krispos staggered, sure his moment was here. His eyes, long used to blackness, filled with tears. How bitter, he thought, to have come just too late.

But nothing further happened, not right then. He heard Anthimos' voice begin a new chant. Whatever magic the Avtokrator was devising, he'd not yet finished it.

Beside Krispos, Mavros also rubbed his eyes. In that moment of fire, though, he'd seen something Krispos had missed. "Only the one guard," he murmured.

Squinting, wary against a new levinbolt, Krispos peered toward Anthimos' house of magics. Sure enough, lit by the glow of a couple of ordinary torches, a single Haloga stood in front of the door.

The northerner was rubbing at his eyes, too, but came to alertness when he heard footfalls on the path. "Who calls?" he said, swinging up his axe.

"Hello, Geirrod." Krispos did his best to sound casual in spite of the nervous sweat trickling down the small of his back. If Anthimos had told the guard why he was incanting here tonight . . .

But he had not. Geirrod lowered his bright-bladed weapon. "A good evening to you, Krispos, and to your friend." Then the Haloga frowned and half raised the axe again. "Why do you come here with brand belted to your body?" Even when he used Videssian, his speech carried the slow, strong rhythms of his cold and distant homeland.

"I've come to deliver a message to his Majesty," Krispos

answered. "As for why I'm wearing my sword, well, only a fool goes out at night without one." He unbuckled the belt and held it out to Geirrod. "Here, keep it if you feel the need, and give it back when I come out."

The big blond guard smiled. "That is well done, friend Krispos. You know what duty means. I shall set your sword aside against your return." As he turned to lean the blade against the wall, Mavros sprang forward, sheathed dagger reversed in his hand. The round lead pommel thudded against the side of Geirrod's head, just in front of his ear. The Haloga groaned and toppled, his mail shirt clinking musically as he fell.

Krispos' fingers dug into the side of Geirrod's thick neck. "He has a pulse. Good," he said, grabbing the sword belt and drawing his blade. If he survived the night, the Halogai would be *his* guards. Slaying one of them would mean he could never trust his own protectors, not with the northern penchant for blood vengeance.

"Come on," Mavros said. He snatched up the Haloga's axe.

"No, wait. Tie and gag him first," Krispos said. Mavros dropped the axe, took off his scarf, and tore it in half. He quickly tied the guardsman's hands behind him, knotting the other piece of silk over his mouth and around his head. Krispos nodded. Together, he and Mavros stepped over Geirrod into the Avtokrator's sorcerous secretum.

The scuffle with the guard had been neither loud nor long. With luck, Anthimos would have been caught up in the intricacies of some elaborate spell and would never have noticed the small disturbance outside. With luck. As it was, he poked his head out into the hallway and called, "What was that, Geirrod?" When he saw Krispos, his eyes widened and his lips skinned back from his teeth. "You!"

"Aye, your Majesty," Krispos said. "Me." He dashed toward the Emperor.

Fast as he was, he was not fast enough. Anthimos ducked back into his chamber and slammed the door. The bar crashed into place just as Krispos' shoulder smote the door. The bar was stout; he bounced away.

Laughing a wild, high-pitched laugh, Anthimos shouted, "Don't you know it's rude to come to the feast before you're invited?" Then he began to chant again, a chant that, even through thick wood, raised prickles of dread along Krispos' arms.

He kicked the door, hard as he could. It held. Mavros shoved him aside. "I have the tool for the job," he said. Geirrod's axe bit into the timbers. Mavros struck again and again. As he hewed at the door, the Avtokrator chanted on in a mad race to see who would finish first—and live.

Mavros weakened the door enough so he and Krispos could kick it open. At the same instant, Anthimos cried out in triumph. As his foes burst in on him, he extended his hands toward them. Fire flowed from his fingertips.

Had Anthimos controlled a true thunderbolt, he would have incinerated Krispos and Mavros. But while his fire flowed, it did not dart. They scrambled backward out of the chamber before the flames reached them. The fire splashed against the far wall and dripped to the floor. The wall was stone. It did not catch, but Krispos gagged on acrid smoke.

"Not so eager to come in and play any more, my dears?" Anthimos said, laughing again. "I'll come out and play with you, then."

He stood in the doorway and shot fire at Krispos. Krispos threw himself flat on the floor. The flames passed over him, close enough that he smelled his hair scorch. He waited for Anthimos to lower his hands and burn him to a cinder.

Anthimos never got the chance. While his attention and his fire were aimed at Krispos, Mavros rushed him with the Haloga war axe. Anthimos whirled, casting flames close enough to Mavros to spoil his stroke. But the Emperor had to duck back into his chamber.

Some of his fire caught on the ruined door. It began to burn. Real, honest flames licked up toward the beams of the ceiling.

Krispos scrambled to his feet. "We have him!" he shouted. "He can't fight both of us at once out here, and trapped in there he'll burn." Already the smoke had grown thicker.

"You think you have me," Anthimos said. "All this fribbling fire is but a distraction. Now to get back to the conjuration I truly had in mind for you, Krispos, the one you so rudely interrupted. And when I finish, you'll wish you'd burned to death, you and your friend both."

The Avtokrator began to incant again. Krispos started through the burning doorway at him, hoping he could not use his flames while busy with this other, more fearful magic. But once summoned, the fire was at Anthimos' command. A blast of it forced Krispos back. Mavros tried too, and was similarly repulsed.

Anthimos chanted on. Krispos knew nothing of magic, but he could sense the magnitude of the forces Anthimos employed. The very air felt thin, and thrummed with power. Icy fear ran through Krispos' veins, for he knew that power would close on him. He could not attack the Emperor; flight, he was sure, would do no good. He stood and waited, coughing more and more as the smoke got worse.

Anthimos was coughing, too, and fairly gabbling his spell in his haste to get it all out before the fire sealed his escape as Krispos had said. Maybe that haste caused him to make his mistake; maybe, being at bottom a headstrong young man who took few pains, he would have made it anyhow.

He knew he'd erred—his chant abruptly broke off. Dread and horror in his voice, he shouted, "Him, not me! I didn't mean to say 'me!' I meant *him*!"

Too late. The power he had summoned did what he had told it to do, and to whom. He screamed, once. Peering through smoky, heat-hazed air, Krispos saw him writhe as if trapped in the grip of an invisible fist of monstrous size. The scream cut off. The sound of snapping bones went on and on. An uprush of flame blocked Krispos' view for a moment. When he could see again, Anthimos, or what was left of him, lay crumpled and unmoving on the floor.

Mavros pounded Krispos' shoulder. "Let's get out of here!" he yelled. "We're just as dead if we toast as if—that happens to us."

"Are we? I wonder." Anthimos was the most definitively dead man Krispos had ever seen. The last sight of the fallen Emperor stayed with him as, eyes streaming and lungs burning from the smoke, he stumbled with Mavros toward the doorway.

Cool, clean night air after that inferno was like cool water after an endless trek through the desert. Krispos sucked in breath after precious breath. Then he knelt beside Geirrod, who was just beginning to groan and stir. "Let's drag him away from here," he said, and listened to the roughness in his own voice. "We don't want him to burn, either."

"Something else first." Slowly and deliberately, Mavros went to his knees before Krispos, then flat on his belly. "Majesty," he declared. "Let me be the first to salute you. Thou conquerest, Krispos, Avtokrator of the Videssians."

Krispos gaped at him. In the desperate struggle with Anthimos, he'd forgotten the prize for which he'd been struggling. He spoke his first words as Emperor: "Get up, fool."

Geirrod's pale eyes were wide and staring, flicking back and forth from one man to the other. Mavros rose, but only to a crouch by the Haloga. "Do you understand what has happened this night, Geirrod? Anthimos sought to slay Krispos by sorcery, but blundered and destroyed himself instead. By the Lord with the great and good mind, I swear neither Krispos nor I wounded him. His death was Phos' own judgment on him."

"My friend—my brother—speaks truly," Krispos said. He drew the sun-circle over his heart. "By the good god I swear it. Believe me or not, Geirrod, as you see fit from what you know of me. But if you believe me, let me ask you in turn: will you serve me as bravely and loyally as you served Anthimos?"

Those eyes of northern blue might have been a hunting beast's rather than a man's, such was the intensity of the gaze Geirrod aimed up at Krispos. Then the guardsman nodded, once.

"Free him, Mavros," Krispos said. Mavros cut through the Haloga's bonds, then through the gag. Geirrod heaved himself upright and started to stagger away from the burning building behind him. "Wait," Krispos told him, then turned to Mavros. "Give him his axe."

"What? No!" Mavros exclaimed. "Even half out on his feet the way he is, with this thing he's more than a match for both of us."

"He's said he will serve me. Give him the axe." Part of that tone of command was borrowed from Petronas; more, Krispos realized, came from Anthimos.

Wherever it came from, it served its purpose. Mavros' eyes were eloquent, but he passed the axe to Geirrod. The Haloga took it, looking at it as a father might look at a long-lost son who has come home. Krispos tensed. If he was wrong and Mavros right, he would have the shortest reign of any Avtokrator Videssos had ever known.

Geirrod raised the axe—in salute. "Lead me, Majesty," he said. "Where now?"

Krispos watched Mavros' hand leave the hilt of his dagger. The little blade would not have kept him or Krispos alive an extra moment against an armed and armored Geirrod, but the protective gesture made Krispos proud once more to have him for foster brother.

"Where now?" the guardsman repeated.

"To the imperial residence," Krispos answered after quick thought. "You, Geirrod, tell your comrades what happened here. I will also speak to them, and to the folk inside."

"What do you want to do about this place here?" Mavros asked, pointing back at Anthimos' sanctum. As he did, part of the roof fell in with a crash.

"Let it burn," Krispos said. "If anyone sees it or gets close enough to hear noise like that, I suppose he'll try and put it out, not that he'll have much luck. But the grove is so thick that odds are no one will notice a thing, and we certainly don't have time to moss about here. Or do you feel otherwise?"

Mavros shook his head. "No indeed. We'll be plenty busy between now and dawn."

"Aye." As he walked back toward the imperial residence, Krispos tried to think of all the things he'd have to do before the sun came up again. If he forgot anything of any importance, he knew, he would not keep the throne he'd claimed.

The Halogai standing guard in front of the imperial residence grew alert when they saw three men approaching. When Krispos and his companions got close enough for torchlight to reveal the state they were in, one of the northerners shouted, "What happened to you?"

Krispos looked down at himself. His robe was torn and scorched and stained with smoke. He glanced over at Mavros, whose face was streaked from soot and sweat. His own, he was sure, could be no cleaner.

"The Avtokrator is dead," he said simply.

The Halogai cried out and came dashing down the stairs, their huge axes at the ready. "Did you slay him?" one of them demanded, his voice fierce.

"No, by Phos, I did not," Krispos said. As he had for Geirrod, he sketched the sun-sign over his breast. "You know he and I had a falling out these past few days." He waited for the northerners to nod, then went on, "This evening I learned—" *Never mind where now,* he thought. "—I learned he'd not forgiven me as he wanted me to believe, but was going to use the wizardry he'd studied to kill me."

He touched the sword that swung on his hip. "I went to defend myself, yes, but I did not kill him. Because I was there, he hurried his magic, and rather than striking me, it ate him up instead. In the name of the Lord with the great and good mind, I tell you I speak the truth."

Geirrod suddenly started talking to the northerners in their own language. They listened for a moment, then began asking questions and talking—sometimes shouting—among themselves. Geirrod turned to Krispos, shifting back to Videssian. "I tell them it be only justice now for you to be Emperor, since he who was Emperor try to slay you but end up killing self instead. I also tell them I fight for you if they say no."

While the Halogai argued, Mavros sidled close to Krispos and whispered, "Well, I admit you did that better than I would have."

Krispos nodded, watching the guards—and their captain. Sometimes, he had read, usurpers gained the imperial guards' backing with promises of gold. He did not think gold would sway Thvari, save only to make him feel contempt. He waited for the guard captain to speak. At last Thvari did. "Majesty." One by one, the Halogai echoed him.

Now Krispos could give rewards. "Half a pound of gold to each of you, a pound to Thvari, and two pounds to Geirrod for being first among you to acknowledge me." The northerners cheered and gathered round him to clasp his hand between their two.

"What do I get?" Mavros asked, mock-plaintively.

"You get to go to the stables, saddle up Progress and a horse for you, and get back here fast as you can," Krispos told him.

"Aye, that's right, give me all the work," Mavros said—but over his shoulder, for he was already heading for the stables at a fast trot.

Krispos climbed the steps to the imperial residence—*his* residence now and for as long as he could keep it, he realized suddenly. He could feel that he was running on nervous energy; if he slowed down even for a moment, he might not get moving again easily. He laughed at himself—when would he find the chance to slow down any time soon?

Barsymes and Tyrovitzes stood waiting a couple of paces inside the entrance. As with the Halogai before, Krispos' dishevelment made the eunuchs stare. Barsymes pointed out toward the guardsmen. "They called you Majesty," he said. Was that accusation in his voice? Krispos could not tell. The chamberlain had long practice in dissimulation.

"Yes, they called me Majesty—Anthimos is dead," Krispos answered bluntly, hoping to startle some more definite reaction from the eunuchs. But for making the sun-circle over their hearts, they gave him none. Their silence compelled him to go on to explain once more how the Emperor had perished.

When he was through, Barsymes nodded; he seemed far from startled. "I did not think Anthimos could destroy you so," he remarked.

Krispos started to take that as a simple compliment, then stopped, his eyes going wide. "You knew," he ground out. Barsymes nodded again. Krispos drew his sword. "You knew, and you did not warn me. How shall I pay you back for that?"

Barsymes did not flinch from the naked blade. "Perhaps while you consider, you should let the Empress Dara know you survived. I am certain she will be even more relieved to hear of it than we are."

Again Krispos started to miss something, again he caught himself. "You knew that, too?" he asked in a small voice. This time both eunuchs nodded back. He looked at his sword, then returned it to its sheath. "How long have you known?" Now he was whispering.

Barsymes and Tyrovitzes looked at each other. "No secret in the palaces is a secret long," Barsymes said with the slightest trace of smugness.

Dizzily, Krispos shook his head. "And you didn't tell Anthimos?"

"If we had, esteemed and—no, forgive me, I beg—your Majesty, would you be holding this conversation with us now?" Barsymes asked.

Krispos shook his head again. "How shall I pay you back for *that*?" he said, then musingly answered himself: "If I'm to be Emperor, I'll need a vestiarios. The post is yours, Barsymes."

The eunuch's long, thin face was not made for showing pleasure, but his smile was less doleful than most Krispos had seen from him. "You honor me, your Majesty. I am delighted to accept, and shall seek to give satisfaction."

"I'm sure you will," Krispos said. He hurried past the two eunuchs and down the hall. He passed the doorway that had been his and paused in front of the one he had entered so many times but that only now belonged to him. He raised a hand to knock softly, then stopped. He did not knock at his own door. He opened it.

He heard Dara's sharp intake of breath—she had to have been wondering who would come through that door. When she saw Krispos, she said, "Oh, Phos be praised, it's you!" and threw herself into his arms. Even as he held her, though, he thought that her words would have done for Anthimos' return just as well—no chance of making a mistake with them. He wondered how long she'd worked to come up with such a safe phrase.

"Tell me what happened," she demanded.

He explained Anthimos' downfall for the fourth time that night. He knew he would have to do it again before dawn. The more he explained it, the more the story got between him and the exertion and terror of the moment. If he told the tale enough times, he thought hopefully, perhaps he'd forget how frightened he'd been.

This was the first time Dara had heard it, which made it seem as real for her as if she'd been there. When he was through, she held him again. "I might have lost you," she said, her face buried against his shoulder. "I don't know what I would have done then."

She'd been sure enough earlier in the evening, he thought, but decided he could not blame her for forgetting that now. And her fear for him made him remember his own fear sharply once more. "You certainly might have," he said. "If he hadn't tripped over his own tongue—"

"You made him do it," she said.

He had to nod. At the end, Anthimos had been badly rattled, too, or likely he never would have made his fatal blunder. "Without you, I never would have known, I wouldn't have been there . . ." This time Krispos hugged Dara, acknowledging the debt he owed, the gratitude he felt.

She must have sensed some of that. She looked up at him; her eyes searched his face. "We need each other," she said slowly.

"Very much," he agreed, "especially now."

She might not have heard him. As if he hadn't spoken, she repeated, "We need each other," then went on, maybe as much to herself as to him, "We please each other, too. Taken together, isn't that a fair start toward . . . love?"

Krispos heard her hesitate before she risked the word. He would also have hesitated to speak it between them. Having been lovers did not guarantee love; that was another of Tanilis' lessons. Even so . . . "A fair start," he said, and did not feel he was lying. Then he added, "One thing more, anyhow."

"What's that?" Dara asked.

"I promise you won't have to worry about minnows with me."

She blinked, then started to laugh. But her voice had a grim edge to it as she warned, "I'd better not. Anthimos didn't have to care about what I thought, whereas you . . ."

She stopped. He thought about what she hadn't said: that he was a peasant-born usurper with no right to the throne whatever, save that his fundament was on it. He knew that was true. If he ruled well, he also knew it eventually would not matter. But eventually was not now. Now anything that linked him to the imperial house he had just toppled would help him hold power long enough for it to seem to belong to him. He could not afford to antagonize Dara.

"I said not a minute ago that you didn't need to worry about such things," he reminded her.

"So you did." She sounded as if she were reminding herself, too.

He kissed her, then said with mock formality so splendid Mavros might have envied it, "And now, your Majesty, if you will forgive me, I have a few small trifles to attend to before the night is through."

"Yes, just a few," she said, smiling, her mood matching his. Almost as an afterthought, she added, "Your Majesty."

He kissed her again, then hurried away. The Halogai outside the imperial residence swung their axes to the ready in salute as he came out. A few minutes later, Mavros rode up, leading Krispos' horse Progress on a line. "Here's your mount, Kris—uh, your Majesty. Now—" His voice sank to a conspiratorial whisper. "—what do you need the beast for?"

"To ride, of course," Krispos said. While his foster brother sputtered, he turned to Thvari and spoke for a couple of minutes. When he was done, he asked, "Do you have that? Can you do it?"

"I have it. If I can do it, I will. If I can't, I'll be dead. So will you, not much later," the northerner answered with the usual bloodthirsty directness of the Halogai.

"I trust you'll do your best, then, for both our sakes," Krispos said. He swung himself up onto Progress' back and loosed the lead line. "Now we ride," he told Mavros.

"I did suspect that, truly I did," Mavros said. "Do you have any place in particular in mind, or shall we just gallivant around the city?"

Krispos had already urged his bay gelding into a trot. "Iakovitzes' house," he said over his shoulder as he rode west toward the plaza of Palamas. "I just hope he's there; the only person I can think of who likes—liked—to carouse more than he does is Anthimos."

"Why are we going to Iakovitzes' house?"

"Because he's still in the habit of keeping lots of grooms," Krispos answered. "If I'm to be Avtokrator, people will have to know I'm Avtokrator. They'll have to see me crowned. That will have to happen as fast as it can, before anyone else gets the idea there's a throne loose for the taking. The grooms can spread word through the city tonight."

"And wake everyone up?" Mavros said. "The people won't love you for that."

"The people of this town love spectacle more than anything else," Krispos said. "They wouldn't forgive me if I didn't wake them up for it. Look at Anthimos—you can be anything in Videssos the city, so long as you're not dull."

"Well, maybe so," Mavros said. "I hope so, by the Lord with the great and good mind."

They reined in in front of Iakovitzes' house, tied their horses to the rail, and went up to the front door. Krispos pounded on it. He kept pounding until Iakovitzes' steward Gomaris opened the little grate in the middle of the door and peered through it. Whatever curses the steward had in mind got left unsaid when he recognized Krispos; he contented himself with growling, "By the good god, Krispos, have you gone mad?"

"No," Krispos said. "I must see Iakovitzes right now. Tell him that, Gomaris, and tell him I won't take no for an answer." He waited tensely—if Gomaris said his master was out, everything was up for grabs again. But the steward just slammed the grate shut and went away.

He returned in a couple of minutes. "He says he doesn't care if it's the Emperor himself who wants to see him."

"It is," Krispos said. "It is the Emperor, Gomaris." The little grate did not show much of Gomaris' face, but he saw the steward's right eye go wide. A moment later, he heard the bar lift. The door swung open.

"What's happened in the palaces?" Gomaris asked eagerly. No, he was more than eager, he was all but panting to hear juicy news before anyone else did. That, to an inhabitant of the city, was treasure more precious than gold.

"You'll know when Iakovitzes does," Krispos promised. "And now, hadn't you better run ahead and tell him you let Mavros and me in after all?"

"Aye, you're right, worse luck," the steward said, his voice suddenly glum. He hurried off toward his master's bedchamber. Krispos and Mavros, who still knew their way around the house where they had once served, followed more slowly.

Iakovitzes met them before they got to his bedroom. The fiery little noble was just knotting the sash of his dressing gown when he came up to his former protegés. He stabbed out a finger at Krispos. "What's this nonsense about the Emperor wanting to see me? I don't see any Emperor. All I see is you, and I wish I didn't."

"Excellent sir, you do see the Emperor," Krispos answered. He touched his own chest.

Iakovitzes snorted. "What *have* you been drinking? Go on home now, and if Phos is merciful I'll fall back to sleep, forget all about this, and never have to tell Anthimos."

"It doesn't matter," Krispos said. "Anthimos is dead, Iakovitzes."

As Gomaris' had just before, Iakovitzes' eyes went wide. "Hold that torch closer to him, Gomaris," he told his steward. Gomaris obeyed. In the better light, Iakovitzes examined Krispos closely. "You're not joking," he said at last.

"No, I'm not." Almost by rote, Krispos told the story he had already told four times that night. He finished, "That's why I've come to you, excellent sir, to have your grooms and servants spread word through the city that something extraordinary has happened and that people should gather at the High Temple to learn what."

To his surprise and indignation, Iakovitzes started to laugh. The noble said, "Your pardon, your Majesty, but when you first came here, I never thought I had a future Avtokrator shoveling out my horseshit. Not many can say that, by Phos. Oh, no indeed!" He laughed again, louder than before.

"You'll help, then?" Krispos said.

Iakovitzes slowly sobered. "Aye, Krispos, I'll help you. Better you with the crown than some dunderheaded general, which is the other choice we'd likely have."

"Thanks, I suppose," Krispos said—Iakovitzes never gave praise without splashing vinegar on it.

"You're welcome, I'm sure," the noble said. He sighed.

"And to think that with a little luck I could have had an Avto-krator in my bed as well as in my stables." Iakovitzes turned a look that was half glower, half leer on Mavros. "Why didn't you overthrow the Emperor?"

"Me? No, thank you," Mavros said. "I wouldn't take the job on a bet. I want to go through life without food tasters—and without using up a few of them along the way."

"Hrmmp." Iakovitzes gave his attention back to Krispos. "You'll have plenty to keep you occupied tonight, won't you? I suppose you'll want me to go and wake up everyone in the household. I may as well. Now that you've ruined my hope for a decent night's sleep, why should I let anyone else have one?"

"You're as generous and considerate as I remember you," Krispos said, just to see him glare. "By the good god, I promise you won't be sorry for this."

"If both our heads go up on the Milestone, I'll make sure mine reminds yours of that," Iakovitzes said. "Now get moving, will you? The faster this is done, the better the chance we all have of avoiding the chap with the cleaver."

Since Krispos had come to the same conclusion, he nodded, clasped Iakovitzes' hand, and hurried away. He and Mavros were just climbing onto their horses when Iakovitzes started making a horrible racket inside the house. Mavros grinned. "He doesn't do things by halves, does he?"

"He never did," Krispos said. "I'm only glad he's with us and not against us. Gnatios won't be so easy."

"You'll persuade him," Mavros said confidently.

"One way or another, I have to," Krispos said as they rode through the dark, quiet streets of the city. Only a few people shared the night with them. A couple of courtesans beckoned as they trotted by; a couple of footpads slunk out of their way; a couple of staggering drunks ignored them altogether. Once, off in the distance, Krispos saw for a moment the clump of torches that proclaimed respectable citizens traveling by night. He rounded a corner and they were gone.

More torches blazed in front of the patriarchal mansion. Krispos and Mavros tied their horses to a couple of the evergreens that grew there and walked up to the entrance. "I am heartily tired of rapping on doors," Krispos said, rapping on the door.

Mavros consoled him. "After this, you can have servants rap on them for you."

The rapping eventually had its result—the priest Badourios

opened the door a crack and demanded, "Who dares disturb the ecumenical patriarch's rest?" Then he recognized Krispos and grew more civil. "I hope it is not a matter of urgency, esteemed and eminent sir."

"Would I be here if it weren't?" Krispos retorted. "I must see the patriarch at once, holy sir."

"May I tell him your business?" Badourios asked.

Mavros snapped, "Were it for you, be assured we would consult you. It is for your master, as Krispos told you. Now go and fetch him." Badourios glared sleepy murder at him, then abruptly turned on his heel and hurried away.

Gnatios appeared a few minutes later. Even fresh-roused from sleep, he looked clever and elegant, if none too happy. Krispos and Mavros bowed. As Gnatios responded with a bow of his own, Krispos saw him take in their dirty faces and torn robes. But his voice was smooth as ever as he asked, "What has so distressed his Majesty that he must have a response in the middle of the night?"

"Let us speak privately, not in this doorway," Krispos said.

The patriarch considered, then shrugged. "As you wish." He led them to a small chamber, lit a couple of lamps, then closed and barred the door. Folding his arms across his chest, he said, "Very well, let me ask you once more, if I may, esteemed and eminent sir: what theological concern has Anthimos so vexed he must needs rout me out of bed for his answer?"

"Most holy sir, you know as well as I that Anthimos never worried much about theology," Krispos said. "Now he doesn't worry about it at all. Or rather, he worries in the only way that truly matters he's walking the narrow bridge, between the light above and the ice below." He saw Gnatios' eyebrows shoot up. He nodded. "Yes, most holy sir, Anthimos is dead."

"And you, most holy sir, have been addressing the Avtokrator of the Videssians by a title far beneath his present dignity," Mavros added. His voice was hard, but one corner of his mouth could not help twitching upward with mischief.

Suave and urbane as he normally was, the patriarch goggled at that. "No," he whispered.

"Yes," Krispos said, and for the half-dozenth time that night told how Anthimos had perished. Listening to himself, he discovered he did have the story down pat; only a few words were different from the ones he'd used with Iakovitzes and Dara. He finished, "And that is why we've come to you now, most holy sir: to have you set the crown on my head at the High Temple in the morning.''

Gnatios had regained his composure while Krispos spoke. Now he shook his head and repeated, ''No,'' this time loudly and firmly. ''No, I will not crown a jumped-up stableboy like you, no matter what has befallen his Majesty. If you speak the truth and he has died, others are far more deserving of imperial rank.''

''By which you mean Petronas—your cousin Petronas,'' Krispos said. ''Let me remind you, most holy sir, that Petronas now wears the blue robe.''

''Vows coerced from a man have been set aside before,'' Gnatios said. ''He would make a better Avtokrator than you, as you must admit.''

''I admit nothing of the sort,'' Krispos growled, ''and you're mad if you think I'd give over the throne to a man whose first act upon it would be to take my head.''

''You're mad if you think I'll crown you,'' Gnatios retorted.

''If you don't, Pyrrhos will,'' Krispos said.

That ploy had worked before with Gnatios, but it failed now. The ecumenical patriarch drew himself up. ''Pyrrhos is but an abbot. For a coronation to have validity, it must be at my hands, the patriarch's hands, and they shall not grant it to you.''

Just then Badourios knocked urgently on the door. Without waiting for a reply, the priest tried the latch. When he found the door barred, he called through it: ''Most holy sir, there's an unseemly disturbance building in the street outside.''

''What's happening in the street outside does not concern me,'' Gnatios said angrily. ''Now go away.''

Krispos and Mavros looked at each other. ''Maybe what's happening in the street *does* concern you, most holy sir,'' Krispos said, his voice silky. ''Shall we go and see?''

The lines on Gnatios' forehead and those running down from beside his nose to the outer ends of his mouth deepened in suspicion. ''As you wish,'' he said reluctantly.

Krispos heard the deep-voiced shouting as soon as he was out of the chamber. He looked at Mavros again. They both smiled. Gnatios scowled at each of them in turn.

When the three men got to the front entrance, the shouting abruptly stopped. Gnatios stared out in dismay at the whole regiment of imperial guards, hundreds of armed and armored Halogai drawn up in line of battle before the patriarchal mansion. He turned to Krispos, nervously wetting his lips. "You would not, ah, loose the barbarians here on, ah, holy ground?"

"How could you think such a thing, most holy sir?" Krispos sounded shocked. He made sure he sounded shocked. "We were just having a nice peaceable talk in there, weren't we?"

Before Gnatios could answer, one of the Halogai detached himself from their ranks and strode toward the mansion. As the warrior drew closer, Krispos saw it was Thvari. Gnatios stood his ground, but still seemed to shrink from the northerner, who along with his mail shirt and axe also bore a large, round bronze-faced shield.

Thvari swung up his axe in salute to Krispos. "Majesty," he said soberly. His gaze swung to Gnatios. He must not have liked what he saw on the patriarch's face, for his already wintry eyes grew colder yet. The axe twitched in his hands, as if with a life of its own.

Gnatios' voice went high. "Call him off me," he said to Krispos. The axe twitched again, a bigger movement this time. Krispos said nothing. Gnatios watched the axe blade with fearful fascination. He jumped when it moved again. "Please call him off me," he said shrilly; a moment later, perhaps realizing what was wrong, he added, "Your Majesty."

"That will be all, Thvari. Thank you," Krispos said. The Haloga nodded, turned, and stalked back to his countrymen.

"There," Gnatios said to Krispos, though his eyes stayed on Thvari till the northerner was back into the ranks of the guardsmen. "I've publicly acknowledged you. Are you satisfied?"

"You haven't yet honored his Majesty with a proskynesis," Mavros observed.

Gnatios looked daggers at him and opened his mouth to say something defiant. Then he glanced over to the Halogai massed in the street. Krispos watched the defiance drain out of him. Slowly he went to his knees, then to his belly. "Majesty," he said as his forehead touched the floor.

"Get up, most holy sir," Krispos said. "So you agree I am the rightful Avtokrator, then?" He waited for Gnatios to nod before he went on, "Then can you show that to the whole city by setting the crown on my head at the High Temple when morning comes?"

"I would seem to have little choice," Gnatios said bleakly.

"If I'm to be master of the Empire, I will be master of all of it," Krispos told him. "That includes the temples."

The ecumenical patriarch did not reply in words, but his expression was eloquent. Though emperors traditionally headed ecclesiastical as well as secular affairs, Anthimos had ignored both impartially, letting Gnatios run Videssos' religious life like an independent prince. The prospect of doing another man's bidding could not have appealed to him.

Mavros pointed down the street; at the same time, Haloga heads turned in the direction his finger showed. A man carrying a large, heavy bundle was coming toward the patriarchal mansion. No, not a man—as the person drew nearer, Krispos saw beardless cheeks and chin. But it was not a woman, either. . . .

"Barsymes!" Krispos exclaimed. "What do you have there?"

Panting a little, the eunuch set down his burden. "If you are to be crowned, your Majesty, you should appear before the people in the proper regalia. I heard your orders to the Halogai, and so I knew I could find you here. I've brought the coronation regalia, a crown, and a pair of red boots. I do hope the rude treatment I've given the silks hasn't wrinkled them too much," he finished anxiously.

"Never mind," Krispos said, touched. "That you thought to bring them to me is all that counts." He put a hand on Barsymes' shoulder. The eunuch, a formal soul if ever there was one, shrugged it off and bowed. Krispos went on, "It was bravely done, and perhaps foolishly done, as well. How would you have fought back if robbers fell upon you and stole this rich clothing?"

"Robbers?" Barsymes gave a contemptuous sniff. "A robber would have to be insane to dare assault one like me, who is so obviously a eunuch of the palace." For the first time, Krispos heard a sort of melancholy pride in Barsymes' description of himself. The eunuch continued, "Besides, even a madman would think three times before he stole the imperial raiment. Who could wear it but the Emperor, when even its possession by another is proof of treason and a capital crime?"

"I'm just glad you got here safely," Krispos said. If thinking himself immune from robbers had helped Barsymes come, he would not contradict the eunuch. Privately he suspected Barsymes had been more lucky than secure.

"Shall I vest you in the regalia now?" Barsymes asked.

Krispos thought for a moment, then shook his head. "No, let's do it at the High Temple, where the ecumenical patriarch will set the crown on my head." He glanced over at Gnatios, who nodded without speaking. Krispos looked eastward. Ever so slightly, the horizon was beginning to gray. He said, "We should go there now, to be ready when the new day comes."

He called to the Halogai. They formed up in a hollow rectangle that took the whole width of the street. Krispos, Mavros, Barsymes, and Gnatios took their places in the middle. Krispos thought Gnatios still wanted to bolt, but the patriarch got no chance. "Forward to the High Temple," Krispos said, and forward they went.

The Temple, as was only fitting, lay but a few steps from the patriarchal mansion. It bulked huge against the brightening sky; the thick piers that supported the weight of its great central dome gave it a squat, almost an ungainly appearance from the outside. But within—Krispos knew the splendor that lay within.

The forecourt to the High Temple was as large as a couple of the smaller plazas in the city. The boots of the Halogai slammed down on slate flags; their measured tramp echoed from the building they approached.

Gnatios peered out between the marching guardsmen. "What are all these people doing, loitering in the forecourt so long before the dawn?" he said.

"A coronation must be witnessed," Krispos reminded him.

The patriarch gave him a look filled with grudging respect. "For an adventurer who has just seized the state, you've planned well. You will prove more difficult to dislodge than I would have guessed when you came pounding on my door."

"I don't intend to be dislodged," Krispos said.

"Neither did Anthimos, your Majesty," Gnatios replied, putting a sardonic edge to the title Krispos was still far from used to.

The forecourt was not yet truly crowded; the Halogai had no trouble making their way toward the High Temple. Men and women scurried out of their path, chattering excitedly: "Look at 'em! Something big *must* be going on." "I wanted to kill the bloody sod who woke me, but now I'm glad I'm here." "Wouldn't want to miss anything. What do you think's happened?" One enterprising fellow had a tray with him. "Sausage and rolls!" he shouted, his eyes, like those of most who lived in Videssos the city, on the main chance. "Buy your sausage and rolls here!"

Priests prayed in the High Temple by night as well as by day. They stared from the top of the stairway at the imperial guards.

Krispos heard them exclaim and call to one another; they sounded as curious as any of the onlookers gathering in front of the temple. But when the Halogai began to climb the low, broad stairs, the priests cried out in alarm and withdrew inside, slamming doors behind them.

Under their officers' direction, most of the northerners deployed on the stairway, facing out toward the forecourt. A band that included Thvari's warriors accompanied Krispos and his Videssian comrades up to the High Temple itself. Krispos looked from the closed doors before them to Gnatios. "I hope you'll be able to do something about this?"

Gnatios nodded. He knocked on the door and called sharply, "Open in there. Open, I say! Your patriarch commands it."

A grill slid open. "Phos preserve us," said the priest peering out. "It *is* the patriarch." A moment later, the doors were flung wide; Krispos had to step back smartly to keep from being hit. Ignoring him, the clerics hurled questions at Gnatios: "What's toward, most holy sir?" "What are all the Halogai doing here?" "Where's the Emperor, if all his guards have come?"

"What's toward? Change," Gnatios answered, raising an eyebrow at Krispos. "I would say that response covers the rest of your queries, as well."

Barsymes spoke up. "Holy sirs, will your kindness permit us to enter the narthex so his Majesty may assume the imperial vestments?"

"I shall also require a vial of the scented oil used in anointings," Gnatios added.

Krispos saw the priests' faces go momentarily slack with surprise, then heard their voices rise as they murmured among themselves. They were city men; they did not need to hear more to know what was in the wind. Without waiting for their leave, Krispos strode into the High Temple. He felt the clerics' eyes on him as they gave way before his confidence, but he did not look toward them. Instead, he told Barsymes, "Aye, this place will do well enough for robing. Help me, if you please."

"Of course, your Majesty." The eunuch turned to the priests. "Could I trouble one of you, holy sirs, for a damp cloth wherewith to wipe clean his Majesty's face?" Not one but four clerics hurried away.

"I'll want to clean off after you do, Kris—your Majesty," Mavros said. "The good god knows I must be as sooty as you are."

The cloth arrived in moments. With exquisite delicacy, Barsymes dabbed and rubbed at Krispos' cheeks, nose, and forehead. When at last he was satisfied, he handed the cloth—now grayish rather than white—to Mavros. While Mavros ran it over his own face, Barsymes began to clothe Krispos in the imperial regalia for the first time.

The garb for the coronation was of antique style, so antique that it was no longer worn at any other time. With Barsymes' help, Krispos donned blue leggings and a gold-belted blue kilt edged in white. His plain sword went into the bejeweled scabbard that hung from the belt. His tunic was scarlet, with gold threads worked through it. Barsymes set a white wool cape on his shoulders and fumbled to work the golden fibula that closed it at his throat.

"And now," the eunuch said, "the red boots."

They were a tight squeeze; Krispos' feet were larger than Anthimos'. They also had higher heels than Krispos was used to. He stumped around uncertainly inside the narthex.

Barsymes took from his bag a simple golden circlet, then a more formal crown: a golden dome set with rubies, sapphires, and glistening pearls. He set both of them aside; for the moment, Krispos remained bareheaded.

Mavros went to the doors to look out. "A lot of people there," he said. "Iakovitzes' lads did their job well." The noise of the crowd, which the closed doors had kept down to a sound like that of the distant sea, suddenly swelled in Krispos' ears.

"Is it sunrise?" he asked.

Mavros looked out again. "Near enough. It's certainly light."

Krispos glanced from him to Barsymes to Gnatios. "Then let's begin."

Mavros opened the doors once more, this time throwing them wide. The boom they made as they slammed back against the wall drew the eyes of the crowd to him. He stood in the doorway for a moment, then cried out as loud as he could, "People of Videssos, Phos himself has made this day! On this day, the good god has given our city and our Empire a new Avtokrator."

The hum from the crowd dropped as people quieted to hear what Mavros said, then redoubled when they took in the import of his words. He held up his hands and waited. Quiet slowly came. Into it, Mavros said, "The Avtokrator Anthimos is dead, laid low by his own sorceries. People of Videssos, behold the Avtokrator Krispos."

Barsymes touched Krispos on the arm, but he was already moving forward to stand in the open doorway as Mavros stepped aside. Below him, on the steps, the Halogai raised their axes in salute—and in warning to any who would oppose him. "Krispos!" they shouted all together, their voices deep and fierce.

"Krispos!" yelled the crowd, save for the inevitable few who heard his name wrong and yelled "Priskos!" instead. "Thou conquerest, Krispos!"—the age-old Videssian shout of acclamation. "Many years to the Avtokrator Krispos!" "Thou conquerest!" "Krispos!"

Krispos remembered the heady feeling he'd had years before, when the nobles who filled the Hall of the Nineteen Couches all cried out his name after he vanquished Beshev, the thick-shouldered wrestler from Kubrat. Now he knew that feeling again, but magnified a hundredfold, for this was not a hallful of people, but rather a plazaful. Buoyed up on that great tide of acclamation, he forgot fatigue.

"The people proclaim you Emperor, Krispos!" Mavros cried.

The acclaim got louder. Shouts of "Thou conquerest, Krispos!" came thick and fast. One burden of worry gone, Krispos thought. Had the crowd not accepted him, he would never have lasted as Avtokrator; no matter what other backing he had, it would have evaporated in the face of popular contempt. The chronicles told of a would-be Emperor named Rhazates, whom the mob had laughed off the steps of the High Temple for no better reason than that he was grossly fat. A rival ousted him within days.

Thvari held up the bronze-faced shield, displaying it to the crowd. The people quieted; they knew what that shield was for. With Mavros behind him, Krispos walked down to where the Haloga waited.

Too quietly for the people in the forecourt to hear, Krispos told Thvari, "I want you, Geirrod, Narvikka, and Vagn."

"It shall be as you wish," the northerner agreed. Geirrod stood close by; neither of the other guardsmen Krispos had named was far away. Thvari would know which soldiers he favored, Krispos thought. At the officer's gesture, the two Halogai set down their axes and hurried over.

Barsymes approached, handing Mavros the golden circlet he'd brought. As Thvari had the bronze-faced shield, Mavros showed the circlet to the crowd. Those at the back of the courtyard could hardly have been able to see it, but they sighed all the same—like the shield, it had its place in the ritual of coronation.

The ritual went on. Mavros offered Krispos the circlet. He held out his hands, palms away from his body, in a gesture of refusal. Mavros offered the circlet again. Again Krispos rejected it. Mavros paused, then tried to present it to Krispos once more. This time Krispos bowed his head in acquiescence.

Mavros set the circle on his brow. The gold was cool against his forehead. "Krispos, with this circlet I join the people in conferring on you the title of Avtokrator!" Mavros said proudly.

As Mavros spoke, as the crowd erupted in fresh cheers, Thvari set the bronze-faced shield flat on the stair beside him. Krispos stepped up onto it. Thvari, Geirrod, Narvikka, and Vagn stooped and grasped the rim of the shield. At a grunted command from Thvari, they lifted together.

Up went the shield to the height of their shoulders, raising Krispos high above them and showing the people that he enjoyed the soldiers' support as well as theirs. "Krispos!" all the Halogai shouted once more. For a moment he felt more like one of their pirate chieftains about to set forth on a plundering expedition than a staid and civilized Avtokrator of the Videssians.

The guardsmen lowered him back to the stone steps. As he got off the shield, he wondered if it was the one upon which Anthimos had stood—and who would be exalted on it after he was gone. *My son, Phos willing, one day many years from now,* he thought, then shoved that concern far away.

He looked up to the top of the stone steps. Gnatios stood in the open doorway, holding a satin cushion on which lay the imperial crown and the vial of oil he would use to anoint Krispos' head. The patriarch nodded. Heart pounding, Krispos climbed the stairs toward him. Having been accepted by the people and the army, he needed only ecclesiastical recognition to complete his coronation.

Gnatios nodded again as Krispos took his place beside him. But instead of beginning the ceremony of anointing, the patriarch looked out to the expectantly waiting crowd in the forecourt below. Pitching his voice to carry to the people, the patriarch said, "Perhaps our new master will honor us with a few brief words before I set the crown on his head."

Krispos turned around to glare at Gnatios, who blandly looked back. He heard Mavros' angry hiss—this was no normal part of the coronation. Krispos knew what it was: it was Gnatios hoping he would play the fool in front of much of the city, and blight his reign before it properly began.

The expanding crowd in the forecourt grew still, waiting to hear what Krispos would say. He paused a moment to gather his thoughts, for he saw he could not keep from speaking. Before he began, though, he scowled at Gnatios again. He would never be able to trust the patriarch, not after this.

But when he looked out to the still-waiting throng, all thoughts of Gnatios vanished from his mind. "People of Videssos," he said, then once more, louder, "people of Videssos, Anthimos is dead. I do not want to speak ill of the dead, but you know as well as I that not everything in the city or in the empire ran as well as it might have while he was Emperor."

He hoped someone would shout out in agreement and bring a laugh from the crowd. No one did. People stood silent, listening, judging. He took a deep breath and reminded himself to try to keep his rustic accent under control; he was glad his years in the city had helped smooth it. He plunged ahead.

"I served Anthimos. I saw how he neglected the Empire for the sake of his own pleasure. Pleasure has its place, aye. But the Avtokrator has to look to Videssos first, then to himself. As far as I can, I will do that."

He paused to think again. "If I did everything I might possibly do, I think I'd need to pack three days into every one." His rueful tone was real; as he stood there, looking out at the people who were under his rule alone, picturing their fellows all the way to the borders of the Empire, he could not imagine why anyone would want the crushing weight of responsibility that went with being Avtokrator. No time to worry about that now, either. He had the responsibility. He would have to bear up under it. He went on, "With the good god's help, I'll be able to do enough to help Videssos. I pray I can. That's all."

As he turned back to Gnatios, he listened to the crowd. No thunderous outpouring of applause, but he hadn't expected one, not after the patriarch ambushed him into coming up with a speech on the spot. But no one jeered or booed or hissed. He'd got through it and hadn't hurt himself. That was plenty.

Gnatios realized it, too. He masked himself well, but could not quite hide his disappointment. "Carry on, most holy sir," Krispos said coldly.

"Yes, of course, your Majesty." Gnatios nodded, bland still.

He raised his voice to speak to the crowd rather than the Emperor. "Bow your head for the anointing."

Krispos obeyed. The patriarch drew the stopper from the vial of scented oil and poured its contents over Krispos' head. He spoke the ritual words: "As Phos' light shines down on us all, so may his blessings pour down on you with this anointing."

"So may it be," Krispos responded, though as he did, he wondered whether a prayer had to be sincerely meant to be effective. If so, Phos' ears were surely closed to Gnatios' words.

The patriarch rubbed the oil through Krispos' hair with his right hand. While he completed the anointing, he recited Phos' creed, intoning, "We bless thee, Phos, Lord with the great and good mind, by thy grace our protector, watchful beforehand that the great test of life may be decided in our favor."

Krispos echoed the prayer, which, since it did not mention him, he supposed the patriarch truly meant. The city folk gathered in the forecourt below also recited the creed. Their voices rose and fell like surf, individual words lost but the prayer's rhythm unmistakable.

And then, at last, Gnatios took the imperial crown in both hands and set it on Krispos' lowered head. It was heavy, literally as well as for what it meant. A sigh ran through the crowd. A new Avtokrator ruled Videssos.

After a moment, the noise began to build again, to a crest of acclamation: "Thou conquerest!" "Krispos!" "Many years!" "Krispos!" "Hurrah for the Emperor!" "Krispos!" "Krispos!" "Krispos!"

He straightened. Suddenly the crown seemed to weigh nothing at all

ABOUT THE AUTHOR

Harry Turtledove is that rarity, a lifelong southern Californian. He is married and has three young daughters. After flunking out of Caltech, he earned a degree in Byzantine history and has taught at UCLA and Cal State Fullerton. Academic jobs being few and precarious, however, his primary work since leaving school has been as a technical writer. He has had fantasy and science fiction published in *Isaac Asimov's Amazing, Analog, Fantasy Book*, and *Playboy*. His hobbies include baseball, chess, and beer.